THE HOUSE ON HONEYSUCKLE LANE

Carole Gift Page

ELM HILL BOOKS
A Division of Thomas Nelson Publishers
Since 1798

www.thomasnelson.com

The House on Honeysuckle Lane ISBN: 1-4041-8579-8

Copyright ©2005 Elm Hill Books, an imprint of J. Countryman®, a division of Thomas Nelson, Inc. Nashville, TN 37214. All rights reserved. Except for brief quotations used in reviews, articles or other media, no part of this book may be reproduced or transmitted in any form or by any means, electronic or mechanical, including photocopying, recording, or by information storage or retrieval system, without the express, written consent of the publisher.

For additions, deletions, corrections or clarifications in future editions of this text, please contact Paul Shepherd, Editor in Chief for Elm Hill Books. Email pshepherd@elmhillbooks.com

Products from Elm Hill Books may be purchased in bulk for educational, business, fundraising, or sales promotional use. For information, please email SpecialMarkets@ThomasNelson.com.

This is a work of fiction. The characters, incidents, and dialogues are products of the author's imagination and are not to be construed as real. Any resemblance to actual events or persons, living or dead, is entirely coincidental.

Previously published by Nelson Books under ISBN: 0-8407-6777-3

Cover design by Patti Evans
Interior by Mark Ross / MJ Ross Design

Printed in the United States of America

THE HOUSE ON HONEYSUCKLE LANE

Heartland Memories Series,
Book 1 of 6

ONE

*The house on Honeysuckle Lane was more than
just the house where I was born. It was more
than the sum total of its rooms, brimming with
memories and love, joy and pain. Three
generations of Reeds had called it home since
the year my Grandfather Reed built the
Victorian two-story for his young bride, Alma.
Through two world wars and a depression, good
times and bad, the house rollicked with life,
shimmered with memories, and exuded nostalgia
like a rare fragrance, stirring the heart with
nameless yearnings.*

*The house on Honeysuckle Lane was everything
to me. In its silence it shaped me, sheltered me,
and nurtured me as much as any person did. And
when I left, I left pieces of myself behind, but
I took with me an enduring connection with that
venerable old house—my home.*

—Annie Reed

The Spring of 1946.

The wheezing, timeworn taxi clattered over the cobbled streets of Willowbrook, its
tires spinning out an eerie siren song, as if protesting the oily wetness of the streets. Annie
Reed shivered in the gloomy darkness of the cab, her body swaying to the rumble of rubber on shiny, rain-slick bricks. How many Midwestern towns still build their roads with
bricks? she wondered absently.

The cab smelled faintly of diesel, old leather, and strong cigars mixed with rain-
soaked wool and wet fur. The fur was on Annie's coat collar—a strip of mink with two
tiny mink heads that nuzzled her chin and made her feel she was sporting an ani-
mal—an odd little pet that kept her company, even while the damp, pungent fur smell
overpowered the sweet fragrance of her perfume.

Annie felt more comfortable with the coat than the perfume anyway. The coat had come from the Salvation Army's second-hand shop back home in L. A. (Yes, she had actually begun to think of Los Angeles as home! Strange, when for so long she had told herself it was only a temporary haven.) But the coat. Rumor had it a Hollywood star had donated it in a spurt of generosity—perhaps Joan Crawford or Bette Davis. Kindhearted Robert, who had worked at the shop much longer than she, had insisted it was far too grand for just anyone, that certainly she should wear it on her cross-country tour. "It accents your beauty, dear Annie," he told her in his booming, take-charge baritone. "Besides, you should look the part of someone famous!"

Look the part! Whether I feel like it or not? she mused now to herself, her gloved hand moving impulsively to what Robert called her long burnished tresses. "Drat!" The rain had played havoc with her pageboy curls, crimping them into frizzy tangles.

Annie didn't realize she had spoken the word aloud until the cabby turned in his seat and looked back at her. "You say something, miss?" He was a wizened, prune-faced little man with a low-slung cap and a fat cigar clamped between his teeth.

"No, I'm sorry. I was talking to myself."

"Bad habit," he muttered. "Some folks say that shows an unstable mind." His gaze lingered on her as if he were debating her mental acuity. Did he actually suppose she was teetering on the brink of lunacy? She imagined she did look rather curious—a young woman alone taking a cab at this hour through the rain-drenched streets of Willowbrook. Annie remembered a voice from the past, her own dear mother's: Don't go out late at night without an escort, Annie. It's not safe!

But that was another decade, another era, Annie wanted to shout back. There's been a war, Mama, and so much more. You can't protect me. I'm not your little Annie Reed anymore!

Annie shivered again. Perhaps it was an act of madness to come back like this to Willowbrook. She marveled over the sudden absurdity of it. What only a few hours before had seemed like a flash of genius now struck her as pure folly, a foolish aberration of her senses.

You can't go home again.

Someone said it once—in a book, a play, on the radio, somewhere she had heard it. Why hadn't she believed it? Now—now it was too late. She was here. There would not be another train back to Chicago for hours.

"Miss, what was that street you said?" the cabby asked, giving her that look, chewing his smelly cigar, blowing smoke rings in the murky air.

"Honeysuckle Lane. The north end of town."

"Right. That's what I thought you said. Nice neighborhood in its time."

"A beautiful neighborhood," she said defensively.

"Yep. Still the nicest houses in Willowbrook. Only—"

"Only what?"

"Only nothing. Now they're building all them new houses out by the highway. Lots of people moving out that way."

Annie didn't reply. Those modern pre-fab, post-war, cracker-box houses couldn't compare with the stately Victorian home her grandfather, Papa Reed, had built for his family before the turn of the century—a magnificent house filled with all the hopes and dreams of a lifetime. Of many lives.

Perhaps that's why she had come back—to retrieve a few of those hopes, resurrect a handful of dreams. Why else had she dared to come back? Why else was she risking everything—her present, her future—if not to find a little piece of the past? The questions assailed her like the pelting rain on the windshield. Would she regret this night? Would it change everything for her? Or would she be able to take one brief glimpse and be satisfied? Or—God forbid!—would she be sucked back irretrievably into the morass of pain she had fled so long ago?

"Miss?" the driver spoke again, craning his neck, his gaze desultory. "Miss, hope ya don't mind my asking. You from around these parts?"

She hesitated, weighing her words. "Yes. Once. Long ago."

"I figured as much. You look mighty familiar—and I'm not saying that just because you're a pretty girl. It's been tugging at my mind since you got in the car. I could swear I seen you just the other day."

Annie's tone turned wary. "That's impossible. I haven't been in Willowbrook in—ages."

He scratched his head, nearly toppling his cap, and turned his gaze back to the road. "Well, I seen you somewhere—and I'm not feeding you no line. Fact is, I got me a nice wife at home. But I could swear I seen your face—big as life—spread across—hey, that's it!" He whirled around, his hand jerking on the wheel so that the vehicle swerved momentarily. "That's where I seen you—in the newspapers. You're somebody famous!"

Annie shrank down in her seat, wishing she could hide behind her sad little minks, or disappear into her coat and become invisible. This was exactly what she didn't want to happen. Be recognized! "There must be some mistake," she murmured.

"No, it was you," declared the cabby. "I can't recollect what it was all about, but something about you making an appearance in Chicago. Hey, are you a movie star?"

She choked on her own laughter. "No, not at all!"

The driver sounded disgruntled. "Well, it was something like that. You appearing for some big event—that's it! Not a movie—an autograph party in Chicago! You're Elizabeth somebody. You wrote that book on the best seller list, didn't you?—that story about Pearl Harbor? You shoulda seen the swell write-up in the Willowbrook News.

Headlines—'Hometown girl makes good'—and a whole page about this war story dedicated to her brother, a local boy. Don't recall his name now."

Annie's face felt prickly warm. She felt trapped by this little man's exuberance. She didn't want his praise, his fawning attention. She wanted only to be anonymous, to clasp her privacy around her like a cloak, a shield. But he was still prattling on, as if the two of them shared a tantalizing secret that bound them together in some absurd alliance.

"Wait'll I tell my wife about this—meeting someone famous, from our own little town," he burbled on. His cigar bobbed furiously as he spoke. "She read your book, you know. Every word. Said it was right good. She knows. She reads everything. You got yourself a real fan in my wife."

"I didn't say I wrote it," Annie managed.

"Have it your way," he chuckled, turning onto Harrington Avenue.

Annie recognized the houses. Only a few blocks to Maypole Drive, where Cath once lived. Then around the corner to her own Honeysuckle Lane. The rain had abated. She cranked open her window and let in a swath of cool, moist air, then inhaled deeply, clearing her head of the cigar fumes and the heavy, stale air of the cab.

"You okay, miss?"

"Yes, I think so."

"You ain't gonna be sick, are ya?"

"No. I just need a little air." If she hadn't set out on this wild goose chase, she could be back in her hotel room in Chicago, wrapped in her comfy robe and sipping hot tea with a wedge of lemon. She breathed in again, hungrily filling her nostrils with the rain-washed air. She could smell the sweet flowers of spring—bell-shaped hyacinth, bountiful lilacs, and lily of the valley—the lush, heady fragrances of her childhood.

"You still got family here?" rasped the cabby. He was grilling her more than the bevy of Chicago reporters.

"I did," she conceded.

"Well, I'm sure they'll be glad to see you, seeing as how you've made it big in the world. Proud as peacocks they'll be—"

"I'm not going to be here that long," she said, her discomfiture growing. The last thing she wanted was to discuss her plans with a stranger. "In fact, I'll be staying only, uh, an hour perhaps. Would you mind coming back for me?"

"An hour?" He craned his neck around, his shaggy brows turning into question marks over his beady eyes. "You want me to come back and pick you up in an hour?" His voice rose to a near soprano trill and hung momentarily in the air.

"Yes," Annie said. "You can do that, can't you?"

"Sure. No trouble. An hour." He sounded puzzled. "Only seems a strange request.

Sure you don't want to wait and telephone? Maybe you'll decide to stay over."

"No. I won't be near a phone. An hour will be enough."

But will it? she wondered as her hungry eyes took in the familiar sprawling yards and towering houses of Honeysuckle Lane. Then, there it was. The corner house. Even in the luminous prism of a rain-drenched night she recognized every shape and shadow of home. Would even a lifetime be enough to relive the memories bursting the seams of that cherished place?

"What's the address, miss?"

She gazed questioningly at her driver, then understood. "Oh, just let me off here at the corner." She was already fumbling in her pocketbook for cash, clasping more bills than necessary, pushing them over the front seat to the man, eager to be out of this stuffy cab, and on the clean wet street, alone.

And suddenly it was so.

In her ears she still heard the cabby's voice edged with a mixture of truculence and astonishment: "Craziest thing I ever heard tell—a classy lady like you out on these dark streets alone! But have it your way, miss. I'll be back in an hour. And pray God you'll be here!"

With mingled relief and trepidation, Annie watched the vintage taxi trundle away with its seasoned driver. She watched until its tail lights shrank to blackness, leaving her standing alone on the corner of Honeysuckle Lane.

Alone. And home.

She focused her gaze on the dusty rose mansion across the street (not quite a mansion, but dubbed the Reed mansion when her grandfather built it in 1890). It was a grand Victorian house with large drafty rooms and dormer windows upstairs and wide bay windows downstairs. It had a steep shingled roof with a dome-shaped cupola and gothic pointed arches, and best of all, a rambling, wrap-around porch with ornamental gables and lots of gingerbread trim.

Many were the hours Annie and her best friend Catherine Herrick had sat on those porch steps in gangly-legged bliss, puzzling over life's deepest enigmas and bedazzled by the seductive promises of fortune, fame, and pure, unsullied romance. Where are you now, Catherine? Do you wonder where I am too?

Annie grimaced and clenched her pocketbook tighter. She would not think of Cath tonight, nor of Knowl Herrick, nor of the Herrick house around the corner, smaller and less imposing than the Reed mansion, and with its own painful legacy. No! Banish such thoughts! She would concentrate only on her own cherished home and pleasant memories.

She shivered. The night wind had already eaten away the remnant warmth of the taxicab. Annie felt the chill seeping under her collar, spreading up her sleeves and around her legs. It was spring now—Chicago's cold, hard-edged version of spring. Willowbrook always inherited Chicago's castoff weather like overworn, outgrown clothing. It never fit, never seemed quite appropriate, always too blustery, too biting, too reckless for solemn, sedate Willowbrook.

She closed her eyes tightly, then opened them and drank in the image of Grandfather Reed's house sitting with tarnished eloquence on its generous, manicured lot. It was ensconced in shadows, of course, like a phantom rising up from the ground with a kind of rickety grace. But Annie knew every line of it as if she were seeing it in bright sunlight. The house was as magnificent as ever. She imagined the gazebo in the back yard with its hanging flower baskets, and the lavish gardens with towering oaks and sweet-smelling rose bushes.

She paused. The lights from the windows drew her, their golden warmth effusing dusky halos. She was too far away to see inside, but she could imagine the rooms—the living room with its velvets and brocades, the long hallways, the sprawling kitchen smelling of ginger and spice, and the parlor, with its French doors opening to the dining room. She had cleaned those small glass panes every Saturday. Meticulously. But that was many years ago when she was just a girl and believed there would never be another house for her but this one.

Surely now the rooms had changed—the walls repapered, the carpet replaced, the old furniture gone. But she would not think of that tonight. She would remember the rooms as they were, filled with the smells of family and familiarity—of mahogany tables with bowls of hydrangea, of freshly ironed organdy and antique lace, of blueberry pies cooling on the windowsill, of Mama's Sunday fried chicken served on her best Staffordshire china, of countless things she could not define but which defined her, the child, Annie Reed.

Recklessly she wondered what the rooms were like now and who the people might be. Did they have any idea of the history in those walls, of the people who had come before? Surely not. It was a secret locked inside Annie's brain—all the memories stored in their safe little niches. Oh, if only she could take them out and examine them again! If she could truly remember. If she could walk straight into that house and once again greet Mama and Papa and Papa Reed and poor Chip and even Alice Marie!

But no. The recollections were dim, smudged with the dark sepia tones of an old, faded filmstrip. Flickering into obscurity. Always just beyond her grasp.

The truth was frightening, disturbing—the fact that nothing and no one familiar remained in this spot, on this street, this place that had been life to her for so many years. She never should have allowed the house to be sold after Papa died. Somehow she should have raised the money to buy it herself.

She trembled. The chill wind beat steadily against her, summoning goose bumps, making the hairs on her arms stand at attention, and stealing into her bones, numbing her. It whistled in her ears, a haunting refrain—your home is gone . . .

She slipped her hands into the pockets of her thick, nubby coat and arched her shoulders until her sodden minks girdled her neck with their clammy collar. Suddenly an automobile roared past, its tires spewing up mud and filth, its engine scream splintering Annie's reverie.

She jumped back from the curb, dazed, her breath stopped in her throat, her heart hammering. Suddenly, in the blazing lights of the careening vehicle, she saw it all as it was—her beloved Honeysuckle Lane—and knew she shouldn't have come. She couldn't recapture the past. Nothing was the same—not the street with its broken bricks and overgrown trees, nor the sidewalk with its cracks and ruts allowing weeds to steal through. She was glad now it was dark and she couldn't see the house. Reality would be rusty and dirty and dismal; reality smelled of garbage cans overflowing and exhaust fumes from too many ramshackle autos grunting at the cross street or sagging by the curb. Reality would snuff out all remnants of the past.

Annie quivered. It was too soon for her taxi to return and too cold to stand here. She had a sudden bold impulse to run across the street and up the porch steps and pound on the door of her house and demand—demand what? That her mother come out and be the same person she was years ago? Her mother wasn't here.

If she knocked now, strangers would answer, and she might mumble something about being lost or looking for a certain street or a neighbor who lived here once. But she would not be convincing, and perhaps they would laugh or grow suspicious or even slam the door in her face. Still, she wished she could warn them, tell them how fleeting and tenuous were these moments they shared, how significant was this hour of living. It would not come again, could not be relived or recaptured, even in memory—for memory was flawed and fickle, at best.

She looked around, straining against the tension in her neck. Her backbone was rigid, her shoulders stiff. She had been standing here too long, lingering like a sentimental fool! She imagined what people would say if they could see her now—a strange young woman given to childish whims, but considering her past, it's a wonder she's not more distraught… people have gone loony for less reason…

Suddenly, Annie heard a noise and knew with a cold, solemn certainty she was not alone. What was it? The crackling of a twig perhaps, the rustle of leaves, the sound of rubber soles on wet pavement? Her pulse quickened, but she saw no one. She waited, listening. The shadows came alive with faint, whispery movement—the breeze stirring the trees, rippling the grasses, rattling a shutter on a distant house.

Someone was with her in the shadows. She sensed his presence. He was stalking her, watching her watch the house, and he was in no hurry to make himself known.

Annie considered running, but where would she go? If he intended to harm her, no matter how fast she ran, he would be there ahead of her, ready to block her path. It would take so little to snuff out her life—sudden, violent pressure on her windpipe, a knife thrust in the ribs, a deadly shot from a revolver which neighbors might dismiss as a car backfiring.

No one, except the taxi driver, knew she was here. No one would think to look for her; her connections with others were loose and transitory these days; she belonged nowhere really, with no one. If she disappeared, who would really miss her? Robert perhaps? But he was far away in California.

With a tremor she imagined the violent scenario followed by the obligatory write-up in the Willowbrook newspaper: Jane Doe, an unidentified woman in her mid-twenties, was gunned down on Honeysuckle Lane last night. Her attacker is unknown. No identification was found on the victim, no missing person's report has been filed, and no one has claimed the body. If anyone has information…

The cabby would notify the police, of course, and tell them he had delivered her to this address. She could hear him explaining in his raspy, fawning voice, "I warned her she was a fool to be out alone like that, but she wouldn't listen. I came back for her an hour later, but it was too late."

Oh, please, little cabby, please come back! she prayed urgently.

From the corner of her eye she glimpsed someone moving closer. She could hear him breathing now, or maybe it was the wind playing tricks on her. Maybe it was only her own heartbeat pumping in her ears. Maybe the shadow was only a bush or tree, a ghastly prank of her own capricious imagination. As much as she lived by her ingenuity, she was hardly a woman given to strange phantasms, fantasies, vagaries of the mind.

She began to walk. Slowly, she told herself. No sudden, exaggerated movements, nothing to tip off the stranger I'm on to him. Walk naturally, as if I take a stroll like this every night through this neighborhood, as if this is where I belong.

She craned her neck around, feigning nonchalance, keeping a steady pace. He was on the sidewalk now—flesh and blood man, a towering, broad-shouldered silhouette breaking forth from the gloomy haze, separating himself from the shadowed mists.

She began to run. She heard the man's footsteps behind her, the soles of his shoes slapping the wet sidewalk, crunching dead branches, slogging through soggy leaves. He had accelerated his pace and, yes, now she knew it was his breathing she heard— deep, quick exhalations as he picked up speed.

He would be upon her in a moment, clamping his hand over her mouth, forcing her down into the grass, ripping her clothing, stealing her money, or her virtue, or her life. Oh, God, where are You when I need You? What irony if it ends like this, where it all began! Surely You wouldn't be so cruel!

She faltered and nearly fell, her foot slipping off the sidewalk into the wet, clinging grass. Her heel turned in the yielding soil and she felt a jolt of pain travel up her ankle. As she hobbled on, breathless, her chest heaving with terror and exhaustion, she knew she had no hope of outrunning her assailant, no chance of being saved. Steeling herself, she felt the stranger's presence even before he touched her.

"Annie! Annie, wait!"

That voice. It was familiar and yet foreign—a voice she loved, a voice she hated, a voice she had nearly forgotten and yet would always remember.

She whirled around, her eyes searching his face in the darkness. "You!" she cried. "It can't be! How did you find me? How did you know I'd come back to Honeysuckle Lane!"

Like a drowning victim whose life flashes before his eyes in a twinkling, Annie's mind jumped decades. She was standing here in the spring of 1946, staring into the face of her past, and at the same time, she was winging back to another spring, that of 1932.

TWO

The Spring of 1932.

"There was a table set out under a tree in front of the house, and the March Hare and the Hatter were having tea at it."

Annie sat in the cherry wood rocker, hugging her slender legs against her bony chest, curling her toes around the hard edge of the seat. She could see herself in her grandfather's dresser mirror—two enormous gray-green eyes in an elfin face, with cropped brown hair nearly as short as her brother Chip's. She looked younger than her twelve years. With a remarkably plain face. Everyone thought so, although no one said it, except Alice Marie. It was Annie's fate to have a sassy older sister whose sole goal in life was to ridicule Annie at every turn. It didn't help that they shared a room—the rosebud room Annie had long coveted for herself. But as long as the two were confined in those four walls, Annie was doomed to suffer Alice Marie's taunts and jibes forever.

Just thinking about Alice Marie's meanness made Annie groan. She jutted out her lower lip and turned her gaze from her own reflection. No sense staring at such an ordinary face if she didn't have to. She focused instead on the pale indigo wallpaper of the blue room (so dubbed by Alice Marie, but it was actually her grandfather's room and almost twice as big as the rosebud room down the hall).

With a stab of guilt Annie realized her mind had wandered. She wasn't listening anymore. She glanced at her grandfather. Dear Papa Reed. His snowy hair looked whiter than usual against his sallow cheeks, and dark circles rimmed his eyes. His lips looked bluish today, but at least he was smiling. Good. He hadn't noticed her lack of attention. He was still reading, his words slow and feeble, but precise. She settled back again, resolving to listen.

"The March Hare took the watch and looked at it gloomily: then he dipped it into his cup of tea, and looked at it again."

A fly droned in the sweet lilac-scented air, its bzzzz blending with Papa Reed's husky voice. Propped up in his great feather bed, he was reading *Alice's Adventures in Wonderland*—the part where Alice joins the Mad Hatter and March Hare for their bizarre tea party.

What a marvelous imagination Mr. Lewis Carroll had, Annie mused dreamily. If only I could create such wonderful creatures as the Jabberwock and Mock Turtle and talking Caterpillar!

Lulled by the golden sun streaming in the window and by the steady rise and fall of Papa's voice, Annie watched the pesky fly circle and land on her toenail. The buzzing stopped, leaving her grandfather's words wafting on the soundless air. She peered at the fly, fascinated; watched its legs move mysteriously, twitching, probing. What did it expect to find on her toenail? Perhaps a bit of black soil from Mama's garden? Slowly she raised her other toe over the tiny trespasser and brought her foot down with a sudden thrust. Missed! Her leg flew out, nearly toppling her, while the fly droned on, oblivious of her attack.

But not Grandfather. He looked up over his spectacles. "Annie, are you listening?"

"Yes, Papa Reed."

"This is the best part, child."

Annie nodded. She was too old to be read to, but she'd never had the heart to tell her grandfather. He'd read to her for as long as she could remember—long after she herself could read. But there was something special about their times together. Something more than the fact that reading started dreams spinning inside her head.

She was her grandfather's favorite—more than Chip or Alice Marie. Not that he ever said so, but she saw it in his eyes, heard it when he said her name. She figured being Papa Reed's favorite made things come out right, fair and square, considering Chip was her father's favorite and Alice Marie was Mama's.

"Are you tired of reading?" she asked, knowing he was, seeing it in the shadows under his eyes.

"No, child. Are you? Is something more exciting than Alice's tea party happening downstairs?"

"No. Mama is baking bread."

"I know. I smell it from here."

"Would you like some?"

"Maybe later, child." But there was no desire for bread in his voice, no hunger for food. Her grandfather didn't eat much these days.

"And Papa is talking politics with Mr. Herrick," she went on brightly. She called her father Papa, but only her grandfather was Papa Reed.

His voice turned gravelly, edged with contempt. "Politics, eh? Are they finding a solution to this drat Depression? Or jobs for the millions of men out of work?"

Annie shrugged, knowing the Depression was off limits with Papa. One wrong word could make his bitterness erupt. Her grandfather had invested heavily in the Great Bull Market, then lost everything in the Crash three years ago. Mama called it "building paper houses in the wind," but Papa Reed refused to discuss it.

"I think Mr. Herrick is trying to sell Papa some brushes," said Annie. "Cath says her father's a Fuller Brush salesman now. Even got his own satchel full of fancy brushes."

"Nothing that man hasn't tried," scoffed Papa. "Wonder if

he'll ever amount to a hill of beans! If he does, I won't live to see it."

"Don't talk like that, Papa."

"Why not? I'm an old man, a sick old man. But as long as I live I'll never have any use for Tom Herrick."

"Cath says her father's the best salesman in the world. She says he can sell anything to anybody."

Papa Reed scowled. "That Herrick fellow's tried often enough. Darkened more doors than any man has a right to." He cleared his throat and looked back at the book. "Don't get me started on Tom Herrick. He's our neighbor and we've got to keep the peace, but I pity his poor wife and those two children of his."

Annie squirmed a little. She felt uncomfortable hearing Papa talk about Cath's daddy that way. After all, Cath thought he was tops, and her brother Knowl seemed proud of his father too. What did Papa know about Mr. Herrick that made him so red-faced angry?

Papa moved his large veined hand over the page and began reading again. But he had lost his place and leaped ahead.

"This piece of rudeness was more than Alice could bear: she got up in great disgust, and walked off…"

In the middle of a line, Papa Reed's words were shattered by a sudden cough, deep, racking. He groped for his water glass on the bedside table, but Annie was there first, handing him the glass, steadying it as he drank. He choked again, a tiny rivulet of water running down his chin and into the folds of his neck. He looked so frail these days, but Annie still thought of him as a strapping man, tall as her father, Jon Reed, Papa's only son. Of course, he hadn't been that tall in years. In fact, now that Annie was in the midst of her growth spurt, she herself was nearly as tall as Papa Reed.

"We can read some more tomorrow," she said, wincing at the weariness in his face. But there was something more. The color had drained out of his skin. He was as pale as the bleached muslin curtains billowing at the open window.

"A little more," he said. "We've got to get Alice away from that dreadful tea party."

Annie laughed. Papa laughed too—and coughed again.

"See?" she said. "You need to rest."

"Humph! Soon I will rest forever. Now I need to read."

Annie sighed. "I told you, Papa, don't say such things. Go on, if you wish. Read." She leaned over and kissed his wrinkled forehead. He was still a handsome man, with a full head of hair as soft and white as eiderdown. And, in spite of the Great Depression, his eyes hadn't lost their crinkly brightness, except for a time after Grandmother Reed died. But that was nearly five years ago now.

Papa was reading again, his voice raspy, but determined. Annie walked over to the window and looked out, listening. Sometimes Papa got so involved in the story, he forgot she was there. She would give him a few minutes more, then insist he stop and rest before lunch.

She closed her eyes, letting the late April breeze wash over

her. It was like summer already—surprising for this Midwestern town just a stone's throw from Chicago. If only summer would come early to Willowbrook this year! She gazed down into the backyard where the trees and flowers were already budding. Mama's garden. Already alive with color.

Suddenly she started, and caught her breath at the sight below. Alice Marie was in the garden with Knowl Herrick—the two walking hand in hand, her head leaning to one side, brushing his shoulder. Knowl, sixteen and almost a man. Annie's secret love. The boy with the brooding eyes and wayward thatch of wheat-brown hair. The boy who had lived next door all her life and still didn't know she existed.

"What is it, child? Something wrong?"

"No, Papa. It's just Alice Marie in the garden—"

"Alone?"

"No. She's with—with Knowl Herrick."

"A nice young man," he ventured, his tired eyes

twinkling. "Don't you think so, child? Nothing like his father.

And he's certainly sweet on your sister."

Annie bristled. "Sweet?"

"Haven't you noticed? I'm an old man confined to my bed, and I see it."

"See what?" Her voice quivered.

"Young love. I suspect we'll be hearing wedding bells one of these days."

Annie spun around. "No, Papa, never! Not Alice Marie and Knowl!"

"Goodness, child, where does all this anger come from?"

She turned back to the window. "I'm not angry, Papa."

"I don't see so well, but I can see you're trembling."

Annie covered her mouth in horror. "They're kissing now,

Papa! What would Mama say?"

He strained forward a little, lifting his hand to her. "Come over here, child. Sit by me. Tell me what is going on with you."

Annie shuffled over and sat down on the bed, crossing her arms on her meager chest. A lump the size of an apricot swelled in her throat; tears welled in her eyes.

"Tell me, child."

"Nothing, Papa. It's just—Alice Marie—"

"Yes, it's always Alice Marie. What has she done now?"

"Nothing." Finally, Annie wrung out the words. "Alice Marie is beautiful and glamorous. And sassy and mean. And she has hips and—and everything!"

"She's fifteen. Nearly a woman."

Annie hung her head. "I'll never be."

"Of course you will, child."

"No, I'll always be what you said—a child! Knowl will never—" Papa's brow arched. "So it is Knowl. I thought so! We're

talking about Knowl here, after all." He put his hand over hers; his was large and warm and mottled with age spots; hers was slender and white and smooth as Ivory soap. "So you are fond of this boy?"

"Will you keep my secret, Papa? Only Cath knows."

"Catherine? Knowl's sister? And she has not told? That is a miracle."

"I've sworn her to secrecy. Knowl would laugh at me."

"Perhaps not, child. I thought your grandmother would laugh

when I proposed—but she said yes! So there's always hope."

They both laughed, then they were silent a moment. She could tell her grandfather was reliving old memories. "You miss her, don't you, Papa?"

"My Alma, my soul? Every day of my life."

"You built this house for her. And brought her here as your bride. You must have loved her very much."

"Yes, and oh, how she loved this house. And how her love filled these rooms, until…" His voice sank to a whisper. "Don't tell a soul I said this—I'll deny it if you do—but if she hadn't died, I wouldn't have been so foolish, so brash. I never would have lost my money and my pride—"

"But you haven't lost her. She's still here, Papa."

"Ah, yes, child. In this room I shared with her, and in the

quilts she stitched, and the curtains she sewed, and in her fancy Monet pictures on the walls…"

"Look, Papa. I adore this photograph on the bureau. You and Grandmother on your wedding day—look how beautiful she looks."

Moisture gathered in the creases around his eyes. His voice broke. "Ah, yes, Alma, we will be together again one day."

"Not too soon, Papa. I need you here."

"And I will be here for you, child. In love and prayers, if not in this rumpled old body."

Annie smiled and patted his white hair. "What would I do without you to read to me and cheer me up?"

"You would do fine. But you make an old man's heart happy by humoring me, pretending you like me reading to you."

"I do! I always will!"

"And for that I love you, child." He coughed again, harder than before. The effort seemed to exhaust him. He put his head back on the pillow and closed his eyes.

Annie searched his face. "You okay, Papa?"

He nodded. "Just tired. Very, very tired."

"It's lunchtime. I'll bring you up a tray."

"No, I'm not hungry. Just tea, with a little sugar and—"

"—Cream. I know. I'll bring up some of Mama's warm bread anyway. You need to keep up your strength."

Annie was gone hardly ten minutes, just long enough to let the kettle boil and prepare a tray with fresh bread and a dollop of strawberry preserves. She carried the tray gingerly up the stairs, taking care that the steaming tea not slosh out of its china cup.

"I'm here," she called as she entered the blue room.

Papa didn't answer.

She set the tray down on the bed stand. "Papa? Wake up, Papa." She shook him gently. "You tea is hot, just the way you

like it."

Sunshine spilled through the window like hot butter, while the fragrant breeze ballooned the curtains. A robin chirped in the apple tree in the garden.

"Papa," she said in alarm, "do you hear me? Wake up! Please, Papa, please!"

Alice's Adventures in Wonderland lay open on the bed. Her grandfather's still hand rested on the page. Annie reached out and touched his smooth face with her fingertips. His hollow cheek, his temple, his chin. They were cool and unmoving, but she drew back her hand as if she'd touched fire. From deep inside her chest a scream gathered and geysered up, splintering the tranquil afternoon. "No, Papa, no, no, no!"

"… then [Alice] walked down the little passage: and then—she found herself at last in the beautiful garden, among the bright flower-beds and the cool fountains."

THREE

They laid Papa Reed out in the parlor in his best suit, with his hands folded on his chest and his lips sealed in a strange, solemn grimace. It wasn't Papa. He never set his mouth that way, not even when he was complaining about the Depression or denouncing Mr. Herrick next door. This odd new expression looked more like the undertaker's face—dour and peevish all at once.

Annie wanted to yell at somebody for not getting this right. Papa's eyes were supposed to crinkle and his mouth should have arced in a sage little smile. The face she remembered rippled and glistened with life; this face was gray and lumpy like clay. And there was something more. She suspected Papa Reed's eyes had been sewn shut. Did they expect him to sit up and look around? Oh, the indignity of death!

And what gloom! The parlor that had brimmed with sunshine and resounded with laughter was dark and heavy now. The velvet drapes were drawn and voices were hushed, and the air was thick with the over-sweet perfume of roses and carnations—flowers Annie had loved until Papa's death. Now, in their porcelain vases, the bouquets looked like sentinels, guarding the shadows.

Only once did Annie bring herself to touch Papa's face. Perhaps fright kept her at arm's length, although in the past, death had stirred more curiosity than terror. But she hadn't stepped so close and stared death in the face before. It was sobering. She shivered as she ran her fingertips over Papa's cheek where she used to kiss him good night. She remembered the softness and warmth, like velvet, with the scent of lavender soap from his shaving mug. Now his cheek was smooth as wax and cold as a stone.

For three days Papa lay on display in the parlor in his gleaming oak casket. And for three days his friends and neighbors streamed through the house with armloads of casseroles and spring blossoms, paying their respects. Annie had never seen anything like it. Against Mama's wishes she stayed home from school and perched like a sentry in a wicker chair just outside the parlor door. She wasn't sure what she was guarding, or why; she just knew she had to do this for Papa.

Worst of all was the endless, monotonous chatter. The first day, everyone gathered around poor Papa, commented on his appearance in mournful tones, then swapped memories of him for hours. Annie had a feeling she'd hear their incessant prattle in her sleep.

"How gaunt he looks," said Mrs. Morrison from down the block. "Wasted away.

Why, Jonathan Reed was such a distinguished man in his day! I remember him in that very suit. He and Alma made such a handsome pair when they walked down the boulevard. Never apart, those two."

"Oh, he took her death hard," said Mrs. Henry, the minister's wife. "Never the same after that. Became a recluse, if you ask me."

"No, the Crash did that," said Deacon Schindler. "Lost his construction company and all his savings and investments, he did. Everything except this house. Good thing his son had money. Would've been a shame if they'd lost this grand old house."

"Built it himself, you know," said Mrs. Morrison. "Built the Herrick house around the corner too. Sold it for a tidy sum. Of course, it's not as large, and the Herricks don't keep it up. It's a shame how they've let it go."

"No wonder, with Tom Herrick always off on some new venture," murmured Mrs. Henry. "We never see him in church. I don't suppose that man will ever settle down."

"Dreadful. Wonder what his roving will do to his children?"

"They'll probably turn out just like him, poor things."

"It's his wife I pity," said Deacon Schindler. "She's a sickly little thing, but she always smiles sweetly like nothing's wrong. Brave woman."

"Or a fool," said Mrs. Morrison. "Truth is, I've heard Betty Herrick makes life miserable for everyone around her, always whining and complaining, or fainting dead away, whenever it suits her."

"Maybe she's truly ill and no one has bothered to notice," suggested Deacon Schindler. "What a tragedy that would be."

"So many tragedies in this world," sighed Mrs. Henry. "Why, think of that poor Lindbergh baby kidnapped last month. Who would have imagined… ?"

Deacon Schindler lowered his head until his chin was lost in the folds of his neck. "I agree. What's the world coming to?"

"It's the Depression," said Mrs. Morrison. "I blame everything on the Depression."

Annie listened to such twaddle for hours, until she was sure her ears would burn. Never had she heard so much gossip. She hadn't imagined that the world was so full of troubles and heartache. The chatter ceased only when Mama or Papa entered the parlor to greet their visitors. Then voices grew solemn and expressions turned somber, and everyone became very decorous and civilized as they paid their respects.

Of course, Mama never liked gossip or small talk. "If you can't say something nice about someone, say nothing at all," she told Annie more than once. Some people interpreted Mama's attitude as priggish or prudish, but Annie knew better. Mama could be as fun-loving and mischievous as anyone when she let her guard down. But that wasn't often, nor with just anybody.

Sometimes, Annie heard her mother and father behind closed doors, giggling like children, and she wondered what magic made her usually staid parents so playful. But, of course, this wasn't the time to think of frivolous things. Not with Papa Reed's funeral just two days away.

Still, on the second day of the wake, Annie began to play a little game. She pictured Papa Reed listening to everything that was said and imagined what his response would be. When Tom Herrick paid his respects and remarked how peaceful Papa Reed looked, Annie imagined her grandfather sitting up stoutly and barking, Of course I'm peaceful! I don't have to hear about your foolhardy ways anymore! Sometimes she had to stifle a chuckle. Once she laughed out loud, and the visitors craned their necks to see who was being so disrespectful of the dead.

But most of the time Annie's vigil left her feeling melancholy and abandoned. She wasn't anyone's favorite anymore. Who would read to her now? Who would laugh with her over Alice's adventures and Huck Finn's shenanigans? There was Cath, of course, dear Cath, her very best friend in the world. But Cath had no interest in books. She wanted only to draw and paint and travel and collect pictures of movie stars. She wanted real adventures, not exploits found in books. Reading was too tame for Cath.

Just before the casket was closed, Annie slipped her copy of Alice's Adventures in Wonderland in beside Papa. It was all she could give him—the last book they'd shared. "For you, Papa," she whispered. "I'll carry you in my heart forever."

On the day of Papa's funeral, Annie wore the only black dress she owned—a castoff of Alice Marie's, with long sleeves and a straight skirt almost to her ankles. It accented the fact she had no curves, an increasingly disturbing fact of life, especially when she saw Knowl Herrick standing with Alice Marie at the cemetery. Even more dismaying, he was holding her hand and wiping her tears. Drat! (Papa's word.) Alice Marie never cried over anything in her life!

At the graveside service, Reverend Henry, looking like a black bird with his natty black suit and generous beak of a nose, spoke eloquently of Papa. Looking over the clusters of family, friends, and townspeople surrounding the oak casket, he intoned, "My beloved, Jonathan Reed will long be remembered by all of us here. In 1875, he helped establish this town. By the turn of the century his construction company had built half the houses in Willowbrook. Fine, well-crafted homes. He was a man of quality and integrity. What the Depression stole from Jonathan Reed it stole from all of us. His loss was our loss. But we'll never forget what he gave us, nor the example he set for us. We were blessed to have known him!"

After Reverend Henry had finished speaking, Alice Marie, looking like an angel in pink chiffon, stepped delicately up on a grassy knoll, taking care that every ruffle was in place. Folding her hands gracefully, she looked heavenward and began to sing "Rock of Ages" in a lilting, bell-clear soprano.

Even the whispering breeze and twittering wrens seemed to hush as Alice Marie sang. The sunlight on her golden curls effused her milk and roses countenance with a resplendent halo. By the time she began the last verse, her voice swelling, resonant with emotion, every eye brimmed with tears:

> *While I draw this fleeting breath,*
> *While mine eyes shall close in death,*
> *When I soar to worlds unknown,*
> *See Thee on Thy judgment throne,*
> *Rock of Ages cleft for me,*
> *Let me hide myself in Thee.*

As Alice Marie's final note faded in the placid air and the fragrant grasses stirred again, Chip—ever the dutiful, attentive brother—came and stood beside Annie. He slipped a comforting arm around her shoulder and whispered, "Papa Reed knows we would have sung to him, too—if we had a voice like our sister's."

While Reverend Henry offered a lengthy closing prayer in his deep, droning voice, Annie's mind wrestled with questions for which she had no answer. Was there really a God who welcomed Papa Reed into a place called heaven? Would Papa be happy there? Or would he tell God he'd rather come back to Willowbrook? Would Papa find someone else to read to in heaven? Would he find any books? There would be the Bible, Annie supposed. But what about Lewis Carroll and Mark Twain and the Bronte sisters? Were they all there, busy writing books in heaven? Annie smiled wistfully. What a marvelous way to spend forever.

After the service, everyone gathered around Alice Marie, bursting with praises. "That was the loveliest tribute your grandfather could have received," declared Deacon Schindler.

"He would have been so proud of you," cried Mrs. Morrison, dabbing her eyes with her lace hanky.

Alice Marie demurely lowered her gaze. "I just wanted my grandfather to know how much I loved him."

Mrs. Morrison gave Alice Marie an impulsive hug. "Oh, I'm sure he heard that splendid voice from the very portals of glory! You must have been your grandfather's favorite!"

Alice Marie stepped back and offered a modest smile. "Yes, Mrs. Morrison. I like to think so."

Mrs. Morrison turned then to Annie. "Well, Elizabeth Anne, you must be awfully proud of your big sister."

"Annie," she corrected. Only Papa called her "Elizabeth Anne," and only when he was angry. But Mrs. Morrison was already off gushing effusively to someone else.

As Annie took one last look at Papa's coffin, huge tears rolled down her cheeks. She sniffed unceremoniously and rubbed her nose. How stupid! She had forgotten her hanky.

She looked up helplessly and met Knowl's gaze across the casket. His crinkly brown eyes were captivating through his wire-rim glasses. He smiled warmly, then broke away from Alice Marie and strode around to her side, where he handed her his handkerchief. Then, without a word he took her in his arms and pressed her head against his chest. He was more than a head taller than she. She held her breath, dazed. She could feel his heart beating through his starched white shirt. Or perhaps it was her own heart pounding in her ears.

He looked down at her, his wind-tossed, wheat-colored hair toppling over his ruddy forehead. "I just wanted to say, Annie, I'm so sorry about your grandfather. I know how much you loved him."

She wiped her nose and said dumbly, "You did? How?"

He gently tweaked her chin. His eyes were merry one moment, brooding the next. "I just know those things."

Annie remained spellbound in Knowl's gaze, until Alice Marie sidled over and took his arm, tossing her flaxen curls. "Knowl, you're going to walk me home from the cemetery, aren't you?"

His handsome, angular face flushed with pleasure. "Of course."

Before Alice Marie strutted away with her prize, she turned to Annie and whispered, "I suppose you'll be happy now. With Papa Reed gone, I'll have the blue room, and the rosebud room will finally belong to you."

Annie was aghast. A knot tightened in her chest, making it hard to breathe. To think that someone—even Alice Marie—would accuse her of being happy about Papa's death! The truth was, if Annie could bring Papa back, she would forever share the rosebud room with Alice Marie—a profound sacrifice, by any measure!

No words of retort came; instead, Annie turned and fled, running alone from the cemetery back to the house, to her familiar rosebud room where she buried her face in her pillow and sobbed.

Catherine found her there—knocked on the door first, but hardly waited for a reply—and came bursting in, exclaiming, "What's wrong? Why didn't you wait for me at the cemetery? Everyone's looking for you! The tables are set up in the garden and spread with heaps of food." She paused, breathless, and wrinkled her freckled nose. "Why are you hiding in your room? Are you crying for Papa Reed?"

Wiping her eyes, Annie told Cath why she wept. Partly Papa, mainly Alice Marie.

Cath was up in arms before Annie had even finished. "I'll pull her fancy curls out of her head and stuff them down her throat for saying such a hateful thing!" Cath made quite a picture when she was angry. Tall and lanky, with freckles and carrot-orange curls as fiery as her personality, she was always waving her emotions in the air like flags for all the world to see. But Annie wouldn't change her for anything.

Cath was still fuming. "If I had a sister like Alice Marie, I'd bundle up her fancy clothes and throw them in the river."

Annie smiled faintly, imagining Alice Marie running about in her petticoats, screaming as her frilly dresses floated by.

Cath reached for Annie's hand. "Come on. You can't run away every time your sister hurts you. You'll be running all your life."

"I can't fight her, Cath. She always wins."

"Not this time. We're going out to the garden—together. And you'll talk to my brother Knowl as if he only had eyes for you."

Annie managed another fleeting smile. "Just as you'll talk with dreamy eyes to my brother, Chip?"

"Of course. Come, Annie. Your grandfather would want you to be with your family today."

"All right, Cath. Give me a minute and I'll be there."

"A minute. That's all."

When Catherine had gone, Annie sat down at the writing desk that had once been Papa Reed's, took out a sheet of paper, and dipped her pen into the ink well. Blinking back tears, she wrote in her best penmanship:

Dear Papa Reed,
I can't sing to you, but I can write to you.
I'll try to be strong without you,
but how can I go on
when there's no one left who loves me best?
I'll always love words the way you loved them,
and I'll try to write stories
you would have loved to read.
And in my heart I will always hear you
reading them to me.
                              — Your Annie.

FOUR

The Summer of 1932.

The rosebud room at the top of the stairs was Annie's now—the first bedroom on the left, with the high dormer windows looking over tree-lined Honeysuckle Lane. Mama had papered the room with pale pink rosebud wallpaper the year Alice Marie was born; hence, the name, the rosebud room. It had been Alice Marie's until Annie came along three years later, on January 8, 1920, the last of Jon and Anna Reed's winsome offspring.

Annie knew how much Alice Marie had detested sharing the small, homey bedroom with her tag-along little sister. Twelve long years, it had been. The two had managed an uneasy truce, broken at times by tantrums, tirades, and angry tears. Annie had grown accustomed to her sister's complaints. "Botheration!" Alice exclaimed in her most caustic tone whenever Annie did something to irritate her.

In response, Annie simply hummed a mindless tune, shutting out her sister's diatribes, which only provoked Alice Marie to more exquisite displays of rage. Sometimes the anger was justified, Annie conceded, remembering the time she operated with a pen knife on the broadcloth stomach of Alice Marie's favorite doll to discover what made it cry.

But now Alice Marie would have her own room—the blue room that had been Papa Reed's and his beloved Alma's for all the years of their marriage. It was the biggest room, and the most mysterious, because no one had entered Papa's door except at his invitation. Annie remembered those days. For a time after her grandmother's death, Papa Reed sequestered himself in the blue room, emerging only for meals, a frail stranger passing through the rooms of his house like a solemn ghost—there for an instant and then gone.

In the past year, he had begun taking his meals in his room, eliminating even that fleeting apparition of himself in the hallways. But he always welcomed Annie for a bedside chat, a good night prayer, or a few moments of reciting a favorite Psalm. And, of course, even after ill health confined him to bed, he still spent countless hours reading to Annie—everything from the classics to the comic strips.

Annie was glad she wasn't moving to the blue room. It would remind her too much of Papa Reed.

After Papa Reed's belongings had been sorted, crated, and carted off to auction (Annie got his Bible and his leather-bound books), Alice Marie began moving her possessions into the empty, freshly scrubbed room. Annie never asked her sister how she liked living in a dead man's room, although the question burned in Annie's mind every time she entered Alice's private domain. Once, Annie realized that Alice Marie must have read her mind, for she eyed Annie coolly and snapped, "It's not so bad in Papa Reed's room. It's better than living with a snippet like you!"

Annie only smiled politely and walked away. She would not stoop to Alice Marie's level. No. She had won the rosebud room, and she needed no further triumph.

As soon as Alice Marie had vacated the premises, Annie began adding her own touches—photographs of her favorite movie stars: Ronald Colman, Norma Shearer, Helen Hayes, and, of course, the three Barrymores—John, Ethel, and Lionel. She hung comical sketches of Charlie Chaplin that Cath had done in charcoal and pastels. She even brought her fine porcelain dolls out of their boxes in the closet and lined them up on the shelf over the bureau. She was too old now for dolls, but she loved waking in the morning and gazing up at their bright satin gowns and flowing silk tresses.

Annie dreamed that someday she would look like one of those dolls, with an hourglass figure and perfect porcelain face. Yes, she could imagine it—dark lashes, pale pink cheeks, red rosebud lips. She would make Alice Marie look dull by comparison.

Alas, Alice Marie, while snooty and insufferable in disposition, possessed a remarkable nose and chin, nearly regal when she tilted her head just so, and the finest mane of golden blonde hair Annie had ever seen. She looked like a smaller version of Mama, although she exhibited none of Mama's compassion and patience.

Annie saw herself as vulnerable, introspective, and quietly fueled by the heat of her emotions, while Alice Marie was outspoken and shrewdly calculating. Annie, if she dared boast of her own character traits, had inherited many of Mama's good qualities—her kindness and sensitivity, her gentleness and love of poetry—but it dismayed Annie that she had been short-changed when it came to Mama's looks. Why had Mama given all of her beauty and grace to Alice Marie? Why couldn't she have made Alice Marie kinder and Annie prettier?

Of course, Annie realized it wasn't really up to Mama. Such decisions were made by her loving Heavenly Father. Surely He knew what He was doing, even if sometimes Annie wished she could be quite frank with Him in her prayers. Maybe it hadn't occurred to Him that she would be much happier with a pretty face instead of a plain one, with blonde hair instead of sable brown, and thick lashes to frame her enormous gray-green eyes. Or maybe God didn't have time for the wishes and whims of a silly young Indiana girl.

Annie considered discussing the matter with Cath during one of their private conversations in the rosebud room as they lay fanning themselves on one of Alma Reed's eiderdown quilts. But Annie wasn't sure she wanted Cath to know how very vain and self-absorbed she was. It was the sort of trait Annie detested in Alice Marie; how could she confess to possessing it herself?

So she kept her lament to herself, while Cath rattled on about what she grandly called her "period," something Annie pretended to know all about. Actually, the whole thing struck her as maddeningly mysterious. She would much rather be outside playing ball with Knowl and Chip, or even army men with figures Knowl had carved from balsa wood. But the boys were in high school now and had little time for little sisters.

"You're doing it again, Annie." Cath sounded irritated.

"Doing what?"

"Day-dreaming. About my brother."

"How can you tell?"

Cath exploded in laughter. "That look you get. All dreamy
eyed, like in the movies."

"I was thinking that Knowl looks like Ronald Colman
without the mustache, but even more charming. Only one flaw. He's in love with Alice Marie." Annie swatted at a fly droning lazily around her head. "Alice Marie says Knowl worships the ground she walks on. Do you think that's true, Cath?"

Cath wrinkled her freckled nose and twisted one of her carrot curls. "He's in love with a pretty face. He can't see her heart. But just you wait. Someday you and I will have a double wedding. I'll marry Chip and you'll marry Knowl, and we'll live happily ever after, just like Janet Gaynor and Charles Farrell in `Seventh Heaven.'"

"This isn't the movies, Cath. It's real life."

"We'll make it happen. We can make anything happen we want, if we try hard enough."

Annie wasn't convinced, but she didn't tell Cath. No sense in both of them being depressed.

"Of course, I'm not sure I want to get married," said Cath.

Annie stared at her as if she had uttered an oath. "Not get married? How can you say such a thing?"

"I have places to go and things to see...." Her voice trailed off. "Besides, what's so grand about marriage?"

Annie nodded. She wasn't sure what married people did that was different from the rest of the world, but she knew it was something special, because every Saturday night, like clockwork, her parents excused themselves and adjourned to their room. And Annie couldn't help noticing the half-smiles they tried to hide as they bid everyone good night.

Annie leaned over close to Cath. "The other night Alice Marie told me she knows what married people do in their bedrooms, but she wouldn't tell me. She just covered her mouth and giggled."

Cath's brows arched with interest. "Maybe she was just bluffing."

"No, because her cheeks flushed beet-red when she talked about Mama and Papa behind their closed doors."

"What do you think she was going to say?"

Annie shrugged. "I don't know." She had pretty much decided she didn't want to know what married people did anyway, if it caused everyone to blush so deeply and act so tittery. She preferred to imagine romance the way it appeared on the big screen when she and Cath went to the picture show on Saturday mornings.

"Then why'd you bring up the subject if there's nothing to tell?" Cath sounded peeved. "Now you've got my curiosity up."

"I figured you might know something Alice Marie isn't telling."

"I've got my suspicions, but I wouldn't say it out loud unless I knew for sure. It's too awful for words."

"Then let's talk about something else," said Annie. She felt a trifle irritated. She wasn't sure why.

"Is your mama going to let you go see that new actress at the Majestic Theater?" asked Cath, fanning herself. Beads of moisture stood out on her upper lip. The curtains at the open window remained limp and lifeless; there wasn't a breeze to be found this side of Chicago.

"What actress? You mean, Katharine Hepburn?"

Cath nodded. "She's in that film, 'Bill of Divorcement.'"

"Mama won't let me see a movie about divorce. She says it's sinful."

Cath slipped off the bed and walked over to the window. She stuck her head out and waved her fan vigorously, stirring up a faint, fleeting breeze. "My mama and daddy talk about divorce all the time."

Annie sat forward, wondering if she had heard correctly. Was Cath talking about the movies or real life? "Your mama and daddy? They talk about divorce?"

Cath sat back down. Her rosy face shone with pinpoints of perspiration. "Yes. They talk about… getting one."

Annie tried to hide her surprise. "Why would they want to get divorced?"

"Because Daddy's gone so much. Selling his brushes. Selling all those Fuller brushes."

"They can't get a divorce. You might move away."

"I'd never go, no matter what. We're friends for life."

"Maybe your mama's joking," offered Annie. She couldn't think of anything else to say. "Maybe she just says that to make your daddy stay home more."

Cath nodded. "But how can he stay home? Mama says there's not enough money to pay the bills. He has to go out selling."

"I'm glad my papa works at the A&P," said Annie. Originally, it was 'The Great Atlantic & Pacific Tea Company,' but Annie was glad the grocery store chain was known these days simply as the A&P. Her father had been a manager there for nearly ten years.

"I wish my father worked at the A&P, too," mused Cath. "Then maybe I'd see him sometime. And maybe then the bill collectors wouldn't be always knocking on our door."

Privately, Annie had to admit that Cath's family had a harder time of it than her family. Her own papa was bringing home a steady paycheck right through the Depression. A lot of husbands and fathers were wearing their best suits and standing on the street corner selling apples for a nickel. "At least we don't live in one of those shanty towns with tar paper shacks, what my papa calls 'Hoovervilles,'" she said at last.

"Thank the good Lord for that!" exclaimed Cath, as if the idea were too preposterous for words.

Annie nodded solemnly. "Papa says we've got to get us a new president. He says Hoover's got to go."

"My papa says so too. He says, 'Hoover told us prosperity's just around the corner, only he never told us which corner!'"

Annie wasn't one to think about presidents and politics, but this summer the subject was on everyone's mind. "My papa says Hoover wasn't responsible for the Crash or Depression, but people have to blame someone, so why not the man who promised them prosperity?"

"Everybody's saying that. Not just your papa."

"Sure, because the election's just months away. Everybody has an opinion."

"Do you?" asked Cath.

"Papa says he's voting for the Democratic candidate, Franklin Roosevelt, and his running mate, John Garner."

"But who would you vote for?"

"I'm with Papa."

"Okay, maybe I wouldn't vote for President Hoover and Vice-President Curtis. But what's so grand about Mr. Roosevelt?"

Annie shrugged. She didn't know much about any of the candidates, but when Papa talked about Mr. Roosevelt, he had a fervency in his voice she hadn't heard before. "He's going to put this country back on its feet," Papa would declare, pounding the table with his massive fist. Annie was still young enough to believe Papa was always right. So lately, when she said her prayers, she added a little postscript: "Dear Lord, please let Mr. Roosevelt be our next president."

"So who are you thinking about now?" asked Cath. "Mr. Roosevelt or my brother Knowl?"

"Neither. I'm remembering something Papa said. 'Change is in the wind.' Do you know what it means?"

"Is it a riddle? A guessing game?" Cath was fanning herself again.

"It's not a game, Cath. Until Papa Reed's death, I thought life would go on the way it always has, with my family living forever in this house. And you'd always live in the house around the corner. But now I see how things change. Papa Reed up and died for no reason."

"He was eighty-two, Annie. Old!"

"Mama and Papa are growing old too!" There, she'd said it! Their sturdy porcelain faces were already lined with fine wrinkles like tiny cracks in a china teacup. "What if they die someday like Papa Reed?" An intolerable thought! "Everything's changing. Chip wants to leave home and join the Navy someday."

"He can't!" exclaimed Cath. "Not until I'm old enough for him to notice me."

"You're thirteen and he hasn't noticed you yet."

"But he will."

"But what if—?" It was too horrible to say.

"What, Annie?"

She forced out the words. "What if your parents get a divorce and you move away? What would happen to us—our friendship?"

Cath was speechless. A rare moment indeed.

Annie hated herself for even raising the question. She wanted to stave off adulthood and remain twelve forever. A perfect age. Old enough to have some sense, young enough to play with the swell paper dolls Cath drew, or slide down a snow bank, or play hooky from school when the circus came to town.

"It's not like we haven't talked about growing up," Annie rushed on. "You want to take the train to New York City to see a vaudeville show and the Statue of Liberty. You'll become a famous artist and study in Europe and paint magazine covers for The Saturday Evening Post."

"That's a whole lifetime away," protested Cath. "Besides, you plan to become a famous writer—a poet like Elizabeth Barrett Browning. You'll travel the world and publish books that say deep things like, 'How do I love thee? Let me count the ways.'"

Annie couldn't argue with that. She yearned to write long, somber gothic novels full of love and heartbreak, sweet heather and dark moors, like the Bronte sisters had done. But she could pen her literary works right here at home on Honeysuckle Lane. No need to upset the apple cart or tread into uncharted waters. No need for lifelong friends to be separated.

"It doesn't matter what careers we choose," Annie declared. "We can be together. I have a foolproof plan."

"Tell me."

"If I marry your brother Knowl, and you marry my brother Chip, we'll be more than friends. We'll be family! We'll be related for the rest of our lives!"

Cath frowned. "But what if something goes wrong? What if we never get married? What if we lose touch with each other?"

Unthinkable!

The two girls sat facing each other in a moment of grave

silence, their legs crossed Indian-style, the heat drawing the sweat out on their faces while flies droned lazily in the muggy air. Annie wiped perspiration from her upper lip and pushed her damp brown hair back from her forehead. In a solemn voice, she told Cath, "We've got to make a pact."

"What sort of pact?" The sun from the window cast flaming streaks across Cath's corkscrew curls. Her head bobbed a little. "You know. A piece of paper we sign in blood saying nothing will ever change between us. We'll always be best friends."

"Why do we need to write it down? We've already said it." "But what if you move? Or what if someday you start acting snooty and smug like Alice Marie and hate me to the core?"

"I'll never act like Alice Marie."

"But suppose you get married to someone beside Chip and your husband says you have to like him better than you like me?"

"I'll never marry anyone but Chip, and he already knows we're best friends."

"I still want to write it down."

"You write everything down."

"Only the important stuff." Annie got off the bed and went to her writing desk. She took out paper, pen, and ink, and wrote, "We, Catherine Herrick and Elizabeth Anne Reed, promise to be best friends forever, and to never like anyone else better, or may heaven strike us dead on the spot." She handed the paper to Cath. "We should sign in blood."

Cath looked doubtful. "Can't we just spit on it?"

"Spit isn't legal."

"Neither is blood."

"It's more legal than spit."

"Well, how do we get blood?"

Annie gazed around the room at the oak night stand with its ceramic blue water pitcher, at the highboy with her albums of stamps from around the world and her worn volumes of Edna St. Vincent Millay and Emily Dickinson. "My brother has a pen knife, but he's doing chores for Mrs. Morrison down the block."

"Mama's pin cushion's in the sewing room," said Cath. "I could run home—"

"My mama's sewing room is closer." Annie ran out of the room and was back moments later, holding up a gleaming needle. She sucked in her breath, closed her eyes, and jabbed the needle into her index finger. A red bubble spouted on the little white pad of flesh. She held her finger still until Cath was ready; then they pressed their fingertips together, blood mixing with blood, and made their prints on the writing paper.

"Sealed in blood," said Annie solemnly.

Cath nodded. "I won't ever care about anybody the way I care about you, Annie. I sign with my blood to prove it."

"Friends forever?" said Annie.

"Friends forever," said Cath.

They signed their names beside the smudged red prints and waited as the sun streaming in the window dried the ink. Then Annie carefully folded the paper and slipped it into Papa Reed's Bible, exactly between the Old Testament and New Testament, where she vowed it would remain until her dying day.

"But why do you get to keep it?" asked Cath. "Why shouldn't I keep it at my house?"

"It was my idea," said Annie. "And my paper."

"But we both signed it."

Annie thought a moment. "We'll take turns. This week I keep it."

That seemed to satisfy Cath. She scooted over beside Annie and hugged her. Their arms were sticky with sweat and their hair damp with humidity, but they didn't care. They laughed as salty tears ran down their cheeks, mixing with perspiration.

"This is the best day of my life," said Annie.

"Me too," said Cath.

But after Cath went home, Annie sat on her bed as the sun sank lower in the sky and wondered why she didn't feel happier about their pact. She wanted that slip of paper to keep them exactly as they were this day—loyal, devoted friends. Friends forever. Friends that nothing and no one could separate.

But she sensed it already. The hours were ticking away, tarnishing the memories, pushing them both beyond these cherished moments to new days and new experiences—a whole lifetime of distractions and diversions, unknown alliances and alienations.

Annie wondered, Could their friendship possibly survive?

FIVE

The Winter of 1936.

Dear Papa Reed,
Mr. Roosevelt has done it again!
He won the election over Governor Alf Landon
for a second term as President
by a landslide of 27 million votes.
His New Deal with its alphabet of programs—
WPA, FERA, CCC, AAA, and NIRA—is sweeping away
the Depression at last. Maybe this time
prosperity really is just around the corner!
Papa says, Now, if Mr. Roosevelt
can just keep us out of war!
We've settled into a routine here at home
of sitting around the radio in the parlor
listening to Mr. Roosevelt's fireside chats.
I like listening to his voice, dear Papa,
because it reminds me of you reading to me
those many years ago.
Now that I'm nearly seventeen,
I want more than ever to be a serious writer.
I would love to write something significant
like Magnificent Obsession or In His Steps.
But do I have the depth and sensitivity
to be a Lloyd Douglas or a Charles Sheldon?
Oh, Papa Reed, what if I am a very shallow person?
Sometimes I think I must be
when I get jealous and angry with Alice Marie.
Or what if I never have any great experiences
in life to write about?
What if I remain insufferably dull?
Papa Reed, I read a book this week
you would have loved to read to me.
It's called Gone with the Wind,
about the Old South in the Civil War,

by an unknown lady writer named Margaret Mitchell.
Her book was published just last June,
and already it's sold hundreds of thousands of copies.
I dreamed last night I was Margaret Mitchell
autographing books for lines of readers going on
forever, and the name I signed was "Annie Reed."
Will all my yearnings always just be dreams
or will they come true one day?
I wish I knew.
I still think of you, Papa Reed.
— Your Annie.

Christmas was still a week away, but tonight was better than Christmas because Chip and Knowl were coming home from Purdue for the holidays. The house was spanking clean—everything from Mama's gleaming brass lamps and mahogany plant stand with its clawed feet to Papa's cherry wood bookcase and his favorite writing desk with its silver blotter and inkwell. Mama had to have everything perfect, making Papa out of sorts and everyone else on edge. Do this, do that, oh, we can't have this, we need more of that, hurry, we'll never be ready on time!

While Papa drove his wheezing Packard through drifts of snow to the depot to meet the evening train, Annie and Cath helped Mama put the finishing touches on the yuletide decorations.

As they worked, "Silent Night" streamed from the handsome floor-model RCA radio Papa bought Mama as an early Christmas present. It stood in the corner of the parlor by the French doors, not far from the freshly cut fir tree Papa had dragged in that morning all the way from the woods behind the house. Sap was oozing from the trunk and the pungent smell of raw, sawed wood and ripe pine needles filled the room.

"My good Persian carpet!" Mama lamented. "Look at all the needles! Look at the wet spots where snow has melted! This rug will never be clean again!"

"Yes, it will, Mama," Annie assured her. "Don't let a little mess spoil this evening. Everything will look wonderful."

"Fiddlesticks! Where's Alice Marie? She promised to help."

Annie fastened a sprig of mistletoe over the paneled door. "She's upstairs in her room, Mama."

"Primping for my brother," said Cath with a hint of exasperation. She sat, legs crossed, in the wing chair, sewing holly berries and popcorn for tree trimmings. "Wait'll Knowl sees Alice Marie prancing in here all painted up like Greta Garbo or Jean Harlow. He doesn't have a chance against her wiles!"

"Maybe he'll think she looks like a hussy," muttered Annie. She still hoped against hope when Knowl walked through the door tonight, he would have eyes only for her. After all, she had grown up a great deal since he began his sophomore year at Purdue in September. Friends and family alike said she was as pretty now as her sister, with her long, burnished tresses and thickly-lashed gray-green eyes. Perhaps Knowl's fondness for Alice Marie had waned during their four-month separation. Alice Marie had certainly swooned over enough handsome beaus during Knowl's absence.

Mama brushed back a wisp of fine blonde hair and wiped her hands on her apron. Tiny beads of perspiration made her face glisten. In the rosy lamplight, she looked like a Christmas angel.

"Catherine, will your mother be joining us tonight?" Mama asked with her customary caution when she inquired about the Herricks. Tom Herrick hadn't been home in several years, except for brief, tension-filled appearances, and even Cath refused to talk to anyone but Annie about her mother's recent binges with alcohol or the financial straits that forced her to take in boarders of questionable character.

"No, Mrs. Reed. My mama's a little under the weather," Cath said politely, "but she'll be fine tomorrow, I'm sure."

"You give her my regards, Catherine. And be sure and take her some of my floating island pudding and homemade fruitcake."

"Thank you, Mrs. Reed. I certainly will."

Mama straightened and rubbed the small of her back. "I hope the road's clear tonight for Papa. Looks like we might get a blizzard blowing in before we're through."

"It should be okay," said Cath. "The road grader was through here earlier, pulled by a team of Mr. Morrison's horses."

Mama shook her head. "Even Mr. Morrison's horses can't hold back these bitter Indiana winters. Any squalls Chicago gets, they send directly our way, never fail."

"Papa'll get through," said Annie. "He's got to." She gazed out the window at the snowflakes whirling and dancing on the crisp night air. The windowpanes were etched with frost—delicate, swirling designs Annie always marveled over in the moonlight before climbing into bed under her mountains of comforters and quilts.

Tonight she stared past the icy hieroglyphics, watching for Papa's automobile. Already her heart was hammering with excitement. Surely Mama must hear. Cath must sense the nervous flutter in her stomach and hear the breathlessness in her voice. Tonight Knowl would truly see her for the first time in his life—the real Annie, the woman she had become, and surely he would begin to feel what she felt.

How was it possible for one human being to feel so much love for another without the other one responding in kind? This time, even though her lips were silent, Knowl would feel the warmth and ardor of her affection. She, who had always had eyes only for him, could love him with profoundly more abandonment than Alice Marie, who dallied with the affections of nearly every young man she met.

"Elizabeth Anne? Did you hear me? What world have you wandered off to?"

Her mother's voice. "What, Mama? I'm sorry. I was just thinking…"

"You're always just thinking. Come back down to earth."

"I know who you were thinking of," smiled Cath.

Annie met Cath's gaze as if to say, I'm thinking of your brother like you're thinking of mine!

Alice Marie swept into the room then, smelling of lavender soap and too-sweet cologne. Her hair hung in shiny golden ringlets and her stylish brocade dress showed the roundness of her bosom and the curve of her hips. Her lashes were long and lush and her lips apple-red. Annie sank down on the settee, her spirits plunging. Drat! Knowl would be as taken as ever by Alice Marie's glamour.

"Mama, are they here yet?" Alice Marie sashayed to the window in her stacked heels. "Where are they, Mama? The train arrived an hour ago. Papa should be back by now."

"It's snowing again," said Cath. "Makes driving slow."

Mama looked Alice Marie up and down. "Looks like you're more ready for a night-club than a home-cooked dinner."

Alice Marie sat down gracefully on the love seat and examined a polished nail. "I'm hoping Knowl will take me dancing, Mama. Anything wrong with that?"

"Tonight's a family time, daughter—your brother home for the first time in months. He'll want to see you."

"He'll want to see Catherine, you mean." She eyed Cath knowingly. "The two of you could join Knowl and me. They play wonderful Jazz at the Stardust Ballroom down-town."

Cath and Annie exchanged quick glances. Cath's glance said Do I dare? Annie's said, You can't go! What about me?

"I don't think so," Cath mumbled without conviction.

"I should hope not," said Mama. "Isn't that where they have those dance marathons where couples dance for hours and days until they faint dead away?"

"Oh, Mama, they don't do that anymore." Alice Marie helped herself to the popcorn Cath was stringing. "The Ballroom has a swell band, Mama. In fact, they—they offered me a job."

Mama's eyes narrowed. "What kind of job?"

"A singing job, Mama. With the band. I'd be their girl singer."

"You sing already," said Mama. "In church."

"But I'd get paid, Mama. It'd be a good job with good pay. A lot better than selling silly hats in the millinery department at J.C. Penney."

"Your papa didn't pay for voice lessons so you could sing with some Jazz band and hobnob with a bunch of traveling musicians."

Alice Marie's voice turned pouty. "You don't know anything about it, Mama. They're swell fellows. From Brooklyn and Detroit and Chicago and St. Louis. They tell such fascinating tales. Listen, Mama, there's a whole lot more to the world than little old Honeysuckle Lane and Willowbrook."

"I have all the world I can handle right here in this house," said Mama, twisting several spiky pine branches into a wreath for the door. "Now go change your dress before—"

Annie jumped up. "Mama, Papa's car! They're here!"

The girls raced Mama through the living room to the marbled foyer where Annie threw open the wide front door. Papa, Knowl, and Chip, their breath making frosty clouds in the air, stomped snow from their galoshes and burst inside. They peeled off wool scarfs and snow-flecked overcoats. Before they were even out of their coats, eager arms circled their necks and smiling lips kissed their cold, ruddy cheeks. The warm, pine-scented house rang with shouts, commotion, and a blur of activity as everyone exchanged hugs and greetings.

"Oh, Chilton—Chip, my son!" cried Mama, dabbing her eyes with her hanky. "You're more grown up than ever. Where's the little boy I rocked in my arms?"

He swept her up and swung her around. "I'm right here, Mama. You're just getting smaller or I'm getting taller!"

Chip gave Annie his usual older-brother hammerlock, kissed Alice Marie on each cheek, then turned his attention to Cath. He took both her hands and drew her to him. "I've seen that red hair in my dreams," he murmured, kissing her gently.

Knowl and Alice Marie embraced as Papa gave Mama a quick peck on the cheek. "I brought your wandering brood home. Now do I get dinner?"

Mama gestured toward the kitchen. "It's almost ready."

Chip sniffed the air. "Mama's pot roast. How I've waited all these months for Mama's pot roast!"

"You're staying for dinner, aren't you, Knowl?" asked Annie.

He released Alice Marie long enough to give Annie an old-fashioned bear hug. "I don't know, Annie. I should get home and see my mama."

"Don't bother," said Cath, her tone brittle. "Mama won't know whether you're there or not."

Knowl's voice lowered. "It's gotten that bad?"

"Worse," said Cath. She turned abruptly from her brother and clasped Chip's hand. "So let's have a nice evening here and we'll face Mama later, okay?"

Knowl nodded and turned to Papa. "Thanks for picking us up at the depot, Mr. Reed." He cleared his throat as he gripped Papa's shoulder. "And thanks for all you've done—the loan—making Purdue possible—treating me like I was one of your own—"

"You are one of my own," said Papa, giving him a fond back slap. "You're a good boy. The loan's just between us, okay? I know you're good for it. Don't mention it again."

"Sure. It's just that college would have been out of the question if—"

"Say no more." Papa turned to Mama. "My dear lady, I could eat a horse!"

She smiled. "A horse? Fine. Mr. Morrison's team was by earlier clearing the road. Or we have pot roast!"

"Pot roast and Christmas all at once?" declared Chip, his eyes sweeping over the candles, holly wreaths, and popcorn garlands. "I think I've died and gone to heaven!"

He bowed gallantly and took Mama's hand, then Cath's, and escorted them to the dining room, where a bountiful table was spread. Alice Marie lingered behind, drawing Knowl aside. Annie paused in the doorway, listening.

She heard Alice Marie whisper, "Knowl, we could go to the Stardust Ballroom later. They have a swell band and I bet Papa would let you take the Packard."

Knowl sounded uncertain. "Not tonight, sweetheart. It's been a long day and I'd better get home after dinner. My mama—"

"I know all about your mama. Don't worry. I'll find someone else to take me to the Ballroom."

"I'll take you, Alice Marie, but not tonight." He seized her arm. "I don't want you going with any other boy, you hear?"

She laughed uneasily. "I was teasing, Knowl. Don't you know teasing when you hear it?"

He kissed her hair. "You've been teasing me all my life!"

Alice Marie tittered coyly until she spotted Annie watching. Her expression sobered. "What is it, Annie? You want something?"

"No. Just dinner. Mama wants us to sit down now."

Cath and Annie helped Mama serve the mashed potatoes, yams, baked apples, creamed peas, buttermilk biscuits, and pot roast. Mama had set the table with her best linen, crystal, and china. Near the table stood an enormous oak hutch displaying Grandmother Reed's Blue Willow ware and fancy crystal containers encased in silver and brimming over with sweet hard candy. Everything gleamed, reflecting the rosy light of the overhead chandelier. Annie felt a warm, heady pleasure tingle through her whenever the family gathered around the table for one of Mama's scrumptious meals. She felt an extra measure of delight tonight with Knowl sitting next to her (her doing, of course). What mattered was that he was beside her, his hard-muscled shoulder mere inches from hers. Forget that his hand moved across the tablecloth to link with Alice Marie's.

"All right, children. Let us pray." Everyone grew quiet as Papa asked the blessing, but the pleasant din quickly resumed amid the clink and clatter of dishes.

Knowl lifted the pitcher of ice water and filled Annie's goblet. "You look very pretty tonight," he told her. "You've grown up."

She felt her mouth go dry. "Do you think so?"

"Of course. Only when you smile do I see the little Annie Reed I used to know in pigtails and bandaged knees."

She flushed. "That was years ago."

"Swell years." Knowl's voice grew wistful. "Sometimes I lie in my dormitory room and picture Honeysuckle Lane and your house and the yard and the garden, and I play back all the memories like they were movie films."

"Don't you think about your house too?"

"No. I remember only happy memories."

Annie felt suddenly ill at ease, as if she'd forced Knowl to admit something none of them put into words. "Pass the gravy, please."

Knowl handed her the china gravy boat. His expression remained reflective. "Are you still writing, Annie?"

She nodded. "Poems mostly. And a few stories."

"So you're still going to be a famous writer someday?"

She stared at her plate. "I hope so."

"You don't sound very confident."

She looked up at him, pleased. He looked genuinely interested. "Oh, Knowl, I want to write deep things like T. S. Eliot or long, wonderful novels like Edna Ferber, but everything I write sounds so—so childish!"

Knowl buttered a biscuit and took a bite. "Tell you what, Annie. I'm studying journalism at the university. Maybe I can give you a few pointers."

Annie gasped. Had she heard right? "Would you?"

"Sure. Be glad to. Your family's like my kith and kin. Your papa's more a daddy to me than mine ever was. Anything I can do for any of you—"

"Tell me, Knowl—Chip," said Papa in his booming voice, "how's life treating you two at Purdue? You learning plenty?"

"Sure are," said Chip. "It's hard, Papa, but I'm doing fine. Especially in math and science."

Knowl turned to Alice Marie. "I wish you could come visit us. I'd take you for a walk along the Wabash River. It's the prettiest sight in the moonlight."

"And you'd love it too, Cath," said Chip. "You should see the art gallery. Paintings from everywhere like you never saw before, except maybe at the World's Fair a few years back."

"I want to go to the Chicago Art Institute next year," Cath said fervently, "but Mama would never let me."

"Mama couldn't stop you if you got a scholarship," said Knowl. "And you could, too. You're good, better than most!"

"You are, Cath," said Annie. "You paint better than those European artists painting all that modern art. I'd go to college in a minute, if Mama let me."

"You, Elizabeth Anne? Go to college? You mean Purdue? That's a boy's school."

"It's not, Mama," said Chip. "Lots of girls go there."

Mama sipped her ice water, holding her goblet with one pinky in the air. "I think college is good for boys, maybe even necessary in these modern times, with jobs so scarce, but a woman still belongs at home with her children."

"What if she has no children?" said Cath. "What if she has no husband? What if she has to support herself?"

Mama looked flustered. "Most young ladies don't have to worry about such an unlikely situation. I think it's very nice that Annie likes to write little stories and poems, and someday she can read them to her children, but she certainly doesn't have to travel off to some faraway university to study literature. She can read all the fine books she wants right here at home."

"Well, I'm not staying home," said Cath. "I'm going to study and paint and travel the world. And I'm not going to paint cornfields and stoic farmers and log shacks like the 'American scene' painters or do glasswork and needlework and iron casting like artists under the WPA. I want more than that. I may go live with my Aunt Jenny in Germany where I can study German and European Expressionism. And I may not have time for a husband and children at all!"

Chip seized her hand and kissed it. "No time for a husband? Then how about time for a suitor, a partner in adventure to travel the world with you, footloose and fancy free—"

Cath's seriousness changed to merriment. She nudged him playfully. "I'd be delighted, dear Chilton. Shall we be vagabond lovers?"

Mama pushed back her chair and stood up abruptly. "I've heard enough fantasies for one night. I'll get dessert. And if we have time we'll decorate that monstrosity of a tree your papa dragged into my parlor!"

Everyone laughed. Years later Annie would recall that frosty December night on Honeysuckle Lane as one of the most cherished in her memory. Everyone was together, filled with hopes and dreams, blithely making plans and promises, never once thinking of the darkness that would one day overtake them.

SIX

The Summer of 1938.

Dear Papa Reed,
The unthinkable has happened.
Last Christmas Knowl gave Alice Marie a ring.
They are engaged to be married on June 25th.
Knowl finished his junior year at Purdue
and will take Alice Marie back with him in the fall.
She is desperate to leave Willowbrook.
I am trying to be brave, but my heart is broken.
Knowl never even knew how much I loved him.
Cath hardly notices my pain she's so in love with Chip.
She promised to be my best friend for life,
but she's like a sophisticated stranger since
completing her first year at the Chicago Art Institute.
Now she's spending the summer in Germany with her aunt.
How I long for the simple days when you were here
and we sat together reading of Alice in her Wonderland.
I graduated magna cum laude from high school this June,
but my "launching" into life has been overshadowed
by wedding plans and talk of trousseaus and honeymoons.
I've resolved to remain forever an old maid and live
out my days in the rosebud room, pouring out my soul
in solemn, ardent words for the world to read.
But what if I find no one who cares to read my soul?

— Your Annie.

Two days before the wedding, Mama fluttered around the house like a wounded magpie, chattering and bemoaning, admonishing and complaining. Nothing was going right, nothing was done, everyone was inept—except Mama. Even poor Papa was the brunt of her agitation. As Annie helped her put the food purchases into the cupboards and ice box, Mama protested the exorbitant prices. "Look, Jon, I shop at your store, and the prices are preposterous. Imagine, the A&P grocery with prices like these!

Hamburger steak nineteen cents a pound! Porterhouse steak, forty-five cents. And pork chops, best center cuts, twenty-five cents! Who do they think we are—the Rockefellers? What is the world coming to?"

"Now, Anna, if you shopped around, you'd know A&P has good prices. Everything everywhere is high these days. You're just nervous about the wedding, but it will be perfect. Trust me."

Mama shook her head. "If it depended on you, I would trust you, but it depends on too many others. Knowl's parents, for instance."

Papa's eyebrows shot up. "Will they both be there?"

"I don't know. Since the divorce, Knowl hasn't seen his father, but who knows? And Betty Herrick—who can predict what she will do? Or what condition she'll be in!"

The doorbell rang and Annie went to answer it, glad to escape Mama's jitters. But when she opened the door and met the dazed, insolent gaze of Knowl's mother, all words failed her.

"Hello, Annie, aren't you going to invite me in?" Without waiting for an invitation, Betty Herrick stepped inside. She was wearing a pea-green suit a size too small and a matching wide-brimmed hat over her flaming red hair. "Where's your mother?"

Annie found her voice. "Mama, it's Mrs. Herrick!"

Mama bustled into the living room, smoothing her housedress and patting a wisp of hair back into the loose bun at the nape of her neck. "Mrs. Herrick—Betty! It's so nice to see you."

Betty Herrick sat down on the flowered divan and fanned herself with her hanky. "So hot for June, isn't it?" She looked around. "You wouldn't happen to have a small glass of wine, would you? I've been suffering the vapors all day."

"No, I'm sorry," said Mama. "We don't indulge. I do have lemonade." She sat down in her favorite Chippendale chair by the window. "Annie, get Mrs. Herrick some lemonade."

Annie left reluctantly. She was dying to hear anything Betty Herrick had to say. When she returned, she heard Betty declaring, "I was so surprised to run into Alice Marie at the Stardust Ballroom the other evening."

Mama looked uncomfortable with the direction this conversation was going. "Alice Marie has gone there a time or two with Knowl, I believe. Not that I entirely approve."

"No, no, she wasn't a guest. She was the girl singer. Actually up there in the spotlight, singing with the band. And the mellow way she crooned, she gave the impression she was born to sing Dixieland and swing."

Mama stiffened. "You know, of course, that Alice Marie works in the millinery department at J. C. Penney—a very respectable job."

"Oh, yes, I know," said Betty Herrick, blotting perspiration from her forehead and upper lip. "I just wanted to mention I'd seen her, seeing as how she's about to become my daughter-in-law. That son of mine never said a word about her singing career."

Mama stood up, her shoulders straight as a soldier's. "I suggest you let Alice Marie tell Knowl about her singing."

Betty Herrick hoisted herself up and ambled toward the foyer. "Oh, I already mentioned it to him. I assumed he knew. He was quite surprised his bride would keep secrets from him. Well, I'd best be going. I'll see you all on Saturday at the wedding."

That evening, Annie wasn't sure there'd be a wedding after all. She could hear Alice Marie and Knowl in the garden talking, their voices rising and falling, stirring up heat in the stifling June night. Annie couldn't make out anything they said, except that both sounded upset. She considered going up to the blue room and listening at the open window, but her conscience got the better of her and she remained in her own beloved rosebud room, waiting and wondering.

Was there a chance Knowl might come to his senses and break off his engagement? But even if he left Alice Marie, what powers under heaven would persuade him to seek out Annie?

It was nearly midnight when Annie heard Alice Marie coming upstairs. Annie peered out her door just as her sister passed by. "Are you okay?" she whispered.

Alice Marie's makeup was smudged and her hair tousled. "Yes, I'm okay—as if you cared."

"I do care." Annie's next question surprised even her. "Do you want to talk?"

Even more surprising, Alice Marie nodded, slipped inside, and sat down on Annie's bed. "I could strangle that witch," she muttered.

"Witch?"

"Knowl's mama. She's just stirring up trouble because she doesn't want to let go of her little boy. She wants him to stay home and take care of her now that Tom Herrick's gone for good."

"Does Knowl believe that?" asked Annie.

"He better. I told him so."

Annie sat down in the maple rocker beside the bed. "Is Knowl angry because you've been singing at the Stardust Ballroom without telling him?"

"He was at first." Alice Marie looked up plaintively at Annie. "I would've told him, but I knew what he'd say. I just had to sing, Annie. You know how it is. It's the same way you feel about writing. And it wasn't enough just singing in church. You don't know what it's like getting up on that stage, and everything's dark, except the spotlight's on you, and you feel nervous and all charged up, like an electric current's going through you, and you start singing and the band is playing behind you, and the sound swells up around you, the saxophones and clarinets, and you know you're sounding so good and mellow. And then there's the applause and you feel like you've got the whole world right in your hand. I couldn't give that up, Annie."

"Is Knowl going to let you keep singing?"

"He didn't say. He just said we'd work it out."

"Then you're still getting married on Saturday?"

"Yes. Knowl still loves me. Nothing will change that."

Annie's heart plummeted. She bit her lip to keep back the tears. "So—so everything's okay, then."

Alice Marie managed a smile. "I—I guess so." She reached out and tentatively touched Annie's hand. "This is the first time we've ever talked like—like sisters, isn't it?"

Annie nodded. It was the first time they'd ever talked like human beings.

"Always before you were just this pesky little kid, but now you're all grown." Alice Marie lowered her gaze. "I know you don't like me much, Annie."

Annie gasped. "Oh, it's not that—!"

"It's okay. I understand. I'm not like you, Annie. I'm spoiled and speak my own mind. All you ever had to do to make people like you was just be. I always had to do. I had to sing best and be prettiest and wear the nicest clothes. No one ever loved me just for being me."

"That's not so. Mama does."

"Mama loves me for performing. For singing like an angel and looking like an angel. For being her perfect look-alike daughter. She doesn't expect that of you. She lets you be you."

Annie was silent. Since she had never had a serious talk with her sister before, she wasn't sure what the ground rules were. She half expected Alice Marie to jump up and leave and resume being her mean, spiteful self, but she remained on the bed, apparently lost in thought.

Finally she said, "Annie, can I tell you a secret?"

Annie swallowed hard. Now what?

"Promise you won't tell Knowl?"

She hesitated. "I promise."

Alice Marie's voice grew light and conspiratorial. "I met a boy in the band. From Ohio. His name is Cary Rose. He's starting his own band—Cary Rose and the Starlighters. He's good, Annie. He could become another Benny Goodman or Ted Lewis. He's going on the road, and he asked me to go with him."

Annie's eyes widened. "Go with him?"

"He wants me to be his girl singer and travel with him to Pittsburgh and New York and Miami. Can you imagine, Annie? Me, little Alice Marie Reed from Willowbrook, Indiana, going to all those wonderful cities and singing on stage, maybe even my name in lights?"

"You sound like you're going."

Alice Marie's expression sobered. "I told Cary I'd only go if he married me."

"Married you? What about Knowl?"

"Don't worry. Cary turned me down. He doesn't want any emotional entanglements."

Annie grasped at straws. "Why don't you go with the band without getting married?"

Alice Marie stood up and examined her face in the dresser mirror. "I'm twenty-one, Annie. It's time I got married. I won't chance being an old maid. And I do love Knowl. He's the only one who's never asked me to be anything but what I am."

Annie sighed. "Then I guess there'll be a wedding."

Alice Marie met Annie's gaze with a directness that unnerved her. "It wasn't my idea, you know, having Knowl fall in love with me. I know you love him. It would have been better if he loved you. But since it's me—maybe no one else will ever love me the way he does. You understand? I can't let him go."

Annie nodded.

Alice Marie walked to the door, her usual confident strut back in place. "I'm glad you're going to be my maid of honor, Annie. You've grown quite beautiful this past year."

Alice Marie's wedding day was everything Mama hoped for—up to a point. Decorated with streamers and bells, the church was bursting with friends, neighbors, relatives, and well-wishers; Reverend Henry was there in his best black suit to officiate the double-ring ceremony; Chip, the "best man," lingered with Papa in the wings, both looking painfully uncomfortable in their tuxedos. Annie and Cath scurried about in their silk, floor-length gowns, frantically adjusting their hairdos or touching up their make-up. Spring bouquets were everywhere, scenting the air with roses and offering a pastel feast for the eyes; and the bridal bouquet was exquisite with small, white spring flowers.

As the organist played the first stanzas of "O Promise Me," the bridegroom paced nervously in his black tie and tails, perhaps anticipating the evening hours of connubial bliss. Annie watched him and pretended he was no one she knew, a stranger with whom she shared no history, no affection, no connection. It was the only way she knew to survive this day.

She held her breath as Tom and Betty Herrick arrived, separately and silently, and allowed themselves to be escorted down the aisle to the groom's side of the sanctuary.

As the wedding march began, Cath turned to Annie and asked, "Where's Alice Marie?"

Annie shrugged. "I checked on her a few minutes ago. She was ready. But she said she wanted a few minutes alone."

"I caught a glimpse of her," Cath whispered, "in a beautiful gown of sequins and satin. Her hair looked like spun gold under her veil. I just hope she'll make my brother happy."

As the organ music crescendoed, Annie said, "Maybe I'd better go see what's keeping her." Lifting her gown to her ankles, she hurried down the hall to the bridal dressing room. She knocked and waited. Silence. She knocked again, then opened the door and peered inside. "Alice Marie? It's time. They're playing the wedding march."

She went inside and looked around. Her breath caught momentarily as she spotted the wedding gown hanging neatly on the closet door. "Alice Marie, where are you?"

She noticed a scrawled, hand-written note on the dressing table. With her heart pumping blood into her temples, she scanned the brief message:

> *Dear Annie:*
> *Cary Rose said yes after all.*
> *He's here for me now.*
> *We're on our way to Pittsburgh,*
> *where we'll be married by a justice of the peace.*
> *Please explain to Knowl and our families.*
> *I can't face them. Please make them understand.*
> *I'm sorry. I didn't mean to hurt anyone.*
> *I'm not like you. I have to follow my heart.*
> *I'll write soon and send you my address.*
>
> *Love, Alice Marie*

SEVEN

The Summer of 1939.

Dear Papa Reed,
The more I hold onto the vestiges of childhood,
the more remnants of my youth slip irretrievably away.
In a handful of months I'll no longer be a teenager,
but a woman with duties, direction, and a future.
I spent an intense year of study at Indiana University
in Bloomington, and learned enough to know
I have a long way to go to become a published writer.
I'm not giving up, but the illusions are gone.
This is an amazing year of change.
We've all dispersed to our tidy worlds
in separate orbits a universe apart.
Alice Marie travels the states with her husband's band
and sends postcards from America's far-flung cities.
Chip and Knowl graduated with honors from Purdue;
Chip joined the Navy; Knowl signed on as a reporter
for the Willowbrook News. He's never said a word
in a whole, long year about Alice Marie
and the wedding that never was.
Cath finished her second year at the Art Institute,
and we're doing something daring before our youth is
gone forever—spending a week together in New York
attending the World's Fair as we did in '33.
Mama and Papa remain at home on Honeysuckle Lane
where I pray they will stay forever, unchanged,
because the farther I wander from home,
the more I want to go home again,
where memories still live of you, dear Papa.

Always, Your Annie.

Annie first saw it in a newsreel at the Majestic Theater—the opening ceremonies for
the Fair. There stood President Roosevelt, bigger than life, in flashing black and white

celluloid, officially cutting the ribbons, while the sonorous voice-over lauded this "Eighth Wonder of the World"—a $155,000,000 wonderland constructed on 1216 acres of wasteland that was once an ash dump in Flushing, Queens.

Then the president himself spoke. Always mesmerized by the voice that sounded so much like Papa Reed's, Annie now saw the man himself, Mr. Roosevelt, on the big screen, lifting his arms, and intoning, "All who come to this World's Fair in New York will receive the heartiest of welcomes. They will find that the eyes of the United States are fixed on the future. Yes, our wagon is still hitched to a star, but it is a star of friendship, a star of international good will, and above all, a star of peace. I hereby dedicate the New York World's Fair of 1939, and I declare it open to all mankind!"

Annie sat forward attentively in the darkened theater, her gloved hands tightening with resolve. She had to see that fair. Somehow it stood for all she was struggling with in her own life; surely she would find her answers at a fair that so boldly proclaimed "the World of Tomorrow." Just as the Fair of '33 had opened the door from childhood to adolescence, so the Fair of '39 offered Annie the perfect threshold to adulthood. Now if only she could persuade Catherine to accompany her. It would be like tying the scattered remnants of their past to a bright, promising piece of the future. How could Cath possibly resist?

In fact, Cath couldn't. She was more than eager to see the fair, especially since her plans to return to Germany had to be shelved because of political unrest in Europe. So, as a long, sweltering summer waned, she and Annie took the train to New York City and rented a room in an aging brownstone within walking distance of the fair.

Their enthusiasm over the boarding house they'd found was short-lived, however. The room was small and boxy, close as a cave, the air boggy with August heat. Its lackluster contents included two narrow twin beds, a modest pine bureau, and nondescript Victorian prints on faded violet wallpaper. A radiator occupied one wall, its nest of pipes looking like some ancient instrument of torture. The adjoining bathroom was tiny as a closet; the wash basin contained a dripping faucet; and an antique tub stood on sculpted feet, rust stains circling the drain.

Neither Cath nor Annie expressed their disappointment, although Annie mused that, even at 75 cents a night, the room seemed an absurd spot to launch a new life of adventure and purpose. Where was the promise of tomorrow in its worn carpet? Where the hope of the future in its gauze curtains framing a bleak window overlooking a smoky gray city?

As they settled in, Cath removed her stylish small-brimmed hat that shaded one eye. "Well, it's not the Waldorf-Astoria, but at least we won't be spending much time here," she noted.

Annie slipped off her jacket, sat down, and tried the bed. "No springs poking through."

"And the view really isn't so bad." Cath wiped a clean spot in the window grime and peered outside. "Look at all the skyscrapers and lights. And look, Annie, we can see the Empire State Building from here!"

Annie nodded reverently. "Tallest building in the world."

The two faced each other. "We're really here, Annie. We've done it. We're taking the adventure of a lifetime."

"Yes, but your trip to Germany last summer must have been more exciting," said Annie.

"It was wonderful, but you weren't there."

"I know how much you wanted to go back this summer—"

"But Aunt Jenny said I shouldn't come."

"Because of all the political turmoil?"

"The country is too unstable. It's Hitler's doing. Aunt Jenny once thought he was the hope of Germany, but now she says he's doing terrible things to the Jews. She has many Jewish friends who have gone into hiding."

"Everyone agrees Hitler is bad, but no one knows what to do about him," mused Annie. "They think if they ignore him he'll go away."

"He won't." Cath lowered her voice even though there was no one else in the room. "Aunt Jenny told me Hitler built a place several years ago near Munich—a prison—called Dachau, a concentration camp for people who oppose him. She says no one talks about it, but she thinks he sends people there to die."

Annie unbuttoned her blouse. It clung to her skin like the stifling humidity weighing down the air. "I don't want to think about evil men like Hitler. I'm going to bed and dream about the fair."

Cath hoisted her satchel on her bed, opened it, and removed a nightgown and toiletries. "It won't go away, you know."

"What won't?"

"The unrest in Europe. No matter how many Neutrality Acts we pass, it's coming."

"War?"

"Yes. I saw the blank terror in Aunt Jenny's eyes last summer, after Germany annexed Austria and declared it a province of the German Reich. She said, 'This is only the beginning.' And she was right. Do you remember last fall? Germans marched into the Sudeten land and partitioned Czechoslovakia."

Annie undressed and slipped on her nightgown. "Yes, I read something about that. But Papa says we should stay out of Europe's problems. He says we're finally out of that drat Depression and we shouldn't go looking for trouble in foreign ports."

"Do you believe that?" Cath's voice was almost accusatory.

"I suppose." Annie studied Cath in the thin, gray light of a single overhead bulb.

"You feel strongly about this, don't you?"

Cath fluffed her pillow and held it against her chest. Her red hair tumbled around her shoulders and her freckles stood out like measles in the merciless light. "I didn't realize it until now, but yes, I do." She tossed her pillow and Annie caught it.

"Help me, Annie. Help me see the world through rose-colored glasses like you, or even through green ones like Dorothy in that new movie, when she saw the Emerald City of Oz."

"Cath, please! First let me get some sleep! The train is still roaring in my ears and I'm still swaying back and forth with that lurching, smoke-filled passenger car."

Cath laughed. "Okay. Shut-eye it is! Shall we toss a coin to see who gets the bathroom first?" They did, giggling like children. Annie won.

Later, when they were both in bed staring up into the darkness, Annie said, "Do you remember the blood pact we made years ago? I've still got it in Papa's Bible back home."

"Our best friends forever pledge?" said Cath, fanning herself. "Isn't it my turn to keep it at my house?"

They laughed again. It seemed like years since they'd laughed like this. Annie listened to a fly drone in the sultry air. From the innards of the rooming house, creaking noises blended with plumbing sounds, layered against the distant, muffled commotion of the streets. Annie's mood mellowed into gentle waves of nostalgia and introspection. "Cath, I thought by now I'd know exactly what I was supposed to do with my life, but I don't. I want to write, but I don't even know what I want to say. How can I offer words to others when I haven't found the words for myself yet?"

The fly buzz-bombed her face and she brushed it away. "You don't have this problem, Cath. You know what you want. You're preparing that exhibit of your work at the Art Institute. And you're sketching a wonderful series of portraits. You're so talented. But me—I'm just—Cath? Cath, are you listening?"

The fly droned on. Cath was asleep.

In spite of their weariness, Cath and Annie were up before dawn, dressing for the fair. With a couple of apples for nourishment, they walked through the humid, pastel-washed dawn down a maze of streets lined with tenements and towering concrete structures, until they reached the throngs of visitors pressing into one of the fair's main entrances. They paid their seventy-five cents admission fee and bought a guidebook for a quarter.

Wearing her best suit, hat, and gloves, Annie felt as elegant and cosmopolitan as any of the ladies surrounding her. She could be a New Yorker, a world traveler, even the mayor's wife, Mrs. Fiorello LaGuardia herself. Annie had worked hard over the years to grasp this sweet measure of self-confidence. Cath looked chic and stylish too, although she didn't take fashion as seriously as Annie did. Cath, like Alice Marie, could look stunning in a potato sack.

Moving now as one with the crowd, they encountered a towering statue of George Washington, with signs proclaiming the 150th anniversary of his inauguration in New York City.

"I've heard of the artist—James Earl Frazier," said Cath. "But I'll never try sculpting anything so big or ambitious."

"It's stunning," said Annie. "But can you imagine taking it home to Mama to put in the garden?"

Cath chuckled. "It's surely too big for a bird bath!"

The two found themselves laughing or uttering exclamations of delight often in the hours that followed, as they made their way through the elegant, color-coded city. They strode along pastel avenues converging on a central stark white globe dominating the landscape—a gargantuan orb housing a scale model of a centrally planned City of Tomorrow, with spotless, poverty-free communities, modern traffic systems with ramped loops, and skyscrapers with landing pads for helicopters.

In the General Motors Building, they watched a film called "The City," showing American slums where millions still lived in poverty, proving that the Depression had never really lifted. The film showcased Greenbelt, Maryland, an example of what the city of the future should be, while a deep male voice intoned, "The future is where we're going to spend the rest of our lives." The genteel voice spoke eloquently of the gleaming salvation of a technological future in which the World of Tomorrow present- ed a designer's carnival of whimsy and wonder, imagination and optimism. Heady stuff for two guileless young women from Willowbrook, Indiana. As Cath and Annie left the building, they were each given a small blue and white button declaring, I have seen the future.

Annie shook her head. "What do you think about all this Futurama business, Cath? Isn't it a bit scary—the way they're so desperately pulling the future out of tomorrow into today?"

"Like the Trojan horse, you mean? Dragging a monstrosity into a naive town where it's welcomed as a gift instead of a deathblow?"

Annie nodded. "You're saying the future may not be the perfect new order the fair claims. But it's more than that, Cath. I feel as if the world is changing even as we stand here. Something's moving away from us, beyond our grasp, and for all the fair's talk about our rosy future, maybe we're really just running about like blind mice in a maze."

"You mean there may be no future at all?"

"Don't you feel that way sometimes?"

"Yes, and so I paint faster and try to squeeze all I can out of every day."

"I try too," said Annie, "but sometimes I feel I can't catch up. I'm always running a little ways behind. It's as if there's something I'm still looking for—a missing piece of the puzzle."

"Don't worry, we won't miss anything today," said Cath. "We'll experience it all if it kills us. Hey, how about a hot dog? I'm starved!"

Cath was true to her word. They indeed crammed every delicious, heart-pounding moment they could into the day, dashing breathlessly from one exotic pavilion to another. Sixty foreign nations displayed their wares. Cath was determined to see them all. They viewed the time capsule and electrified farm at the Westinghouse Exhibit; marveled over an electric dishwasher and a Coldspot refrigerator in a modern kitchen; saw themselves on a genuine television camera purported to be the wave of the future; and crossed Fountain Lake and Rainbow Avenue to the amusement park to ride the Cyclone roller coaster.

But the most significant event of the day, as Annie would later recall it, still lay ahead. It began as they passed the British Pavilion. A young, limber, bearded man stood on the corner handing out leaflets. As soon as Cath spotted him, she whispered, "Look, Annie, wouldn't he be wonderful to sketch? He looks like Savonarola."

"Who?"

"An Italian religious reformer who lived during Michaelangelo's time and impressed him with his apocalyptic vision. I studied him in art history. That man on the corner has the same fire in his eyes and zeal in his gestures. Look, he nearly dances. His whole face lights with passion."

As they approached, Annie met the bearded man's gaze. It was as direct and startling as Cath described. The wiry chap darted toward her holding out his pamphlet, and Annie took it without question.

"Have you been born again?" he asked with a guttural German accent and an urgency that struck right to the marrow. Cath accepted a leaflet too.

"What?" asked Annie, not sure she'd heard right, her gaze locked with his.

He quoted a Scripture verse Annie recognized. John 3:16. For God so loved the world that he gave his only begotten son. "Oh, yes, I believe that," she said quickly. "I'm a Christian. I've gone to church with my family all my life."

Her response failed to satisfy the strange fellow. "Have you been born again?" he repeated, thickly enunciating each word.

Annie was ready to dismiss this over-eager zealot and walk on, but Cath was already approaching him, extending a hand. "Would you mind if I sketched you?" she asked boldly. "I'd be no bother. You could continue your preaching."

Her request took him by surprise. He shrugged off his evangelical stance and stared blankly at her. "You want to draw me? Right here on the street?"

Cath quickly explained she was a struggling art student preparing sketches of interesting people for an upcoming art show. The man thought a moment, then replied, "You may sketch me if you will also listen to me."

Cath turned the pamphlet over to its blank side. "I will, if you have a pencil I may use."

Annie glared at Cath, as if to say, We don't have time for this. "Listen, Cath, can't we go somewhere? You can't draw with all these people milling around."

"There's a little cafe near here," said the man, gesturing with long, graceful hands that might have been painted by El Greco. He reminded Annie of a Rumpelstiltskin or a leprechaun—a lithe, leaping sprinter, all elbows and knees, with limbs springing like elastic bands—a fanciful character from some Mother Goose tale. And yet in his gaunt, powerful features Annie glimpsed the spiritual intensity of an Elijah.

They walked to the cafe, the man handing out his leaflets to all who would take them. At the top of the page, Annie noted the words, REPENT BEFORE IT IS TOO LATE! Bible verses in small print followed.

What are we getting into? she wondered, but kept her reservations to herself, since Cath was obviously ecstatic. They sat at a small, outside table in a narrow strip of shade and ordered iced tea with lemon. Cath began drawing; the man began talking; and Annie felt herself slip into an exhausted, heat-induced reverie.

She only vaguely heard the man say he was Helmut Schwarz, an itinerant, self-proclaimed evangelist; his parents had come to America from Germany in the twenties where as a boy he walked the sawdust trail at a Billy Sunday tent meeting. "Now I preach hellfire and brimstone," he admitted, "whatever it takes to bring lost souls to Jesus Christ."

Cath kept drawing, intent on the hypnotic passion in Helmut's expression but oblivious to his words. Annie nodded politely at appropriate moments, but didn't rivet her attention on him until he said, "I am a German Jew. A Jew who has found his Messiah in Christ. I returned to Germany last winter to let my people know of their redemption, but I found death already stalking them. Relatives have already died at Hitler's hand."

"That's awful," said Annie. "Can't someone do something?"

"Everyone looks the other way. They hum and smile and go about their business, pretending such horrors do not exist."

"My aunt is German," said Cath, "and she has Jewish friends who have gone into hiding."

"Well they should. You've heard of Kristallnacht?"

"It sounds—vaguely familiar," said Annie.

"It was in the paper months ago, on a back page. A young Jew killed a German diplomat in Paris. Last November Nazi thugs retaliated. They attacked Jewish homes and businesses across Germany."

"Aunt Jenny wrote and told me about it," said Cath. "Several of her Jewish friends were hurt and their property destroyed."

"I remember now," said Annie. "The Nazis were criticized for such barbaric behavior."

"We do nothing but offer a slap on the wrist," said Helmut.

Annie's voice was small and solemn. "What can we do?" "I warned my family to come to America," he said, "but they will not, so I shall return to them before the year is out." For a while they talked on about world events. "We are in the last days," said Helmut fervently. "Death is coming to mankind. God cannot continue to tolerate evil." He leaned forward with renewed urgency, his gaze pinning Annie to the wall. "Are you saved, Miss Reed?"

She shifted uncomfortably. "You don't understand. My family is very religious. We go to church every Sunday. I've been a Christian all my life."

His eyes maintained their intensity; his voice resonated with an impassioned eloquence. "I believe you are a very religious person, Miss Reed, but I am not talking about rules and rituals or doctrines and creeds. I am speaking of a Person—the person of Christ. Does He live in your heart? Do you know Him as your most intimate companion? Has He made you a new creation by His Spirit?"

Annie felt her protests dwindle. She sank back in her chair. She turned her iced tea glass around and ran her finger over the lemon wedge perched on its rim. She looked over at Cath, who was still drawing intently, capturing the fine curve of the reformer's aquiline nose.

"I pray," she said defensively, knowing even as she spoke that it was more ritual than genuine dialogue with the Almighty.

"But when Christ ascended to heaven, He gave His Holy Spirit to live in our hearts. I am speaking of a personal relationship, not mere religion," Helmut continued, his voice ardent, drilling her mind with its reasoned veracity. "If we depend only on religion, our generation is doomed; we can transform our world only through the power of His Spirit. Imagine it. He spun the galaxies into place, yet He chooses to reside within the fragile membrane of a human soul. We need only repent and Christ will gather us into His arms as the mother hen gathers her chicks, as the shepherd clasps the lost lamb to his breast."

Annie felt dazed. The sun had moved, throwing their table into the golden, glaring light. She felt warm and excited, agitated and dazzled. Cath was still caught up in her drawing, nodding occasionally or making a sound as if responding, but certainly not listening.

"Do you want to be saved, Miss Reed?" His luminous eyes read to the depths of her sensibilities.

"Yes," she said, her voice light as air. "Yes, I do."

Cath looked at her. "Annie, you're already a Christian."

"Not like this."

She prayed with the Jewish preacher who had claimed his Messiah, and invited the Christ of Scripture to plant His Spirit deep in her being.

Afterward, Helmut pressed a Gospel of John into her hand. "I pray you will never be satisfied again to merely live your religion. Let Christ live His life through you. He is your Lord, your Redeemer, and your most cherished Friend." He turned to Cath as she finished the portrait. "Will you pray also, Miss Herrick?"

"No," she said quickly, holding up the sketch for Helmut to see. "God and I already have an understanding."

He eyed her shrewdly, then murmured, "You are a fine artist. God has given you a wonderful gift."

"I worked hard for it." Cath looked at Annie. "Shall we go? We have a lot to see before the fireworks tonight."

Later that evening, as they walked back to their rooming house, Cath said sullenly, "I can't believe you let that fanatic intimidate you."

"I didn't," said Annie. "He made sense."

"He's a radical. He thinks he has to save the world."

Annie said softly, "Someone does."

"But not you. You go to church. You worship God. You've got your religion. You don't need some revolutionary coming along and knocking your traditions out from under you."

"He didn't. He gave me something very precious."

"He gave you nothing but extremist gobbledygook."

"He gave me a personal Jesus."

Cath shrugged. "And I've got a prize-winning drawing!"

"Then we're both happy," said Annie.

"You won't let this change anything, will you?"

"I think it already has."

"Oh, swell. Some religious conversion is going to spoil our whole week at the fair."

"Why should it spoil anything?" protested Annie.

"I don't know. It just will." Cath caught Annie's arm. "Promise it won't spoil our friendship."

"Don't be silly, Cath. How could Jesus come between us?"

Cath chuckled. "You're right. He didn't sign our blood pact."

That night, as they entered their little crackerbox room, Annie was startled by the moonglow spilling in the window, turning everything milky with starlight. Everything looked the same; yet everything was different. Even the creaks and groans of the time-ravaged brownstone echoed in Annie's ears like soundless music.

Truth crept in with a sweet, hard reality. Annie wasn't Annie anymore. Annie was a newborn colt, trying her limbs, gulping clean air, blinking at sunlight, shivering with the shock of nativity.

EIGHT

WAR DEADLINE SET FOR NOON SUNDAY, SEPTEMBER 3, 1939

FINAL ANGLO-FRENCH ULTIMATUM SENT TO HITLER

Adolf Hitler was given until noon today to evacuate his armed forces from Poland or risk immediate war with England and France. Unless the Fuehrer complies, the French and British Parliaments simultaneously will declare their countries to be in a state of war with Germany in accordance with their treaty obligations to Poland.

War was perched at the world's doorstep. War was beating down the door. By September, the effusive hope and blind optimism of the World's Fair were long gone. It had been only a month since Cath and Annie had spent their blissful week at the fair. Yet somehow eternity had passed through that month and left the world irretrievably changed. Germany had attacked Poland, and now the glorious "World of Tomorrow" blazoned by the fair was merely a haunting memory.

While Annie grieved the loss of the fair's—and the world's—lofty hopes and dreams— thanks to the street preacher, she had something else now to console her—an undergirding strength, the Holy Spirit's quiet, empowering presence. And she had her studies to look forward to—although it seemed almost frivolous to be packing for her return to Indiana University when the world stood on the brink of war.

But what else was she to do? Surely the actions of an anonymous Indiana girl wouldn't change the course of world events or spin time backward to the carefree days of August. So she continued to pack, her motions automatic. Yes, her tailored suits and fur-trimmed dresses would fit in the large valise; cardigans and cashmere sweaters in the small one; felt hats, berets, and handbags in their boxes; her lingerie, silk chiffon hose, and doeskin gloves in the leather tote. On the train, she would wear her moss green rayon taffeta with the squared shoulders and flared skirt, and her suede pumps with the Cuban heels.

But what about coats? With the lingering autumn summer heat, she wouldn't need her silver fox or herringbone tweed for weeks yet. Better pack them in the trunk. As usual, her mother would accuse her of marching off with half the house in tow.

As she artfully folded each article of clothing, Annie's mind drifted with the languid, sensual strains of Gershwin's Porgy and Bess wafting from the Philco radio on the bureau. Only one more night at home with Mama and Papa. Annie was reluctant to trade the cozy solitude of her beloved rosebud room for the communal noise and commotion of the dormitory, but such was the price of an education.

Annie smiled inwardly, reflecting that Cath loved dormitory life, and thrived on roommates, chaos, and confusion. Thanks to Knowl's generosity and a partial scholarship, Cath would be able to afford another year at the Art Institute. She was already no doubt settling back in and savoring the lavish, bawdy night life of Chicago—so different from quiet, serene Willowbrook. Strange how she and Cath could be best friends and yet such opposites. Cath was always so eager to get away from Willowbrook; Annie was always so eager to come home.

A knock sounded on Annie's door, jarring her from her reverie. She called, "Come in," and looked up in surprise to see Knowl standing in the doorway. He looked as dashing as ever in his double-breasted worsted suit and polished wing-tip shoes. She was always struck by the impeccable image he presented. With his sandy blond hair and ruddy good looks, he could be a model in a fashion magazine, Annie noted, her gaze lingering longer than she intended.

"I suppose you're busy," he said, sounding apologetic.

"Never too busy for you," she replied, and flushed a bit, wondering if he guessed the greater implication of her words.

"I know you'll be leaving tomorrow, and I planned to stop by sooner, but things have been insane at the paper since Friday. You know, don't you—?"

"Yes. The Germans invaded Poland. It's all anyone talks of these days."

Knowl removed his glasses and massaged the bridge of his nose. "It's been especially stressful at the paper, Annie. I don't think you knew—I received a promotion—"

"You did? Tell me!"

He smiled abashedly. She loved his innate modesty. "Believe it or not, I'm managing editor now. Old man Hoopes resigned, so they needed someone with a business and journalism background. Fortunately, that's what I got my degree in."

"That's wonderful, Knowl!" Spontaneously she embraced him, as she would Chip had he confided good news. Knowl received the embrace and gave her an extra squeeze. Annie suspected it was merely a brotherly gesture. "When, Knowl? When did this happen?"

"Last week. I didn't want to say anything until I'd spent a few days at the helm, so to speak." He held his glasses up to the light, examined the lenses, then slipped them back on. "I couldn't have picked a more turbulent time to step into the old man's shoes. War in Europe! The whole world's going crazy!"

"No wonder we haven't seen you lately." She corrected herself. "I mean, Mama mentioned you hadn't been over lately."

"I know, and I miss this house. You're all like family. How are your mama and papa these days?"

"Fine. Some mornings Mama's in the doldrums with Chip so far away in the Navy. She misses him terribly."

"How's our boy doing?"

"Swell. You know he applied to Officer's Candidate School and passed with flying colors. He's very excited about his future."

Knowl nodded. "Chip always was an adventurer at heart. As long as I've known him, it's been his dream to be a commissioned officer in the Navy and travel the world on some glorious ship."

"Quite a few travelers in our family," mused Annie, thinking of Alice Marie traveling the country with her husband's jazz band. But that was a sore subject with Knowl, so she swiftly returned to the "safe" topic of her brother. "No matter how rosy a picture Chip paints of military life, Mama worries about him going off to fight a possible war."

Knowl smiled. "I suspect your mama would worry even if there wasn't a war looming. She's like a mother hen gathering her chicks, and if one or two are out of the fold, she frets."   "You do know my mama. But as long as she has her old reliable bromide powders and her Lydia Pinkham's Vegetable Compound, she's okay. And Papa—he's happy as long as he's got his crossword puzzles and the radio tuned to Lum and Abner or Major Bowes' Amateur Hour on Thursday nights."

Knowl sat down in the rocker by the window. "And you, Annie? How are you?"

She crossed her arms nervously. Her face felt flushed. She could feel a fine mist of perspiration on the back of her neck. "I'm fine, Knowl. Why do you ask?"

He shrugged. "I don't know. I guess it's because I go along taking everything for granted for years, thinking nothing will ever change, and then suddenly there's a war, and everything looks different. Everything's at stake." He rocked backward until the chair nearly hit the rosebud wallpaper.

Annie held her breath.

"I'm not making any sense, am I?" He looked around. "Now, take this room, for instance. It doesn't change. I like that. It looks the same as it did when you and Cath were little and chased fireflies and caught them in milk bottles and sat in your closet watching them flicker."

Annie gasped. "How could you possibly remember that?"

He grinned. "Chip and I were in the closet with you."

"Yes, I remember. You always caught more lightning bugs than we did." She walked over to the window and looked out. "But you're wrong, Knowl. This room has changed. I put away the dolls and took down the movie star posters. Everything changes. You just haven't noticed."

"That's what concerns me, Annie." He sat forward and put his fingertips together in contemplation. "You see, now that I have a position of responsibility—I am responsible to my readers, you know, Annie—and that's a serious matter. How can I guide them through this thing if I don't know my own mind?"

Annie sat down on her bed and gazed across at him so that their eyes were level. "You mean the war? Guide them through the war?"

"More than that, Annie. Sentiment is riding so high these days. Passions are inflamed. Everyone has an opinion. I don't want to come across as a fatalist, and yet I'm not sure I can agree one hundred percent with my colleagues."

Annie shrugged. "You've lost me."

"I'm speaking about our involvement in the war, Annie. I believe it's coming. I don't think we can stay out of it." He removed a sheet of paper from his vest pocket, unfolded it, and handed it to her.

"What is this?"

"A report of what other editors around the country are advising about the war. I'm printing it tomorrow. Read it."

Annie silently scanned the paper.

The New York Times: "We must close our ranks."

The New York World Telegram: "The first law of man is self-preservation."

The New York Sun: "The government at Washington must be neutral."

The Cincinnati Times-Star: "May we steel ourselves against the propaganda and emotionalism... of the European conflict from the outset."

The Denver Post: "The American people don't have to go crazy just because Europe is in the throes of war lunacy. But we will be crazy if we do not attend strictly to our business, remain neutral and keep out of European feuds."

Annie looked at Knowl. "They all say we should stay neutral and not get involved.

Don't you agree?"

Knowl wrung his hands with an intensity Annie rarely saw. "I wish I agreed, but I don't think Hitler can be stopped unless America joins forces with the Allies."

Annie sat back. "That would mean another world war."

Knowl nodded. His features glistened with an exquisite agony. "Remember my aunt in Germany? Jenny Weiss? We received a letter today. She says Germany is gearing up for war, with long trains carrying big guns and thousands of troops, all laughing and waving like they're going to a picnic. She says the Rhine, a peaceful little river with old ruined castles, is frantic with activity—boats being loaded with coal and lumber, trains loaded with freight. She says, 'Germany is mobilizing right before my eyes.' Listen, Annie, she wrote this letter on August 26th, the day before Germany struck Poland. What does that tell you?"

"It scares me," she whispered. "I think of Chip. I think of you."

"Chip's always been a fighter. I bet he's itching to have a go at Hitler. As for me, I'll enlist, but they probably won't let me serve with my bad eyesight." He sighed heavily. "I'm afraid people will say it's easy for me to talk up a good war when I don't have to go fight it."

They were silent a moment. The room was close, the air still. A dog barked somewhere down the block; a June bug buzzed against the window screen. Annie met Knowl's gaze, read the turmoil in the deep wells of his umber-brown eyes. "I don't know what to say," she murmured. "I just know you'll always do what's right and honest and true."

The intensity in his expression softened. "But how do I know what's true, Annie? Even Henry Ford, our nation's top industrialist, says the world will never tolerate another war because memories of 1917 are still too fresh."

"He knows cars, but he doesn't know the future."

Knowl smiled. "Then you don't think I'm obligated to echo the sentiments of the rest of the country?"

"You've got to be your own man, Knowl. Tell it the way you see it."

Knowl's voice grew heavy with emotion. "I see a world on the verge of cataclysm, Annie. London's gearing up even as we speak. It came over the telegraph wires this morning. They have their antiaircraft ground defenses manned, air raid service mobilized, and police, firemen, and demolition squads with steel helmets and gas masks posted everywhere. They've sandbagged and shuttered all their public buildings, including the U.S. Embassy. Every city building has a basement air raid shelter, and they're practicing nationwide blackouts. Three hundred thousand school children were evacuated from London on Friday, and before tomorrow three million people will have been evacuated to the country. Does that sound like a country anticipating a mild skirmish?"

"But that doesn't mean we have to fight too," said Annie.

"I hope to God we don't," said Knowl, "but if Hitler gets a foothold over there, who's to say any place in the world will be safe from his tyranny? He's a madman, Annie. And all we want to do is rap his knuckles like a naughty schoolboy."

"If you feel so strongly about it, Knowl, then that's what you should say in your editorial. You're our link to the world; you're our eyes and ears. We won't know what's happening over there except from what we read in the papers or hear on the radio."

Knowl nodded. "This will be the first war in history the whole world can hear."

"But it's what we read that we remember most, Knowl. You have a wonderful chance to serve your country through the Willowbrook News."

"I know. It's an amazing opportunity. In fact, you should try your hand at writing a column sometime yourself, Annie."

"Me? You mean, be an advice columnist like Emily Post or Dorothy Dix?"

"No. Like Annie Reed. An original. You'd be terrific."

"No thanks. The Great American Novel someday, maybe. But I'll leave the editorializing to you. You're the expert."

Knowl stood up and ran his fingers through his thick hair. "I just hope I'm up to it, Annie. I don't have the experience Hoopes had. He was the real expert."

She went to him and touched his arm. "I believe in you, Knowl. And I'm very proud of you."

He put his hand over hers. "Thanks, Annie. I can always count on you." His expression grew animated. "I am excited, actually. I won't publish rumors or unconfirmed reports. No sensationalism. I'll verify every news flash before I print it. I'm determined to protect my readers from propaganda, misinformation, or false reports. You know Hitler's already bombarding the news services with tales of his incredible exploits."

"Won't the news services weed out such falsehoods and distortions?"

"Sure. I'll work closely with all three of them—the Associated Press, United Press, and International News Service. All American papers depend on them for the lion's share of their news. But I won't expect them to do my work for me."

Annie smiled. It was wonderful seeing Knowl so impassioned about his work.

He caught the whimsy in her eyes and chuckled. "I hope I'm not boring you with all of this. I just had to talk to someone. There's no one around my house...."

"Your mom?"

He grimaced. "Same as ever. The bottle's her best friend."

"And your dad?"

"Haven't seen him in months. I think he's taken up with some woman in Kokomo."

"I'm sorry. It must be awfully painful—"

A tendon in his neck tightened, but he smiled and pinched her cheek. "We can't all have a perfect family like yours, can we, Annie?" With a cheery gesture of bravado, he turned and started for the door.

She went after him. "Are you going already?"

"Looks like you still have packing to do—and an early train to catch tomorrow, I bet."

"Yes, but—"

"I don't want to bore you with any more newspaper talk."

"You weren't. I always enjoy talking with you, Knowl."

"I know. That's what I love about you, Annie. You always make me feel like I'm tops in your book."

"You are." She accompanied him into the hallway. "Did Mama offer you any lemonade when you arrived?"

"No, I came straight up."

"Then you must have some lemonade before you go, and we'll sip it on the porch. Surely there's a breeze blowing by now."

He laughed. "You win."

A faint breeze stirred the tepid air as they settled into the porch swing with their lemonades. Annie savored Knowl's closeness—the scent of his sweet cologne and his muscled arm against her shoulder. Through an open window she could hear Bing Crosby crooning a love song on the console radio in the parlor. Oh, if only Knowl would see her through the eyes of love. If only he could feel the enchantment of this moment—the two of them sitting together in the moonlight. If only he could hear the pounding of her heart and know it beat for him alone!

"Have you heard anything from Alice Marie?" he asked.

"Alice Marie?" Annie felt a sudden chill. Knowl hadn't uttered her name since the day she left him at the church to run off with her musician-paramour. "My sister doesn't write often."

"But she's happy?"

"I suppose. She sings with her husband's band, you know. They've played all over—New York, Hollywood, St. Louis, Miami. She's even sung on the radio and seen her name in lights."

"What do your folks think about her new life?"

"Oh, Papa doesn't say much, but, of course, Mama frets and worries. She thinks any dance music with bodily contact is suspect. She says jazz appeals to our baser impulses, and modern dancing bewitches people and makes them do evil things. She thinks Alice Marie is headed for trouble."

"What do you think?"

"I don't know. Cath gives art lessons to school children in Chicago, and she has them warm up by performing these modern dances. She says it makes them much freer and more creative. Somehow, they translate the rhythm and grace of dancing into their painting."

"That sounds like something Cath would claim. But we're not talking about jazz. We're talking about your sister. You still haven't answered me. What do you think about Alice Marie?"

Annie groaned inwardly. Why was her older sister still so important to Knowl? Why couldn't he just forget her? "I think Alice Marie loves adventure, and she loves singing and being the center of attention. So I imagine she's in her glory."

"I suspect so," said Knowl gloomily. "I never could have made her happy. I'm too tame, too serious, too predictable."

"You're wrong, Knowl. You could have made her happy—if she'd only given you a chance."

"Well, it's all in the past," he said matter-of-factly.

Annie studied the way the moonlight crossed his face, illuminating his handsome features. "Is it, Knowl?"

He sat forward, his elbows on his knees, his voice resonant with emotion. "I haven't talked about Alice Marie since our wedding day—the last time I saw her. Actually, I didn't see her then. It was considered unlucky for the groom to see his bride before the wedding. I don't even know how she looked in her wedding gown."

Annie sipped her lemonade, but the liquid formed a cold bubble in her throat. "She looked beautiful, Knowl, as usual."

"I try not to think about her, Annie. I don't even know why I loved her. She was selfish and spoiled, but she made me feel like anything was possible. She made the world seem bigger than Willowbrook, bigger than Indiana, bigger than anything. She was like magic, a flash of lightning, a song you can't get out of your mind, a rainbow you think you've caught in your fingers, but you haven't. It's only an illusion."

Annie listened silently. She had a feeling Knowl was weeping, but it was too dark to see. Her heart ached, as if someone were squeezing it with his bare hands.

"Growing up, I didn't think I could be anything without Alice Marie," Knowl continued. "She was my life, my light, my hope. But now I know I can succeed; I can go on without her. That doesn't make it hurt any less. Do you understand, Annie?"

"I do," she whispered. "I know exactly how you feel."

He gazed at her, the moonlight glinting in his eyes, and suddenly, Annie was in his arms and his mouth was on hers, and she could feel the wetness of his tears on her face. They kissed with a sweet, delicious urgency born of yearning and heartbreak. Then, as suddenly as he had embraced her, he released her and stood up. "I'm sorry, Annie. I didn't mean to do that."

She sank back in the swing, dazed, the taste of his lips still burning on hers. "It's okay, Knowl. Don't apologize."

He straightened his jacket and smoothed back his hair. "I've stayed too long. I'd better go. Thanks for letting me talk your ear off. And please don't think me weak and foolish." He managed a smile. "Have a great year at the university, okay?"

She stood up, her knees weak, uncertain. "Knowl, wait!"

Already halfway down the porch steps, he looked back quizzically. "Yes, Annie?"

"I—I'll miss you!"

"I'll miss you too."

Annie watched Knowl stride off down Honeysuckle Lane and disappear into the darkness. On this warm September night when the world stood on the verge of war, she sensed she stood on the threshold of something nearly as immense and unknowable—events that would forever bind her to Knowl Herrick, and a paradoxical future promising great happiness or lifelong misery.

NINE

The Winter of 1939.

*October 9th—Hitler Threatens Offensive across
Low Countries*

*November 4th—U.S. Neutrality Act Modified to
Aid Allies*

*December First—Allied Losses Total 73 Ships;
U-Boats Sink 25*

*December 23rd—First Canadian Troops Arrive in
United Kingdom*

In Willowbrook, the snows of December blanketed the earth and, for a time, muffled the sounds of war in Europe. As in Christmases past, Papa brought home a tree from the woods, and Mama strung berries and popcorn into garlands. Papa shoveled snow from the walks and brought in wood for the fireplace. Mama baked sugar cookies and made fruitcakes bursting with sweet cherries, candied orange peel, and meaty pecans.

Four days before Christmas, Annie arrived home from the university. Chip, home on his first leave since completing Officer's Candidate School, picked her up at the depot in Papa's new Nash LaFayette Sedan with its gleaming white sidewall tires. Her brother, tanned, blonder than ever, and looking handsome in his crisp blue uniform, was brimming over with good humor and enthusiasm. He regaled her with marvelous tales of Navy life, embellishing every detail with a gilt edge. "It's everything I hoped for, Annie—gritty, hard, exciting, full of challenges. The guys are swell, too, even my commanding officers. And you'd love San Diego's sun and sea, Annie, especially after one of Indiana's frostbitten winters. I'm hoping to be assigned to Pearl Harbor—that's in Hawaii—where there's enough sun and surf to last me a lifetime."

"Well, no matter how wonderful the Navy is, it's even more wonderful to be home with you again in Willowbrook!" declared Annie. "And it's going to be wonderful to see Cath and Knowl again. It'll be like old times. The Four Musketeers!"

Chip winked at her. "The loves of our lives, right?"

Annie studied her brother's bronzed features. "You do love Cath, don't you?"

He kept his eyes on the snow-crusted road, his gloved hands confidently on the wheel. "As much as you love Knowl."

Annie sighed. "If only we could all live happily ever after."

Chip looked over, raising one eyebrow. "Why can't we?"

"The truth? I don't think Knowl will ever get over Alice Marie."

"Sure, he's over her. Our sister's history in his book."

"How do you know?"

"It's just a hunch. Knowl's too bright to pine over a lost cause, even our starstruck, globe-trotting sister."

Annie smiled grimly. "What about me? That's what I've been doing for years. Pining over—"

"Knowl's no lost cause. He's a man with a future. Look how fast he got that promotion at the paper."

"I'm thrilled for him, of course, but I'm not thinking about his future; I just want to be part of his present."

"Then stop running off to Bloomington every autumn."

"Quit college? Now you sound like Mama. She thinks I should stay home, get married, and have babies like other women my age."

Chip laughed. "You've never been like other women, Annie. You want something out of life other women haven't even thought to look for."

She considered that. "It's true, isn't it, Chip? I've always felt different from the others. I used to think that was bad, but maybe it's not. Maybe you're right. Maybe wanting more out of life makes me special."

He reached over and touched his gloved hand to her cheek. "Someday Knowl will realize that and glimpse the remarkable Annie I see."

They arrived home as the slate-gray sky took on a faint pink wash and the snowdrifts became sculpted mounds in shimmering shades of blue. Her heart pounding with anticipation, Annie drew her white fox collar around her neck and crunched through the snow over the walk and up the sprawling porch, its bric-a-brac trim accented with glittering icicles of varying lengths.

Mama and Papa had heard the automobile and were already opening the door, allowing a burst of warm, sweet-scented air to push back the chill, biting wind. They welcomed Annie with enormous smiles and joyous acclamations, both speaking at once, arms open for hugs. After a heady round of kisses and embraces, Annie hung her fur on the coatrack and looked around, savoring the sweet familiarity of home.

Strains of "Silent Night" drifted from the console in the parlor. No, it was actually Mama's new electric record player that connected with the radio and needed no winding. Aromas of gingerbread and the piney fragrance of Christmas wreaths filled her nostrils as her eyes scanned the cozy rooms with their comfortable furnishings and cherished curios and antiques.

"Thank goodness, no matter how insane the rest of the world may be, my dear home on Honeysuckle Lane never changes!"

Mama and Papa looked older, though. The lines in Papa's face were deeper, and Mama's expression was pinched and her eyes shadowed with worry. They both fussed over Annie, Papa gesturing for her to sit down, while Mama offered a cup of eggnog or steaming hot tea with lemon.

"Annie, my girl," Papa declared as she settled back on the flowered love seat, "you look as pretty as a picture!"

"A little thin maybe, but we'll fatten you up," said Mama, surveying her with a proud, pleased smile.

Chip shrugged off his peacoat. "Papa's right, Annie. You're pretty enough to model for those J.C. Penney ads in the newspaper. In fact, you could give Alice Marie a run for her money."

"You really think so?" In spite of the lingering chill, Annie suddenly felt warm to her toes. Chip had rarely compared her favorably with her older sister. Annie did feel attractive in her slim-waisted, full-skirted frock and sheer batiste blouse, showing just the hint of a frill between her jacket lapels.

Friends told her she had the perfect figure for the approaching forties. The hourglass shape of '39 was out. Now, fashion demanded a long-stemmed, willowy shape, high bosom, and a firm and supple midriff, with no curves or bulges. At last, fashion was on her side! As long as Mama didn't fatten her up too much!

But would Knowl notice her new sophistication? Would he care? Annie discovered she would find out soon enough. Mama had invited Knowl and Cath to dinner tonight to celebrate her home-coming.

They arrived shortly after seven. "I'm sorry we're a tad late," said Knowl. "I was tied up with a deadline at the paper." "Not to worry," said Mama, her hands fan-dancing the air. "I have baked ham and scalloped potatoes in the oven. They will keep for hours!"

"In that case—" Knowl tossed his wool scarf back around his neck, pretending to leave.

"No, no, it's ready now!" cried Mama. Everyone laughed.

They paired off as they headed for the dining room—Mama and Papa, Chip and Cath, Knowl and Annie. The table was stunning, set with Mama's best linen, china and silver, including her favorite silver candlesticks—a wedding present from her parents.

"It's beautiful, Mama. Just the way I knew it'd be!"

As Knowl held Annie's chair for her, his fingertips lightly brushed her hair. Was it an accident? Or a small gesture of affection? As they ate, it seemed Knowl had eyes only for Annie. Perhaps absence had truly made his heart grow fonder. Or perhaps Annie's overactive imagination was all too eager to read signs that were not there.

After dinner, while Mama went to the kitchen for dessert and Papa retired to the parlor to listen to Lowell Thomas, Chip held up his crystal goblet of ice water and said briskly, "Let's drink a toast, shall we?"

"With water? questioned Knowl in amusement.

Chip smiled. "You'll find nothing stronger in the Reed household, I'm afraid."

"Then water it is," said Cath, holding up her goblet and meeting Chip's gaze. "What shall we drink to?"

"How about, 'to the four of us,'" said Knowl. "May we each find our dreams and never let them go."

"To the four of us and our dreams," said Chip.

The goblets clinked, the etched crystal glittering in the flickering glow of candlelight. Annie sipped her drink, then looked at Knowl. His eyes were on her, surrounding her, mesmerizing her. She felt weak, tongue-tied.

"You're beautiful, Annie," he whispered.

She flushed and glanced self-consciously at Cath and Chip. But they were engaged in a long, tender kiss—until Mama returned and exclaimed, "Oh, my goodness, I thought I was serving dessert!"

Everyone laughed. Levity seemed to come easily this evening, as if everyone and everything were touched with a gossamer sprinkle of merriment. As Mama served her special floating island pudding and sugar cookies, Papa returned to the table and insisted on blowing out the candles. "It's enough that I couldn't see my dinner. By George, I'm going to see my dessert!"

Laughter again, sweet and rare and wonderful. Annie savored it like the delectable taste of Mama's cooking.

When all had had their fill, Papa sat back in his chair and cleared his throat ceremoniously, the way he always did when he was going to make one of his little speeches. "While much of the world is in great pain and turmoil tonight, we in this room have much to be thankful for this Christmas season—shelter and safety, a warm, comfortable home, and Mama's wonderful meals. And love, lots of love—and the company of dear friends. Let us be faithful in thanking our Heavenly Father for all He has given us. And let us pray for Alice Marie, our only child missing from the fold tonight."

Mama dabbed at her eyes with her lace hanky, then reached into her apron pocket. "I have a surprise, children. We received a Christmas greeting from Alice Marie today. She enclosed this letter. Let me read it aloud, and perhaps we'll feel Alice Marie's presence here with us after all." She read in her light, bell-clear voice that sounded so much like Alice Marie's:

> *Dear Mama and Papa, Chip and Annie:*
>
> *I hope you have a wonderful Christmas.*
> *I'd love to be there with you in Willowbrook,*
> *but Cary and I are here in Hollywood with the band.*
> *We have an engagement at the Palladium on Christmas Eve and our names are in lights on the marquee: CARY ROSE AND THE STARLIGHTERS, FEATURING ALICE MARIE. Isn't that incredible? It's like a dream come true. I'm here in our hotel room dashing off this note before our next jam session. I wish I could tell you all I've seen and done these past months. Cary and I*
> *have met so many celebrities in these beautiful*
> *ballrooms. Stars like Joan Bennett, Hedy Lamarr, and*
> *Henry Fonda. Rhumba dancing is the craze in Hollywood night clubs these days. Everyone's doing it.*
> *It's fun hobnobbing with movie stars and learning*
> *their secrets. If I don't hear it on the dance floor,*
> *I can always read it in Louella Parsons' column the*
> *next morning. Lots of material for your stories,*
> *Annie, but you'd be too horrified to write them!*
> *Speaking of writing, Annie, I met an author*
> *who writes about the stars, Adela Rogers St. Johns.*
> *I told her about you, and she wishes you success*
> *in your writing. She says, never give up, never.*
> *That's good advice for all of us, isn't it?*
> *Tell Cath I expect to see her art work someday*
> *in the Saturday Evening Post, and tell Knowl*
> *congratulations on his promotion last fall.*
> *Forgive me for not writing more often.*
> *You know me, always caught up in my own little world.*
> *But I love you all even though I may not show it.*

As always, Alice Marie

Mama folded the letter and tucked it back in her apron pocket. "So now, Papa, we have heard from all our children."

Annie looked at Knowl, tried to read his expression. Did he still have deep feelings for Alice Marie? He met her gaze and smiled—his eyes direct, frank, as if to say, You have nothing to worry about anymore.

She smiled too—with relief and gratitude, then looked around the table from face to face. "This has been a grand homecoming. Thank you, Mama and Papa. And Chip—it's so good to have you home. How long can you stay?"

"Just till after Christmas. I love the Navy, but I sure have missed Mama's cooking!" He swung an arm casually around Cath's shoulder. "And my best girl's kisses!"

"What do you think about the war in Europe?" asked Knowl.

Mama groaned. "Not more war talk on this fine evening!"

"We can't ignore it, Mama," said Chip. We can't hide our heads in the sand—or the snow! Life goes blindly on like it always has here in Indiana, but terrible things are happening overseas, and one day soon we'll have to deal with it."

"Then you do think America will get involved," said Knowl.

"We will if we want to keep that madman Hitler from ruling the world. I'm ready, and the Navy's ready. We can't just—"

Papa interrupted, his voice low and menacing in a way Annie had never heard before. "Listen to me, Chilton. It's easy enough for you young upstarts to swagger around and talk about fighting a war. Sure, we just run over to Europe and put Hitler in his place and make the world behave the way we think it should. Easy to say. I was a doughboy in the World War, and when I came home I told myself I'd do anything to keep from fighting like that again. Sure, you talk bravely and wave flags, but before you agree to fight a war, you imagine what it's like to hold your dying buddy in your arms and feel yourself get wet with his blood. War is about dying. I say, let Europe fight its battles and leave us alone!"

"But it's not that simple, Papa," said Chip. "There are reports that German submarines are cruising off our coasts."

"As long as they're over the three mile limit, they have as much right to be there as anyone. After all, America is neutral in this war."

"Are we neutral—or spineless?" Knowl interjected. "It's because the democracies haven't exercised enough leadership in the past twenty years that Hitler got his foothold in the first place. That, plus the bankrupt statesmanship of England and France. We've allowed Italy and Japan to become bandits and Russia to become an opportunist. Where will it end?"

Papa shook his head. "Mark my words. War is a futile instrument for settling international affairs."

"Then what is the answer, Papa?" asked Chip.

Mama stood up and straightened her shoulders. "Enough talk about war. Who's going to help me wash dishes?"

"I'll help you," said Papa, getting up. "Let the young people spend an hour alone. They have little enough time together."

"Fine. You children go to the parlor. Relax. Play the radio. I'll bring you some hot tea."

"Listen, Mama," said Chip, "Cath and I are going to her house for awhile. See her Mama, maybe take her some cookies."

Mama smiled. "That's a thoughtful thing to do, Chilton."

Knowl leaned over and whispered to Annie, "Don't believe a word of it. Mama fell asleep hours ago. They just want to be alone."

"Oh, Knowl, don't be so cynical!"

Chip got up and ambled over to Knowl. "What say the four of us spend tomorrow in the snow, sledding, skating, whatever? Like old times."

"I have to put the paper to bed, but I may be able to sneak away for a few hours."

After Chip and Cath had gone, Knowl and Annie took their teacups and settled in the parlor on the flowered love seat, listening to the romantic melodies of Fred Waring and Guy Lombardo. For a while they gazed in silence at her Grandmother Reed's Monet prints hanging on the wall, one on each side of the rustic brick fireplace, where a warm fire crackled.

At last, Knowl reached over and took Annie's hand, and she allowed her head to rest on his shoulder. For all the outward appearance of serenity and calm, her heart was pounding in her breast like a bass drum. Surely, Knowl could hear and feel the pulsing excitement. But, if he sensed her sweet agitation, he chose to ignore it. They chatted on quietly about mundane things—the weather, the holidays, his work, her schooling, their families.

"I've noticed a change in you this year," he remarked, his eyes on the bone china teacup in his hand.

"A change? How?"

He set his cup on the table and looked at her. "There's something about you—a tranquility, a quiet maturity, as if you've resolved some fundamental things in your life."

"I have." She drew in a deep breath. "Last summer at the fair I met a street preacher who helped me see my Christian faith in a new light."

"Really?" Knowl sounded amused. "What new spin did he put on things?"

She smiled. "I still believe what I always have, Knowl, just as you do. But it's no longer mere pomp and circumstance, or ritual and ceremony. More important than what I believe is whom I believe in."

"I'm listening," said Knowl, rubbing her hand gently.

"I made a personal commitment to Jesus. I accepted Him as my Lord and Savior."

"How is that different from what you've always done—going to church, worshipping, praying, reading the Bible?"

"Those were actions, things I did because it was expected of me. Don't you see, Knowl? I only went through the motions."

"You're saying you didn't believe in Christ then?"

"Oh, yes, I believed the Bible. I believed everything I was taught. Just as I believed what I was taught in school about the history of England, or the principles of math, or the rules of grammar. I believed with my mind, but it was never real in my heart. It wasn't a personal, life-changing experience."

"I'm not sure I understand, Annie."

Her heart was pounding again, this time with urgency and conviction. "Don't you see, Knowl? For all the years I went to church and worshipped God, I was never shown how I could have His Spirit living in my heart."

Knowl shrugged. "I think you're making this difficult, Annie. You know God by going to church, by going through the motions, as you say. That's what worship is all about."

"But that isn't all of it, Knowl. In the Scriptures, Christ promises to come and live in us if we repent of our sins and invite Him in. Imagine! He not only saves us, but He gives us His Holy Spirit to be our most intimate Companion. That's what He has become to me, Knowl. Not just a creed to live by or doctrines to believe in. His Spirit inhabits my heart and His love flames my passion for Him. He's my life, Knowl—my Savior, my lover, my closest friend."

"You say that eloquently, Annie. I'm quite impressed."

She blushed. "I've never spoken of it like this before. It's a very personal thing to me."

"And I suppose you're suggesting I might want to experience this flaming of the Spirit in my own life?"

"I can only tell you it has made all the difference for me."

"And a very appealing difference it is. Your zeal becomes you, my dear." He lifted her hand to his lips and kissed her fingertips. "I'll give your impassioned claims some thought."

When Annie walked Knowl to the door that evening, he put his hands on her waist and drew her close. He kissed her hair, her cheeks, and the hollow of her neck. She yearned to lose herself in his warmth, his closeness, the spicy fragrance of his cologne. But as quickly as he embraced her, he released her, reached for his topcoat, and stepped to the door. "Good night, Annie. I'll see you tomorrow, and we'll play in the snow."

Play in the snow, they did—the four of them, as they had in the past so many years ago. Booted and bundled in their heaviest coats and muffs, swaddled in scarves like mummies, they dragged their rusting childhood sleds from the cellar and crunched through heavy snowdrifts to the hill at the edge of the woods. They climbed on, stomachs down, pushed off, and careened down the rutted, jagged, snow-crusted slope, their steel runners skimming swiftly over gleaming ice, their tousled hair flying in the wind, as they banked to the right, then the left, screaming and laughing all the way.

They ended up in crumpled heaps at the foot of the hill, their sleds toppled, muffs battered, scarfs tangled, and their cheeks biting red. When they grew weary of sledding, they built a snowman, with black-coal eyes, a carrot nose, and a crooked button smile. Then Chip started a snowball fight, pelting Cath, then Annie. Knowl joined in, only to be attacked by both girls, who rubbed handfuls of snow in his face. He retaliated by chasing them halfway home and tackling Annie. The two collapsed as one into the snow, laughing and panting, their breath forming frosty puffs in the chill air. Chip pulled Cath down, too, and they rolled in the snow, giggling and tussling like children.

At last the four stopped to catch their breath and sat back, gulping air. Snow, twigs, and debris clung to their woolen coats and leggings and caught in their hair. Annie shivered. The icy wetness was seeping through her garments to her skin. "I—I'm freezing," she chattered.

Knowl scrambled over beside her and wrapped her in his arms. "I'll keep you warm," he promised. "And if that won't do, I'll take you home and build a roaring fire in the fireplace."

"Wait," said Chip, holding out his arms grandly. "We have one more winter ritual in honor and memory of our precious Hoosier childhoods."

Cath laughed. "What more is there? We've done it all!"

"This!" he declared, and lay down in a patch of virgin white and spread his arms and legs like scissors, cutting butterfly swaths in the powdery snow.

"Snow angels!" cried Cath. "We loved making snow angels!"

They all found places where the snow was pristine smooth, and one by one they made angels in the snow. Annie and Knowl lay side by side, their arms outstretched, fingers touching. The icy cold had pervaded her flesh and numbed her fingers and toes, but she had never felt more alive or in tune with the earth. She gazed up into the eternal gray sky and at the naked oaks towering overhead with splintery limbs decked out in glittery spangles.

Cath looked over at her, her face ruddy with cold, ice crystals dotting her lashes. "This is one of those moments, isn't it, Annie? One of those timeless flashes that can't be tied to the past."

"Like the fair, you mean?"

"Yes. Like the fair. It'll always just be. As long as the four of us live, we're bound together by this memory. We're part of one another—the four of us, just as the two of us were connected by our blood pact as children. Remember, Annie?"

"Oh, dear Cath, how could I ever forget?"

Chip rolled over beside Cath. "Anyone have the faintest idea what these delirious ladies are talking about?"

"Don't you see, Chip?" Annie exclaimed. "No matter where we go or how far apart we are, nothing can separate the four of us, because of moments like these. They're eternal; they go beyond time and place. They live forever in our hearts."

Knowl stood up, brushed off the snow, and helped Annie to her feet. "The girls are right, Chip. They've got us. We're tied to one another. We might as well surrender peacefully."

"I'm all for surrender," said Chip, "when it comes to love, not war."

Annie looked at her brother and felt a chill that had nothing to do with the frigid air. War! He'd said the word in jest, but the bitter reality of war—distant, yet frighteningly imminent—hung in the silence between them.

Chip helped Cath up and dusted the gauzy layer of snow from her fur-trimmed coat. "The sun will be setting soon," he said. "I hate to break the spell of this day, but maybe we'd better head home."

While Chip walked Cath to her house around the corner, Knowl walked Annie to her door. He lingered on the porch, smoothing her tangled hair with his gloved hand. "You're my snow angel," he murmured. "I wish you weren't going back to Bloomington next week."

Annie held her breath. Around her, the wintry wonderland with its twilight frosts grew soundless, as hushed as pale stars peeping through the silver dome of sky. Had she heard correctly? Was Knowl suggesting more than a passing fondness?

"I've dreamed of you since September, since the kiss we shared," he said, gathering her against him as much as their coats and muffs would allow.

And I've dreamed of you forever, she acknowledged silently.

"I wondered what it would be like to kiss you again," he continued, "and last night I found out. And, my darling Annie, it was every bit as wonderful as before."

She struggled for words, for air, for composure. "Knowl—"

He kissed her with a sweet urgency, and she returned the kiss, as tears beaded on her lids.

He whispered against her ear, "I think I'm falling in love with you, Annie."

Breathlessly, she answered, "And I've always loved you, Knowl."

TEN

The Spring of 1940.
On March 24th, the headlines in the Willowbrook News for Easter Sunday
read:

TORN EUROPE HONORS PRINCE OF PEACE
(The Associated Press) Mankind at war paused
in troubled Europe today to celebrate
in restrained Easter festivities
the Resurrection of the Prince of Peace,
more than 1,900 years ago. Under the shadow of guns
threatening to speak out in the long-feared total war,
Christians of all sects raised their voices
in song and prayer amidst ceremony and custom
handed down through the centuries.

On that troubled Easter Sunday morning, Annie awoke in her own bed in the rose-bud room, comfortably at home for a slim week of vacation from Indiana University. She heard Mama and Papa rise early as usual, and knew Mama was busying herself in the kitchen, stirring up waffles or eggs and ham, while Papa sat at the table, sipping his coffee and bending over his newspaper. She imagined him scanning the headlines, then turning abruptly to the comic section where Barney Google and Snuffy Smith and The Katzenjammer Kids would paint over the deadly, glaring headlines of war with their garish, cartoon-colored ink.

But for Annie, and the rest of America that spring, the questions wouldn't go away:

Will Germany send air fleets against England?

Will Russia move against Rumania?

Will Scandinavia be drawn into the war?

Will there be an offensive on the western front?

Will there ever be peace?

But, perplexing and onerous as the questions were, no one voiced them aloud in the Reed household that Easter morning. Mama served a bountiful breakfast and wondered when the spring flowers would bloom. Papa chuckled over Blondie and Bringing up Father, while Annie quelled her larger concerns with dreamy recollections of Knowl's kisses the night before. After breakfast, the threesome piled into Papa's Nash Sedan and headed for church, anticipating a suitably moving sermon from old Reverend Henry.

Knowl sat with them during the service and afterward joined them for one of Mama's scrumptious fried chicken dinners. Chip hadn't been able to secure an Easter leave, and Cath had remained at the Art Institute to work on her junior art exhibition, so, instead of the "Four Musketeers," it was just the two of them. But Annie relished this time alone with Knowl. She felt closer to him than ever, and sensed that his fondness for her was growing too.

After dinner they took a walk in the garden. The air was nippy but fresh from a recent spring rain; the ground was greening with tender new grass, and fragrant with blossoms and buds. Annie wore her ivory cashmere sweater over a tiny-waisted pink frock with bustle bows. Knowl's suit was a stylish herringbone tweed that accented the handsome silhouette of his broad shoulders and narrow waist and hips.

They walked slowly, hand in hand, just as Annie remembered him walking with Alice Marie the day she spied him from Papa Reed's window so long ago. But that was another lifetime, and a young girl Annie scarcely recognized now. She wanted to shout to the world, It's the first Easter Sunday of a new decade, and Annie Reed is walking with Knowl Herrick and basking in his approving gaze. God, in His grace, has smiled on her and given her these priceless moments with the man she loves!

She was too grateful to ask for more, perhaps even a bit too proud to beg God to give her Knowl for a lifetime. Still, it was her constant unspoken prayer. The desire of her heart. A verse in Scripture spoke of God giving His children the desires of their hearts. At Christmas, Knowl had said, I think I'm falling in love with you. Since then, he had remained silent. Was it possible God would spark genuine, enduring love in Knowl's heart for Annie? The question had played over and over in her thoughts like a favorite, unforgettable melody. Today it appeared the question might be answered.

"Shall we sit down in the gazebo?" Knowl suggested.

"It's one of my favorite spots," she replied. "From there you can see Mama's entire garden."

They crossed the lawn and entered the little pavilion with its white lattice trim, and sat down side by side on a narrow bench seat. Knowl took her hand and held it between both of his. "I've missed you, Annie," he said softly. "More than you know."

Her voice was light with anticipation. "I've missed you too, Knowl."

"It's very lonely in Willowbrook without you. I miss Chip and Cath, too, of course, but mostly you. When I'm at the newspaper doing my work, I find myself wondering what you're doing at that precise moment in Bloomington, and at night as I fall asleep I wonder if you might be thinking of me as well." His eyes searched hers. "I hope you don't think it improper of me to reflect on you at such times, Annie. I'm only trying to say you're on my mind day and night, at work or repose."

She felt her face flushing with pleasure and astonishment. She had prayed for Knowl's affection, but had never dared dream she might actually stir such heartfelt passions.

He removed his glasses, placed them on the bench beside him, and gently gathered her into his arms. "What I'm trying to say, dear Annie, is that I love you very much. I'd be honored if you'd consider becoming my wife."

Annie felt suddenly weak, dazed with euphoria. Tears welled in her eyes and spilled onto her cheeks. "Oh, Knowl, do you even have to ask? Of course I'll marry you. I love you with all my heart."

He kissed her face, her tears, her hair, crushing her against him so that she could scarcely breathe. She revelled in his warmth, his touch, the robust scent of his cologne.

Then, as if a chill wind had overtaken her, she thought of Alice Marie. She gazed up imploringly at him. "Knowl, dearest, I have to ask—"

He smiled with his eyes. "I think I know—"

"Alice Marie. You loved her so. She almost became your wife."

He nodded. "I don't deny it. I loved her desperately. I loved her for her confidence when I had none. I loved her for her gaiety when I was full of gloom. I loved her for her boldness when I felt painfully timid. But I've realized, Annie, that was a hollow man seeking love for all the wrong reasons. I'm not that man anymore. I've got my relationships in order—with man and God. I come to you not out of neediness, but out of wholeness, because I think we have much to offer each other."

"Then you're over your feelings for my sister?"

His eyes grew serious. "I must be frank with you, Annie. I'll always be fond of Alice Marie, but it's as if I've locked her in a room of my heart and thrown away the key. I don't choose to visit that room anymore. It's part of the past."

Annie nodded uncertainly. She would have felt better if Knowl had said he had banished Alice Marie from his heart altogether. "You said your relationships are in order, with man and God. Does that mean—?"

"Yes. I've prayed the sinner's prayer, as you encouraged me to do. I'm not sure I'll ever have the intimacy with God that comes so natural for you, but I know I am, as you say, redeemed."

"I'm so glad, Knowl. I was afraid—"

"Afraid of what, love?"

"Afraid you'd have Cath's attitude. She resents my conversion. She thinks I've become something of a fanatic."

Knowl chuckled. "Cath has no room to talk. She's always running off to extremes or throwing herself into some pet project or cause. She shouldn't begrudge you—"

"I'm not running to extremes, Knowl—"

"No, but by your very zeal, you bring into question the people who sit in church pews every week, yet never personally invite Christ into their lives."

"I'm not judging them, Knowl. All I know is I went through the motions all my life without knowing the Person I worshipped. I missed so much."

"What about your parents? Are they going through the motions, as you say?"

She thought a moment. "They don't talk about it, but at some point in their lives they must have quietly recognized Christ as their Savior. Their faith is real—I've seen the evidence of it in their lives—but it's taken for granted. They seem content knowing God from a distance."

"That's your opinion," said Knowl.

"Yes, my opinion. I only know that a distant God isn't enough for me. I feel an intense yearning to know Christ better." She looked up questioningly at him. "Am I sounding like a foolish saint, Knowl? I don't mean to. I just want you to know the woman you're marrying—the real Annie Reed. You see, I've discovered I'm more comfortable with God than with anyone else, even you. I'm most myself when I'm in His presence. He must come first. Can you accept that about me?"

Knowl leaned over and kissed the tip of her nose. "If that's the worst you can tell me about the hidden Annie Reed, I'll consider myself most fortunate."

She smiled teasingly. "And what is the worst about yourself? What dark secrets do you harbor?"

With a mocking twinkle, his eyes narrowed, and he uttered a malevolent laugh. "The worst about me? I am mad," he embraced her and smothered her neck with kisses, "about you!"

She laughed and pretended to push him away.

"I may go mad waiting for our wedding day," he warned, his mouth moving against her cheek. "Say you'll agree. We'll be married in June, as soon as you get home from the university."

She drew back in surprise. "This June?"

"Yes, of course. The sooner, the better. I realize you'll want to finish out the school year. Otherwise, we could make it an April wedding."

"Oh, Knowl, I hadn't thought about school. I want to get my degree. I've worked so hard. I still have two more years."

He looked at her with consternation. "Annie, there's no way you can continue at the university and still be married. I just assumed you'd realize you'd have to come home to Willowbrook for good."

She contemplated this new reality. "Yes, you're right, of course, Knowl. Willowbrook will be our home. I just never expected a marriage proposal. I thought I would always go on with my own life, loving you from afar."

Knowl laughed. "No long distance relationships for us, my love. I want you in my home, in my room, in my bed."

Annie blushed. Then she looked up into his face. "Knowl, you said, your home? What home do you mean?"

He stared blankly at her. "Why, the house where I live, of course. Right around the corner."

She straightened her shoulders. "I never stopped to think about where we would live."

He smiled agreeably. "Where else, but in my house?"

"It's your mother's house."

"It's mine, too. You've always known, since my father left, my mother couldn't afford that house without my salary. I won't have her struggling alone or taking in questionable boarders. You know how troubled she is. She needs me, Annie."

Annie stood up and walked over to the railing. "I just never thought—I never pictured myself living in your house. I guess I never imagined myself anywhere but here in my parents' house on Honeysuckle Lane."

Knowl laughed dryly. "Well, we certainly can't live here with your mother and father."

"But you expect us to live with your mother."

He stood up and approached her. Frustration edged his voice. "You know how my mother is, Annie. You know how she's been since the day my father walked out on us. I can't walk out on her too."

Annie turned back to Knowl and touched his chin. "I know, darling. I wouldn't ask that of you. It's just—well, it'll take some time for me to get used to the idea. You understand, don't you? I've always lived in this house with Mama and Papa. This house has been my life, my heritage, sometimes even my consolation."

"And look how close we'll be—practically next door. You can walk over and visit your parents any time you wish."

Annie smiled. "You're right, of course. It's time I stopped thinking of my silly old house and started thinking of our home, the one I'll be sharing with my own dear husband. It's what I've always dreamed of, Knowl."

He clasped her hands and swung her around. "Then let's go tell your parents and my mother. We'll tell them to prepare for a June wedding. Perhaps Chip can steal away from the Navy long enough to be my best man."

"And Cath can be my maid of honor!"

"It'll be grand! The 'Four Musketeers'—together again!"

On a warm, sunny Saturday, the twenty-second day of June, Annie awoke to the thought, Today is my wedding day! At last I'll be Mrs. Knowl Herrick! Everyone would be there in the romantic little chapel. Chip, granted a forty-eight hour liberty, had flown to Chicago, then caught the train to Willowbrook to be best man. Cath, who had completed her third year at the Art Institute, had come a week earlier to help Annie with the final alterations on her formal satin and lace gown.

Even Knowl's parents would be attending the wedding, although not together, of course.

The only person missing would be Alice Marie, who had an engagement with the band in San Francisco. Although she didn't admit it, Annie felt more relieved than saddened by the prospect of her older sister's absence.

Just before the ceremony, Cath handed Annie a folded slip of paper. "It's something 'old' and 'borrowed,' Annie—our friendship pact we made as children. It's your turn to keep it. Friends forever, right?"

Annie tucked the fragile, faded paper into her bodice. "Friends forever, Cath."

As they embraced, Cath whispered, "It's turning out the way we always dreamed. You're marrying my brother and coming to live in my house. Someday I'll marry your brother and live in your house. We'll always be family. Nothing can come between us."

Annie eagerly searched Cath's face. "Is this an announcement? Are you and Chip—?"

"No, we're not engaged. Neither of us wants to settle down for years yet. He has the Navy. I have my art. But we're very much in love, like you and Knowl—"

Cath's confidential words were interrupted by majestic strains of "The Wedding March" peeling from the organ and filling the chapel. "Oh, Cath, it's time!" Annie said breathlessly.

Moments later, as she walked proudly down the aisle on her father's arm, she reflected, Yes, Cath is right. It's all turning out as I've always prayed! Knowl Herrick is waiting at the altar to make me his wife, and I'm not about to disappoint him, the way Alice Marie did.

Still, Annie couldn't escape the nagging thought that the wedding of her dreams was hauntingly reminiscent of that other wedding that almost was. Was Knowl remembering, too, as he repeated his vows and slipped a gold ring on her finger, that he had almost stood at this altar with Alice Marie two years ago? Even more dismaying, did he wish Alice Marie was standing beside him now? Was Annie only second best?

No! Surely the tender expression in Knowl's eyes told her everything she needed to know. He had eyes for her alone. And she would make him happy. Whatever it took.

The reception was filled with food and music, conversation and laughter, delightful in every way, except that Tom Herrick bragged a bit too shrilly about his latest sales exploits while glaring menacingly at his former wife. He looked much older than Annie remembered—graying, his face deeply wrinkled, his suit a size too small for his girth. Unfortunately, Knowl's mother, Betty, who was obviously a trifle tipsy, wasn't about to ignore her ex-husband. In a loud, rancorous voice, she demanded to know why someone had allowed a louse like Tom Herrick inside a hallowed church.

Refusing to let anyone spoil their wedding, Mr. and Mrs. Knowl Herrick left on their honeymoon amid a flurry of rice and well wishes. They drove across the state line to Detroit in his spanking new Hudson Country Club Sedan and spent the weekend in the honeymoon suite of a luxurious downtown hotel. It was the amorous, fantasy kind of honeymoon from which romance novels are born, Annie mused in retrospect. Unfortunately, it was entirely too short.

They returned to Willowbrook on Monday morning, because Knowl had pressing responsibilities back at the newspaper. He dropped Annie off at her house so she could pack the rest of her belongings. After work, he picked her up and delivered her with all her worldly goods at his house around the corner.

The moment Annie stepped across the threshold of the Herrick house, she felt a sudden gloom, almost an oppression of the spirit. Naturally, she had visited the rambling old residence from time to time over the years, but only as a momentary guest. She had rarely bothered to notice its dark, dull atmosphere, nor had she considered how unaccommodating it might be as one's permanent abode.

It was hard to imagine that such a house existed only a stone's throw from her own precious house on Honeysuckle Lane. It was startling, too, to realize that her closest friend, Cath, and her dear husband, Knowl, had been raised in these sunless rooms with their yellowed wallpaper and dreary carpets.

Whereas Annie's home evidenced her mother's loving care in every gleaming nook and cranny, the Herrick house was stark testimony of a family torn asunder and barely warding off poverty. The furniture was sparse and utilitarian, and placed haphazardly. The walls were stark, devoid of paintings or decorations, except for a few of Cath's early sketches. The heavy drapes were closed, allowing only a sliver of sun to enter. Where's the love? Annie wondered desperately. Where's the warmth, the joy?

Knowl must have sensed her dismay and caught a glimpse of the house through her eyes. "I know it's nothing like your home," he said quickly, "but we can fix it up. Ma's never cared a whit about the place, and Cath and I spend as little time here as possible." He laughed mirthlessly. "I guess you already know that. We spent half our lives at your house!"

Annie walked through the parlor to the kitchen. "It's okay, Knowl. I've got a little of my mother's knack for sprucing things up. Maybe we could hang some lighter curtains and let the sun in." She walked over to the large bay window and opened the drapes. "There. Isn't that better?"

"Close it, Annie. It's too bright."

Annie whirled around at the sound of Betty Herrick's voice. The woman stood in the doorway in a faded robe, her orange hair mussed and her eyelids heavy, as if she'd just awakened from a deep sleep. "The light bothers my eyes," she said thickly, "so I keep the drapes closed. Of course, you're new here, Annie, so I don't expect you to know all our little quirks and idiosyncrasies yet. But you'll learn soon enough." She shuffled over and patted Knowl's cheek. "My son will see to that, won't you, Knowl, dear?"

ELEVEN

While the war in Europe raged, Annie waged her own private war with Betty Herrick. Not a war of words or deeds, but a war of nuances and insinuations, of steely glances and insolent tones, of words left unsaid—a psychological war of minds and wills, a tedious war of endurance.

Betty Herrick was cunning in communicating her hostilities to Annie without incurring the wrath of her son. She was devious, clever, and dauntless in maintaining the status quo. Whenever Annie fixed dinner, Betty managed to suffer indigestion; when Annie longed for an hour in the evening alone with her husband, Betty managed to succumb to some ailment that required her son's attention. When Annie brightened the dreary rooms with her family's garden flowers, Betty complained of her allergies. And when Annie made any effort to renovate that sorry carcass of a house, Betty quickly squelched her plans, insisting she was happy with things as they were. So the house remained unchanged, except when Annie managed to slip something past her cantankerous mother-in-law.

Annie found consolation in her daily prayer times in the little sewing room upstairs, in her husband when he wasn't wrestling with his latest newspaper deadline, and in Cath, whenever she was home long enough to visit. But it seemed Cath found every excuse imaginable to slip away from the house for an afternoon of trekking the countryside for watercolor subjects, or a few days of landscape painting in Brown County, or even two weeks of private portrait instruction in faraway Greenwich Village. It peeved Annie that Cath could escape her mother's melancholy house to traipse off to Lower Manhattan in New York City to indulge her bohemian leanings.

But even when she was home, Cath and her mother sparred back and forth with withering verbal attacks, each one attempting to out-shout the other. Several times during that first summer, Annie considered packing her things and moving back home.

In fact, during one especially trying afternoon, Annie tossed a few garments into a valise and trudged home. Tearfully, she told her surprised mother, "I've come home to stay. I can't live in that awful place with that awful woman another day!"

Instead of showing sympathy, Mama placed her hands on Annie's shoulders and turned her back toward the door. "Daughter," she said sternly, "you may come home to visit anytime you wish, but not to stay. You've made your choice. You have a husband and you must make him a home. No one said it would be easy, but you're smart enough to figure out a way to do it. Now get back there before someone discovers you've gone."

At the moment, Annie felt betrayed and forsaken by her own kin, but as the waves of hurt and futility ebbed, she knew Mama was right. She had committed herself to Knowl. She couldn't allow an angry, hysterical woman to come between them. But so far she felt powerless to intervene or resolve her dilemma.

From time to time Annie also vented her frustration to Cath, but Cath offered little sympathy either. "Why do you think I spent half my life at your house?" she countered. "If you had any gumption, you'd tell my spineless brother to pack up and move you out of here, before Mama dictates every aspect of your life the way she tries to dictate ours."

Annie shook her head in resignation. "I'm not like you, Cath. I'm no good at confrontations. You like to shake things up, make demands, put people on the spot. I prefer the line of least resistance."

"Then you'll never survive in this house," Cath replied.

During that summer, Annie thought often about Cath's dire pronouncement. She found herself walking aimlessly through the gloomy rooms of the Herrick house, searching for some nameless remedy, some means of escape. She meandered about in a daze, her arms crossed on her chest in an instinctive protective gesture, wondering how she had stumbled into this curious predicament. By what quirk of fate was she expected to call this creaking monstrosity home?

There was something else Annie hadn't counted on—how much she would miss university life. She hungered for the stimulating literary and cultural camaraderie she'd grown accustomed to in Bloomington—the teas, the readings, the concerts, the art galleries and museums. She missed writing essays, stories, and poems, and receiving her instructors' glowing critiques. She felt her mind growing dull and flabby, her body listless, her spirits numb. How could she be deteriorating so rapidly when she was finally with the man she loved?

When she approached Knowl about her concerns, he seemed helpless to offer a solution. In fact, her dissatisfaction stymied, even irritated, him. He obviously hadn't counted on Annie needing more from him than he could give.

In desperation Annie suggested, "Maybe I should find a job."

Knowl retorted, "I won't have my wife working. I'm quite able to support this family."

"But I need something to do," she protested.

"You may have your chance," he warned. "If America gets into the war, men will go off to fight. Women and children will be put to work so industries essential to warfare won't suffer."

Annie retaliated in exasperation. "It seems as if we've been talking war forever! When will it ever stop?"

Knowl's brows furrowed darkly. "One of these days talk won't be enough." After a few moments of silence, he said in a conciliatory tone, "If you want to be useful, why don't you write a column for the newspaper?"

"A column? About what?"

"Anything. Whatever you please."

"I wouldn't know what to say. I wouldn't want to write about ordinary things, like canning peaches, or making quilts, or growing roses. What could I write that anyone would want to read?"

Knowl adjusted his glasses. "You say you're a writer, Annie. It's what you've always wanted to do. So find something to write."

She nodded. How could she argue with such rhetoric? If she were truly a writer, she would indeed write!

"But I haven't had any profound experiences, Knowl. All I know is Willowbrook and Honeysuckle Lane. Life in a small town."

"Well, look what Booth Tarkington did with that. He won the Pulitzer Prize for The Magnificent Ambersons and Alice Adams. I'd say, as an Indiana author who writes about small-town, midwestern life, he's made quite a success of it."

Annie couldn't argue with that either. The larger question that loomed in her mind was whether she possessed the talent to take commonplace events and imbue them with magic. The possibility that she had only a modicum of talent was too painful even to consider.

The next day, Annie assumed Knowl had forgotten their conversation about her writing, but when he arrived home from work that evening, he was carrying an enormous box. He marched into the study and placed it on the desk. "This is for you, Annie. Now you'll have no excuse not to write."

With eager, awkward fingers, Annie tore open the box and peered inside. "Oh, Knowl, is this what I think it is?"

He reached in, removed the contents, and set the instrument squarely on the desk. "There. Write till your heart's content!"

Annie lovingly examined the handsome machine. "Oh, Knowl, it's wonderful! A Remington typewriter! How can I thank you?"

He drew her into his arms. "Ask me again tonight, love."   Annie felt as if she'd been given a new lease on life. Whenever the Herrick house or Knowl's mother became too much to endure, Annie retreated to her revered Remington in the study. There, she lost herself in other worlds and wonderlands limited only by her own imagination. She wrote, not for a critical, sophisticated audience, but for herself alone—fanciful stories about imaginary characters accomplishing unbelievable feats. She reconstructed the capricious stories she and Cath had invented and played out as youngsters. And the adventurous tales of chivalry and bravery, of knights and pirates and Indians and kings that Chip and Knowl had acted out in their dauntless, magical youth.

As the months passed, Annie began to feel creative again, invigorated, productive. In fact, one day she even summoned the courage to lovingly confront Betty Herrick. She was clearing the table after lunch while Betty sat nursing a glass of wine and spouting her usual complaints. "You put too much onion in that salad, Annie. You know it gives me heartburn. By the way, be careful when you wash those china cups. I found one chipped the other day. Oh, and Annie, I heard you at your typewriter early this morning. The clatter of those keys woke me out of a sound sleep. You've got to consider other people, dear."

Annie felt her blood rising, prompting the familiar headache that came whenever she squelched her anger and smiled sweetly in the face of Betty Herrick's barbs. But today something snapped in her usual chain of reactions. She sat down across from Betty and looked her directly in the eye.

"I've never spoken crossly with you, have I, Mrs. Herrick?"

The woman looked taken aback. "Why, no, not that I recall."

"I've always shown you the greatest respect," Annie continued, her voice filling with emotion. "Even when you haven't deserved it."

"Why, I—"

"I've lived here nearly half a year, and I think it's time I stopped feeling like a guest— or a servant. I realize we can't both be the lady of the house, Mrs. Herrick. I don't want to take your place, but I need my own place here. I don't want to take over your home, but I need to feel it's my home too. I don't want to take your son away from you, but there are times when I need my husband with me. I'm quite willing to share, and I think there's more than enough love, time, and possessions here for all of us."

Betty Herrick swallowed another sip of wine.

"Do you realize," Annie plunged on boldly, "that both Knowl and Cath avoid this house whenever they can? They don't enjoy being here. They feel the tension. It does-n't have to be that way, Mrs. Herrick."

Betty finished her wine and poured another glass.

"I could help you change things," said Annie. "I could help you make this house attractive, and we could set up a system that would allow you time with your son and daughter. Isn't that what you're afraid I'll take away?"

Betty's eyes riveted on Annie. "It's been that way all my life," she rasped. "Why should it change now? I could never compete with you and your perfect family for my children's affections. They always preferred your company."

"That's not so—"

"Of course, it's so! What did I have to offer them? No adoring husband and father, no loving family. Just one bitter, broken-hearted mother in a rundown house with too many bills and no money to pay them."

Annie felt a sudden wave of compassion sweep over her. "I'm sorry, Mrs. Herrick. I didn't realize—"

"What? That I had feelings too? That I saw what was happening to my home, my children? Of course, I knew! Why do you think I drink? It makes me forget what might have been!"

Impulsively Annie got up, went around the table, and embraced Betty Herrick. The woman flinched and stiffened, but she didn't push Annie away.

"Will you let me help you?" asked Annie. "Will you let me make a few of the rooms more attractive? Nothing drastic. A little paint, some lighter curtains, a few knickknacks here and there, even some of Cath's paintings. They would look lovely in your house."

"I never asked her for any. I was too proud to beg."

"But maybe she thinks you don't like them. Maybe she's just waiting for you to notice her work and enjoy it."

Betty's gray eyes narrowed. "I don't want you touching my room or the guest rooms upstairs."

Annie nodded. "I won't do anything without your approval." She paused, then added, "I know you miss having Knowl to yourself in the evenings. Perhaps if he spent an hour visiting with you in the parlor after dinner while I wash dishes, you wouldn't mind me having him the rest of the evening."

Betty frowned. "Make an appointment to see my own son? Is that what it's come to?"

"You would have him all to yourself for that hour. Isn't that better than now, when he comes in and avoids even ten minutes of conversation?"

Betty quizzically arched one brow. "You could persuade him to spend an hour with me each evening?"

"I think so, if you promise not to pursue him with contrived ailments at all hours of the night."

Betty sipped her wine. "I see. I'll give it some thought."

In the months that followed, Annie couldn't claim a miraculous transformation in the Herrick household, but there was a decided improvement. Betty Herrick complained less and took Annie at her word, allowing her to spruce up the living room and parlor with fresh paint, new drapes, and several of Cath's best paintings. Cath was incredulous—and immensely delighted—that her mother actually wanted to hang her art work on the walls.

Even Knowl was amazed by the change in his mother. She nagged less and drank less, and most of all, she seemed truly grateful to have an hour of his time to herself each evening. And, keeping her part of the bargain, Betty stopped harassing and interrupting Knowl and Annie during their evenings together. Gradually, with the passing of weeks and months, Annie began to feel that perhaps it wasn't so bad living in the Herrick house after all.

T W E L V E

The Summer of 1941.

In August, Chip returned home to Willowbrook with a one-week leave from the Navy and a secret that kept him humming and smiling. On a humid, airless Saturday night, he and Cath, and Knowl and Annie, drove into town to celebrate his homecoming. They saw The Philadelphia Story in the cool comfort of the Majestic Theater, then walked arm in arm down the block to Walgreen's Drug Store for chocolate milkshakes.

While waiting to give their order, they sat on swivel stools at the soda fountain, where a large, round sign urged, "Drink Coca-Cola" and soda and sundae glasses graced little doilies and stood in rows on glass shelves. Lulled by the movie and feeling pleasantly satisfied, Annie watched their reflections in the sprawling mirror behind the counter, as the four of them made small talk and lame jokes, whirled their stools, and laughed like carefree children.

While the soda jerk dawdled, cleaning the marbled countertop and polishing the spigots that delivered carbonated beverages, Chip pretended to help himself to a bowl of fresh fruit on the counter and Knowl eyed a crystal cake container filled with glazed doughnuts. Finally, when Chip reached over and knocked on the red, gleaming Coca-Cola cooler, the sandy-haired soda jerk snapped to attention, took their orders, and served their shakes. With Knowl and Chip making private jokes about the boy being more jerk than soda, they carried their shakes over to a table opposite the counter.

"So, how did you girls like the movie?" Chip asked as they settled at their places.

"I adored Katharine Hepburn!" Cath exclaimed, looking like Kate herself with her flowing red hair, green pinafore dress, and saddle oxfords. "I tell you, she deserves an academy award for that bravura performance."

"I loved James Stewart and Cary Grant," said Annie. "I've never seen two more handsome men, unless it's our dear brothers."

"Ah, little sister, are you speaking sincerely or in jest?" queried Chip, drumming his fingers on the shiny black tabletop.

"Oh, she's serious," said Cath. "You're much more handsome in your white Navy uniform than you ever were in your old, smelly football jersey."

"Football? That's ancient history!" teased Knowl. "But I suppose sipping shakes at the malt shop does bring back old school memories, doesn't it?"

"Not for me," said Chip. "I'm on to bigger and better things. The world is waiting at my door!" He turned slightly, straightening his torso and lifting his chin. "Cath, sweetheart, what do you think of my shoulder marks now that I'm a Lieutenant, Junior Grade? Some insignia, huh?"

She ran her fingertips over the tiny star and stripes. "Very impressive, darling, but it's the man who makes the uniform." She leaned over, her face upturned to his. "And I love this man more than I can say!"

He bent over and kissed her lips.

Annie nudged Knowl. "Looks like the lovebirds want to be alone."

He clasped her shoulder. "That's all right. I wouldn't mind some time alone with my sweet bride."

Chip grinned. "That's what I like to see—a guy who knows how to take good care of my sister."

"You took the words right out of my mouth," said Knowl, eyeing Cath meaningfully. "When are you two going to become more than pen pals?"

Cath stirred her milkshake. "You know Chip and I will never be homebodies like you and Annie. It's not our nature."

Chip flattened his straw paper. "Then again, you never know...."

"Are you saying there's hope for the old boy yet?" quizzed Knowl. "You've been acting like you had a secret to tell..."

"You might say, after globe-trotting for awhile, I have a new appreciation of home," said Chip. "With all my travels, there's no place like Willowbrook, and nobody like my Cath."

She looked longingly at him. "I just wish you weren't shipping out so soon, honey."

"Where are you going this time?" asked Knowl.

"Hawaii. A sweet little place called Pearl Harbor, the jewel of the Pacific, where the sun always shines and the girls wear grass skirts and welcome you with exotic orchid leis."

Knowl grinned. "Is this a vacation or an official assignment?"

"Both, I hope," said Chip. "I figure while Britain and Europe are fighting it out with Hitler, I'll be relaxing on some sandy beach in my island paradise. Actually, I'll be stationed on the battleship, Arizona. Not a bad way to spend a war."

"Then you don't think America will enter the skirmish?" asked Knowl.

Chip traced a water ring on the table. "FDR won his third term by promising to keep us out of the war. So far so good."

"He was bowing to the political power of the isolationists," murmured Knowl, "including men like Charles Lindbergh. I hope we don't discover we've been living in a fool's paradise."

Annie nodded. "Since Knowl and I married, the war has become so remote to me. I hear the news reports and simply tune them out. It was weeks before I realized France had surrendered to Germany on our wedding day. And then it just dawned on me that Hitler attacked Russia on our first anniversary. I know I should keep up with what's happening in Europe, but life at home is so demanding—"

Knowl chuckled. "What she's trying to say is, she's so busy battling my mother, she's too weary to worry about Europe's battles."

Annie playfully slapped Knowl's arm. "That's not true. I get along quite well with your mother these days."

"She's right," said Cath. "It's amazing. I can't be in the same room with my mother without both of us screaming. But Mama goes along with whatever Annie says. Annie can do no wrong."

"It wasn't like that at first. Now I simply try to be firm, but agreeable, that's all."

"Anyone who can be agreeable around my mother is a saint."

"Amen!" Knowl emptied the rest of his shake from the frosty metal decanter into his glass. "That's why I married my Annie. She's the only girl I know who could get along with Mama."

"I hope you had other reasons besides that," Annie protested.

Knowl leaned over and whispered invitingly, "I'll tell you all the other reasons tonight."

Cath nudged Chip. "Look at them! Do you think we'd be that lovey-dovey after a year of marriage?"

Chip laughed. "I give up! I can't keep this under wraps any longer! I was going to wait for an evening of music and romance, but I guess movies and milkshakes will have to do."

Cath stared at him. "What are you talking about?"

"What I've been dying to tell you," said Chip.

"I knew you had a secret," cried Annie. "Tell us!"

He looked at Cath. "Forgive me for making this the night you'll always remember instead of an evening of moonlight and roses. Somehow it seems right—the four of us together for this."

"For what? Just tell me, before I die of curiosity."

"This," said Chip. He reached into his pants pocket, then set a tiny black box on the table before Cath.

She opened the box with exquisite care, as if it might shatter in her hands. A gleaming diamond ring winked out at her. She gasped, "Oh, Chip, it can't be. This is a joke, right? You found this in a box of Crackerjack?"

"No, Cath." He reached over, removed the ring, and slipped it on her finger. "Will you marry me?"

She began to weep, but quickly brushed the tears away, and sniffled noisily. "How can you do this to me—here, in a place like this? Everyone's watching! No one gets engaged in Walgreen's Drug Store!"

"We do—if you say yes."

"But we're both adventurers at heart, not homebodies."

"Who says we can't travel and have adventures together?"

"But when would we marry? Where would we live?"

"I'll get a furlough in December. We'll have a Christmas wedding here in Willowbrook. Then I'll arrange some way for you to come live with me in my Pacific Paradise."

Laughter mixed now with her tears. "I've always loved you, Chip, since I was a scrawny little girl with red pigtails. I'll never love anyone else."

"Then say yes, Cath."

She drew in a deep breath. "Yes!"

Chip stood up with the imposing dignity of his uniform and swept Catherine into his arms. They kissed tenderly, while their delighted siblings looked politely away. Knowl drew Annie close and pressed his cheek against her hair. "Looks like they're finally going to tie the knot," he whispered. "Your brother, my sister. What a grand pair!"

Annie nodded, tears streaming down her cheeks. It was like Cath had always said. Their dreams would come true. They'd be family forever. Suddenly, Walgreen's had never looked more enchanting.

December 7, 1941.

It was the most commonplace of mornings. Annie would always remember it that way. A typical Sunday morning, except that Cath was there. She had come home from Chicago after only three months at the Art Institute. She explained vaguely that she was suffering from some minor complaint, but Annie suspected she came home early to prepare for her Christmas wedding. In fact, for days she had been consumed with designing her own wedding dress, which Annie's mother had promised to make.

Now, at breakfast on this brisk, snowy morning, Cath showed Annie the sketch. "What do you think of it? Will it do?"

"It's magnificent!" declared Annie, studying the sketch while her ham and eggs grew cold.

In her enthusiasm, Cath had forgotten her breakfast, too, although she rarely had more than a cup of black coffee and dry toast these days. "Do you really like it?" she cried with unabashed pleasure. "Do you see, Annie? The gown will be ivory satin with hand-beaded lace and a Queen Anne neckline. It'll have long sleeves, a fitted bodice, and a large bow in back with a cathedral train."

"You'll be a beautiful bride, Cath."

"It's not too gaudy or showy, is it? Not too outrageous for Willowbrook?"

"Willowbrook has never seen a finer wedding dress!"

Cath beamed. "I know Chip will love it. Oh, Annie, I can't wait! I miss him so much."

"You've waited twenty-two years. You can wait another two weeks."

"I just pray nothing will happen to cancel his furlough. It's all he writes about. I read you his last letter, didn't I?"

Annie smiled. "Yes, but go ahead. Read it to me again."

Cath removed an envelope from the pocket of her full bodiced, loose waisted frock and took out a thin sheet of stationery. She read the words as if she knew them by heart.

> *My dearest Cath:*
>
> *How I miss you! I think of you all day*
> *and dream of you all night. I close my eyes*
> *and pretend I'm holding you in my arms.*
> *Everything is quiet and peaceful here as usual.*
> *You'd love the sun-washed, flower-covered hillsides,*
> *especially now that you're knee-deep in snow.*
> *We have 75,000 American military people in Hawaii,*
> *and we spend most of our time drilling and running*
> *through simulated alerts. Most of us feel lucky we're*
> *away from the war in Europe. In fact, some of the guys*
> *sit around, have a few beers, and congratulate*
> *themselves for being here instead of in the thick of*
> *battle. A lot of the guys spend Saturday nights*
> *dancing or partying at Hickam Field, but I'm spending*
> *Saturday night writing you. I can hear the big band*
> *music in the distance, and it makes me even lonelier*
> *for your arms. I can't wait until Christmas.*
> *My furlough's been approved. On December 20th,*
> *I'll hop a clipper for San Francisco and arrive*

in less than twenty-four hours. Then I'll catch the
first train east and pray that every other soldier
isn't taking the same train home for the holidays.
God-willing, I'll be home by Christmas Eve.
We'll be married in Willowbrook and honeymoon in
Honolulu, where bright posters promise the tourists,
"A World of Happiness in an Ocean of Peace."
It's all waiting for you here, sweetheart.
I pray for you every day, Cath. God be with you.
They say there are no atheists in foxholes.
Well, I may never see a foxhole, but I've seen
enough of life to know only God can see us through.
Listen to Annie, Cath. She knows Him better than
any of us. If you're ever in a pinch, she'll
steer you right. Tell her to take good care of you
until we're together again.
Give Annie and my folks a great big hug,
but keep the best hug for yourself.
See you soon, my dreamy stardust girl!

With all my love, Chip

P.S. Merry Christmas in Hawaiian! "Mele Kalikimake."

That December morning, Annie, Knowl, and Cath were almost late to church, so absorbed were they with the wedding dress sketch and Chip's latest letter from glorious Hawaii. They stole into the sanctuary as quietly as possible in their snow boots, and sat in the last pew, still bundled in their heavy coats.

Elderly Reverend Henry was growing a tad forgetful these days, so his sermons often ran an extra ten minutes while he repeated favorite anecdotes he'd already presented. But he always delivered a morsel of truth that Annie found helpful for the week to come. Today's tidbit: "It's not the war in Europe that can destroy us; it's the war of the spirit that defeats us when we don't keep Christ our first priority in life."

On the ride home from church, Cath mused, "Maybe I'm mellowing, but I'm actually starting to enjoy Reverend Henry's messages. Does that mean I'm becoming a homebody like Annie?"

"Happiness does that to you, sis," said Knowl. "Or maybe it's the fact that you're going to be an old married lady yourself in a couple of weeks."

"Watch it, dear brother. I'm getting married, not buried. And, no matter what, I'll always be a free spirit at heart."

Shortly after noon, Annie, Cath, and Knowl walked around the corner through drifting snow to the Reed house for one of Mama's delectable leg of lamb dinners. Besides a few hours of pleasant company with her children, Mama would have a chance to measure Cath for her wedding gown.

"My goodness," Mama exclaimed when she examined Cath's sketch, "I've got only two weeks to turn this lovely picture into a genuine satin bridal gown!"

"You'd better measure me after dinner," Cath warned, "so I'll have plenty of room in that dress to breathe."

Knowl playfully pinched his sister's waist. "You have been putting on a pound or two. I think it's called, 'happy fat.'"

Cath ignored the remark and sashayed over to the console radio. "Shall we have dinner music?"

"Yes, let's," said Annie. "Good music, good food."

"Let me," said Papa. He turned the dial. "It's nearly one p.m. Time for the Longine Symphonette. Ah, there! Wonderful Sunday dinner music!"

They sat down at the dining room table and held hands while Papa prayed. He closed with, "And may God bless Chilton so far away in the Pacific. Please, God, let there be peace in our world soon. In Jesus' name, amen." He looked up with a smile and said, "Now pass the bread."

For a while, everyone ate in silence, savoring Mama's browned potatoes and tender lamb with its piquant mint sauce. Then, as appetites were sated, ripples of conversation began, first about Christmas, then about the wedding and all that must be accomplished before these two momentous events arrived. "We all must work together," said Mama. "Remember all the last minute details before your wedding, Annie?"

"Do I! I thought I'd never be ready on time!"

"I don't remember anything about it," Knowl interjected, his voice full of whimsy, "until I saw Annie walk down that aisle."

"Men are that way," scoffed Mama. "Oblivious to everything, until they've got their bride in their arms. Weddings are for women. Men come along for the ride."

"That's telling him, Mama," said Annie.

Cath was about to speak, but the music in the parlor stopped suddenly and a sonorous male voice boomed over the speaker. Papa clambered out of his chair and ambled to the parlor. "Might be news about Europe," he said, turning up the volume.

There was a burst of static; then a deep, resonant voice thundered over the air waves. "I repeat, we have just received word that the Japs have bombed Pearl Harbor. The damage is not yet known, but first reports confirm the bombing has been heavy. Please stay tuned for further information."

The music resumed, but everyone remained silent and motionless, as if the bulletin had cast a paralyzing spell on them. In an instant, the spell was broken, and everyone moved and spoke at once. Papa began turning the dial for other stations that might offer more details. Mama ran to his side, a bowl of creamed peas still in her hands. Knowl jumped up and ran to the telephone. Cath and Annie stood up uncertainly and stared in mute astonishment at each other.

Mama set the peas on the radio and clasped Papa's arm. "What about Chilton? He's there, at Pearl Harbor."

"Chilton's fine," said Papa gruffly. "Go sit down."

Mama seemed to accept his words. She returned to the table, her expression blank. She sat down and folded her hands in her lap. Her eyes were wide, her lips parted in bewilderment.

Knowl returned from the phone and drew Cath and Annie into his arms. "It's true. It just came over the wire service. The Japanese attacked Pearl Harbor. No news yet on how bad it is."

"What about Chip?" cried Cath. "He could be hurt!"

"I'm sorry, sis. We probably won't know for days."

"What can we do?" said Annie. "We've got to do something!"

"I've got to go to the newspaper office," said Knowl. "Things are popping. There's pandemonium—"

Annie stared up incredulously at Knowl. "We're at war, aren't we? We're really at war."

He nodded. A tendon in his jaw tightened. "Yes. War."

Cath clutched Knowl's arm, her voice shrill. "How can this be? We were afraid of the Nazis, not the Japanese. They're not warriors. They're near-sighted little toy-makers! No one takes them seriously!"

"Maybe that's the problem," said Knowl. He walked to the hatrack in the hallway and removed his overcoat. "I'm sorry. I've got to go. I'll call if there's any news."

"When will you be back?" asked Annie, knowing there were other, more important questions she wanted to ask, but she had no words to frame them.

"I don't know when I'll be home, Annie. I'll be late."

Mama called from the table, "But your dinner—! No one finished dinner."

Papa went over and put his arms around her. "I'm sorry I snapped at you. We'll be okay. Everything will be okay."

Mama looked up at him, her eyes filling with tears. "But my son—my baby! He's over there. He could be hurt. He could be—Oh, God, no!" She began to weep.

Cath went to the window and looked out. She put her hands on the glass and ran her nails over the frosty film, then pressed her head against the cold pane. "Oh, God, he's got to be okay. Please, I love him so much. Let him be okay!"

Annie stood in the dining room, her gaze moving from Knowl striding out the door, to Cath at the window, to Mama and Papa at the table. She felt immobilized, stymied, powerless to move. Mama needed her. Cath needed her. But it was as if she had stepped outside of time, outside of her own body. She was watching from a distance, a remote observer witnessing the frantic, useless motions of people in crisis.

And there was nothing she could do to help, except marvel that the world still looked the same. She still stood in the safe haven of her home on Honeysuckle Lane. Mama's wonderful dinner sat half-eaten on the table. Music was playing again on the radio. Everything was as it ought to be. Except that the picture lied, the apparent serenity of the moment had become a travesty, a sorry remnant of the world that was, a happy, predictable world that promised Christmas and a wedding.

This new world, this unknown quantity, offered only horror and grief. It didn't mesh yet with this pleasant room, and a table laden with food, and the lull of music from the same radio that had just leveled a deathblow to their peace.

Annie wanted to sit back down at the table and continue eating as if nothing had happened; she wanted to go on, untouched and unshaken by the appalling announcement on the radio.

What to do? What to do now that the world had been rocked on its axis? What to do now that her universe was exploding in her face? And yet, irony of ironies, she was still captive to the tranquil moments left over from a life that no longer existed.

She sat down at the table beside Mama. She picked up her fork and poked at the cold lamb on her plate. She looked over at Cath and said, "Come sit down."

What was there to do but to go on with the mundane details of living, which had been set in motion before the announcer's dire words put their lives in limbo? Go on living, breathing, eating, and speaking, until there was something concrete to hold on to, until this terrible new reality struck home and changed their lives forever.

THIRTEEN

JAPS BOMB HAWAII
Guam, Midway, and Wake also attacked

It was a long, sleepless night. Annie and her parents sat huddled by the parlor radio, listening to scant news bulletins broken by static and delivered by stunned reporters. Cath sat staring out the window at the swirling flurries, as if she expected Chip to come striding through the darkness and up the snowy walk. Secretly, Annie watched for him, too, expecting him to burst inside and declare, "I'm home! Where else would I be on a night like this?"

That was the question that burned in their minds like a hot coal in the hand. Where's Chip tonight? Is he dead or alive? Wounded or thanking God in heaven he got out without a scratch?

Knowl spent the night at the newspaper, writing and rewriting copy as fast as reports came in. He telephoned home with brief updates gleaned from the rapid influx of news items and dispatches from around the world, some coming in staccato bursts, others jumbled and confused, a few bordering on hysteria.

Rumors were flying across America. The Japanese were going to bomb California, or Oregon, or New York City. Reports had it that the entire West Coast was blacked out that night. Sightings of the Japanese fleet were reported off Los Angeles, and dive bombers were rumored to be approaching San Francisco. One reporter summed it up succinctly: "If the Japs can bomb Pearl Harbor, they can attack anywhere!"

As the morning of December 8th dawned with faint streamers of light on the horizon, Cath and Annie were still gathered with Annie's parents around the console radio. At last came the official word from Washington. President Roosevelt's voice resounded over the air waves, announcing, "Yesterday, December 7th, 1941, a date which will live in infamy, the United States of America was suddenly and deliberately attacked by naval and air forces of the Empire of Japan.… I ask that the Congress declare that since the unprovoked and dastardly attack by Japan, a state of war has existed between the United States and the Japanese Empire."

It was settled then, Annie reflected solemnly. America and Japan were at war. It would be a fight to the finish. Only one nation could come through victorious.

But that didn't answer a more pressing question. What of Chip? There was still no word of her brother!

Late in the afternoon, Knowl arrived at the Reed house for a quick meal before heading back to the paper. He looked weary, distracted, his hair tousled, his eyes shadowed. Annie went to him and embraced him, holding back her own fears and concerns. "Have you had any sleep?" she asked.

He shook his head. "No, maybe an hour in my chair between news bulletins."

"Any word about the damage in Pearl Harbor—was the Arizona hit?" asked Cath urgently.

"The fleet was hit, Cath, but we don't have specifics yet."

They went to the kitchen where Mama was already stirring a pot of vegetable soup on the stove. "Smells good," said Knowl wearily. He sat down at the table and arched his shoulders, as if to relieve muscle tension. "Annie, I stopped by home and told my mother we'd be staying here until we hear word of Chip. I told her she was welcome to come over, too, but she'd rather stay there, of course, nursing her favorite bottle of wine."

"I'll go home and check on her regularly," said Cath.

Mama set a steaming bowl of soup before Knowl.

"Thanks, Mama Reed. I've lived on nothing but coffee since that delicious lamb dinner of yours yesterday."

"That dinner seems like a hundred years ago." She handed him saltines and a glass of milk. "Knowl, do you have any news that hasn't come over the radio?"

"All I know is that it's been mayhem at the paper, everyone running from the newsroom to the wire room to the copy desk. The printers are going crazy—bulletins and flashes coming in over the teletype, the wire services doing a jitterbug, dispatches from Reuters, phones ringing off the hook. We got a Wirephoto from the Associated Press underscoring that we've been hit in our own Western hemisphere. Most folks figured we were invincible. Now we know better."

He spooned down several mouthfuls of soup, then said, "The irony is that the Japanese envoys, Nomura and Kurusu, were meeting with Secretary of State Cordell Hull in his office at the very moment the bombs were being dropped on Pearl Harbor! Can you imagine such audacity? Evidently, Japan hadn't bothered to inform their emissaries they were attacking."

Papa shuffled into the kitchen, looking haggard, still wearing yesterday's shirt. "I don't understand, Knowl. How did it happen? How did our country let this happen?"

"I don't know, Papa Reed. I think our commanders were too busy preparing to fight the last war, not this one. A war of battleships, not aircraft. We overlooked or underestimated the advances Japan was making in aviation technology."

"But why did they attack us?" demanded Cath. "What did we ever do to them?"

Knowl crumbled a cracker into his soup. "I think Japan sees us as their only rival for control over the Pacific. They think we're determined to keep them a second-class power."

Annie sat down across from Knowl. "I thought Hitler was the power-happy one, not Japan."

"Not true," said Knowl. "Japan has been quietly amassing colonies and territories and carrying out aggression in Asia for years. We've warned them, to no avail. Recently we stopped buying Japanese products, and just last August we froze all Japanese assets in the United States and put an embargo on oil to Japan. They can't survive without oil."

"Are you suggesting our government knew Japan would retaliate?" asked Cath.

"I think Roosevelt thought General Tojo might attack the Philippines, but never Pearl Harbor." Knowl looked over at Annie, his brow furrowed. "Sweetheart, I guess I'd better tell you. I stopped by the recruitment office today and tried to sign up. I want to be in this fight. I belong over there with Chip."

"Oh, Knowl, did they accept you?"

His jaw twisted slightly. "No. They turned me down flat. It's my poor eyesight, as I expected. They said I'd serve my country best by remaining at the helm of the Willowbrook News, giving civilians the daily lowdown on the war."

"It's true, Knowl," said Annie. "No one puts out a better newspaper than you."

Knowl stared down at his soup bowl, his expression desolate. "You don't understand, Annie. I want to be in the thick of it. In uniform like Chip. Yesterday you hardly saw a uniform anywhere; today, guys in uniform are everywhere. They're rushing to enlist. I want to go with them. I want to battle it out with the Japs and Nazis face to face."

"Roosevelt hasn't declared war with Germany yet," said Mama.

"No, but it's coming. We're in another world war, whether it's official or not. The attack on Pearl Harbor is only the beginning."

Sure enough, on Thursday, December 11th, Germany declared war on the United States. But, for the moment, the Nazis were old news. Everyone was waiting for specifics about Pearl Harbor.

Details of the devastation trickled in over the next few days after Japan's attack, but the reports were maddeningly vague and incomplete, as if America were reluctant to let Japan know how crushing their blows had been. The battleship West Virginia was hit first, then the Oklahoma. The U.S.S. Arizona was attacked by torpedoes, then by bombers; torpedoes also struck the California. In all, eighteen warships were sunk or damaged, including five battleships. One hundred and eighty-eight planes were destroyed. And gradually the toll in human life was revealed. Over two thousand four hundred Americans were killed at Pearl Harbor.

But many of those painful statistics were still unknown in the Reed household as Thursday, December 11th arrived. Cath and Annie had remained since Sunday, partly to offer and receive consolation from Annie's parents, but also to await news of Chip. Any news would come to the house on Honeysuckle Lane, his childhood home.

That afternoon, shortly after a radio bulletin informed America of Hitler's declaration of war, Cath and Annie went upstairs to the rosebud room. Annie took comfort in the familiarity of its pale pink wallpaper, high dormer windows framed by lace curtains, sturdy oak bureau, and the dressing table with its cozy vanity lamp. They sat on the comfortable old bed that had been Annie's throughout childhood and gazed nostalgically at the familiar paintings and keepsakes.

"I wish we could go back," Cath said softly, "and be children again with nothing more to worry about than homework and chores and which toys to play with."

Annie nodded, tracing squares in the patchwork quilt. "We didn't realize what a wonderful world we had."

"Oh, it wasn't perfect," said Cath. "The Depression kept us poor, and my parents fought, but at least I didn't have to worry about whether the world would destroy itself in war or whether someone I loved was dead or alive."

"Chip's got to be alive," said Annie fervently. "I'd know it if he wasn't. He's my only brother. The world would feel dark if he weren't in it anymore."

"It feels dark to me," said Cath. She reached over and picked up an old mohair teddy bear and hugged it against her chest. "I'm scared to the very marrow of my bones. I have a feeling I'll never see Chip again."

"Don't say that, Cath. He'll be okay. I know. God will take care of him!"

"Maybe He will, and maybe He won't. I'm sorry, Annie, I'm not much of a believer. Everything in my life has been hard won." She pressed her cheek against the bear's furry head. "I've lost most of the people I've loved—my father to other women, my mother to alcohol. I don't think God likes me much."

"He loves you, Cath. More than you'll ever know."

"Maybe, but I don't feel very loved. I feel—alone."

"You're not, you know. I'll always be here for you."

"Will you, Annie? Even if—?"

"If what, Cath?" Annie studied her dear friend's face. Cath looked frail and vulnerable as a child—her freckled face slightly flushed, her red hair cascading around her shoulder's like a young girl's, her blue-green eyes wide and luminous with pain.

"Would you love me if you knew I wasn't good like you, Annie? If you knew I'd done something terribly wrong?"

Annie felt an alarm go off somewhere in her head. She replied carefully, "Of course, Cath. We all make mistakes."

"Not you, Annie. Not like this."

Annie reached over for Cath's hand. It felt small and cold, like a lifeless dove. "What is it, Cath? What's wrong?"

Large tears rolled from Cath's eyes. "I prayed it wasn't so. Every day I prayed. But I knew. I knew!"

"Knew what? Tell me."

Cath set the teddy aside and moved her hands over the small curve of her stomach. "I'm in a family way, Annie. I'm going to have Chip's baby."

Annie recoiled, as if someone had slapped her hard on the back, knocking the breath from her lungs. At last she found her voice. "A baby? Chip's baby?"

The tears came faster now. "I didn't mean to, Annie. Chip said it was all right. He said we were engaged, practically married. He said nothing could happen the first time."

"You and Chip—? When?" She answered her own question. "It had to be his August leave."

Cath slipped off the bed and went to the bureau for a tissue. "I'm four months along. I'm already starting to show a little."

"That's why you were worried about your wedding dress fitting."

"I didn't want anyone to guess." Cath gazed out the window overlooking Honeysuckle Lane. "I never even told Chip. I figured we'd be married by Christmas, and we could tell people the baby came early."

Annie joined Cath at the window and embraced her as if comforting a child. They stood, arms entwined, watching snow flurries fall silently, light and slow as feathers. The world outside the window looked peaceful and inviting—houses and street lamps already decorated with wreaths and garlands for Christmas. Annie's voice was soothing. "It'll be all right, Cath. Chip will be home for Christmas, and you'll be married just as you planned, and you'll have a darling little baby to raise."

"If Chip's not dead," Cath said, her voice a dark monotone. "If he is dead, I want to die too."

"He's not dead!" Annie said shrilly. "Do you hear me? My brother's not dead!"

Cath held Annie close. "I'm sorry, I'm sorry. Forgive me."

Regaining her composure, Annie repeated softly, "He's not dead. Don't ever say those words aloud again. Don't even think them."

"I won't. I promise, I won't." Cath stared back out the window. Suddenly, her body stiffened and she gripped Annie's arm hard. "Look," she whispered.

Annie looked down. Her heart froze within her. A Western Union truck was rumbling down the street toward her house. She watched in silent horror as the truck stopped and a man stepped out, a telegram in his hands. She watched him walk gingerly up the ice-glazed walk and scale the porch steps. She heard the cheerful ring of the doorbell. After a moment, she heard the front door open.

Annie held her breath. She and Cath locked arms with a wordless desperation, as if they were free-falling through miles of sky. Tears coursed down Cath's cheeks and her wide, full lips contorted in a soundless scream.

The sound came from downstairs—her mother's anguished, harrowing shriek that would resound hauntingly through the rooms of her beloved house for as long as Annie lived.

FOURTEEN

A Service of Memory for
Chilton "Chip" Reed
Born May 13, 1916
Willowbrook, Indiana
Passed away December 7, 1941
Pearl Harbor, Hawaii
Service held 1:00 p.m., December 21, 1941
at the Willowbrook Christian Church
Service conducted by The Reverend Miles Henry

There was an unearthly quality about it, as if the events of the moment were being played out in some surreal memory or a subconscious crevice of the mind. The surroundings were mundane and familiar. The church Annie had attended all her life. A snow-shrouded landscape with dead trees, their shorn branches burdened with ice. And the quaint, fenced yard of a cemetery beyond the knoll.

But the participants seemed caught in some bizarre rehearsal, moving through preordained actions, reciting someone else's quirky lines. The day, in all its facets, seemed illusory, the illogical events of a dream, the grisly fodder of a nightmare. And yet, everyone was moving in step, accepting the dream as truth. And Annie was expected to concede that it was real as well.

She could do no such thing. That would mean risking insanity. No. Only under silent protest would she play her part as the script was written. Enter the sanctuary as a mourner, sit in the straight-back pew, sing a familiar hymn. Hadn't she sat through a service like this for Papa Reed ten years ago?

But this was something else. The memorial service for her brother, Chip. And

Reverend Henry, in his usual blackbird garb, stood at the altar like a dark prophet of doom, intoning in his sonorous baritone, "Lieutenant Chilton Reed—along with nearly twelve hundred of his countrymen—gave his life on that great ship, the U.S.S. Arizona. All of us who knew him and loved him will miss him immensely. But we will never forget him. His dreams, his youth, and his future may be buried with him beneath the bloody, oil-slick waters of Pearl Harbor, but his bravery and passion for life will live on in our hearts for as long as freedom lives."

Annie tried to play her part. She listened dutifully to Reverend Henry's words of tribute, but they sounded small and hollow, as if coming at her from a great distance. She stared above the altar at the stained glass window showing Jesus the Good Shepherd carrying a lost lamb in his arms. Jesus. Her Jesus. Why then did she suddenly feel like a lost sheep waiting to be found? Where was her Good Shepherd when she needed Him most?

This was supposed to be a wedding! Annie wanted to shout, not a funeral! How can this be a funeral without a body? And how can I believe Chip is dead just because a telegram said so?

The service proceeded, an orderly progression of moments, one after another, holding Annie captive. She sat stoically between her mother and her husband, in no way making a spectacle of herself. She dabbed her eyes politely with her hanky. She bowed her head when Reverend Henry prayed. She went through the proper motions, behaving in a most mannerly fashion, holding her emotions hostage. After all, if she were to deviate from the script, she might veer off into madness. She yearned to cry, to dissolve in grief, to shut out the world. She craved comfort and reassurance that life still had meaning, that loving someone didn't always lead to pain and disappointment.

And then it was over. A tidy, respectable service. Everyone said so. Annie filed out of the church with her family, shaking hands, receiving condolences, uttering words of appreciation that faded in the brittle air.

And finally they were on the way home, squeezed together in the warm automobile, everyone silent, turned inward, perhaps mulling over private pain, fractured dreams, or cherished memories.

Then, unexpectedly, Mama spoke, her voice jarring the stillness with its tenuous lilt. "Did you know why we called him 'Chip'?"

"What, Mama?" asked Alice Marie, her usual porcelain beauty marred by smudged makeup and tears. She looked older, her blonde hair curled in a sophisticated bob, her makeup too stark for Willowbrook. She had come home alone while her husband traveled on with the band to Indianapolis.

"I said, did you know why we called Chilton, 'Chip'?"

"No, Mama. I never thought about it before," Alice Marie replied distractedly. "He was just Chip, that's all."

"We called him 'Chip,'" said Mama, her voice filling with emotion, "because when he was born, your papa kept saying, 'He's a chip off the old block.' I wanted to call him 'Chilton.' It sounded so noble, so strong. But from then on it was 'Chip.'"

"He was noble and strong no matter what people called him," said Annie, suddenly tearful. The script was gone, the dam broken. Emotions spilled out like hot lava. "He was the best brother ever, and he was supposed to come home and get married this Christmas! I'll never be the same without him; I'll never feel whole again!"

The day after Chip's funeral, Papa hung an American flag from the porch and placed a gold star in the window—a silent declaration that this family had lost a son in the war. Annie reluctantly left Mama and Papa alone in their melancholy home on Honeysuckle Lane, and returned to the Herrick house around the corner, dutifully rejoining Knowl and Cath. But she wasn't the same person who had left her husband's house. Now, she nursed homesickness; she slogged through sorrow; at night she couldn't sleep; during the day she couldn't stay awake. Nightmares mixed with daydreams. Maybe she was going crazy.

But it was nothing compared with what Cath was experiencing—Cath with a baby in her belly to remind her in her innermost being what had been ripped away forever.

Annie forfeited any spirit of Christmas this year. In fact, she found herself resenting the merriment of others. How could people celebrate the holidays, give gifts, and sing carols when her brother was dead? Even the war had lost its fascination. What did she care about battles and blitzkriegs and bombings when the war's star player had fallen?

As the final days of December dwindled away, Annie admitted she was succumbing to the paralyzing dregs of bitterness. Her spirits had turned as brittle as the icicles hanging from the eaves of the Herrick house. This wouldn't do. She had to be strong for Mama and Papa, and for Cath. They needed her now more than ever. So, with grim determination, she bottled up her grief, dried her eyes, forced a smile in place, and went about the business of cheering her family, offering a hug, sharing tears.

Only Knowl seemed reluctant to grieve with her. Whenever Annie turned to him for consolation, he grew aloof and refused to speak of Chip; his eyes hardened, his jaw tightened, and he retreated to innocuous discourse. He threw himself into his work, spending days and evenings, and sometimes even weekends, at the newspaper office. Annie suspected that Knowl's grief was mingled with guilt—guilt that he, too, hadn't died serving his country, that for the first time in their lives, fate had separated him from his lifelong comrade. "I should have been there with Chip," Knowl muttered to himself more than once.

"What could you have done?" Annie demanded. "You might have died too."

"That would have been better than living with regrets."

At night, while everyone slept, Annie tried to find comfort in God, seeking the solace that had come so readily before Chip's death. But, for the first time since her conversion, she felt as if God had turned His back on her. Was He no longer listening? Did He no longer care? Why had He snatched away her beloved brother at the pinnacle of his joy and achievement? Why was He allowing those she loved to suffer this unbearable pain?

Annie grieved not only for Chip, but also for what his death was doing to Mama and Papa. Her parents had always seemed so strong, so self-sufficient and capable. There seemed to be nothing they couldn't handle. Hadn't they held on steadily through the Depression, maintaining a secure home and protecting their children, when other families faltered and fell by the wayside? Papa had remained stalwart and unshakable even after Papa Reed lost his business, his money, and his pride. And Papa stood tall and brave even after his dear Papa Reed died.

But now, Papa had lost his only son, and suddenly, he seemed like a weary, defeated old man. He seemed to be shriveling and dying before Annie's eyes. And Mama—always the strongest woman Annie had ever known—seemed to be sinking right along with Papa.

Whenever Annie walked over for a visit, she found Mama and Papa sitting listlessly by the radio, a book or a newspaper lying unopened in their laps. Mama would be listening to her favorite dramas, Ma Perkins, Hilltop House, and The Guiding Light, and weeping along with the characters. Papa would sit and listen to The Great Gildersleeve or Fibber McGee and Molly, but the antics of the outrageous Jordans, Gale Gordon, and Harold Peary no longer amused him.

And then there was Cath. She moped about the Herrick house in her bathrobe or locked herself in her room, refusing to see or talk with anyone. She shrank from any suggestion of company and even refused to dip into her oils or watercolors to try a painting. Annie helplessly watched her best friend withdrawing from life and shutting down all feeling. But how could Annie help Cath, when she couldn't even help herself?

One night in mid-January Annie realized how serious the situation with Cath had become. Shortly after midnight, Annie awoke out of a sound sleep, startled by a strange sound. She got up and padded quietly down the hall to the bathroom. There she found Cath in her nightgown, bent over the toilet, retching violently.

She knelt beside her. "Cath, what's wrong? Do you want me to call Dr. Galway?"

Cath turned sharply, a frail, wraithlike figure. Dark, haunted eyes stared out of a ghostly, bleached muslin face. Annie stepped back in shock. Cath was dying before her eyes. "What have you done?"

Cath collapsed into Annie's arm, weeping, her cotton gown wet with perspiration, and they sank to the floor together, Annie mopping Cath's fevered brow. "I'm sorry, Annie," Cath sobbed. "I thought I could—get rid of it!"

"Rid of—you mean, the baby? Oh, Cath, no! What did you take?"

"Castor oil. Someone said— But it didn't work. It just made me violently ill."

Annie rocked Cath in her arms, the way she might rock a naughty child she deeply loved. "Cath, Cath, oh, my dear Cath, how could you? Your baby! It's all we have left of Chip!"

Cath pulled away and swept the wild tangles of hair from her forehead. "I can't keep from showing anymore. People will know. I can't bear their pity and scorn. I can't live with the shame, Annie. I'd rather die!"

Impulsively, Annie gripped Cath's shoulders and shook her hard. The words erupted in a torrent of fury and pain. "Don't you dare say you'd rather die! Chip couldn't help dying, but he would have fought it with every ounce of his breath. Don't you dishonor his memory with such talk! You're going to live, and your baby's going to live, do you hear me?"

They wept and embraced each other, until Annie heard Knowl's concerned voice at the door. "Hey, everything okay in there?"

"It's Cath," Annie said quickly. "She's not feeling well."

"Is there anything I can do to help?"

"No, we'll be fine. Go back to sleep, dear."

When Knowl had gone, Annie helped Cath back to her room. She sat at her bedside and rubbed her forehead until she fell asleep. "Don't worry, dear Cath, we'll figure something out," Annie whispered into the darkness.

Instead of returning to Knowl's bed, Annie slipped downstairs and curled up in the old oak rocker by the window. She gazed out at the feathery snow floating in a wonderland of black velvet; she felt herself growing quiet as the snow, so quiet that, for the first time since Chip's death, she could hear the still, small voice she cherished. Father God, You're still there! I've just been making too much noise to hear You!

"Will you weep with me, Jesus?" she whispered urgently. "I need to know You feel my pain. Will You see Cath and me through this mine field of grief, and show us the answer for her baby? I'm angry with You for letting Chip die. There's so much about You I don't understand. Hold me, Jesus! Don't let me go!"

The next morning, Annie entered Cath's room with a tray of biscuits and hot tea. "Wake up, sunshine," she trilled.

Cath buried her head under her pillow, then peered out with one shadowed eye. "It can't be morning. This must be some sort of purgatory. I feel like I was run over by a train."

"Drink your tea and you'll feel better." Annie handed Cath the tray and sat down in the chair by the bed. "I have something to say. An idea. Don't say no until you've heard me out."

Cath nibbled her biscuit. "What is it?"

"It's about your baby." Annie's burst of confidence wavered a little. "If you honestly don't feel you can raise my brother's child, perhaps I know someone who could."

"Who?"

"Knowl and I."

Cath's narrow brows arched quizzically. "What are you saying, Annie?"

"I'm talking about your baby. You don't want anyone to know you're pregnant. Well, they won't have to know. There's a way we can keep Chip's baby in the family. Knowl and I could adopt it and raise it. No one would have to know whose baby it is."

"You've gone absolutely daft," cried Cath. "That's impossible. It would never work."

Annie's tone grew serious. "What other choice do we have?"

Cath sipped her tea, her hand trembling slightly. "You mean, I'd have the baby secretly and give it to you and Knowl? You'd be the mother and I'd be the aunt?"

"Something like that. Think of it, Cath. Your baby would be raised by a Reed and a Herrick. Knowl and I both have blood ties to your baby. It's the one way you could have a part in your baby's life and still keep your freedom and your good name."

A faint light gleamed in Cath's eyes. "I see what you mean, Annie. Remember the blood pact we made as children? We'll always be part of each other. And you're part of my baby through Chip. And Knowl's part of my baby through me, his sister!"

"No one would have to know you're the real mother, except our families."

"But would Knowl want to raise my baby?"

"Of course! He loves you. You're his sister." Annie's tone turned confidential. "Besides, we've wanted children since the day we were married, but it just hasn't happened. We may never be able to have children of our own."

Cath's expression grew animated. "If that's true, then my baby could be my gift to the two of you."

"We'd love her as if she were our own."

Cath put her tray aside and sat up in bed. She moved her hand wonderingly over her swollen belly. "Annie, give me your hand. I just felt the baby move. Press right here. Can you feel it, Annie? The baby—your baby—is kicking!"

That evening, when Knowl arrived home from work and went upstairs to change out of his suit, Annie followed him into their room and shut the door quietly behind her. He looked around, startled, then smiled. "Hi, sweetheart. What's up?"

She struggled to find her voice. Her heart pounded furiously, and her tongue felt thick and dry. What had seemed like such a natural idea this morning now struck her as rash and infeasible. The two of them raise Cath's child? How could she begin to convince Knowl of such an absurd proposition?

Knowl was waiting, eyeing her with his scrutinizing gaze.

"It's Cath," she began unevenly. She considered a dozen ways of leading into the matter, but they all seemed lame and pointless. So she simply blurted, "Your sister's going to have a baby."

Knowl was incredulous. "Whose baby? You mean Chip's?"

"Yes. It happened last August."

"He never told me, never said a word."

"He didn't know. Cath never told him."

Shock turned to anger. "How could he do it? He was my best friend. How could I compromise my sister's virtue when he knew how uncertain the future was?"

Annie slipped her arms around her husband's neck. "It was wrong, but they loved each other. They were going to be married."

"It's this hellish war," said Knowl darkly. "It makes all of us a little crazy. But what's my sister supposed to do now?"

Before Annie lost her nerve, she spelled out the plan she'd presented to Cath that morning. "Please don't decide until you've had time to think about it, Knowl."

He ran his fingers through his thick, wheat-colored hair. "It just wouldn't work, Annie. How can you expect my sister to simply turn her baby over to us? And what would we tell people?"

"We'd tell them just what they needed to know. We adopted a baby. Wouldn't it be better for us to raise the child than strangers? The baby's already part of us—you and me. And it's part of Chip. It's all we have left of Chip."

Knowl searched her eyes. "This means everything to you, doesn't it?"

She hadn't realized it until now, but yes. She wanted this baby desperately. "It's the only answer, Knowl—for Cath, for the baby, for all of us."

"I'll think about it," he said, pulling his tie from around his collar. "Right now I want to go have a talk with my sister." That same night Knowl told Annie they could keep the baby. "Cath convinced me it's what she wants too. But we're going to have to tell my mother and your parents. It'll be a shock, but I think the blow will be softened when they realize they're going to be grandparents."

Knowl was right. His mother took the news sullenly at first, throwing a handful of bitter accusations at her "wayward" daughter; but after her initial outburst, she became surprisingly sentimental and assured Cath, "You'll be okay, daughter. You're made of sturdy stock. You and your baby, both."

Once Annie's parents recovered from their initial astonishment, they seemed genuinely delighted to realize they would be grandparents to Chip's offspring. They comforted Cath as if she were their own daughter and marveled over God's unexpected miracle. It was the first time Annie had seen her parents smile since the terrible day that heart-shattering telegram had arrived.

FIFTEEN

The Spring of 1942.

The war was in full swing. Most of the strong, young men of Willowbrook had enlisted and were being shipped off to such exotic, far-flung locales as Bataan and Corregidor in the Philippines, or Australia, New Guinea, the Bismarcks and the Solomons in the Southwest Pacific—under General MacArthur's command—or the British Isles for the American buildup in Britain to prepare for a second front.

Knowl was Annie's daily source of information on the war. As managing editor of the Willowbrook News, he was consumed with keeping track of every battle, every bombing raid, every U-Boat campaign, every torpedoed carrier. It was as if the world had become an immense chess game, and since, by some quirk of fate, Knowl wasn't allowed to participate, he was determined at least to monitor all the strategies.

He stuck pins in a map of the Dutch East Indies to show military bases controlled by Japan, and on a map of Burma, he traced the Japanese invasion and the British retreat through Rangoon, Mandalay, and a score of other cities with foreign names Annie would never remember. Knowl seemed obsessed with what was happening in the Philippines, the Mediterranean, the Indian Ocean, and even the Atlantic, where German U-boats were reported off the Florida coast.

It worried Annie that Knowl seemed to consider the war effort and the Allies' ultimate victory his personal responsibility. She had a feeling he was trying to carry on for Chip and make up for his own 4-F classification, but, if so, she was the loser. Knowl's fixation with the war was keeping him at an emotional distance from his family. How can I possibly break through his preoccupation and restore our close, loving relationship? Annie wondered.

Worse yet, Knowl's career demands mounted as more of his staff enlisted or were drafted. One night in early May he arrived home after midnight, looking weary and disheveled, and announced, "I lost another linotype operator to the draft, so I had to pitch in and help with the presswork. I put on my black apron, and the guys and I put the type together, hot metal and all. Somehow we got the paper ready for the morning edition. Now if we can just keep getting the newsprint we need."

"You work too hard," Annie told him, knowing her words were wasted. "You're too conscientious about trying to cover all the war news, Knowl. You're not the New York Times or the Boston Globe. You can't do it all yourself!"

But Knowl heard only what he wanted to hear. "I consider it my duty to keep our people informed," he retorted. "You know as well as I do that most provincial and small town papers—dailies and weeklies alike—carry only local news. The Nazis could invade New York, and you wouldn't read about it in their papers. I don't work that way. I want Willowbrook to know what's happening here and in the rest of the world as well."

Annie wanted to counter with, Then you might start by finding out what's happening in your own house! But if she were completely honest, she had to admit she herself was preoccupied much of the time lately—not just with the war, but with managing the household and caring for Cath during the final weeks of her pregnancy.

It had been a test of Annie's wits just to keep the fact of Cath's pregnancy concealed from friends and neighbors. Once her pregnancy became obvious, Cath stopped leaving the house, except to spend time in the sequestered privacy of the garden. When people came to visit—which was rare—Cath remained in her room, surrounded by her paintings, easel, and art books. Town folk assumed Cath was still at the Art Institute in Chicago, except for the good Dr. Galway, who came routinely to check the progress of Cath's pregnancy.

Cath's self-imposed exile from her former life and acquaintances, coupled with her lingering grief over Chip, drove her to the edge of derangement. At times she paced the floor, ranting and raving over life's inequities; at other times, she shut herself in her room and sobbed for hours. She had no one to vent her pain and frustration on, except Annie, and Annie considered it her duty to carry as much of Cath's burden as she was able. After all, by having Chip's baby, Cath was giving the Reed family a precious legacy—a fact which added an unexpected dimension to Cath and Annie's friendship.

In fact, at times Annie sensed that Knowl was jealous of the bond she shared with his sister. It wasn't that Annie intentionally ignored him; it was just that he had a paper to put to bed and she and Cath had Chip's baby to prepare for. But, like Knowl, Annie felt exhausted and emotionally drained much of the time.

The war, of course, didn't make life any easier. Staples most people took for granted were now restricted, including meat, cheese, fat, butter, coffee, and sugar. Knowl was limited to three gallons of gasoline a week for his automobile. War ration books were issued and hoarded like gold. There were coupons for all sorts of things, even tires and shoes.

But Annie didn't mind the shortages and inconveniences; they were minor compared with what America's servicemen were facing overseas. With food rationing in effect, Annie was learning, as a matter of course, to serve Spam instead of hamburger, to make sausage patties out of oatmeal, to forego butter for the tasteless white oleo that turned yellow when its bag was kneaded. She and Cath even planted a "victory garden" in the backyard, raising precious carrots, beans, corn, and peas. Tender green shoots, stalks, and stems were already spiraling up out of the dark earth in response to the warm May sunshine. Ripe vegetables would be on the table long before summer waned.

But May brought with it a stark reality: Cath's baby was due by the end of the month. Annie could tell the time was drawing near by the way Cath walked—sluggishly, more a clumsy waddle than a walk—and by the way she held her aching back or eased her swollen frame into a chair.

Cath complained constantly these days too. "It's so awfully hot, Annie. There's not the slightest breeze…Oh, Annie, look how my feet are swollen. Can you rub them for me?…Isn't there a bit more sugar for my tea, Annie?…Oh, Annie, I can't go on like this! Look! I'm as big as a house, and everything aches from my head to my toes."

Annie tried to remain patient; she told herself it was natural for Cath to be grumpy and irritable; anyone who had to carry around all those extra pounds and put up with someone kicking her from the inside out had a right to be peevish. But just as often Annie felt irritable herself and wanted to tell Cath to go wait on herself or rub her own feet—if she could still reach them.

As the middle of May approached, Cath had a new complaint. "I get these strange feelings, Annie. My whole belly is tightening up hard as a ball. It happens as regular as clockwork. What do you suppose it means?"

Annie replied the way she always answered such questions. "Why don't you telephone Dr. Galway and ask his advice?"

"You know why," pouted Cath, curling up under her flowered afghan. "He keeps telling me I must have my baby in the hospital."

"He's right. It's the safest way, Cath. You've got to decide now. Your baby is due in just a couple of weeks."

"I've told you over and over, Annie. I'm having my baby here at home. That's how my mama had me, in her very own bed."

"But these days women go to the hospital," Annie protested. Besides, how could Cath have her baby in this room cluttered with canvases and sketches, brushes and palettes? "It's dangerous having a baby at home," she pressed on. "What if there are complications?"

"We'll manage, Annie." Cath offered a triumphant little smile. "Besides, Dr. Galway said he would come here if I insist on having the baby at home. Don't worry. He won't let me face childbirth alone."

"I don't find his promise reassuring," said Annie. "What if he doesn't arrive in time? What am I supposed to do?"

"Help me birth my baby. I couldn't do it without you beside me. And my mama will be here. She knows about these things. She's had two babies!"

Some help she'll be! Annie wanted to argue. Betty Herrick spent most of her days in her room listening to the radio and nursing a glass of wine. But no sense in upsetting Cath with complaints about her mother. "Do you think the baby will come early?" Annie asked instead.

A wistful expression crossed Cath's face. "I'm hoping it will be born on May thirteenth, Chip's birthday. It's fitting somehow—a tribute to Chip's memory."

"That's swell, Cath, but it's only two days away."

Cath ran her palm over her great, round tummy. "I know."

That evening, as Knowl and Annie prepared for bed, she lingered before the dresser mirror, brushing her long hair, and wondered whether her husband even remembered there'd be a baby in the house any day now. He sat at their small writing desk, shuffling papers he had brought home from his office. He was filled as usual with talk about the latest war news—this time, the Battle of the Coral Sea.

"Our carriers, the Lexington and the Yorktown were damaged," he told her, "but the Japanese were forced to abandon their attack on Port Moresby. Do you know what this means, Annie?"

She was thinking about Cath, the baby. "No, Knowl, what?"

"This is the first time we've stopped the Japanese advance. It's a strategic victory for the Americans."

"I'm glad, Knowl," she said distractedly, slipping on her dressing gown. "But there's something I want to talk about—"

He stood up, pulled off his shirt, and tossed it on the bed. "There's something I want to talk to you about, too, Annie."

She looked up at him. "What? A problem?"

"No, sweetheart. An opportunity. You know old man Hobart who owns the newspaper?"

She nodded. "We've met a few times. A nice old man."

"Right. Well, all of his sons are overseas fighting for our country. That leaves Hobart watching out for his sons' wives and children. He's facing a cash flow problem, with the war and all the extra mouths to feed—"

"What are you getting at, Knowl?"

He turned her toward him and put his hands on her shoulders. "Hobart offered me a half interest in the paper, honey. We'd be partners. I'd be half owner of the Willowbrook News."

"Oh, Knowl—!"

"I know. It would mean using up our savings, Annie."

"Is this what you want—to own half the paper?"

Knowl's face was animated, his brown eyes glinting with excitement. "I never thought I'd have this chance, Annie. I'll have more say on policy, editorials, everything. It'll be a real partnership. Yes, it's what I want. More than anything."

She went into his arms. "Then you should do it, Knowl."

He removed his glasses and set them on the bureau, then kissed her properly. "It's been a long time," he whispered.

She nodded. "Our lives are so busy—"

"Too busy. I've missed times like this."

She nestled her head against his muscled chest. "Me too, darling. And I'm afraid things are only going to get busier."

He looked blankly at her. "Why?"

"The baby. It's due any day. Sometimes I think you've forgotten. You're going to be a father."

Knowl's expression grew remote. "I'm going to be an uncle, not a father."

Annie stared up at him in surprise. "What are you saying, Knowl? You agreed to raise Cath's baby!"

He steered her over to the wide, four-poster bed and they sat down. "Yes, we've agreed to raise Cath's baby, but I'm not entirely convinced she'll give it up. When that day comes and Cath goes off to make her own life, then I'll start thinking of her baby as ours."

Annie felt shaken. "Do you think she won't go through with it?"

"I'm not sure. I don't think Cath's sure either."

Annie didn't sleep well that night. She tossed and turned and dreamed of a baby with two mothers who both desperately wanted their child. While both women wailed, a Solomonlike figure made dire pronouncements about what calamities awaited if one mother didn't surrender the infant to the other.

Annie woke with a start and stared up into the silent darkness. Dear God, do I want this too much? Am I unwittingly pressuring Cath to give up her child? Help me accept whatever happens with Your loving kindness and grace.

The next day, as Cath and Annie sorted tiny kimonos and gowns that had been part of the Herrick layette over twenty years ago, Annie said cautiously, "Cath, whatever we've decided about the baby isn't cast in stone, you know."

Cath examined a pair of satin booties. "What are you saying, Annie?"

"I'm saying, if you changed your mind and decided you wanted to keep your baby, it would be all right."

Cath dropped the booties in her bountiful lap. Her lips parted in surprise. "Keep my baby? What do you mean? Have you changed your mind, Annie? Has Knowl?"

"No, of course not. I just don't want you to feel we're pushing you to do something you'll regret."

"Regret?" Cath moved her fingertips over a spot where the baby kicked. "Don't you understand, Annie? If it weren't for you and Knowl agreeing to keep the baby, I would have found a way to get rid of it. My baby's alive today because of you."

Annie felt a wave of relief sweep over her, but guilt followed on its heels. "I just wanted to make sure, Cath."

Cath's eyes welled with tears. "I thought it was all settled, Annie. I won't raise a fatherless child. I won't make my baby live in shame. She needs a good home and two parents."

"That's what she'll have, Cath. I won't mention it again."

Several minutes of awkward silence hung between them before Annie asked, "What do you plan to do after the baby's birth?"

Cath shrugged. "I haven't thought that far ahead. Maybe I'll go to New York City or Greenwich Village. I have friends there. Maybe I'll try some illustrations for magazines, something that will pay the bills. No one's buying paintings these days. But whatever I—"

Cath sat forward suddenly, clutching her abdomen. "Annie, something's happening. Something feels different. I feel water. A lot of water!"

Annie jumped up. "Oh, Cath, it must be time! I'll call the doctor. Do you need help getting into bed?"

"No, just get Dr. Galway. Hurry, Annie!"

Dr. Galway arrived within the hour, the picture of confidence and composure. "Yes, young lady, you're in labor," he said after checking Cath. "But it'll be a while. First ones always take their time. You just relax. Get a little shut-eye. I'd guess this baby will be born sometime in the morning."

"May thirteenth?" murmured Cath. "That's Chip's birthday."

"Is everything okay with the baby?" asked Annie.

The gray-haired physician nodded. "Don't worry, Annie, I'm an old hand at this. I delivered you and Catherine and your siblings many years ago." He picked up his satchel and started for the door. "I'll be going, but I'll check back on Catherine this evening. Just keep her comfortable. It's going to get a lot harder for her before it gets easier."

Annie spent the rest of the day at Cath's bedside, holding her hand as the contractions came on, feeding her chips of ice when her mouth was dry, and whispering words of encouragement when her body grew exhausted.

Even Betty Herrick left the sanctuary of her room to peek in on her daughter from time to time. Once she brought the girls cups of broth; later, she came with Jell-o and hot tea with lemon. "Sometimes it helps the pains if you reach back and hold on to the headboard," she told Cath. "Or try twisting a sheet as tight as you can. Anything to take your mind off what's happening in your belly."

"Go away, Mama! Let me be!" Cath had no patience for any of her mother's home remedies. She only groaned louder and thrashed around on the bed like someone in combat with an invisible assailant.

Betty Herrick left, obviously grateful not to be needed at a time like this. "Call me when something happens, Annie."

Annie nodded. She felt nearly as exhausted as Cath. It seemed that every pain Cath felt, Annie felt too. Each time, she allowed Cath to squeeze her hand until the violent upheaval receded, leaving Cath panting and feverish.

"It hurts bad, Annie," Cath moaned. "No one told me it would be like this."

"I didn't know, Cath. I'm sorry. I didn't know."

After several tension-filled hours of sitting, waiting, and praying, Annie rolled her shoulders, stretching achy muscles. She looked around, startled. The room was darkening. Looming shadows stretched across the walls and absorbed the last faint rays of daylight. Cath's paintings, stacked everywhere, looked eerie in the shadows, especially the portraits. It seemed as if silent, anonymous faces watched and waited with them.

Annie realized she had lost all track of time. In fact, it seemed she and Cath were suspended in a timeless realm that demanded all their energies and concentration if they were to survive. In reality, of course, they were still in Cath's canvas-cluttered bedroom, waiting for her baby to make its appearance.

More hours passed, agonizingly slow. Annie wondered with increasing concern when Dr. Galway would return. It was nearly midnight, and Cath was becoming more agitated and vocal. "Leave me alone! Don't touch me!" she screamed when Annie tried to hold her hand during an especially hard contraction. "Make it go away, Annie!" she shrieked. "Don't make me do this!" Cath was panting so hard now that Annie feared she might hyperventilate.

Cold, hard fear settled in Annie's chest. Would Cath survive this birth? She looked like a mad woman, her red hair tangled and matted with perspiration, her flushed face beaded with moisture, her luminous green eyes wide and desperate, her lips parched and pleading for relief.

Annie felt fresh tears gather. To think that Cath would endure such pain for a baby that would be Annie's! If only she could take on Cath's pain and ease her torment!

Unexpectedly, Cath reached out and gripped Annie's wrist. "I've got to push, Annie. I can't stop it!"

Annie screamed for Dr. Galway.

Betty Herrick appeared in the doorway. "I called his home. He's on the way. And I called Knowl at the paper. He's coming, Annie."

"So is Cath's baby! Hurry, Betty, bring some clean sheets. We may have to deliver this child ourselves!"

As it turned out, Dr. Galway arrived just as the baby was crowning. He took over with a skilled, practiced hand, and with profound relief Annie stepped back to become an observer.

She watched as Dr. Galway pressed Cath's abdomen. "Okay, Catherine. Take a deep breath, and with the next contraction, give it all you've got. That's it. Now, push, push, push!"

Annie gazed in mute fascination as the baby's head emerged, its cupid face pinched, its dark hair matted." "Okay, get ready to push again!" With a deft turn of the wrist, Dr. Galway guided the shoulders out, followed quickly by the supple, glistening body of Cath's child.

"It's a girl, Catherine!"

Cath lay back, her chest heaving. "I knew she'd be a girl!"

Dr. Galway suctioned the infant's nose and mouth until she sputtered and screamed in protest. Then he laid the waxy, wriggling baby on Cath's chest, the two still bound together by the pulsing, blue umbilical cord.

"She's beautiful! Look at her, Annie!" Cath panted. "Can you imagine such a beauty responsible for all those fierce kicks in my ribs?"

Annie bent close to Cath and gazed in awe at the tiny, squirming newborn. "She's a miracle if I ever saw one, Cath."

"Put her to the breast, if you'd like," said the doctor, "while I finish up here. She's a little one and probably has a big appetite."

Cath looked up questioningly at Annie.

"Go ahead," Annie whispered.

Awkwardly Cath cradled her daughter and helped her suckle. "She's doing it, Annie. She's a smart one. She knows just what to do."

"Of course, she's smart," said Annie with a wistful half-smile. "Look who she's got for a mother!"

"Born at twelve-fifteen, Wednesday, May thirteenth," Dr. Galway announced in his deep, resonant voice.

"Chip's birthday," Cath and Annie said in unison.

SIXTEEN

Cath remained in Willowbrook for three months, helping Annie care for her new-born daughter. After much discussion, they named the child, Jennifer Reed Herrick. It was Cath's idea. "Jennifer, for my Aunt Jenny in Germany," said Cath, "and Reed because she would have been a Reed if I'd married Chip."

Annie had her own ideas for names, but she acquiesced to Cath; it seemed a small enough favor to let Cath name her child. After all, Annie would have all the years ahead to raise the youngster as she wished.

Throughout the summer of 1942, Annie's life remained in limbo. She had a new daughter, and yet she didn't quite have a daughter. She was a mother now, and yet not exactly a mother. Whenever she watched Cath nurse the baby, Annie felt an odd sensation of standing on the outside looking in. She struggled with jealousy that Cath could so naturally fulfill the needs of her hungry infant. The two looked so lovely and perfect together—Cath with her flowing red hair and Jenny with soft wisps of auburn hair to match. The quintessential portrait of motherhood, Cath could have posed for one of those Renaissance paintings of Madonna with Child.

But when people come to visit or the family attended church, Annie became the devoted mother presenting Jenny as her newly adopted daughter, and Cath became the doting aunt, hovering in the background. Once guests left or the family arrived home from their outing, Cath whisked Jenny off to a private corner to suckle her, and Annie was left empty-handed, wondering if this bizarre charade would ever end.

Just as Annie began to fear that life would always be like this—two women sharing one child—Cath began to paint again. She converted a small workshop in the backyard into an artist's studio, explaining that she couldn't paint in the house because turpentine smells were bad for the baby.

When it was feeding time, Annie would stalk out across the lawn to Cath's studio with Jenny wailing in her arms, and inquire, "When are you coming in to nurse the baby? She's been crying for twenty minutes!"

Cath would answer, "Oh, Annie, could you please mix some formula? I'm painting those glorious garden flowers, and if I stop now, the sun won't be right."

So Annie would trudge back to the house and mix the formula and feed Jenny her bottle, while her resentment mushroomed. Why couldn't Cath make up her mind and either be a mother or not be a mother? And why was Annie so weak that she allowed Cath to keep them locked in limbo?

And then one hot, August day, to Annie's amazement, she found Cath packing. "Where are you going?" she asked as Cath rolled up her canvases and piled her belongings in a large black trunk.

"New York," said Cath. "I have a friend from the Art Institute—Jeffrey Granger. We spent a lot of time together in Chicago. Now he's in New York doing covers for the Saturday Evening Post and other magazines. He says he can get me some work illustrating stories."

"How long will you be gone?" Annie ventured.

Cath met her gaze with a frank, solemn expression. "I won't be back, Annie. It's time I got on with my life and let you and Jenny get on with yours." She reached out and gave Annie an impulsive hug. "Thanks for everything—for putting up with me through my pregnancy and for not pressuring me about Jenny. I think I'm finally ready to let her go."

"Oh, Cath, I'll miss you!"

"I'll miss you too. Friends forever, right?"

"Friends forever," whispered Annie.

Cath blinked back tears. "And you'll send me some snapshots in New York, okay? Pictures of Jenny? And I'll send her a doll or something. Don't worry. It'll be from Aunt Cath."

In the months after Cath left for New York, Annie settled into the routines of motherhood with joy and wonder. Jenny was a delightful baby, who learned quickly, smiled easily, and thrived on Annie's love. Knowl, too, took to fatherhood with unexpected pleasure, now that he knew his sister was serious about relinquishing her parental rights to the child.

Knowl managed to get home earlier in the evenings, so that he could spend an hour or two with his wife and daughter before Jenny's bedtime. And Annie made a point of greeting him at the door with Jenny in her arms. "Here's Daddy, sweetheart," she would croon. "Go see Daddy."

Knowl would swing Jenny up in his arms until she laughed and squealed. "What's my girl been up to all day?" he would ask in his most buoyant voice.

"She sat up by herself," Annie would report, or "She ate all of her pablum," or "She said 'Da-da' just as clear as a bell.'"

Both Knowl and Annie felt more relaxed these days. In fact, as she watched Knowl playing with Jenny or rocking her to sleep at night, she found herself falling in love with him all over again. He was a gentler, more peaceful man, sensitive and loving and kind.

As autumn swept in, working its alchemy with a golden, burnished eloquence, Knowl and Annie bundled Jenny up in her woolly coat and leggings and took her to the park in her fancy buggy carriage. This year, more than ever before, Annie loved the smudgy, smoked-glass aura of fall—the toasty aroma of bonfires, the ghostly silhouettes of gnarled oaks, and the crackle of green velvet leaves dried into russet lace.

On Sundays Annie dressed Jenny in frilly pinafores and jumpers and they took her proudly to church, where everyone remarked how much she looked like the two of them—and wasn't it simply amazing, considering she was adopted!

In spite of the family's continuing grief over Chip's death, Annie found that life had taken on a rosy hue as the Christmas of '42 rolled around. The days no longer seemed marked by pain and loss; if anything, they were both heartwarming and bittersweet. Jenny made all the difference. In little ways, she reminded Annie of Chip—the way she crinkled her eyes when she laughed, the way her strawberry-blonde hair glistened in the sunlight, the way her chin dimpled when she smiled. Mama and Papa noticed the similarities too. More than once, Annie heard her mother declare, "Jenny is the spitting image of Chilton at that age!"

Jenny was having a positive effect on Betty Herrick too. At first she watched from the sidelines, as if she felt uncertain about her role in Jenny's life, but gradually she reached out and assumed the grandmotherly role that was naturally hers. She took Jenny for walks in her carriage and rocked her sometimes in the antique rocker by the window in the parlor. Knowl told Annie confidentially, "If anyone can soften my mother's heart, it's Jenny."

With Jenny's laughter and love filling the old Herrick house, even the war seemed less threatening and more distant. Knowl himself seemed less consumed with battles and military strategies and combat statistics. In fact, he was becoming a real father, as absorbed in Jenny's growth and development as Annie was. Sometimes, he was even a bit too eager. For Christmas, he brought home a painted wheelbarrow, a carved, pine rocking horse, and a porcelain doll with real hair. Annie laughed and said, "Knowl, darling, Jenny won't be ready for these for months yet!"

"I know, but I just want to be ready," he replied, holding a bewildered Jenny on the back of her polished wood horse. "She'll be all grown up before we know it!"

It did seem that Jenny was growing by leaps and bounds. She was already too big for her bassinet and outgrowing the little kimonos Mama had sewn with such loving care. Often, she held her own bottle now, her pudgy little fingers wrapped awkwardly around the glass. Annie wanted to reject such signs of budding independence; she wanted to hold on to every moment of babyhood, lest suddenly she find her sweet child grown and gone.

Knowl, on the other hand, watched Jenny's progress with obvious paternal pride. "Look how big my girl's getting!" he would exclaim when he arrived home each evening. Then he would ask expectantly, "What's she learned to do today?"

"She pulled herself up to the sofa," Annie would report. Or, "She smeared apple-sauce all over me, herself, and the kitchen!" Or, "She held her arms out and made the saddest little face when I put her down to nap. So I held her until she fell asleep."

In fact, rocking Jenny to sleep every afternoon had become a regular routine for Annie, giving her ample time to savor her dreaming, angel-faced child—until one day Knowl warned, "If you keep doing that every day, you'll never get anything else done."

"What do I have to do around this big old house but clean, fix meals, and take care of our baby?" Annie countered.

Knowl eyed her shrewdly. "One of these days you'll want to get back to your writing. When's the last time you even scribbled a few lines in your journal?"

"Months, I guess," Annie admitted sheepishly, "but I'm always so tired and distract-ed."

Knowl was unrelenting. "You've always said you wanted to pen great literature."

"I do," she agreed with a wan little smile, "but great writing comes out of great suf-fering, and these days, thanks to Jenny, I'm much too happy—and exhausted—to write deep, solemn prose."

Knowl kissed Annie lightly on the lips. "Then why don't you write a few articles for the paper? Short, simple essays. I'm sending the paper free to the servicemen from Willowbrook. They would love to read light friendly articles about their hometown."

"Oh, Knowl, I'm sure you have better columnists than me."

"No, to tell the truth, we're short on columnists. All the good men are off fighting the war." He twisted one of her chestnut curls around his finger. "Besides, you write with real feeling, Annie. You could capture the warm sentiments and atmosphere of home these guys are missing so desperately."

Annie put her hand over Knowl's. "I'll think about it. It might be fun, if I can find a few moments between diapers and formula and buggy rides and laundry."

The more Annie thought about Knowl's suggestion, the more tempting the idea became. Wasn't it a writer's dream come true? She could write about ordinary homey things that mattered to her, and the Willowbrook News would publish her humble mus-ings!

One evening in late December, Annie sat down at her desk and wrote an essay about what it was like growing up in a small Midwestern town. She wrote about picking wild-flowers in June, playing with cornhusk and rag-mop dolls in the gazebo, and going to church ice cream socials with Mama and Papa. She described the rousing band concerts in the park on starry summer nights and the country fair with its cotton candy and pop-corn wagons, its carousels and merry-go-rounds, its midways and calliopes. She closed the article by thanking "our fighting boys overseas for ensuring that our children will enjoy the same wonderful, carefree childhood we experienced."

Knowl seemed pleased with the article. "I think this will remind a lot of soldiers what they're fighting for." He tilted her chin up to his. "Can you have another article for me by next week, sweetheart?"

Annie swallowed her panic and said, "I suppose so, Knowl."

As the new year—1943—dawned, so did Annie's writing career. At first Knowl pub-lished one article a week, then two, and finally, before Annie quite realized what was happening, she was writing a daily column, Monday through Friday. To her amazement, she began to receive letters back from servicemen around the world, thanking her for bringing them a taste of home. Typical of the letters was one from a sailor in the Philippines: "My family and friends write me every week, but it's never quite enough. They tell me the news, but they don't know how to make home sound like you do. I'm always hungry for another glimpse of what I left behind. Please keep writing. My ship-mates are subscribing to the Willowbrook News just to read your column!"

Knowl was delighted with the flood of responses Annie's column generated. "These letters are great," he declared. "Look, these boys are writing you things their families would love to read. Let's select the best and get their permission to publish them. Hometown families will feel like they're hearing from their own sons."

Knowl was right. No matter how many letters families on the home front received from their sons overseas, they were always eager to read another letter from a home-sick soldier or sailor. After all, even if the letters weren't from their sons, they were from someone's son.

By spring Annie was writing dozens of letters a week to servicemen around the globe, in addition to her daily newspaper column, "Letters from Home." She had written about every aspect of hometown life she could imagine—everything from shopping on Main Street with ration coupons to women raising victory crops down on the farm; from pro-files of "Rosie the Riveter" making airplane parts in the local factories to the heroic deeds ordinary citizens were performing to help the war effort, including tirelessly writing V-Mail to the fighting men. She wrote of victory drives, war bond sales, service star mothers, vol-unteer air raid wardens, and Red Cross and Salvation Army workers. She wrote a lot about food; soldiers loved to imagine eating Mama's homecooked meals, especially Sunday din-ners of country fried chicken and buttermilk biscuits.

Annie also wrote about Willowbrook families who had boys in the service, featuring a different family every week. And when she received word that someone's son had died serving his country, she wrote a tribute to honor his memory and made sure his name was added to the Willowbrook Honor Role in the town square. And every tribute she wrote was, in essence, paying homage to her brother, Chip.

Subscriptions to the Willowbrook News multiplied from week to week as families from neighboring towns clamored to read or be part of the "Letters from Home" column. "Even some of the big city newspapers are starting to look our way," Knowl told Annie one evening in May. "You're putting Willowbrook on the map, sweetheart. There're talking about syndicating your column across the country, the way they do those gossip columns by Louella Parsons and Adela Rogers St. Johns in Hollywood, or that advice column by Dorothy Dix." His dark eyes twinkled with a mixture of mirth and amusement. "Think of it, Annie! You could be the Emily Post of nostalgia."

She was sitting at her dressing table brushing her hair in slow, languorous strokes, watching Knowl in her mirror. She met his gaze with an expression of uncertainty. "I'm not sure that's what I want. I imagined myself writing something more enduring, more substantial than a syndicated column. A book perhaps."

He tightened the sash on his robe. "I thought you said serious literature would be too demanding while you're raising Jenny."

Annie put down her brush. "Now that she's almost a year old, I'm not nearly so consumed with her care. And between your mother and my mother, Jenny would have plenty of attention. I really think I'm ready to tackle a serious work."

Knowl was the doubtful one now. "What would you write about?"

She hesitated, then said softly, "I'd write about Chip and Pearl Harbor. I don't even know what I'd say, but there are so many unresolved feelings about my brother inside me. Somehow, if I could just make sense of his life and death, I think I could help a lot of people who've lost someone they loved."

"That's a noble goal, Annie. But when would you write this book about Chip?"

"I wouldn't neglect the column, if that's what you're afraid of. I could do my serious writing at night, so I'd still have time to spend with Jenny and write my column during the day."

Knowl stood behind her now, his arms circling her shoulders. He pressed his cheek against the top of her head. "Save a little night time for your husband, too, okay?"

She pivoted on her dressing stool, facing him, and embraced him around the waist. "I'll always have time for you, Knowl. You're my life."

"And you're mine, Annie. I thank God for you." He lifted her up in an ardent embrace, his mouth moving in whispers down her neck. "Enough talk of business. Now let's talk of us!"

"My favorite subject," she said beguilingly. Knowl's presence always made her feel a trifle weak and bedazzled. She inhaled, breathing in his scent, savoring his closeness. No one else on earth could make her feel this way!

On Jenny's birthday that year, Knowl and Annie took her to visit Grandma and Grandpa Reed around the corner on Honeysuckle Lane. Jenny was already taking her first awkward steps and speaking several words. Mama, Da-da, Bye-bye, No, no! She was always eager to visit her grandparents, because Grandpa Reed kept orange and lemon slices in his pocket for her. But today he wasn't waiting with candy. He wasn't anywhere in sight.

"Where's Papa?" Annie asked her mother as they made their way from the parlor to the kitchen. Mama stood at her cast iron stove, ready to slip a loaf of homemade bread into the warming oven. Her china tea tins and bisque crockery sat on the linoleum countertop, near the open window, where Grandmother Reed's delicate lace curtains fluttered in the breeze.

"Papa's in his room," said Mama, her feathery brows knitted in a frown. "In bed."

"What's wrong? Is he ill?"

Mama sighed, as if debating how much to divulge. "You might as well know, Annie. Your papa hasn't been well for a long time. Since Chip died, it's like he's given up his zest for life. He doesn't eat. He doesn't take care of himself."

"Has he seen the doctor?" asked Annie, her concern mounting.

"Yes, Dr. Galway has been here several times. He thinks it's Papa's heart. He used words I don't remember. None of them were good."

Annie reached for her mother's hand. "Papa's not—he's not dying, is he?"

Mama turned away and buried her face in her hanky.

Annie gathered Jenny in her arms and hurried up the stairs. She passed the rosebud room and blue room and strode down the hall to her parents' bedroom. She knocked gently and waited until she heard the familiar voice, bidding her enter. She went in, walking quietly, and set Jenny on Papa's bed, beside him.

He nestled the child against him. "How's my Jenny girl?"

She reached out and pressed a chubby finger against his bulbous nose. He laughed and she laughed too. "Bye-bye," she chirped.

"Bye-bye already? You just got here, little one!"

She hasn't learned to say hello yet, Papa," said Annie, valiantly striving to quell her mushrooming fears. "How are you feeling, Papa? Mama says you're a little under the weather."

"Aw, your mama worries too much. I'm healthy as a horse."

"You look a bit pale. Thinner too. Are you eating enough?"

He managed a wan smile. "Did you ever know anyone who didn't eat with Mama around?" He coughed sharply. "It's just my ol' ticker acting up, giving me a little trouble."

Annie leaned over and kissed her father's high forehead. "Well, you follow the doctor's orders, you hear?" She felt a sudden sickening jolt in the pit of her stomach. Papa looked just the way she remembered Papa Reed looking during the final days of his life. She scooped up Jenny and hid her sudden tears in Jenny's golden angel hair.

"You leaving already?" Papa asked.

"We don't want to tire you."

"No, you're not. Sit by my bed. Let me look at my precious granddaughter. When I look into her face, I imagine I'm twenty years younger and looking into Chilton's eyes. She's the spitting image—"

"I know, Papa, but she's Knowl's daughter now. She can't hear us always saying how much she looks like Chip or Cath."

"I know," he said, reaching for Annie's hand. She felt his hand swallow hers up; it felt so much bigger and stronger, reassuringly capable. And yet something in the lines of Papa's face made him look shockingly vulnerable and old. "When Jenny's older, I'll keep mum about Chip, but right now she's the only one who can ease this old man's broken heart."

"I—I'm writing a book about Chip," Annie ventured, not sure she wanted to share this very personal bit of news. But perhaps it would cheer Papa to know his son wouldn't be forgotten.

"A book? About Chip? What will you say about Chip?"

Annie averted her gaze under Papa's sudden scrutiny. "I'm not sure yet, Papa. I want to write about Pearl Harbor and how Chip and so many other strong young men died bravely for their country."

Papa looked away. "How can you write about something like that?" He sounded almost angry. "What do you know of it? My son is dead. Who can explain it? Who can make it okay again?"

"I know, Papa. I know nothing I write will change what happened to Chip. But there's something inside me that has to be said. I thought in time it would go away, but it keeps growing. I don't know what it is or how it will turn out. I just know I've got to try to make sense of it and put it down in words."

"There is no sense to it!" Papa rasped, visibly shaken. "Some men die, and other men's hearts are broken, and they, too, die bit by bit, unnoticed, unmourned."

"Not true, Papa. No matter what happens, God still loves us and wants the best for us. I have to believe that. Otherwise, nothing in this world makes sense."

"God could have spared Chip's life," grunted Papa.

Annie blinked back tears. "He could have spared His own Son's life, too, but then we'd all be without hope."

"I am without hope," Papa murmured, looking away.

Annie flinched. Yes, it could be Papa Reed lying in that bed! "Just because we don't understand God doesn't mean we shouldn't trust Him," Annie said quietly. "I was angry at first too, Papa. Then I realized I had nowhere else to go but to God. He's so vast, so beyond us, Papa. And yet, sometimes, I feel the whole of Him compressed within me, a joyous Spirit that feeds me peace no matter how tilted the world is. And that's what I hold onto, Papa, that little piece of Spirit swelling out the walls of the universe in this tiny dark cubicle of my heart."

Papa briefly met her gaze. "Calm down, daughter. I would never utter a word of disrespect against the Almighty, but He has broken me, and I don't know how to fix things. I suppose I'll never get where you are in your faith."

Annie lifted her father's arm and kissed the rough, mottled back of his hand. "I don't know how to say it in words, Papa. Some days I feel God so close. Other days I don't know where He is. I know He's here inside me, but sometimes He seems so distant, as if He's speaking to me from the dark side of the moon." Her voice wavered slightly. "I'm trying to listen to Him, Papa. And sometimes I hear Him in my heart clearer than I hear your voice. And when I hear Him, I feel as if this is what I was born for, and all's right no matter what's wrong outside. That's why I know God has so much to say, if we only knew how to listen better."

Papa patted her hand. "I'll try to listen, Annie. For your sake."

SEVENTEEN

The Summer of 1943.

Mama's voice came thin and strangled over the telephone wire. "Annie, come quick! It's Papa. He's gone, Annie!"

With those few words, Annie's safe, ordered world collapsed again. "I'm coming, Mama!"

But there was nothing Annie or anyone else could do. That strong rock of a man who had survived the Depression, two world wars, and the death of his only son, was dead.

Mama was beside herself with grief. "I never needed your papa more than I do right now," she lamented, "and he's gone! What do I do, Annie? He made everything run smoothly. He earned the money and paid the bills and made repairs and took care of me. He always told me not to worry—to raise the children and make a good home, and he would do the rest. But there is no home left without Papa!"

Annie yearned to comfort her mother, but her own grief left her feeling immobilized. She couldn't think what they ought to do. Call people? Make funeral arrangements? Prepare an obituary? Fortunately, Knowl stepped in and took over the burdensome details. He called Cath and Alice Marie and promised to pick them up at the train depot. He telephoned Reverend Henry and contacted the Willowbrook Funeral Home about burial plans.

For the next few days, Annie felt as if she were walking in a dream. Voices came at her from a distance; people seemed remote, as if she were viewing them on a movie screen. She seemed to be standing outside herself, looking on, watching without involvement as she greeted her sister and best friend, as she received the condolences of acquaintances, even as she held her mother in her arms and whispered words of consolation.

The scene seemed staged somehow, her words lines of dialogue scripted by someone else and recited without conviction. No matter how she tried, she could not break through the shadowy sensation that the passing hours were rites to be endured, that grieving had imposed its own rigid rules of conduct and propriety.

What she wanted most was to connect with those she loved on some raw, instinctive level that would get to the root of her pain, that would break through the numbness to the enormous anguish beneath. But no one in the broken circle of family seemed able to reach beyond the self-imposed strictures of mourning.

On June 26, 1943, Papa was buried in the family plot next to his parents, Jonathan and Alma Reed, in the shade of a weeping willow. The gnarled, ancient tree stood sentry on a grassy knoll in the rustic cemetery behind the church. After the graveside service, the ladies of the church served a simple buffet luncheon in the backyard of the Reed home. Annie was amazed at the number of mourners. Many were people she didn't know or hadn't seen in years; others were only nodding acquaintances.

Several filed by and clasped her hand and said, "You don't know me, but I worked for your father at the A&P, and I want to tell you what a good man he was," or, "Your father was my boss at the A&P, and he was always kind and fair. Everyone in the store will miss him."

Annie hadn't stopped to think about this whole area of her father's life that she had never shared. She simply knew that he went off to work each morning and returned each evening. He rarely talked about work and never complained, so she had assumed there was nothing interesting about working with a dozen clerks and checkers among cabbages, condiments, canned goods, and the whole cornucopia of grocery items offered by the A&P.

But, catching a glimpse of her father's secret workaday world in the loving accolades of his employees, she realized how much she would never know about the valiant, steadfast man she had called Papa.

That evening, after the mourners had gone, Papa's family meandered around his roomy old house, aimless and dazed. Suddenly there seemed to be no more script to follow, no roles to play, no visitors to greet, no pressing tasks at hand. Mama, her blonde hair flecked with gray, puttered in the kitchen, bemoaning the fact that there was no room in the ice box for all the left-over food. Alice Marie, looking more sophisticated than ever with her thickly penciled brows and dark red lips, found places on tables and bureaus for the endless bouquets of fresh, fragrant carnations, roses, and lilies.

Knowl sorted through some of Papa's important papers, and Cath fed Jenny vegetable soup and applesauce. Annie watched silently, fighting off twinges of jealousy as Cath played "dive bomber" with the spoon, making Jenny shake with laughter. Annie chided herself. Surely Cath had a right to spend time with Jenny, the way any aunt might enjoy a favorite niece.

As deep blue hues darkened the skyline and stars winked out from the heavens, Annie stepped out on the sprawling front porch and stood by the carved oak rail. She gazed up and down tree-lined Honeysuckle Lane, listened to the ratchety song of crickets, and watched fireflies blink green bobbins of light in the sultry summer air.

Annie loved this porch. It possessed an eternal quality, stayed the same, year in, year out; whatever the season, she could stand here and see the world from the same perspective. People came and went, but this porch remained.

In the stillness she could almost hear whispers in the wind, random wisps of conversations from years gone by. Papa Reed, Chip, and now her own beloved Papa lived on in memories that lingered here. As long as this dear old house stood, they would be here for her in bittersweet recollections from the past. Tears ran unchecked down Annie's cheeks. The terrible wall of deadness and apathy barricading her responses had ruptured long enough to allow a gush of fresh, sweeping emotion—painful, yet strangely satisfying.

Reluctantly Annie left the comforting silence of the porch and returned inside where lamplight glowed, warding off shadows, and a radio droned on, too low for anyone to hear. The air was muggy and still and June bugs buzzed against the screened windows—ironic evidence of life in the ravaging wake of death. In the parlor, Cath was rocking a slumbering Jenny in the maple rocker and Alice Marie sat curled on the love seat browsing through family photo albums. "I'm keeping some of these pictures," she said. "Mama told me once I could keep some."

"Only the ones Mama has doubles of," said Annie from the doorway.

"That's not fair," said Alice Marie, patting her short, wavy blonde hair into place. "You live here. You can see the family anytime. I travel. Sometimes years go by before I get home again."

"Whose fault is that?" asked Cath.

"You should talk," said Alice Marie. "How long has it been since you've been home?"

"I get home more often than you do."

"Maybe if I'd left a baby behind, I'd get home more often too. I bet I'd—"

Annie broke in. "Stop it, Alice Marie. Do you think I want Jenny hearing remarks like that?"

"She's a baby. What does she know?"

Annie sat down in the upholstered chair by the fireplace. "We're all on edge. We're all grieving. And we're not children anymore. Let's try to get along."

After a long moment of silence, Cath asked Alice Marie, "Why didn't your husband come home with you? I'd think he'd want to be supportive at a time like this."

"Cary wanted to come," said Alice Marie sullenly, "but the band is booked solid through Labor Day."

"You still enjoy singing and traveling with the band?" asked Cath, her fingers mindlessly weaving through Jenny's carrot-top curls.

"I love singing. Traveling gets a little tedious. Cary promised we'd settle down as soon as we've made enough money."

"You mean, you'll settle down in Willowbrook?" asked Annie.

"Why not? Or maybe Chicago or Detroit or Fort Wayne."

Annie studied Alice Marie's expression. There was an edge of defensiveness in her voice and a sadness in her eyes that Annie suspected had nothing to do with Papa's death. "When will you be rejoining Cary and the band?" she asked.

Alice Marie avoided her gaze. "I don't know. There's no hurry. Cary has a—a new girl singer. Someone he's training. So he won't need me for a few weeks."

Annie flinched slightly. "You're staying that long?"

"Yes. I want to be here for Mama. She'll need someone."

She has me! Annie wanted to say, but refrained. She looked instead at Cath. "How about you, Cath? I suppose you're eager to get back to New York and your work with Jeffrey Granger."

"I told Jeff I'd be gone a few weeks. He understands. Like Alice Marie says, this is an important time to be in Willowbrook. Your mama needs us all to rally around her." Cath kissed Jenny's hair. "I need to be here too. Your papa was like a father to Knowl and me. I miss him more than I can say."

Annie stood up abruptly. She felt unnerved, threatened somehow, in a way she couldn't put into words. "I'd better go shoo Mama out of the kitchen and get her upstairs to bed." She looked at Cath. "Do you want me to take Jenny upstairs too?"

Cath looked up pleadingly. "Let me hold her a little longer. This whole house smells and feels like death. Jenny's like a sweet breath of life."

Annie nodded, but she felt uneasy, as if she were allowing something to be set in motion that couldn't be stopped.

Annie's uneasiness grew during the next two weeks. Nothing about her life seemed normal anymore. Alice Marie settled in with Mama, reclaiming her favorite blue room, and Cath moved back into her old bedroom at the Herrick house. Knowl frequently spent his evenings at the Reed house helping Mama with Papa's business matters, and Cath passed the days with Jenny, playing with her, taking her for walks over to Grandma Reed's, and sketching her in the garden or the gazebo.

Annie wasn't sure how to handle these new events. Should she let Knowl know she didn't like him spending so much time in the same house with Alice Marie? Surely he would consider her a jealous school girl. Should she tell Cath how much her time spent with Jenny bothered her? Cath would consider her less than a friend for her selfishness and small-mindedness. No, better to remain silent and try to quell such small jealousies and resentments.

Annie's grief over Papa's death and her daily household concerns overshadowed ongoing news of the war. Distractedly she scanned the headlines each evening: RAF Command Bombs Hamburg—Success!; Battle of Kursk Rages On—Seen as Largest

Tank Battle of War; Roosevelt and Churchill Urge Italian Surrender—"Oust Mussolini!" But no matter how much Annie tried to take an interest in world and national events, her own erratic homelife consumed all her energies.

Just as Annie lamented over how unsettled her days had become, a new situation threatened to throw her life into even greater turmoil. It happened one evening when she paid her mother a visit. The two sat together on the porch swing in the twilight, savoring the faint stirrings of a breeze, when Mama said the words that shattered Annie's already tenuous sense of security.

"I'm thinking of selling the house, Annie." The words seemed wrung from a sob and hung in the air like a death knell.

Annie stared at her mother. "Sell the house? You can't."

"I don't want to, Annie, but there may be no other choice."

"Of course, there are other choices. The house is us, our family. It's home. Where else would you live? What would you do?"

Mama absently twisted her wedding ring around her finger. "Aunt Martha has invited me to come live with her, Annie."

"Aunt Martha? You mean, Aunt Martha in Chicago? Aunt Martha with all the cats?"

"She's been quite ill lately and needs someone to care for her. And I need somewhere to live. It might be the best answer for both of us."

"You have somewhere to live, Mama! Right here!"

"It's too big a house now, Annie. I'm the only one left. I'd feel useless rattling around in it all by myself. And I can't afford the upkeep now that Papa's gone."

Tears of frustration spilled out of Annie's eyes. "We can't lose you and this house, Mama. We can't. Knowl and I will help out. We'll figure out something!"

"Knowl's already put all his money into his newspaper. You children don't have anything extra. It's best this way. You'll see."

Annie stopped swinging and sat forward, her back stiffening. "I won't let you do it, Mama. I won't let this house go. I'd do anything before I'd see strangers living in our house. You'd never forgive yourself either, Mama."

Her mother was silent for what seemed an eternity. When she spoke again, her voice was edged with something Annie had never heard in her mother before—a defenselessness that made Annie shiver, as if she were exposing something immensely private and tender. "Annie," she said quietly, "I love this house. You know that. But it has too many memories. I see your papa in every room. I hear his voice on the stairs and in the walls. I smell him and feel him—his hair, his face, his clothes. He's everywhere and yet he's nowhere. I walk through the house all day and night searching for him. I stand in his closet and bury my face in his clothing to catch the scent of him. Sometimes he feels so close. I'm always on the verge of reaching out for him, but my arms are still empty.

Better I should go live with Aunt Martha and her cats than live like this."

Annie sat back and embraced her mother. The woman who had always seemed so self-reliant seemed almost frail in her arms. "It's so unfair, Mama," she whispered.

"No, Annie. It's just life. It changes. It goes on. It'll be good for me to spend time with Martha. She's my older sister, and she needs me. I need to feel needed, Annie. I need to be useful."

In the weeks that followed, Annie channeled all of her grief and inner turmoil into her writing. With Cath helping to care for Jenny, Annie had time to spend at her old Remington typewriter, her fingers moving tirelessly over the keys as she poured out her feelings about Chip and the war. She realized the book was taking shape more as a novel than a biography. There was so much she didn't know about Chip's experiences at Pearl Harbor. But at least the writing was cathartic. Annie was feeling more in control of her emotions, girding her strength for the vast changes taking place in her life.

In mid-August, while British and American military leaders met with Roosevelt and Churchill in Quebec to plan war strategies, Annie put the finishing touches on the first draft of her book. On one especially scorching evening, when Knowl arrived home early from the paper, Annie nervously showed him the manuscript. She sat beside him all evening while he read, both of them enduring the humidity, her heart pounding and her mouth dry as she waited for his opinion.

"I like it," he told her after skimming the first hundred pages. "It really shows how you felt about Chip."

"Do you think it's something I could—get published?"

Knowl rubbed his jaw. "I don't know much about book publishing, but I think it's worth a try. I've got some connections through the paper. Let me get the name and address of a New York publisher for you." He gave her a big bear hug and kissed her soundly on the lips. "Who knows? Maybe I'm kissing the world's next best selling author!"

With immense fear and self-doubt, Annie put her manuscript in the mail to Sanders and Browne Publishers in New York City. For three weeks she watched intently for the mailman, her palms sweaty, her heart doing somersaults. Finally the postman handed her a large package postmarked New York. With mounting excitement, she tore off the brown paper, but her heart sank as she recognized her own manuscript. Rejected! Tears swam in her eyes as she picked up the enclosed letter and began reading.

Mrs. Elizabeth Anne Herrick
1334 Maypole Drive
Willowbrook, Indiana

Dear Mrs. Herrick:

Thank you for submitting your manuscript, PACIFIC DAWN, for our consideration. While we regret that we cannot offer you a contract, we do feel your book shows promise. Your work demonstrates great feeling and conviction, but it lacks a certain authenticity that would be necessary for its commercial success.

We suggest you invest some time in direct communication with several of our military men who were stationed at Pearl Harbor and experienced the Japanese attack firsthand. Their first-person accounts may lend the credibility your novel presently lacks.

You may wish to contact Mr. Robert Wayne of Los Angeles, a former editor with Sanders and Browne, who is presently recuperating from wounds suffered at Pearl Harbor. As an officer in the Navy, he experienced the devastation firsthand. He may be willing to read your manuscript and offer the kind of critical evaluation it needs. His address is listed below.

Thank you for considering Sanders and Browne. We wish you success in the placement of your work.

Sincerely,
Randolph L. Simmons, Editor
SANDERS AND BROWNE PUBLISHERS

Swallowing the painful lump in her throat, Annie carefully folded the letter and slipped it inside her Bible beside the faded little paper containing the friendship pact she had made with Cath so many years ago. Silently she vowed that she would never make such a foolish mistake again. Best to stay where she belonged—writing her simple little newspaper columns that everybody liked. Forget writing serious literature. She simply didn't have it in her, as the prestigious New York publishers, Sanders and Browne, had so officially pronounced.

By September, as General Eisenhower announced the surrender of Italy to the Allies, Annie's personal woes increased. Mama sold the house on Honeysuckle Lane. The papers were signed. The house now belonged to somebody else—a family from Cincinnati named Rosarno. Mama told her children to take whatever furniture, knickknacks, and personal possessions they wanted. The rest would be auctioned off in an estate sale in the backyard.

Annie kept her furniture from the rosebud room; Alice Marie stored the furniture from the blue room in Knowl's basement, saving it for the time "when I have my own house." Annie, Cath, and Knowl selected the best of the oak pieces for the Herrick house. "When everything's in place, you'll feel like you're back in your old home," Knowl told Annie as the movers carried out desks and tables, upholstered sofas and Queen Anne chairs.

Annie cried anyway, even if the furniture was going to the Herrick house around the corner where she lived. It wouldn't be the same. Her life was being dismantled piece by piece before her eyes, and there was nothing she could do about it.

The auction was even worse. Shortly after dawn, on a cloudy September Saturday, strangers came and moved everything that remained out of Annie's childhood home and placed it in random clusters in the backyard. Long before everything was in place, townspeople converged on Honeysuckle Lane and swarmed over the lawn, picking over and examining the items like annoying bees. Annie, holding Jenny in her arms, watched with her mother from a distance as her family's private treasures were bartered and haggled over by callous intruders.

Before the auctioneer had sold even half a dozen items, the swollen rain clouds burst overhead, drenching the Reeds' cherished possessions and memorabilia. Annie's heart broke as she watched velvet love seats and paintings, fragile curios and linens ruined by the downpour.

But the auctioneer and his clients simply raised their umbrellas and went on with the auction. They looked like birds of prey in their black raincoats, their heads down, shoulders bent against the rain, shiny umbrellas warding off the storm. Watching them, Annie wanted to scream, Get out of here, all of you! Leave our things alone! Let us be!

But she looked over at her mother's stricken face and held her tongue. "Let me take Jenny inside," Mama whispered, her cheeks streaming with tears and rain. With the child in her arms, she turned on her heel and hurried back into the house.

But Annie stood her ground. She would see this horrible auction through to the end. She didn't care that her hair and clothing were soaked or that dampness was chilling her skin, striking with a savage iciness to the very bone.

Annie watched mutely as the auctioneer trilled his little spiel, "Who'll give me ten, I say ten, who'll make it twenty, I've got twenty, twenty once, who'll make it thirty, I've got thirty, going once, going twice, gone!"

Gone. Yes. That stormy day, all the patchwork pieces that made up the fabric of Annie's childhood and youth were gone—ripped apart and scattered like confetti in the wind.

But if Annie thought she couldn't be more miserable, she was wrong.

EIGHTEEN

The Fall of 1943.

Annie wept aloud the day she and Knowl put Mama on the train for Chicago. Mama kept insisting she was looking forward to living with Aunt Martha and her cats, but Annie knew Mama had never had a fondness for cats. "If you want to come home to Willowbrook, Mama, just say the word," Annie told her firmly. "You'll always have a place to live with Knowl and me."

Mama dismissed that notion with a wave of her hand. "You and Knowl have all you can handle with Catherine and his mother there. You don't need me hovering around too."

"Cath's only visiting," Annie argued. "She'll be going back to New York any day now."

"Will she?" Mama asked meaningfully, raising one eyebrow.

Although neither of them put it into words, Annie knew what her mother was insinuating. Cath had grown much too comfortable living at home again, and in dozens of trifling ways she was reclaiming her child—taking Jenny for walks, reading to her, giving her baths, tucking her into bed at night. Her overtures were always explained away as helpful gestures: "Here, Annie, let me feed her. You go ahead and finish typing that page," or, "I'll rock Jenny to sleep. You go spend some time with your husband."

Annie had grown accustomed to taking the road of least resistance, but even as she gave in to Cath in inconsequential ways, she felt a growing uneasiness. Cath was becoming too emotionally involved with Jenny. They were right back at the impasse they faced at her birth—two mothers for one child.

The last thing Annie wanted to do was hurt Cath; they had been soul-mates all their lives. But Annie longed to have her little family to herself once again. If only Cath would return to her life in New York. Her good friend, Jeffrey Granger, telephoned often enough asking her to come back. Cath admitted they were more than friends. Perhaps they even loved each other, although Cath wasn't ready yet to make such a commitment. Privately, she told Annie, "I care deeply for Jeffrey, but I'll never love him the way I loved Chip. He was the great love of my life. Maybe there'll never be another."

"You won't know unless you give him a chance," Annie warned. Even as she said the words, she felt a twinge of guilt, knowing she wanted Cath to leave so she could have Jenny to herself again.

And then there was Alice Marie. As long as Mama remained in her house on Honeysuckle Lane, Alice Marie stayed on with her. Annie found it peculiar that, for the first time in her life, Alice Marie was putting Mama's needs above her own, but she tried not to question her sister's motivations. Nevertheless, when two months had passed and Alice Marie had still made no effort to rejoin her husband and his band, Annie couldn't help wondering what was going on.

The truth became evident the day Knowl and Annie drove Mama to the train station. On the way home, Annie turned and said to Alice Marie in the back seat, "I suppose now that Mama's gone to Chicago, you'll be eager to rejoin Cary and the band."

Her sister's expression turned as icy as an early frost. "No, Annie," she said abruptly, "I won't be joining Cary."

Annie felt a sinking sensation deep in her chest. "Why not? What happened? Did you two have a fight?"

"I don't wish to talk about it," Alice Marie declared, raising her chin proudly and gazing out the window.

"But where will you stay now that Mama's house is sold?"

For the first time, Alice Marie's china-doll pout cracked slightly. Her voice wavered as she said, "I don't know where I'll stay. Maybe in a hotel somewhere."

"I don't understand," Annie protested. "What about your marriage? Your career? Aren't you going back to Cary at all?"

Annie couldn't recall ever seeing her sister weep before, except in a very controlled manner at funerals, but suddenly, here she was, in the back seat of Knowl's automobile, heaving with sobs. Knowl was so shocked by Alice Marie's outburst, he nearly lost control of the vehicle. And Annie, blaming herself for prompting her sister's fountain of tears, felt beside herself with dismay.

Knowl pulled over to the curb and parked, and at last they got the truth out of Alice Marie. "Cary sent me home," she cried. "He's found—somebody else!"

Annie was confused. "A new singer, you mean? That new girl singer he hired?"

"She—she's more than his singer! She's his mistress too!" Alice Marie buried her face in her hands and continued to weep. For the first time in her life, Annie felt a wave of sympathy for her glamorous older sister. It was startling to realize that Alice Marie could hurt just like any other girl who was jilted.

"You mean, Cary doesn't want you to come back to him and the band?"

"No-o-o," Alice Marie wailed. "When I came home for Papa's funeral, I thought Cary would call and beg me to come back. But he hasn't. And he won't take my calls either!"

Knowl was struggling to contain his anger. "I'd like to get hold of that rat and show him a thing or two." He handed Alice Marie his handkerchief. "Don't worry. You'll always have a place to stay with us. Right, Annie?"

Annie stared back dumbly. Had she heard right?

"Oh, Knowl, I couldn't," Alice Marie protested, a bit too demurely.

"Sure, you can. You're family. We have a big house and plenty of room. You can stay until you get back on your feet."

And that was how it came to be that Annie found herself living under the same roof with what seemed suddenly like a menagerie of humanity—her often inebriated mother-in-law, her beautiful, betrayed sister whom her husband had once adored, and her best friend, the mother of Annie's adopted child.

The Herrick house had never been Annie's favorite abode. It lacked all the warmth, refinement, and class of her family home on Honeysuckle Lane. But at least Annie had been able to escape the dreariness of the place with frequent visits to her mother's home around the corner. Now her cherished house was locked to her. Strangers lived there now. The facade looked the same, but it was a painful illusion of what once was.

The Herrick house was Annie's only residence, but it was peopled with an assortment of individuals who clashed and grated against one another mercilessly. Alice Marie loathed Betty Herrick and often complained to Annie, "That woman's a depressing drunk who skulks around this place like the witch of Endor. She gives me the creeps."

Betty Herrick was equally chilling in her assessment of Alice Marie: "That girl is a contemptible opportunist. She's trying to get her hooks back in my poor Knowl, and he's foolish enough to let her!"

Cath was little help as a referee. She fought with her mother and argued with Alice Marie. Knowl was no help either. He spent longer hours at the newspaper, claiming that the war news was more demanding than ever. Bulletins were coming in daily from the Eastern Front, Italy, New Guinea, the Central Pacific, and the Solomons, not to mention air operations over Europe, China, and the Pacific.

Knowl pointed out that Annie had only to take a look at the headlines for October to see all that was happening: Italy Declares War on Germany; British Cruiser Charybdis sunk in English Channel; US 34th Division Takes Sant 'Angelo; Soviets Capture Chaplinka, Cut Off German Supplies. Every area of the globe seemed to be bristling with war activity, and Knowl was determined to report it all.

When Annie fretted that he was gone too much, he told her, "You know how I feel about this, Annie. I can't be over there fighting this war, but I can write about it in a way that brings it home to the people here. I owe it to our servicemen. They're dying, Annie, and we go about our business as if the war were nothing more than another entertaining radio show. We talk about battles like they're baseball scores. When do we start sacrificing, Annie?"

Duly chagrined, Annie vowed never to complain about Knowl's tardiness again. He was right, of course. The war was so much more significant in the larger scope of world events than her paltry problems. What did it matter in the long run if Alice Marie pursued Knowl or if Cath played mother to little Jenny? Life would right itself in time, if Annie just held her peace. Why then did she feel as if she were about to be sucked away into some nether world? Why did she feel as if she herself were the object of a war being waged, with enemies at every front?

Perhaps she was being paranoid. Perhaps grief over Chip and her father's death and the loss of her dear home and mother were driving her to the edge of lunacy. Could she trust her own intuition? Even when she prayed, she felt a shadow of doubt that God was still listening. What had happened? Her great God had once been her most intimate friend. Now, He—like everyone who mattered most to her—seemed somehow remote.

One evening late in October, Annie experienced what she could only describe later as an epiphany—a sudden, terrifying insight into the very nature of her existence. Her life and her relationships were shockingly different from what she had assumed.

The revelation began innocently enough. After spending an hour or so in her room writing in her journal, she went downstairs and was about to enter the parlor when an odd, oppressive sensation stopped her. From the darkened hallway, she stared into the parlor and there in the rosy lamplight saw Cath serenely rocking baby Jenny, and on the love seat sat Knowl and Alice Marie chatting and laughing comfortably together. The scene seemed so stunningly correct and complete that Annie felt an impulse to run back upstairs to her room, lest she break the spell of that homey setting.

The truth hit her with shattering clarity: She didn't belong! Like the tag-along child of yesteryear, she was superfluous, a bothersome appendage, useless and unnecessary in this pleasant family circle. If she didn't exist, Cath could have her child and Knowl his true love. Her very presence created a distortion that skewed what could have been a straight course.

Annie shook off the crushing sensation almost immediately, and entered the room as she had planned. Cath handed her the sleeping child and Alice Marie excused herself and went upstairs to bed, leaving Annie to enjoy a few priceless moments with her husband and daughter.

But Annie couldn't completely dismiss her sense of foreboding. She pressed close to Knowl and whispered, "Do you think we made a mistake accepting Cath's child as our own?"

Knowl was less than reassuring. "We didn't make a mistake, but I wonder if Cath thinks she did?"

"Can't you talk to her? Reassure her we're the best family for Jenny?"

"How can I tell her that, Annie? She's my sister. She's got to see it and believe it for herself. My words won't change anything. What about you saying something? She's your best friend."

"I know, but we can't talk about Jenny. She's created a wedge between us. I feel so uneasy, Knowl. I don't know where it's all going to end." In the silence of the moment, Annie decided to risk revealing even more of her concerns. "In fact, where both Cath and Alice Marie are concerned, I feel like I'm walking on egg shells." She smiled mirthlessly. "Or worse, on quicksand!"

Knowl looked at her. "Where is that coming from? Is it fear? Jealousy? No one's a threat to you, Annie. Especially not Alice Marie."

Annie studied the way lamplight glinted streaks of rainbow off the diamond in her wedding ring. "I suppose I'm being foolish, Knowl, but I can't help remembering how much you loved her. You almost married her."

He lifted Annie's chin to his. "But I married you, didn't I? I love you, Annie. But that doesn't mean I can't care about Alice Marie. She'll always be a good friend. If I seem to be spending more time with her than usual, it's because I'm worried about her."

"Worried? Why?"

Knowl's brow furrowed. "She doesn't want you or anyone else to know how bad her marriage was. She's struggling with quite a broken heart—and a wounded spirit."

Annie felt clashing waves of jealousy and concern. "What happened, Knowl? What did Alice Marie tell you?"

"Let's just say Cary Rose is a bully and a two-timing jerk. This girl singer your sister mentioned isn't the first of Cary's conquests. Alice Marie put up with it for as long as she could, but there was more—"

"More? What more could there possibly be?"

Knowl hesitated. "Beatings. The brute broke a couple of your sister's ribs. She was in the hospital twice. I think she's terrified of the man."

Annie shook her head, dazed. It hardly seemed possible. Her capable, confident older sister—the victim of a cruel, cheating monster? "Are you sure about this, Knowl?"

He nodded. "Alice Marie told me herself. I feel sorry for her, Annie. I wish there was something we could do to help."

"We are helping. We've taken her in. She's become part of the family. What more can we do?"

Knowl held her close, rubbing the back of her neck. "I knew you'd understand, sweetheart. That's what I love about you."

But Annie didn't understand. Events were moving on beyond her grasp, beyond her ability to influence or change them. She sensed she was on a collision course, heading for catastrophe, but she was powerless to alter her destiny. Her life was being written for her by an unknown hand, and she was too small in the scheme of things to make a difference.

NINETEEN

The Spring of 1944.

For the next few months, everyone in the Herrick household settled into a some-times strained but often surprisingly convivial routine. Alice Marie found a job in a local munitions factory during the week and took the train to Chicago on weekends to sing in a canteen for the Great Lakes servicemen. To her occasional annoyance, she lodged with Mama, Aunt Martha, and her cats, and, on returning to Willowbrook, she often expressed her gratitude to the heavens that she had to endure such a menagerie only on weekends. Mama, she reported, seemed to have adjusted to the stealthy felines with astonishing forbearance and seemed quite at peace nursing Aunt Martha back to health.

Through Jeffrey Granger's connections, Cath received a long-coveted assignment to paint a cover for the Saturday Evening Post. She was both ecstatic and full of trepidation. To think that her work would grace the same cover that boasted the homespun genius of Norman Rockwell! She had to have exactly the right subject—a scene that would com-municate both passion and pathos. Something as elemental and profound as mother and child, Madonna and infant. She asked Annie if she would pose in the antique rocker holding Jenny, with the light from the parlor window filtering through the lace curtains just so. It would make a universal statement of maternal love and yet capture the essence of a particular mother and child. Annie was reluctant at first, then finally agreed.

She wore an evergreen velvet dress with snowy white collar and cuffs, a princess waistline, and a full circle skirt that hung in gentle folds to mid-calf. Her thick, sable-brown hair cascaded around her shoulders in loose curls and showed honey-gold high-lights where the sunlight washed in from the window. A touch of mascara and moss green eyeshadow accented her large, gray-green eyes and her ivory complexion offered a flawless contrast to the matte red of her full, faintly smiling lips.

Jenny, with her auburn hair in a mass of Shirley Temple curls, wore a white lacy pinafore dress with yards of ruffles, lacy anklets, and shiny black patent leather shoes. With her enormous blue eyes, rosebud lips, and ruddy, chipmunk cheeks, she had an irre-sistible way of smiling and batting her long lashes that Cath was determined to capture.

But sitting still wasn't an easy feat for a bouncy, rambunctious two year old. Cath had to work quickly in brief sittings, and when Jenny finally fell asleep in Annie's arms, she had to finish the painting from memory. Nevertheless, the portrait Cath produced was extraordinary in every way—not only her best work, but capturing an aura of tenderness and warmth unparalleled in any of her previous work.

Annie continued writing her daily columns for the Willowbrook News and persevered with her novel, Pacific Dawn, meticulously writing and rewriting each chapter. She finally worked up enough courage to write Robert Wayne in Los Angeles, the former editor who had been wounded at Pearl Harbor. He wrote back to tell her he would be glad to read her manuscript and offer his suggestions. But the very thought of sending her work off for a stranger to read left her feeling panicky and unworthy. So she tucked his letter in her Bible beside the rejection letter from Sanders and Browne. Perhaps some day she would summon the fortitude to risk facing rejection once more.

On the first Sunday of May, Cath and Annie surprised Knowl with a special home-cooked dinner—with meat! "Whatever you're cooking, it smells delicious!" he exclaimed, bounding into the kitchen with Jenny riding his shoulders.

"It's fried pork chops," said Cath, "with boiled potatoes and milk gravy."

"And fresh peas from the garden," Annie added as she shelled the peas into a colander.

"As you know, dear brother," Cath continued with a flourish, "as of last Thursday, all meats have been taken off ration except for steaks and certain choice cuts of beef. Thus, we have pork chops at last!"

Knowl jounced Jenny in the air. "Looks like we got back just in time for a royal feast, Sweet Pea!"

Annie tickled Jenny's tummy under her polo shirt. "You sweet little ragamuffin! Where did Daddy take you?"

"We took a horsey ride around the garden," said Knowl with an impish grin. "Three times. This tired ol' horsey is ready to be put out to pasture!"

Jenny held out her chubby arms and Annie scooped her up and nuzzled her cornsilk hair. "And I bet this little cowgirl is ready for her nap!"

Jenny's fat cheeks were flushed with sun and excitement. "No, Mommy! Tickle Jenny! Tickle Daddy! Tickle Aunt Cath!"

Annie laughed. "No more tickling until you've had a nap!"

After Annie had put Jenny to bed, she and Cath set the dining room table with their best silver and bone china. The white linen tablecloth offered a striking contrast to the red velvet drapes framing the high, narrow windows. Knowl hovered nearby, helping himself to a carrot stick and a wedge of tomato. He had changed out of his pinstripe suit into a polo shirt and khaki slacks. "Is this a special occasion?" he asked. "I haven't seen a meal like this in months."

"It is, sort of," said Annie. "Cath recently finished her painting for the Post cover. She's shipping it off tomorrow."

"Really? Congratulations!" He gave Cath an affectionate squeeze. "Actually, I was growing rather fond of that painting. It was of my two favorite girls—next to my little sister, of course."

"I just hope they like it at the Post," said Cath.

"They'll love it," said Annie. "It's your best work yet."

"I think Jeffrey will like it too," said Cath.

"When are we going to meet this Jeffrey fellow?" asked Knowl with a wink. "Isn't it about time he met the family?"

"I don't want to scare him off, brother dear."

"Then it is getting serious? You think he might propose?"

"It's not that serious, yet. But it could be someday."

"You won't just run off and get married, will you?"

Cath tossed her honey-red hair. "Are you kidding? I'm going to let you give me away at a grand, expensive wedding. Annie will be my matron of honor and Jenny will be my flower girl. Wouldn't she make the prettiest little...." Cath's words drifted off. She seemed momentarily lost in thought. Then, as quickly, her reverie broke. She looked up and said brightly, "Let's eat. Before the food gets cold!"

That evening, while Jenny slept and Knowl drove to the depot to pick up Alice Marie coming in from Chicago, Cath and Annie sat beside the parlor radio listening to the soothing music of Guy Lombardo. The room contained several pieces of Mama's furniture and resembled the parlor on Honeysuckle Lane. Annie sat on a striped love seat; across from her, Cath occupied a Queen Anne chair. After a while, Cath looked up and said, "Annie, do you remember the pact we made as children?"

Annie smiled. "Of course. How could I forget? It's in my Bible upstairs. Why do you ask?"

Cath twisted a strand of her flowing, crimson hair. Her green eyes shone with a strange sort of urgency. "Are we still best friends, Annie? After all these years?"

Annie felt a small alarm sound somewhere in her head. "Of course, we're best friends. Friends forever, right?"

"Right. That's why I feel I can say this—"

"Say what, Cath."

Cath sat forward in her chair, her elbows resting loosely on her knees. She wore a casual cotton print dress with peach blossoms that accented her hair. "I'm leaving soon, Annie." She said the words matter-of-factly.

"Leaving?"

"Yes. I'm going back to New York. Back to Jeffrey. He's arranged an exhibition of my work in one of the city's most prestigious galleries."

"That's wonderful, Cath. You deserve your success."

Cath was silent a moment. Then she said quietly, "Success is hollow without the people you love."

Annie winced inwardly. She wasn't sure what was coming, but she sensed she wouldn't want to hear it. "What are you saying, Cath? Are you still thinking of Chip?"

Cath shook her head, tossing back her thick mane of hair. "No, not Chip." She met Annie's gaze frankly. "It's Jenny. Will you let me have her, Annie? Will you let me take her with me?"

Annie was certain she hadn't heard right. She parted her lips to frame a question, but no sound would come. A high, shrill whistle seemed to be ringing in her head, a pressure expanding so painfully in her skull she couldn't think straight.

"It's only right," Cath continued softly, her gaze still pinning Annie to the wall. "You know it's right. She's mine, Annie. She's always been mine."

Annie still couldn't reply. Her tongue felt thick and sluggish, unnatural in her mouth.

"Did you hear me, Annie? Say something."

At last Annie found her voice. "I can't give her up, Cath."

"Why not?"

"I'm her mother. The only mother she's known."

"No, Annie, I'm her mother."

"You bore her. You haven't raised her."

"She loves me too, Annie. I've held her, played with her. She's young. She'll forget. She'll adjust. Let's make things right now before it's too late."

"It is too late," said Annie abruptly. "We shouldn't even be having this conversation. We settled this the day you asked Knowl and me to raise Jenny."

Cath lowered her gaze. "We were all a little crazy after Chip died. Don't make me pay for my mistake for the rest of my life, Annie. Think what we've meant to each other all these years. What was that friendship about? What did it mean?"

Annie's heart pounded hard in her chest. "It didn't mean you could give me your baby to love and care for, and then on a whim come marching back and snatch her away."

"This is no whim, Annie." Cath's eyes widened with unshed tears. "I fought this. I wish you could hear all the arguments I've had with myself. But I can't fight anymore. I need my child. I'll never be whole without her. I need Jenny!"

Annie brushed away her own tears. "I need her too! She means everything to—" Annie stopped. She heard the front door open and close."

"We'll talk later," said Cath. "Just think about what I said."

"I won't think about anything else."

Annie looked around just as Knowl and Alice Marie came strolling down the hall together, laughing merrily. They stopped when they saw Cath and Annie.

There was an awkward silence, then Alice Marie said in her bubbliest voice, "Knowl was just telling me about the swell dinner you had today. I hope there are left-overs. I worked up a big appetite singing to all our boys in uniform." She sashayed across the room and sat down in the Queen Anne chair opposite Cath's, crossing her legs so that her knees showed. She was wearing a tight-fitting black dress, stacked heels, and a winsome little hat cocked just so on her stylish blond curls. Her brows were heavily drawn and her lips a deep matte red. And Annie noticed that Knowl hadn't taken his eyes off her since they entered the room.

"So you had a good weekend?" Annie asked politely.

"The best. Except for dodging Aunt Martha's cats. I wish I could sing all the time and get paid for it. It sure beats playing Rosie the Riveter."

"How was Mama?"

"Doing remarkably well. You know Mama. She thrives on taking care of people. She's got Aunt Martha taking walks in the sunshine, and going to Saturday night band concerts in the park and Sunday morning services at the Methodist Church. She's even got me going. And she's actually nursed a few of Aunt Martha's sickly cats back to health."

"That's our Mama!" said Annie, forcing a smile.

She endured a few more minutes of meaningless chitchat before announcing that she was going to bed.

Knowl looked quizzically at her. "Are you feeling okay?"

"I—I have a little headache," she replied shakily.

The headache lasted for two weeks. All the fears and misgivings that had assailed Annie in the past surged back with debilitating force. She couldn't sleep. She couldn't eat. She couldn't think straight. Constantly echoing through her mind were Cath's ominous words: I want Jenny. I need my child. Don't make me pay for my mistake for the rest of my life.

No matter what Annie did, she could still hear Cath's voice entreating her to relinquish her child. Long after Knowl went to bed each night, Annie sat in the maple rocker by the window and stared out bleakly at the pale, distant stars. What am I going to do? she wondered. How can I possibly survive without Jenny?

She couldn't tell Knowl what had happened. It would devastate him. So she kept her conversation with Cath to herself, valiantly but unsuccessfully striving to push it out of her mind. One evening, when the weight of Cath's demand became too oppressive, Annie ventured to ask Knowl, "What would you do if your sister decided she wanted Jenny back?"

Knowl removed his glasses and rubbed the bridge of his nose. "I don't know. I suppose I'd try my best to talk her out of it."

"And if that didn't work?"

"Then I guess I'd have no choice."

"You'd let her have Jenny?"

"We have no contract, Annie, no adoption papers, nothing in writing. Cath is legally Jenny's mother."

"We should have made it legal. Why didn't we make her sign something? Why did we just accept her word?"

"Because she's my sister and your best friend." Knowl drew Annie to him. "Has Cath said something? Is that what this is about?"

Annie buried her face against Knowl's chest. "Nothing you need to worry about, darling."

He held her at arms' length and studied her face. "But something's clearly wrong, Annie. What is it? Something besides Cath?"

Annie looked away. "You'll think me silly."

"No, tell me."

She met his gaze and said entreatingly, "I—I wish it could be just the three of us in this house—you and Jenny and me. Sometimes I feel—I feel like an outsider—as if I didn't belong, as if this weren't even my home—"

"I thought you got over that feeling long ago. My mother gets along better with you than with anyone else in this house."

"It's not your mother—"

A knowing expression crossed Knowl's face. "Is it Alice Marie? You're not still jealous of your sister, are you?"

Annie lowered her gaze. "I feel foolish, but I can't help it, Knowl."

He pulled her back against him. "It's you I love, Annie."

"But do you ever regret losing her?"

"I didn't lose anything. I gained everything. Do you want me to tell her to move out, Annie? I will, if that will give you some peace."

"Where would she go?"

"Chicago maybe? She could go live with your mother."

Annie chuckled in spite of herself. She could just imagine finicky, persnickety Alice Marie living with Aunt Martha's cats full time. "It wouldn't work, Knowl. Alice Marie can hardly tolerate Aunt Martha's cats on the weekends."

"Then what do you suggest?"

"I don't know. Apartments are hard to find these days."

"And this house is so big, it seems a shame to have the rooms sitting vacant when someone needs a place to stay. Especially family."

Annie searched his eyes. "You want her to stay, don't you?"

Knowl smiled. "I've told you before, Annie. I care about your sister. I enjoy her company. We've all managed to get along under one roof so far. I see no reason for her to move."

Annie pulled away and walked over to the window. The venetian blind was closed, blocking out the evening sky. "Forget I mentioned it, Knowl."

In the middle of the night, Annie awoke from a troubled sleep. She reached over instinctively for Knowl and felt the reassuring rise and fall of his chest as he slumbered. She got out of bed and padded quietly down the hall to Jenny's room. She gazed at her sleeping child as the moonlight cast a starry glow over her countenance. "Angel baby," Annie whispered. "I'll always love you. You'll always be my sweet princess."

Like a sudden rush of wind, apprehension chilled her. Why is it I always seem to be fighting a war only I know is in progress? Am I delusional? Paranoid? Oh, God, help me! I don't know how to help myself!

As the blistering days of summer dwindled away—as the Allies made their triumphal entry into Rome and landed on the beaches of Normandy to begin D-Day, thus liberating western Europe; and as the Allies invaded Southern France and liberated Paris—Annie pondered her own liberation. How could she escape the tightening chains of her spiraling fears and anxieties?

She sensed that Cath was preparing to make a move. She had grown increasingly distant over the summer, emotionally remote and given to long silences, so that Annie could only guess what she was thinking or feeling. The old lighthearted Cath was evident only when she played with Jenny, but even then, Annie sensed a guardedness, even a possessiveness in her behavior, as if she expected Annie to come at any moment and snatch Jenny away from her. Annie wanted to, in fact, but she stoically refrained from interrupting their playtime.

Then, on the first Sunday evening in September, what Annie had dreaded for so long, became reality. While Knowl was at the depot picking up Alice Marie from her usual Chicago weekend, Cath called Annie into her room. Frank Sinatra was singing "I'll Never Smile Again" on the radio. From the open suitcases on the bed, Annie could see that Cath was packing. "Are you going to New York?" Annie asked faintly, hardly daring to ask.

Cath faced her squarely. "Yes, Annie. I'm doing what I should have done months ago."

"No one says you have to leave. This was your house long before it was mine."

"I'm well aware of that," said Cath. "That's not what I wanted to tell you."

"What then?"

Cath went over to the radio and turned it off. Her voice wavered slightly as she said, "I talked with a lawyer, Annie."

"A lawyer? Why?"

Cath pushed her hair back behind her ear. "I wanted to find out what rights I had—whether Jenny was still mine or not."

Annie gripped the oak bedpost. "And?"

"And my attorney says she's as much mine as the day I bore her. I never signed her away, Annie. You know that." Cath's expression remained firm, but her eyes glistened with tears. "I have a right to take my baby, and that's what I'm going to do. I'm taking her with me to New York and starting a new life with Jeffrey. This is my chance to be happy."

Tears coursed down Annie's cheeks. "Can't you just stay here? Can't we keep sharing Jenny like we've been doing?"

Cath's voice broke. "No, Annie, we can't. We've tried it, and it doesn't work. We both want her. We can't both be mama to her!"

Annie sobbed, "I can't let you do this, Cath."

Cath was weeping now too. "You can't stop me, Annie. You can fight me in court, but you know I'll win. We don't want to put Jenny through that."

Annie sank down weakly on the bed. "Have you told Knowl?"

"No. But I will. Tonight. I'm hoping you'll help me pack up Jenny's things so we can catch the train tomorrow." She paused, then said, "Or, if you don't want me taking Jenny's belongings, I can buy her new clothes and toys in New York."

"No, you can take them," Annie said dazedly. "She'd be lost without her favorite teddy bear and blankets."

Cath sat down on the bed beside Annie. She reached out as if to offer an embrace, then apparently thought better of the idea and dropped her hands into her lap. "I'm sorry, Annie. I didn't mean to hurt you. I've always loved you as my closest friend. But no one told me how much a mother loves her baby. No one told me about the connection you feel that never breaks. My mama wasn't like that, so I didn't know how it would be. If I had known, I'd never have let Jenny go."

Annie pulled herself up off the bed and shuffled to the door. "Knowl should be home any minute now. I'd better go."

She left Cath's room and walked down the hall to her own room. She had to compose herself before she went downstairs and faced Knowl. For his sake, she had to be strong. Even if everything was shriveling and dying inside her, she couldn't let him see her collapse. Somehow, they would find solace in each other. Together, with God's help, they would survive.

Twilight was already casting long shadows across the walls and, outside her window, the first stars were studding the sky with magical pinpoints of light. Annie went to the window and looked out. Her gaze traveled across the expansive garden, so much like Mama's garden on Honeysuckle Lane, but not as nice. Mama had a green thumb like no one else. Still, the Herrick garden had its own lovely flowers and shrubs.

Suddenly Annie spotted someone on the garden walk—two people. Knowl and Alice Marie. They must have just arrived home from the depot and were taking a detour through the garden. Annie watched with mounting curiosity as Alice Marie clasped Knowl's hand and pulled him toward a rose bush, like one child beckoning another to play. Her beautiful face bright with laughter, she plucked a pink rosebud and fastened it in his lapel. He laughed and stepped back, turning toward the house. But she caught his hand and stopped him.

What happened next shook Annie with waves of horror and disbelief. Alice Marie went into Knowl's arms and held him fast and lifted her lips to his and kissed him ardently. Their embrace kindled memories in Annie like heat lightning—of another kiss in another garden a lifetime ago, when she was only twelve and watched from Papa Reed's window.

Annie turned away sharply and allowed herself to sink down on the hard oak floor. She curled herself into a ball and rocked back and forth, her chest heaving with soundless screams.

CHAPTER TWENTY

The remaining hours of that first Sunday evening in September, 1944, were a blur for Annie. Somehow, her body took over and compelled her to get up, dry her eyes, powder her nose, straighten her dress, and go downstairs. In a bizarre, unexpected way, she was able to shut down her emotions and move and react reflexively. Annie herself was locked away in a dark corner of her consciousness, still coiled in a fetal scream. But the Annie she presented to Cath and Knowl and Alice Marie was quite composed, if a bit subdued.

Knowl and Alice Marie had already entered the house and were talking with Cath in the parlor. Annie greeted them, careful to smile and not quite meet their gaze. At a moment like this, she could not bear to look deeply into Knowl's eyes, so she turned her attention to the rosebud still in his buttonhole. "How pretty," she said, as lightly as she was able. "Where did this come from?"

"The garden," said Knowl, with just the hint of discomfiture. "Alice Marie seemed to think I needed a flower in my lapel."

"Distinguished men always wear a flower in their lapel," Alice Marie insisted, lifting her hand with a little flourish of the wrist.

Annie sat down in an upholstered chair that had graced Mama's parlor before she sold the house. It felt comfortable and inviting. Annie hadn't realized how weak she felt, how unsteady her ankles were. She had to see this ordeal through as quickly as possible. She turned to Knowl and said, "Your sister has something to tell you. It's about Jenny."

Cath looked wide-eyed at Annie, obviously taken aback that she had plunged so directly into this most difficult topic.

"Tell him, Cath," Annie prompted.

Briefly, Cath told Knowl and Alice Marie what she had told Annie earlier. She finished with, "I've already talked this over with Annie, and she's agreed that I can take Jenny with me to New York. We'll be leaving tomorrow."

Alice Marie spoke up first, her voice honed razor-sharp with indignation. "How can you do that to your brother and my sister, Cath? Look at all they've done for you! This is a fine way to repay them after they've raised your child as their own! What a selfish—"

Cath shot back with, "Keep out of it, Alice Marie. You're the last person on earth to talk about selfishness!"

"Let's keep things civil, okay?" said Knowl. He stood up, walked over to the fireplace, and ran his fingers through his honey-brown hair. He removed his glasses and set them on the mantle. "Can't we talk this over, Cath? We all love Jenny. Surely there's some way we can all share in her life, like we've done this past year."

Cath shook her head. "I've put my life on hold long enough. I want a marriage and home like you and Annie have. I want the same kind of happiness you two have found."

At the idea of her happy marriage, Annie flinched visibly and steeled her jaw to keep her lower lip from trembling. "So you see, Knowl, it's settled." Her voice came out small and breathy. "Cath has made it clear that there's no way we can fight this. For Jenny's sake, we've got to make the transition as smooth as possible."

Knowl stared hard at her. "Look at me, Annie. Have you been imbibing some of my mother's wine? You're the last person I expected to give up where Jenny's concerned."

Tears started, but Annie cut them off with a silent, brutal reminder of what she had just seen in the garden. "Maybe it's best for Jenny to be raised by her real mother, Knowl. There's no earthly love stronger than a mother's love."

"I don't believe what I'm hearing, Annie." Knowl doubled his fist and pummeled his palm in frustration. "Together we might have been able to change Cath's mind. I could still check with our attorney about our rights. But if you've already given up—"

Annie stood up and walked toward the stairs, her shoulders straight. "Yes, it's too late. I've given up, Knowl. I'm going to go pack Jenny's things." She turned to Cath and said, "I want to drive you to the depot tomorrow."

"You hardly ever drive, Annie," Knowl protested. "I'll take off work and drive Cath and Jenny to the train."

"No," Annie said sharply. "I want to do this myself, Knowl. I have to do this."

"Then I'll go with you. You can't go through this alone."

"No, Knowl, I want to do it alone. You need to be at the paper. Say your good-byes to Jenny in the morning before you leave." Before he could argue further with her, Annie turned on her heel and strode out of the room. She hurried up the stairs before anyone could guess the suffocating grief constricting her heart. She spent the night packing Jenny's belongings, and after Knowl was asleep, she packed her own things, placing her Bible, some money Mama had given her, and her manuscript, Pacific Dawn, in among her clothes. She had no idea where she was going or what she would do, but she knew she could not spend another night in this house.

When she had finished packing, Annie sat in the rocker by the window and stared numbly into the darkness. A cool breeze wafted against the filigrees of lace curtain, and Annie shivered involuntarily. She hugged her trembling body and continued rocking. She could not bear the thought of climbing into bed beside Knowl and feeling his body next to hers. That was a privilege she would never allow herself again.

Hours later, as the first rays of dawn sent faint shafts of light through the window,

Annie stirred from her rocker and carried her suitcases down to Knowl's automobile and placed them in the trunk. She would have Knowl take Jenny's things downstairs and load them in the back seat before he left for work.

That afternoon, Cath and Annie said little during the drive to the depot. It was as if they had exhausted all their fond words of friendship and all their years of close camaraderie. Now they were empty. There was nothing left, except two silent women who were less than strangers.

Jenny alone, sitting between them in her pink jumper and lacy white blouse, carried on a steady stream of chatter, pretending to feed a saltine to her floppy brown teddy bear. "Teddy go bye-bye," she chirped. "Teddy go bye-bye!"

Jenny was still prattling on when they arrived at the depot twenty minutes later. "Twain! Twain!" she squealed as they entered the crowded station and headed for the ticket counter. She toddled between them, clutching Cath's hand and Annie's.

"We're riding a train all the way to New York City," Cath told Jenny shortly, as they settled down on a bench to wait for the conductor's call.

Jenny looked questioningly at Annie. "Mama go bye-bye?"

"No," Annie said quickly, gathering Jenny into her arms. She felt a physical ache travel through her, as if her body were already experiencing the withdrawals of separation. She gazed intently at Jenny, trying to memorize every dimple, every curve and curl. She touched the velvet ribbons in Jenny's hair and wound a tangerine ringlet around her finger.

"Mama can't come with you," she said haltingly, touching the tip of Jenny's button nose. "But I'll think of you every day, and Jesus will take care of you." She choked on a sob. "His angels will watch you wherever you go, Jenny, and they'll be watching me too. So whenever you want to talk to me, just whisper the words, and angels will bring me your words on the wind. And when you hear the wind, that'll be Mommy whispering to you."

Jenny held her stuffed bear up for Annie to kiss. "Teddy loves Mommy," she chortled.

Suddenly, over a crackling loud speaker, a deep, echoing voice called, "All abo-oard for Toledo, Cleveland, and New York City!"

Cath jumped up and reached for Jenny's hand. She looked entreatingly at Annie, her green eyes glistening. "I'm sorry, Annie. Please forgive me!"

Don't do this, Cath! Annie wanted to scream. Don't take my baby away! Dear God, how can I be letting this happen?

Somehow, Annie held her tongue, bent down, clasped Jenny in her arms, and buried her face in her soft curls. She felt her tears spill out on Jenny's head; she inhaled Jenny's sweet baby scent and pressed her wet cheek against Jenny's round one, until the child wriggled out of her grasp and stared up at her. "Why Mama cry?" The cherub-faced toddler reached out and touched the wetness with her chubby fingers. Her rosebud lips puckered. "Mama don't cry!"

"I won't, Jenny, if you promise not to cry either!" But in my heart of hearts, I'll be crying for the rest of my life!

Annie stepped back as Cath caught the child up in her arms and hoisted her onto one hip. She slung her travel bag over her shoulder and strode with Jenny down the platform toward the train, her heels clacking a rhythmic rat-a-tat on the planked wood floor. Cath offered a faltering wave before the two disappeared among clusters of servicemen and civilians boarding the train. Annie caught another glimpse of them as Cath stepped with Jenny into the immense passenger car. Annie swallowed her sobs and waved frantically. "Bye, Jenny! Bye, my sweet baby!"

She was still waving as the leviathan train gained steam and moved down the tracks, roaring a deep, reverberating chuga-chuga as it pulled away from the station. Diesel fumes replaced the baby smell in Annie's nostrils. The horn blasted, erasing the echo of Jenny's lyrical voice.

When the train was out of sight, Annie walked back into the station and approached a ticket counter. Her dreadful ache of loss was already hardening into a heavy weight in her chest; it was as if her emotional pain demanded physical expression. She looked at the gray-haired clerk and said, "I'd like to buy a ticket."

"Where you goin', miss?"

Annie hesitated, her mind fighting the numbing chaos of shock. "I—I don't know."

The man's bushy brows crouched over his beady eyes. "I can't sell you a ticket unless you know where you're going."

"Chicago," she said, breaking through her confusion. "The next train leaving." Of course. Mama was in Chicago.

Before boarding the train, Annie telephoned home and told Betty Herrick she would be going to Chicago to visit her mother. "Knowl will have to come pick up the car at the depot. Tell him I'm sorry to leave like this, but I—I have to get away for a few days."

The train west was as packed as the train east had been. Mainly servicemen, but a lot of ordinary folk were traveling too. Annie had read something about train stations becoming the hub of activity for Americans these days. No wonder. With gas rationing, one could travel only so far in an automobile.

Annie found a seat by the window at the back of the car beside two sailors who were snoozing loudly. She squeezed by them and sat down, taking care not to disturb their slumber. Then, as the train heaved forward and rumbled down the tracks, she sank back in her seat and allowed her body to sway with the rhythmic, jostling motion.

Hours later, when she disembarked in Chicago, she stared up in amazement at the huge, sprawling station, so different from the homey small town depots made of rustic brick or stone. Clutching her valises in sweaty palms and feeling faint-hearted and dazed—a tiny pebble carried by the tide in a vast ocean, she mused—Annie let herself be carried along with the masses of travelers streaming into the station.

Not until she sat down on a crowded bench and debated how to get to Aunt Martha's, did she realize she couldn't visit her mother after all. It would mean telling Mama all the painful things that had happened. It would break Mama's heart to know she had lost Jenny and that Knowl had betrayed her with Alice Marie. Mama had endured enough suffering these past few years. No matter how bad things might be, Annie vowed not to contribute to her mother's anguish.

Instead, Annie took a taxi to a modest hotel near the station and rented a room for the night—a room that reminded her of the New York City brownstone where she and Cath had stayed while visiting the World's Fair. She winced, recalling those carefree, idealistic days. Neither of them could have guessed the heartaches that awaited them, nor the agonizing choices that would one day splinter their friendship.

Annie grabbed a quick bowl of soup in the drab hotel dining room; then, fighting waves of anxiety, she telephoned home, yearning to hear Knowl's voice in spite of everything. But Alice Marie answered and told her Knowl wasn't there.

"Please tell him I won't be at Aunt Martha's after all," she said, recoiling at the idea of even carrying on a conversation with her conniving sister. "I'm not sure what I'm going to do, but I don't want him calling Mama and worrying her."

"You sound like you don't plan on coming home right away," said Alice Marie knowingly.

"I don't know, yet. I can't explain it, but I've got to have some time to myself. I'll be at this number for a few days. If Knowl wants to talk to me, tell him to call me here."

"You're wise to go away for awhile," said Alice Marie in a voice layered with meaning. "I think it's best for everyone. Knowl wouldn't admit it, but I think you and I know it's true."

"We'll see," said Annie coolly. "Be sure and give him my message." She hung up feeling worse than ever, as if someone had replaced her heart with a cold, hard stone. Was it possible Knowl actually wanted her to leave so he could be with Alice Marie?

Annie spent the next three days in her cramped, airless hotel room, waiting for Knowl's call. It never came. Finally, with tears cascading down her cheeks, she removed her wedding ring and slipped it into her pocketbook. The gold band was too painful a reminder of all she had lost. She spent the hours that followed in a dark reverie of the soul, pining for Jenny, her spirits languishing as she imagined Knowl and Alice Marie rekindling a smoldering romance.

Her room's one redeeming feature was an old Philco radio, which Annie played day and night, listening to the amorous strains of Stan Kenton, Johnny Mercer, Perry Como, and Vaughn Monroe. She wept as Doris Day, accompanied by Les Brown's band, sang "Sentimental Journey." Annie was on her own "sentimental journey," but she had no idea where it would take her.

On the fourth day, Annie decided she could no longer remain in limbo. She would either have to go home or move on. But where? That evening, as she thumbed listlessly through her Bible, an envelope fell out on the floor. She picked it up and gazed at the return address. Los Angeles. It was from Robert Wayne, the man who had been wounded at Pearl Harbor.

Suddenly, Annie felt an inexorable need to talk with this man who had been there when her brother had died. But how could she possibly communicate with him? He was a stranger living across the continent. She couldn't just get on a train and go to California. Or could she?

The idea tantalized her. Why not go to California? If she were ever to do something bold and unthinkable, this was the time. Who could stop her? This man—Robert Wayne—had even offered to help her with her book. He was willing to read and critique it. When would she ever have another chance like this?

For the first time in days, Annie felt hope blossom inside her. Perhaps life was still worth living; perhaps she still had a future even without her beloved Jenny and Knowl.

What happened in the days that followed seemed more like a dream than reality. Out of desperation or blind optimism, Annie followed her heart, purchased a one-way ticket to Los Angeles, using the name of a character from her novel (on a lark, just to be daring), and found herself ensconced on a cushioned seat in a train car heading for sunny California.

Day faded into night and night into day as the monolithic engine surged onward through country and towns, over mountains and deserts, across trestles and bridges. Crossing the Mississippi River to Kansas City and following the route of the Santa Fe Trail, the Super Chief wended its way through midwestern farmlands and headed toward open plains. It crossed Colorado's Pike's Peak, and sped through Albuquerque, Flagstaff, and Needles, traveling from high mountain plains to California desert. Between catnaps, and for hours at a time, Annie sat staring out the window at passing scenes—bustling cities made of concrete and steel and the back sides of towns with their tenements and trash, crumbling buildings and coal-blackened shantytowns. She held her breath at the beauty of rugged, majestic mountains, the pure, jaded color of lush green forests, and the steepness of sheer, plunging cliffs.

On the third day, the train chugged into Los Angeles and wheezed to a stop at Union Station—grander than any building Annie had ever seen, with its high beamed ceilings, rich mahogany woodwork, and gargantuan rooms with gleaming marble floors. It possessed the reverential quality of a cathedral, as if significant things had happened there or would happen in years to come.

With luggage in hand, Annie walked outside Union Station into bright California sunlight. She set down her baggage and looked around. This certainly wasn't Indiana; rather, it seemed like an exotic island paradise, its landscape dotted with spiky, towering palm trees with bushy crowns. Mountains rose up in a purple haze on the distant skyline, and the warmth of the sun caressed her like an embrace.

Annie hailed a taxi and showed the driver Robert Wayne's address on the envelope. Within twenty minutes he pulled up in front of a large, anonymous-looking adobe building in what appeared to be an older, dilapidated section of Los Angeles. A sign in big black letters over the door read, SALVATION ARMY RESCUE MISSION AND SEC-OND-HAND STORE. Annie stared at the humble stucco exterior and at a red neon sign in the window, flashing JESUS SAVES. "There must be some mistake, driver," she said quickly, "I'm looking for someone's residence, not a rescue mission."

"This is the address you gave me," said the driver, his voice a gravelly monotone. "Take it or leave it."

"I—I'll take it," she replied, handing him his fare.

What am I doing here? Annie wondered as she stepped out onto the curb, her pulse quickening with dread. I've come on a wild goose chase, and now I have nowhere to go!

The cabby set her luggage on the sidewalk, returned to his taxi, and drove off, leaving her standing alone on an unfamiliar street in a vast, strange city across the world from Willowbrook. With mounting trepidation, Annie approached the mission, passing two old men in grimy work clothes sweeping the sidewalk and clipping a hedge. One glanced up and silently eyed her attire. She felt out of place in her slim black suit and white frilly blouse with its immense bow. Ignoring his gaze, she opened the door and strode inside, purposefully crossing the room to a desk where a young Negro woman sat. The woman looked up and smiled. "Hello. I'm Francenna. May I help you?"

"I'm not sure," said Annie, tentatively holding out her letter. "I'm looking for someone. He wrote and gave me this return address. I thought it was a residence. I'm sure there must be some mistake."

The woman looked at the address and grinned broadly. "Oh, that's correct, all right. You received a letter from Robert." She saw Annie's puzzlement and added, "Robert Wayne. He sent you the letter, right?"

Annie caught her breath. "Yes, he did. You mean, he lives here—at this mission?"

"He sure does. A real fine man. He's over in the soup kitchen right now. You want me to go call him for you?"

Annie gazed around at the modest surroundings—plain walls, worn, overstuffed furniture, a threadbare carpet. She looked back at the girl. "Yes, please call him for me."

Annie sat down in a nearby chair and waited, thrumming her fingers nervously on her pocketbook. Finally, a tall lumberjack of a man emerged from a side door and took long strides toward her, moving with just the hint of a limp. He had a sturdy, rough-hewn face and dark curly hair that tumbled over his wide forehead in unruly locks. Reaching her, he held out his hand and met her gaze with riveting, luminous blue eyes. "I hear you're looking for me, miss?"

"Yes, I am—if you're Robert Wayne."

His wide, generous mouth spread into an easy grin. "I was, last time I checked. How can I help you?"

Annie felt suddenly flustered. "I—I'm Annie Reed. You wrote me once. It's been a long time. You probably don't even remember." She held out his letter and he took it in his large, graceful hands and scanned it quickly.

"Yes, I remember writing you. Never heard back, as I recall."

Her face reddened. "I wanted to write, but I was afraid to. I was afraid you wouldn't like my book."

"Is that why you've come all the way from—" He paused and look at her address on the envelope. "—All the way from Willowbrook, Indiana? Goodness, Miss Reed, you're a long way from home!"

"I know. It's a long story. I feel rather foolish now for even tracking you down."

He handed her back her letter. "It's no problem. If you brought your manuscript, I'd still be glad to take a look at it."

"I did, but—" She looked down helplessly at her suitcases.

"Does that luggage mean you haven't found a place to stay yet?" he asked.

"I'm afraid so. I just came from the train station, and I—I don't know any hotels in the area."

"You've come for a little vacation, I suspect?"

"Not exactly. It's a long story, and—"

"And you look exhausted. And hungry. I bet you haven't had any lunch."

"I haven't. And you're right. I'm famished."

"The grub here isn't fancy, but it's good. I should know. I help cook it." He beckoned her to follow him and she fell into step beside him. He pointed toward several rooms, explaining, "Our offices are down that hall; sleeping accommodations for men are to your left; women are in the next building. We have a few rooms for families, but never enough. And the chapel's just off the courtyard. I'll give you the grand tour later, if you're interested."

"Yes, I am," said Annie, fascinated by the man's enthusiasm.

He showed her to a table in a large dining room peopled by an assortment of humanity—scores of military men, a few families with small children, a handful of women with babies, and several elderly men and women. "Sit down, and I'll bring you a plate from the kitchen. No sense standing in line when you're weary."

He was back minutes later with a plate for each of them. Then he left again and was back with coffee. He sat down, bowed his head, and said grace. Then he looked up and smiled. "Hope you like meatloaf and scalloped potatoes, Miss Reed. Or is it Mrs?"

"It's just plain Annie, and yes, I do like meatloaf."

"All right, just plain Annie, tell me why you've come all the way from Indiana just to see me."

TWENTY-ONE

"I was hoping you'd help me with my book," Annie told Robert Wayne over lunch in the mission dining room. "Your publisher suggested I contact you. My novel needs work, and because you were at Pearl Harbor, I thought—" Her words faltered.

Robert nodded. "You wanted the realism only someone who had been there could give."

"Something like that. Will you help me?"

"Yes, I said I would in my letter. If my fellow editors at Sanders and Browne think you have promise, who am I to deny you the help you need?" He spooned up a mouthful of potatoes. "But, tell me, what are your plans? How do you intend to live while you're here? Do you need a job?"

"I haven't thought that far ahead," Annie admitted sheepishly. "I have enough money to last me a couple of weeks, through September perhaps, but yes, after that, I suppose I will need some kind of work if I'm to stay in Los Angeles."

He eyed her with a wry sort of merriment. "I have an idea. Please don't think I'm overstepping my bounds, but suppose I talk with Reverend Briggs about you. There's always something around here to do—"

"I don't understand. Who is this—?"

"I'm sorry. I'm running ahead, as usual. Marshall Briggs is director of the mission. You'll like him. An unpretentious, salt of the earth type. Like me. He's run the mission for ten years, and I consider him my closest friend."

Annie studied Robert Wayne's ruggedly handsome features. "Somehow I thought perhaps you ran the mission. You seem to know your way around so well."

He flashed his wide, boyish grin. "I know my way around here all right, but not because I'm the preacher. Sure, I do speak from time to time, but no heavy theology. Just practical, no nonsense stuff to help these guys get on with their lives." He paused. "Most of the guys we see here these days are just like I was when I came here."

"And how was that?" asked Annie, sipping her coffee.

"I'll tell you all about it sometime—when you're ready to stop being 'just plain Annie' and willing to talk about what brought you here."

"I told you. My brother. He died at Pearl Harbor."

"I know. But there's more. I can see it in your eyes. I know a person in pain when I see one."

Annie looked down at her coffee cup. "They say it takes one to know one."

"And they're right, Miss Reed… Annie." He finished his coffee and sat back in his chair. "If you're interested, I'll talk to Marshall about you working here for your room and board. How does that sound?"

She smiled faintly. "It sounds a little overwhelming. And quite exciting."

Robert Wayne was true to his word. He introduced Annie to Reverend Briggs, who readily accepted his friend's recommendation. "If you say she's a good worker, Rob, that's all I've got to hear," he declared in a deep, booming voice. "You have Francenna show her to her room." He turned back to Annie. "We'll want you to pitch in wherever we need you. Sometimes that'll be the soup kitchen. You do cook, don't you?"

Annie nodded uncertainly. She had cooked for a handful of people, but not for hundreds!

"We may also need you to clerk in the second-hand store from time to time. That's how the mission earns money for food. You have had experience in retail sales, haven't you?"

The words caught in Annie's throat. "Not exactly, but I—I learn fast."

If Annie had known what she was getting into when she agreed to work at the mission, she might have fled back to Union Station for a return ticket to Willowbrook. In the weeks that followed her first meeting with Robert Wayne, she found herself immersed in scullery duties and assigned to a room no larger than the sewing room back home. However, after working in the stifling soup kitchen from morning until night, peeling potatoes, preparing hot meals, and washing dishes until midnight, Annie soon considered the humble cubicle her special haven.

When Robert suggested that perhaps people were working her too hard, Annie protested and assured him she was doing fine. Privately, she admitted that the hard physical labor was a godsend, for it kept her mind off Knowl and Jenny.

As the weeks of autumn passed, Annie caught glimpses into the character of this unusual man, Robert Wayne. He said little about himself, but he constantly showed his kindness and generous spirit in small deeds. When tired mothers needed help with their children, Robert was there, playing with the youngsters; when soldiers or sailors returning from battle needed a friendly ear, Robert was there, listening to their agonizing tales; when the kitchen was short of help, Robert donned a chef's hat and apron, rolled up his sleeves, and tackled his duties with energy and good humor. In his "spare" time, he was reading Annie's novel, a chapter here, a chapter there. Annie insisted there was no hurry. They could tackle the project anytime. She herself was too busy—and, yes, terrified—to face the prospect of a rewrite.

In fact, Annie had a hard time keeping up with Robert Wayne on any level. One moment he was scrubbing pots and pans in the hot, noisy kitchen; next, he was in the pulpit in the chapel, an imposing, animated figure standing between the Christian flag and the American flag, declaring how much God loved every man, woman, and child in that humble sanctuary. "You were created with such a need to worship," he declared one November evening, "that if you don't worship God, you will worship something else!" He looked from face to face. "What are you worshipping tonight?"

Annie felt a twinge of conscience. How long had it been since God was more than a nodding acquaintance? How could she begin to draw close to Him again? It seemed that all of her feelings—love, affection, joy, and trust—had been locked away from her grasp, and she had no idea how to free them again.

Annie's perplexity lingered as autumn eased seamlessly into winter. One evening, two days before Christmas, as she helped Robert serve hot soup in the mission kitchen, he said to her, "How long has it been since you've had a night out on the town?"

She looked up in surprise and laughed. "A night out? I don't suppose I've had one since I came to Los Angeles. You know that, Robert. I started working here the day I arrived, and there hasn't been time since for frivolous jaunts."

"That's a mistake we've got to remedy immediately."

"What do you mean?"

He wiped his hands on a towel and reached for her hand. "You've worked tirelessly for months without complaint, and I think you deserve an evening of fun and relaxation. And I'd like to be your escort, if you'll allow me."

Annie's face grew warm. "Why, that would be nice, Robert."

"Swell. Go change into something party-like, and I'll see if I can borrow Marshall's car for the evening."

Annie went quickly to her little room in the women's dormitory and changed into a soft Angora sweater and a pencil-slim damask skirt. The outfit wasn't a fancy evening dress, but it made her feel feminine. She had grown so accustomed to wearing her thick, curly hair pulled back or up in a bun, but now she removed the pins and brushed it down in long, cascading waves. She even dabbed on a hint of rouge and eye color and lined her lips in red. The results amazed her. It had been months since she had cared about her looks; it surprised her to realize how pretty she could be with just a little effort.

Within the hour Annie was settled in Marshall's gleaming red DeSoto beside Robert Wayne, looking heroic in his naval uniform. "You look very gallant and courageous," she said approvingly.

"And you look quite beautiful," he told Annie as he pulled out onto the street and merged with early evening traffic.

"Where are we going?" she asked, nervously fingering her handbag. She felt as excited as a school girl on her first date.

"You'll see, Annie. All I'll tell you is that it's near Hollywood and Vine."

Annie's heart quickened. "I've wanted to see Hollywood since I arrived in Los Angeles."

"It's not just Hollywood," said Robert. "You're going to see the USO's Hollywood Canteen."

"Oh, I've heard of it," said Annie. "It's where the servicemen can go and be entertained by actual movie stars."

"Right. The place itself is nondescript. It was once an old stable that was turned into a theater. Right after the war started, a bunch of studio musicians wanted to boost the spirit of our troops, so somehow they got the support of forty-two unions and transformed this old stable-theater into the most jumping night spot in town. They even got Bette Davis to help run the thing. You can't beat Bette Davis."

Annie nodded. "You're right. I adore Bette Davis. But isn't the canteen just for servicemen?"

He winked. "What do I look like? Don't worry, I've got my connections. I'll get us in." He pulled over to the curb and turned off the ignition. "See that line of servicemen? They're waiting to get into the canteen a block from here."

"You mean we're going to stand in that line?"

"You got anything better to do tonight?"

She smiled. "Not a thing."

They waited in line nearly an hour before they reached the entrance of the makeshift club. Robert was right. He managed to get them inside. While the air outside the canteen was cool and brisk, the atmosphere inside was warm and close, bristling with energy and excitement. The band was playing a lilting rendition of "Don't Sit Under the Apple Tree." The plaster walls were adorned with Christmas garlands and wreaths, and a decorated tree held a prominent place on stage. Cozy tables and chairs lined the walls, pushed together almost too close for comfort.

There was standing room only as pretty hostesses greeted the servicemen. Soldiers and sailors crowded onto the dance floor with their glamorous partners, or stood in line for refreshments at the tall pine counter, or clustered around the stage waiting for the next show.

Robert looked at Annie. "I think they assumed you were just another hostess coming to entertain the troops. By the way, I should warn you I'm not much for dancing. Hope you don't mind."

She laughed. "If you're talking about jitterbugging, that's not my style either."

"Actually, I meant slow dancing. Looks like they've got one of the best jazz bands in the country here tonight. Harry James' orchestra. But I still have two left feet."

"Then let's just sit down and enjoy the entertainment."

They found a table and Annie sat down while Robert went for refreshments. He came back with sandwiches and coffee. "You wouldn't believe who served me. I'm sure it was Betty Grable."

Annie replied brightly, "And I could swear I saw Rita Hayworth on the dance floor."

"You probably did. She can really cut a rug." He leaned over close to her ear. "If the noise and the crowd get to be too much, just let me know. We can go somewhere quieter."

Annie looked around as lines of servicemen kept streaming inside. "This reminds me of the crowds at Union Station. How many boys come here?"

"Over two thousand a night. Quite a production, right?"

Annie nodded. "And I'm glad I got to see it first hand."

They stayed another hour, long enough to hear Eddie Cantor's comedy routine and Fred MacMurray's humorous repartee with Dorothy Lamour, followed by a rousing medley of Christmas tunes by Harry James's orchestra.

Later, as they left the canteen, Annie gazed up at the swaths of light cutting across the night sky over the hills of North Hollywood. "I never get used to those searchlights," she mused. "We didn't have them in Indiana."

Robert smiled. "In Indiana you didn't have to worry about Japs dive-bombing you or Nazi subs attacking your shores."

"No, but we weren't far from the Great Lakes and Chicago, and there was some concern there."

"Which is why we all have our air raid wardens faithfully doing their jobs and watching the skies day and night," said Robert. He helped her into the car. "Do you wish to head back to the mission, or would you like to take a drive down by the beach? The Santa Monica pier is delightful in the moonlight."

"That sounds wonderful. I haven't seen the ocean yet." She paused. "But won't you use up Marshall's gas coupons?"

Robert turned onto Santa Monica Boulevard. "Let's live dangerously for one evening, okay, Annie?"

Minutes later, he pulled the DeSoto off the road onto the beach and turned off the engine. "It's a bit chilly, but we could take a walk, if you like."

"All right."

They left the car and began walking along a dark, sodden expanse of beach. Pungent salt spray was heavy in the air; the moisture cooled Annie's skin and left the taste of sea on her lips. The low sound of tide lulled its easy rhythm in her ears—waves washing shore and ebbing back into darkness, only to surge forward again.

"It's a beautiful night," Annie said with a sigh. "So peaceful and serene. It's hard to believe there's a war going on, and so many people fighting and being killed. Why can't it always be calm and lovely like this, the way God intended?"

"Because God allowed man to have his way, and we've all gone our own ways ever since," said Robert, his voice sounding lyrical and faintly philosophical at once. "We never learn, do we, Annie? We keep making the same mistakes again and again, each new generation thinking it can settle the evils of the world once and for all. We thought we had it settled in the Great World War, and now, hardly a generation later, we're in the middle of a second World War. Where does it end? With a third? A fourth? When we totally annihilate one another?"

"When we can't have peace with those we love, how can we have peace with strangers?" mused Annie.

"What a dark thought coming from such a pretty face," said Robert with an edge of whimsy.

"I don't mean to sound so tragic, Robert. It's just that—" Unexpectedly, her platform heels sank into the moist sand. She grabbed Robert's arm in alarm.

"You might want to go barefoot, Annie."

"A good idea!" She carefully removed her shoes and stockings and carried them. "Goodness, the sand is cold," she said, laughing, "but at least I can walk."

Robert removed his shoes and socks and rolled up his pant legs. "Can you imagine walking barefoot on the beach just two days before Christmas?"

They strolled down to the water's edge and gazed out at the ocean glittering with moonlight. "In Indiana it's probably snowing right now," said Annie. "I'd be bundled in a fur coat and putting another log on the fire."

Robert looked over at her. "I'd like to know more about your life in Indiana, Annie. After all these months you're still a stranger to me. We work together, laugh together, but I know nothing about you, except for what I gleaned from your novel."

"I could say the same about you, Robert. You've told me nothing about your life before you came to the mission. I know you were an editor with Sanders and Browne before the war. That means you must have lived in New York."

"Yes, I was born and raised there—"

"Then why didn't you go back to your job after you were wounded at Pearl Harbor? Why, with all your talent, did you come to Los Angeles and accept menial labor in a Gospel mission?"

He grimaced. "I told you once it was a long story."

"I have my own long story, Robert," Annie said softly. "Perhaps it's time we told our stories."

"I'm willing to listen if you are."

She shivered. "Maybe we should talk in the car."

They walked back to the automobile and got in. Through the windshield they could see the ocean, dark and silent, except where moonlight shimmered on the surface, spreading out ripples of incandescence.

"Who goes first?" asked Robert. "I have a feeling this is going to be painful for both of us. Dredging up old memories, probing festering wounds."

Annie met his gaze. "I've tried so hard to put the past behind me, Robert, but hard work and new surroundings don't change anything, do they? I'm still the same person inside."

"Who is that person, Annie? And what has hurt you so badly that you had to run half a continent away to forget?"

Slowly, with halting voice, Annie told Robert about her life in Willowbrook—about Chip and her father dying; her mother selling her beloved home and moving away; Knowl rekindling his love for Alice Marie; and Cath taking back the baby Annie had grown to love as her own. Somehow she kept back her tears as she spoke, but the pain was evident in the throb in her voice.

Robert reached over and took her hand. "No wonder you've kept silent so long. I'm sorry, Annie. You must have felt betrayed by everyone you loved. You didn't deserve that."

He paused for a long moment, then said, "I understand losing the things you love and feeling like you've failed at all the important issues in life. I've never told anyone, other than Marshall, what it's been like for me since Pearl Harbor. I'd like to tell you about it now."

She squeezed his hand. "I'm listening, Robert."

He stretched in his seat and cupped his hands behind his head. "I was a gung-ho officer in the Navy, Annie, ready to win the war bare-handed, with my eyes closed. Then, when I was assigned to Pearl Harbor, I foolishly thought, Wow, if this is war, give me more! We spent our time playing soldier and sailor—drilling, marching, and enjoying the tropical sunshine. We figured the Nazis were a world away in Europe, and the Japs were preoccupied with Asia. We never thought they'd have the gall to strike American troops directly."

"What were you doing that Sunday morning, Robert?"

"December seventh? Strange. I remember it with such mixed metaphors. I was assigned to the battleship Nevada, just off Ford Island. It was a beautiful morning, peaceful and warm, the kind any tourist would love. I got up earlier than a lot of my shipmates who had partied late the night before. I remember I had corned beef hash and eggs for breakfast. Very tasty. On my way back to quarters, I noticed the ship's band on deck preparing to play "The Star Spangled Banner" for morning colors at 0800.

"Around 7:50 a.m., I sat down at my desk to address Christmas cards. I was listening to radio station KGMB play the top ten tunes, when I heard this distant rumble, like thunder. Suddenly, I realized it was the high-pitched sound of airplanes in a dive. I looked out the window and saw two planes going into a dive right before my eyes. At first I thought they must be our own planes taking practice dives, but then I saw the red moons on their wings. The Rising Sun. I couldn't believe it. Torpedo planes were heading for Battleship Row. We didn't have torpedo nets because torpedoes weren't supposed to work in shallow water. But the Japs had figured out a way to do it.

"The West Virginia was hit first, then the Oklahoma. And the California. There was total shock and confusion. The air raid siren sounded; ship horns and bugles were blowing. I heard a terrible explosion. Everything shook. I ran topside. I didn't even have time to grab my life jacket. Everyone was running every which way, screaming, shouting commands, just trying to survive. Incredibly, while torpedoes pelted Battleship Row and bullets whizzed all around us, the band kept right on playing our national anthem."

Robert paused, his voice hoarse with emotion. Annie reached out and touched his face with her fingertips. "You don't have to continue, unless you want to."

He stretched his hands out toward the dashboard and cracked his knuckles. "I've got to get this all out, Annie, from start to finish." His voice grew still more somber. "Next in line to us in the harbor was the USS Arizona. It was attacked first by torpedoes, and then by bombers. At about 8:10, we saw this great billowing smoke fill the sky. A bomb had detonated her forward ammunition magazine. The noise was deafening and the concussion knocked our own crew members off their feet.

"Hundreds of men from the Arizona were thrown into the water, and we could see them swimming and drowning in burning oil, breaking through the slick surface to breathe and then sinking again. We tried our best to rescue as many as we could, but the ship sank like lead."

Wiping tears from her eyes, Annie murmured, "Chip could have been one of those men you tried to rescue."

"Yes, he could have been," said Robert quietly. "It dawned on us that we were the only battleship not put out of commission, so we jumped into action and headed her out to sea. But the Japs spotted us and bombed us. We fired wildly, scared out of our wits, but they got us. Finally, we ran our ship aground so she wouldn't block the harbor. Somehow, in that last barrage of bombs and bullets, I got my leg blown up. I don't remember what happened after that. I woke up in the hospital with doctors debating whether or not to let me keep my leg."

Robert stared absently out the window. "I kept my leg, but I nearly lost my soul. During my months of recuperation, I was filled with anger and bitterness—and guilt. I didn't know why I had survived Pearl Harbor when so many good men died there. I wanted to die too. The girl I had left behind married someone else. I was too burned out emotionally to return to my editorial position at Sanders and Browne."

Annie studied him intently. "What did you do?"

Robert's voice took on a sinister edge. "I got drunk and stayed drunk for six months. I didn't want to think or feel anything. I came to California because that's where I had been stationed. San Diego. But I made my way north and settled here in Los Angeles. One night I stumbled into Marshall Briggs' Salvation Army mission and collapsed. He fed me, gave me a bed, and helped me get my life back on track. It took some doing, but I stopped drinking and started helping out around the mission. It's been my home ever since."

There was silence as Annie digested this new information about Robert. "Are you saying you're a reformed alcoholic?"

He nodded. "I take life one day at a time."

"But you seem so confident and capable. I can't imagine you being helpless, out of control."

Robert chuckled. "It's not me, Annie. It's God. It may sound trite, but He was there when I had nothing else to hold onto. Even in my drunken stupors, I knew I could never measure up to what God expected of me. There was always this huge gap between God and me. Marshall helped me understand that I didn't have to try to bridge that gap myself, because Christ had already done it for me. All I had to do was admit I was a sinner who needed saving. If I knew nothing else at that time, I knew that much. I threw myself on Christ's mercy, Annie. I pleaded for His Spirit to inhabit me and turn my life around. You know the rest. He made me a new man and gave me a new purpose in life."

"I know what Christ can do for a person," Annie agreed. "I must admit, though, that I've allowed that relationship to grow cold recently. I don't feel the closeness anymore. I only remember that I once felt it passionately."

"It's never too late to rekindle the flame, Annie. His Spirit's still there within you, waiting, ready to help. But He won't force you to love Him or serve Him. He respects you enough to let you make your own choices—and your own mistakes."

Annie gazed out the window at the dark sea. "I want to feel that divine passion pulsing in my heart again," she whispered. "I want to break through this terrible numbness I've felt for so long. Help me, Robert, please."

"I'll help, Annie. I'll do what I can. But it's got to start with you."

TWENTY-TWO

The next day, Christmas Eve, Annie tried telephoning Knowl at the Herrick house in Willowbrook. His mother answered, her slurred voice belying her drunken condition.

"Betty, is Knowl there?" Annie asked urgently.

"No, he's gone. Everybody's gone."

"Listen, Betty, this is Annie. I need to know what's happening there. Are Cath and Jenny okay? Is Knowl—is he making a new life with Alice Marie?"

"They're all gone," Betty Herrick muttered thickly. "Knowl and your sister, Catherine and the baby, all of them. Moved out. Left me alone."

"Betty, will you tell them I called? Tell them I'm okay. Take down this number, Betty. Knowl can reach me here if he wants to." She slowly repeated the number. "Tell him I called."

"All alone," said Betty vaguely. "Here in this miserable house. Left me just like my husband Tom. Every last one of them left me. You too, Annie. You left too. I'll never forgive any of you. And when I'm gone, may none of you forgive yourselves!"

Annie said good-bye and carefully replaced the receiver in its cradle. She bit her lip to keep back tears. Last night, when she was with Robert, she had felt almost strong enough to cope with the crises back home in Willowbrook. But hearing Betty Herrick's pitiful voice again, Annie knew she still had a long way to go. Jesus, Jesus, help me draw strength from You. Heal these hurts in me so I can face my family again.

She gazed at her reflection in her bureau mirror. Little Annie Reed, Little Orphan Annie. The wide, empty eyes of a child in pain still stared back at her. With Robert at the canteen, she had felt so hopeful and whole. Why couldn't she hold on to that feeling?

A knock sounded on Annie's door. She grabbed a tissue and quickly blotted tears from her eyelashes, then opened the door. It was Francenna, holding a gift-wrapped package. "This is for you, Annie. I wanted to drop it by before we get too busy with the mission Christmas program tonight."

Annie drew her inside. "Thank you, Francenna. I needed to see a friendly face right now."

"What's wrong, Annie? Are you okay?"

"I will be. It's just that I—I tried calling home. And it made me realize I can't go back and change anything in my past. I have to accept the fact that that part of my life is over. The people I loved have gone on with their lives without me."

Francenna wrapped Annie in her arms. "We're here for you, Annie. Robert and Marshall and I and all the people you help every day. We all love you and need you."

Annie smiled through her tears. "I love you too, Francenna. You've been a wonderful friend to me."

"Well, if there's anything I can do to help, you come and tell me, you hear? I'm right next door."

"I do have a favor to ask, Francenna." Annie walked over to the phone. "Would you call my mother for me? Tell her I'm fine and wish her Merry Christmas. And one day, when I'm stronger, I'll come to Aunt Martha's to see her."

"Are you sure you don't want to make the call, Annie?"

"I can't. Mama would ask too many questions. She probably knows by now I gave up Jenny, but I don't think she knows about Knowl and Alice Marie. It might kill her to think her favorite daughter could betray her own sister."

"I understand." Francenna made the call, explaining that she was a friend of Annie's and that Annie was happy and well, but needed more time alone to get over losing Jenny. "She wanted to talk to you, Annie. She sounded like she had a lot to say."

"But she's well? She's okay?"

"Yes, she said she's fine."

Annie smiled wanly. "That's all I needed to know."

Francenna looked at the wall clock. "We'd better get to the sanctuary for the Christmas program. If we don't start on time, we'll never get out. You know how long-winded Marshall can be!"

Marshall began the service that night with a request for prayer for American troops overseas. "We know that over a week ago the German Luftwaffe began a major offensive in the Ardennes, and now they have attacked Bastogne, creating a sort of 'Bulge.' Let us pray with new urgency for the Allies' victory. And let us trust God that next Christmas, 1945, a free world will celebrate Christ's birth!" He paused and added, almost as an aside, "You all probably realize that, here at home, beef products are being rationed once more, and new quotas have been set for most commodities. Our mission will continue to do all we can to feed hungry, needy people, but we will also be compelled to conserve and be even more frugal with what we have." He lifted his arms high. "But no matter how lean our cupboards may be, let us continue to praise our great God from whom all blessings flow!"

Christmas was over before Annie realized it—her first Christmas away from her family. She could only imagine what Jenny must look like now. She was old enough to get excited about Christmas gifts, but Annie had no idea where Cath had taken the child. Somewhere in New York City.

A few days into the new year, Robert came to Annie with a concerned expression on his face. "I've got something to show you, and you may find it disturbing."

She stared curiously at him. "What, Robert? What is it?"

He held out a copy of the Saturday Evening Post. Annie immediately recognized Cath's painting on the cover. "I posed for that with Jenny," she said, almost in awe. She took the magazine and studied it intently, moving her fingertips over the shiny paper where Jenny's smiling face was printed. "I'd nearly forgotten about this, but here it is, in beautiful color. Jenny and me. For all the world to see." She hugged it against her chest. "May I keep this, Robert?"

"If you're sure it won't upset you too much."

She managed a smile. "It'll upset me, but it's all I have to remind me I was once Jenny's mother."

He put his hand lightly on her shoulder. "Do you ever think about going back home, Annie?"

"All the time." Her lower lip quivered. "But don't you understand? There's nothing left, Robert. No home. No husband. No baby. All I have left are memories."

"Then maybe it's time to put the memories behind you."

"I'm trying." Annie took the magazine back to her room and sat on her bed, staring at the picture. Mother and child. Where was Jenny now? Would she remember that Annie had once been her mother? Was she happy with Cath? Annie tacked the picture on the wall next to her bureau. Somehow it made Jenny seem closer to her heart.

In mid-January, while Robert and Annie worked together in the second-hand store, he said to her, "One of these days we need to get to work on your book, young lady."

She looked at him in surprise. "What do you mean?"

"I mean, I finished reading your manuscript a few weeks ago, and I figured you'd be after me, wanting to know what I thought."

Her face flushed. "I didn't want to pressure you. I knew you'd talk to me about it when the time was right. And, to be honest, I was afraid your silence meant you didn't like it."

He smiled. "Not true. I just thought we'd better get the holidays behind us. But now that we have some free time, we can roll up our sleeves and get to work. You've got some rewriting to do."

Annie felt her throat tighten. "Is the manuscript that bad? It's only the first draft, Robert, and I'm sure I can—"

"It's not bad at all, Annie." He put a price tag on a brown tweed sports jacket and hung it on the rack. "You've done an exceptional job, for a first novel. You write with real feeling, your characters are believable, and you have a credible plot."

"Then what's wrong with it? What needs to be changed?"

He handed her a stack of tea towels to be priced. "The way I see it, you need to write with more of a universal tone. Your story has to appeal to a wide readership. Right now it has a very private quality to it. I'm sure it was cathartic to write, but it becomes a bit tedious in places to read."

Annie's heart fluttered with dismay. "Then you're saying it's not publishable?"

"I'm saying I think I can help you make it publishable. But it won't be easy. Are you game?

She smiled. "I am if you are!"

In the months that followed, Robert and Annie met several days a week in the little mission office just off the foyer. The nondescript room was cramped but adequate. Robert worked closely with her, going over her manuscript chapter by chapter, editing, making changes, asking questions, urging her to probe more deeply into herself— her feelings, her insights, her motivations.

"Ask yourself the hard questions, Annie," he urged. "Don't let your characters off easy. Convince your readers the people in your story are made of flesh and blood, of feelings and needs; they're not just a bunch of fancy words on a page."

"It's hard," said Annie. "I feel as if my brain were stretching with the effort to create. Whatever I'm doing, I hear my characters in my head, talking, talking. I want to stop and listen. And then I feel silly. It's as if I'm going around with a secret no one else knows. I may be serving hash in the soup kitchen or sorting merchandise in the thrift shop, but in my mind this whole other world is going on." She looked up at Robert and smiled. "Am I a little bit crazy."

He nudged her chin. His dark curly hair tumbled over his forehead, his tie was askew, and his shirt sleeves were rolled up to the elbow. "You're not crazy, Annie. You're a novelist in the throes of creation. You're suffering birth pangs."

When Annie wrote about Pearl Harbor, Robert was there beside her, helping her see the events from his perspective, imparting glimpses and experiences only one who had been there could know. As he spoke, the dingy office walls seemed to fade into a pastel haze of memories. "The war came suddenly, from far away," he told her solemnly, "and without warning, we were in the midst of it. It was happening to us. We weren't ready. We thought we were, but we had only been playing games, like tin soldiers.

"I remember the billowing black clouds most of all," he said, his tone unexpectedly dispassionate. "They looked like they had mushroomed up from the underbelly of hades, and the smoke smelled hellish as brimstone, like the flames of Dante's Inferno. And the impact struck with a shuddering sensation, like earthquakes happening over and over, reverberating through the islands. And I recall the noise whistling through my ears, screaming in my head, and I was screaming with it. The terrible sounds came from without and within."

Robert's voice throbbed now, growing deep and distant. "What haunts me even today are the nightmare images of the aftermath. Even from my hospital room where I was recuperating, I could see it in the distance—the harbor with those blackened, twisted vessels jutting up from dark waters, like fallen mastodons or ancient dinosaurs, their massive, battered skeletons cutting stark gashes in the skyline, as if the sea had vomited up some prehistoric burial ground. But it was our own men who were buried there, hundreds in the steel bellies of their ships, or floating face down in an oily grave. For weeks body parts washed ashore with the debris from those supposedly invincible battleships."

Annie placed a comforting hand on Robert's shoulder. "You don't have to keep talking."

"No, I want to talk—just as you need to write. It helps. It's like rubbing a sore muscle. It hurts like the dickens, but somehow it feels better." He took her hand in his and squeezed it. His blue eyes shone with a rare intensity. "You mean a lot to me, Annie Reed. You know that, don't you?"

She could feel her neck and shoulders growing warm under her cotton shirtwaist dress. She reached back instinctively and touched her hair pinned in a loose bun at the nape of her neck. "You mean a lot to me too, Robert Wayne. You've been a wonderful friend and mentor."

He returned a smile rimmed with sadness. "I think you know I'd like to offer more if you were free, truly free."

Annie looked away, her cheeks growing pink. "I'm sorry, Robert."

"Don't be. I won't ever speak of this again, but I thought you should know there's so much more I want to be to you than just a mentor and friend."

Annie mindlessly curled a corner of her manuscript page. "I care deeply about you, too, Robert. But no matter what my husband does, in my heart I'll always be his."

"I know, Annie, and perhaps that's what I love most of all about you—your deep, eternal loyalty. Don't ever change."

Blinking away uninvited tears, she looked back into his eyes, and said, "Did you know, Robert, that Francenna said I could use the office typewriter to type my final draft?"

He laughed grimly. "I had hoped you might say something consoling or romantic, but if you insist on changing the subject to something safe and practical, then, yes, she told me. She's as excited about your book as I am."

Annie set her manuscript back on the office desk. "Once I've made all the changes, I should be able to type a final draft by May—if the mission can get by without my usual evening hours."

"I've already talked to Marshall," said Robert, "and he's eager for you to finish your book too. I let him read part of it, where your characters deal with some spiritual issues, and he thinks it will have a significant message for all Americans. Especially now that the war is winding down. We've spent so many years fighting battles. When the conflict ends, we will all have some new soul-searching to do. I think your book will help people put the war in perspective and glean hope for the future."

Annie smiled. "I'd be very happy if it accomplished all that, but mainly I just want to tell a good story that honors Chip's memory and communicates some of the emotional and spiritual truths I've discovered these past few years. And which I'm still discovering, thanks to you and Marshall and this mission."

"I'm glad we've been a help to you, Annie."

She met his gaze again. "Robert, you're the inspiring one. You're a brilliant editor. Have you thought about going back to New York and reclaiming your old position?"

He cleared his throat. She could tell by his expression that the question made him uncomfortable. "To tell you the truth, Annie—"

"I'm sorry, Robert. I didn't mean to put you on the spot."

"That's okay. I think often about going back to my old position. I know I could tackle it with a new verve, but I'm afraid I'd lose more than I'd gain."

Annie studied him. "What do you mean?"

He sat back and cracked his knuckles, the way he always did when he was speaking of serious matters. "Since I came to live and work at the mission, I've felt a real partnership with God. I sense His peace when I wake up in the morning, and when I go to bed at night I sleep like a baby, knowing I've got my life on track with the Almighty. I wouldn't want to jeopardize that closeness with His Spirit."

Annie nodded. "I know what you're saying, Robert. I've tasted that closeness with Christ when you know He's right there. It's almost as if you're breathing His breath, thinking His thoughts, living His passion and joy. No matter what happens, you feel as if you can rise above it, because as long as you've got Him, you're complete and fulfilled."

"That describes it very well, Annie."

She gazed down at her hands. "But there are all too many other times when I feel myself push God into the background of my life while I muddle through alone. I know He's still there, but His voice is so small and the joy remains just out of reach."

"There's a remedy, you know," said Robert. "Oh, so simple, but we tend to ignore it."

"A remedy? I suppose you mean the Bible."

"I do. Wash your mind with His Word every day, and spend time daily in His presence, even if all you do is listen."

Annie smiled mischievously. "Does Marshall worry that you may take over his pulpit? You preach very well, dear Robert."

He cracked his knuckles again and said slyly, "I'm not sure whether that was a compliment, Annie, or a complaint."

She shifted coyly in her chair and answered with a wink, "I think I'll just let you stew about it for a while, Robert, if you don't mind."

TWENTY-THREE

The Spring of 1945.
The headlines for April 12, 1945, blared the
shocking news:

ROOSEVELT DEAD!

Franklin Delano Roosevelt, 32nd President of the United States, died today of a cerebral hemorrhage at Warm Springs, Georgia. Born in Hyde Park, New York, in 1882, Roosevelt overcame crippling poliomyelitis to become the only president to be elected to a fourth term...

Annie could read no more. She threw down the newspaper and buried her face in her hands. How could her beloved president be dead when the world finally hovered on the verge of peace? All the anguish Annie had suffered at Papa Reed's death and later at Chip's and her own Papa's came rushing back like flood waters bursting a levee.

She wept for her brave leader who had fallen when the battle was about to be won, but she mourned even more for herself. There would be no more fireside chats from the man whose voice reminded her so much of Papa Reed's. The war would end, but she would never see the expansive smile of victory on Mr. Roosevelt's face. The great nation of America, leader of the world's nations, was suddenly without its own greatly esteemed leader.

The mood in the dining room that evening was somber. Servicemen and civilians alike talked in a stunned monotone; some were visibly distressed and wept openly; others steeled their expressions and kept their feelings to themselves.

When Annie saw Robert in the kitchen, she could tell by his red-rimmed eyes that he, too, had wept at the news. She went to him and they embraced wordlessly. What could either of them say?

Later, while they were cleaning up, Robert opened up and expressed his thoughts. "Roosevelt didn't look well back in February in those photos of him with Churchill and Stalin at Yalta. The pressure on him then must have been incredible—negotiating with so many world powers and deciding all the details of what a post-war world would be like. He just didn't seem quite on top of things the way I expected him to be. I felt he gave away too much. It had to be his illness."

"At least he knew the war in Europe was virtually over," said Annie. "That had to have been some comfort to him."

By mid-April, the president had just been put to rest when news began to filter through from Europe of the atrocities committed against humanity by Hitler's Nazis. British and American forces liberating Belsen and Buchenwald discovered concentration camps where millions had been put to death. Annie read the statistics with horror and disbelief. How was it possible that while Americans were carrying on rather normal lives during the war, on the other side of the world millions of innocent people were being slain in such hideous fashion?

Annie asked Robert about it, and he was as incredulous as she was. "We heard rumors, and some of us suspected that the Germans were abusing their power, but I had no inkling it was this bad. No one else did either, or surely, something would have been done to stop that madman."

"I remember Catherine's Aunt Jenny wrote her years ago from Germany about the Jews being persecuted and having to go into hiding. But who would have thought it would go this far—that Hitler would try to annihilate an entire race?" Annie clasped her hand over her mouth. "I just thought of something else."

"What, Annie? What is it?"

"The street preacher who led me into a personal relationship with Christ—his name was Helmut Schwarz, and he was a German Jew. He was going back to Germany to witness of his conversion to other Jews. I wonder if he was one of the millions to die?"

"I don't think you'll ever know, Annie, this side of heaven."

As the impact of the president's death and Hitler's massacre struck Annie with full force, she turned in desperation to the one Source she knew that offered solace. Instead of thumbing through her large Bible, she found the small Gospel of John that Helmut Schwarz had given her years ago. For several days she pored over it day and night, burning its truths into her consciousness, committing favorite portions to memory: In the beginning was the Word...All things were made by him...n him was life...And the light shineth in darkness...as many as received him, to them gave he power to become the sons of God...And the Word was made flesh, and dwelt among us.

Yes, she was finding her way back, experiencing His love again like a fountain overflowing in her heart.

During the early days of May, Annie finished typing her novel while keeping one ear tuned to the radio. World events were happening so quickly, there was hardly time to digest one piece of news before another was announced. On May first Hamburg radio announced that Hitler was dead. He and Eva Braun had committed suicide in Hitler's Bunker the day before. Mussolini and his mistress Clara Petacci and other Fascist leaders had been shot and killed two days earlier.

On May second, Berlin fell, and the German army surrendered in Italy and part of Austria; on May fifth, the Germans surrendered in Holland, Northwestern Germany, and Denmark; and on May sixth, they surrendered the rest of Austria and Bavaria. By May seventh, Germany's land, sea, and air forces had surrendered unconditionally. The war in Europe was over.

On May eighth, as Annie carefully packaged her finished manuscript to take to the post office, she listened to the celebrations mingling with static on her table radio. It was V-E Day—Victory in Europe. President Truman, Winston Churchill, and King George VI all made special broadcasts to announce the long-awaited news. Twenty-five million men had stopped fighting the largest, costliest war in history. However, Truman's speech included a warning that the fighting wouldn't be done until "the last Japanese division has surrendered unconditionally."

When Annie returned to the mission after mailing her manuscript, she encountered Robert mopping the hardwood floor in the hallway. He was pleased by the news of victory, but also a bit skeptical. "Like Truman says, we still have the Japanese to deal with. The war's not over until it's over."

Annie nodded. "It's hard to rejoice over peace, when I read of all the atrocities Hitler has committed. You've read the accounts, haven't you, Robert? Our troops have reported finding huge piles of naked, emaciated human bodies, as many as five hundred in one pile. One soldier described the smell as the worst stench imaginable, something that will haunt him for the rest of his life."

Robert propped his mop against the wall and gently squeezed Annie's hand. "I know how you feel, Annie. I feel that same sense of outrage. I want to do something to right those terrible wrongs, but we can't change what has happened. All we can do is to start working now to make sure such evils never happen again."

"But how do we do that, Robert? We work here in our little mission, doing what we can to help the people who come to us, but it's so little in the larger scheme of things. There must be something more we can do."

He took out his handkerchief and wiped his brow. "You are a little crusader, aren't you, Annie Reed? That's good. Because that passion and fire will fill your writings and perhaps someday you will change the world."

She studied him intently. "Are you laughing at me, Robert? Am I so naive that you find my frustration amusing?"

"No, dear Annie, not at all!" He replaced his handkerchief, then drew her over against his chest and held her for a moment. "No, I am charmed by your zeal. I am even a bit jealous of your ability to feel so deeply about life and its injustices. I'm afraid the war has made me too cynical, maybe even a bit callous." He held her at arm's length. "You're good for me, Annie. You help me stay balanced."

"And you do the same for me, Robert."

"We make a good team," he noted meaningfully.

Annie looked away, unsure how to reply. As Robert returned to his mopping, she said, "I suppose you know, I just came from mailing my manuscript to Sanders and Browne."

He looked at her and grinned. "Congratulations, Annie. You do realize I'm sending them a personal letter telling them I highly recommend that they publish your book."

Annie looked back, pleased and surprised. "You'll do that for me—actually recommend that they publish my novel?"

"I'm not doing it just for you, Annie. I'm doing it because your book deserves to be published. And I think Sanders and Browne will make a bundle on it, so you see, it's just good business."

"Whatever you call it, I can't thank you enough, Robert." She leaned up and lightly kissed his cheek.

His eyes twinkled with merriment. "Now let's pray that my publisher has the same good sense I do!"

Three months later, Annie received the news she had seemingly waited a lifetime to hear. She tore open the envelope and eagerly scanned the letter from Sanders and Browne. One sentence jumped out at her: We are pleased to inform you that your manuscript, Pacific Dawn, has been accepted for publication.

She raced over to the second-hand shop where Robert was stocking merchandise and thrust the letter under his eyes. He set down a box of china figurines and scanned the letter silently. Then he let out a loud whoop, swept her up in his arms, and swung her around. "You did it, Annie! You did it!"

She collapsed, laughing, against his chest. "No, you did it, Robert. You helped me when no one else could."

He stepped back against the counter and took her flushed face in his large hands. "We've got to go celebrate, gal! Go put on your fanciest duds and we'll go out on the town. Dinner and a movie. How about it?"

She picked up a figurine from the box and examined it. "We can't, Robert. Who will serve in the soup kitchen tonight?"

"I'll talk to Marshall. Maybe he and Francenna will take our place if they know how important this is. It's not every day a writer sells her first novel." He took the figurine from her and set it on a shelf, then looked back at her, his eyes misting with unexpected emotion. "Think of it, Annie. You're going to be a published author. I expect to see your name on the New York Times best-seller list about this time next year."

Annie swept back her auburn hair and shook her head dazedly. "I feel so giddy, Robert, like a child who discovers that all the toys under the Christmas tree are hers. How can I thank you?"

He twisted a ringlet of her hair around his finger. "Just be happy, Annie. Enjoy whatever success and fame come your way."

She stared blankly at him. "Fame? I don't expect fame."

"But it will likely come, Annie. You've written a marvelous book that taps into the sentiment of our troubled times. I think your book will experience widespread popularity. Will that bother you?"

She bent down and removed another figurine from the box—a porcelain princess in a flowing gown. She handed it to Robert. "I've felt anonymous for so long," she murmured. "I wonder what will happen when my family sees my name on a book cover?"

"I'm sure they'll be pleased for you," said Robert softly, setting the figurine on the shelf beside the other. "Maybe you should consider contacting your husband again. You can't leave the past unfinished forever."

"In my mind it is finished. If I thought it weren't—if I thought Knowl still wanted or needed me—"

"What, Annie? What would you do?"

She fingered the wide bow on her silk blouse. "I don't know what I would do, Robert. I can't imagine Knowl wanting me back. Too much has happened—for both of us."

Robert cupped her elbow in his hand. "You won't go back. And yet you have the loyal heart of a married woman. You can't keep living in limbo, Annie. You need to resolve things. Either reconcile with your husband or finalize your separation with a divorce."

"I can't." Annie stiffened, averting her gaze to the china statues. "I couldn't bear to face Knowl. I couldn't stand to hear him say he doesn't love me."

Robert pulled her back to him and rubbed her tears away with his thumb. "I didn't mean to upset you, especially not at a joyous time like this. Forget what I said. Now go get ready for our gala evening."

Within the hour Annie was ready, and the two walked to a nearby steak house on Vine Street, where they ordered sizzling porterhouse steaks and baked potatoes. They ate by candlelight, savoring the atmosphere, the food, and the company. After dinner, Robert raised his water glass and proposed a toast. "To tomorrow's best seller. May it give hope and joy to all who read it."

Annie raised her long-stemmed goblet and clinked his lightly. "Tell me, Robert," she said quietly, "is it normal to feel petrified at a time like this? So many people will be reading my book. What if they don't like it?"

He sat forward, meeting her gaze with a smile. "They'll love it, Annie. Take my word for it."

With one fingertip, she thoughtfully traced the rim of her glass. "But it seems almost trivial compared with all that's happened in the world lately. I wrote my book for one kind of world, but since last week when our country bombed Hiroshima and Nagasaki, since this atomic bomb, which erases civilizations in a mere handful of moments, I feel as if I live in a vastly different world."

He nodded. "Tell me how you feel, Annie."

"I feel—alarmed and shocked. Growing up in a little Indiana town, even with my far-reaching imagination, I never pictured a world where people could destroy one another with such swiftness and ease—where millions could be systematically murdered in monstrous ovens by one man's decree or where entire cities could be decimated by the small cargo of a single plane. Where will it all lead, Robert? What more are we capable of? Do you feel this same sense of foreboding? Or is it just me?"

"No, I feel it too. But it came earlier for me. It came when I stared at the twisted, blackened ruin of Pearl Harbor. That's partly why I turned to alcohol, and later, that's why I turned to God. He created us and gave us guidelines for living that would keep us on track. But we threw out the instruction manual, convinced we could come up with a better plan. So far we haven't done it. And now, if we're not careful, we'll self-destruct. It's happened to other civilizations. And it could happen to us."

"It's as if we've seized some of God's power, and now that we have it, what are we going to do with it?"

Robert reached across the table for her hand. "This is supposed to be an evening of lighthearted celebration, not mournful introspection. Let's think about pleasant things, like the rest of the evening we have to spend together."

Annie smiled. "I can't wait for our second course—popcorn and a movie."

Leaving the restaurant, they walked two blocks to the Bijou Theater, where they bought popcorn and Coca-Colas and watched a moody, intriguing film called Gaslight, starring Charles Boyer and Ingrid Bergman. Afterward, they walked home at a leisurely pace, holding hands.

"Thanks for a wonderful evening, Robert," Annie told him. "I loved the movie, and I haven't had steak like that in years—if ever. It was delicious!"

"We can thank the government for loosening their restrictions on meat. I can't tell you how delightful it is not to be eating Spam for a change!"

She laughed. "I know. In the soup kitchen, I'm known as the Queen of Spam, I've fixed it so many ways."

"A tribute to your ingenious talents, Miss Reed," he teased.

When they reached the mission, Robert stopped Annie on the sidewalk, under the moonlight, and lifted her face to his. "Dear Annie," he whispered, "I wish to heaven I had the right to tell you how I feel." He bent to touch her lips with his, but she turned aside, her lashes wet with tears.

"I'm sorry, Robert," she whispered. "I can't. It would spoil everything between us."

He straightened his shoulders and mopped back a thatch of stray hair in a gesture of futility. "Forgive me, Annie. God help me, I don't want to ruin what was one of the most beautiful evenings of my life." He walked her promptly to the women's dormitory, opened the door for her, then pivoted sharply and strode away, his heels clacking decisively on the rough cement.

On the evening of August 14, 1945, Annie was listening to George Burns and Gracie Allen on the radio, when an announcer broke in and declared, "Japan has surrendered unconditionally!" President Truman came on then and made appropriate remarks about the end of the war and America's final victory. Annie listened with an immense sense of relief and also a twinge of sadness. How different this day was from the day her family had been listening to the radio and heard the appalling news of Japan's attack on Pearl Harbor. How much her own life had changed in the intervening years!

During the next hour, Annie sat by the radio in her modest dormitory room, listening to the reports flooding in of Americans everywhere celebrating V-J Day. Soldiers and sailors were kissing girls in Times Square. Bands were playing. Confetti was flying and balloons soared heavenward. People poured out of their homes and crowds gathered in the streets. Couples danced and jitterbugged. Everyone was shouting and cheering and throwing streamers.

But the celebrations weren't limited to the radio. Annie could already hear the sounds of victory outside her own window. Sirens blasted, church bells rang, car horns honked, radios and jukeboxes blared. Lights that had been darkened for years turned on all over the city. Annie gazed out the window as soldiers and civilians swarmed into the streets, their voices jubilant. The mission's occupants spilled out into the street as well, shouting and waving. Annie knew she should go find Robert and celebrate with the others, but for just a little longer she wanted to sit here alone in the privacy of her room and offer up a silent prayer—of thanksgiving and regret.

On September 2—the same day the Japanese surrender was signed in Tokyo Bay aboard the battleship Missouri—Annie signed her book contract with Sanders and Browne. After that, the brisk, gusty months of autumn flittered by like dry leaves in a chill wind. As autumn faded into winter and winter into spring, Annie's life took on a surprising placidity. She continued her work at the mission and the thrift shop, working comfortably along-side Robert, who was careful not to insinuate himself too aggressively into her life. She enjoyed her friendship with Francenna and marveled over all she learned from Marshall. It was as if she had indeed found her niche and God was blessing.

Early in the spring of 1946, Annie met the postman to collect the mail and was handed a surprise—a package containing the first copy of her published novel, Pacific Dawn. Her fingers trembled as she opened the box and removed a shiny hardcover book with her name, Elizabeth Anne Reed, scrolled across the front. Above her name was a compelling illustration of Pearl Harbor with the Arizona silhouetted against a pink sunrise.

Uttering an exclamation of delight, Annie clutched the book to her bosom and ran through the mission, seeking Robert. When she found him in the office hunting and pecking over an old Remington typewriter, she held the handsome volume out to him, barely suppressing her glee.

Robert clasped the book and jumped to his feet, nearly overturning his spindle chair. "It's here! Incredible, Annie! It's finally here. Your first book!"

"Isn't it the most beautiful book you ever saw?"

"Penned by the most beautiful author," he told her.

She flushed. "I want to go to the bookstore, Robert, and look at my book on the shelf. Will you take me?"

"You couldn't keep me away." He opened the book slowly, careful not to break the spine. "Have you heard directly from Sanders and Browne? I assume they'll want you to go on a publicity tour to promote your novel."

"Yes, they wrote me. They want me to make appearances in half a dozen cities between here and Chicago to autograph books. San Francisco, Denver, Kansas City, St. Louis. They've scheduled the tour for April, but I wrote and told them I wasn't sure I could go."

Robert looked sharply at her. "You've got to go, Annie. This is your big chance. You've got to let people everywhere know about your book."

She was silent for a long moment. Then she said solemnly, "It will mean going to Chicago. I'll be only a couple of hours away from Willowbrook. It would be almost like going home."

Robert squeezed her arm. "Maybe it was meant to be, Annie. Maybe it's time to face the ghosts of the past."

"I don't know if I can, Robert. I'm so afraid."

"Well, at least telephone your mother in Chicago and tell her you'll be in town."

"I will, if you stay here with me while I call." Annie's hands turned clammy with panic as she dialed Aunt Martha's number. She waited, until a strange voice came on the line and announced, "I'm sorry, that line has been disconnected." Annie tried again, convinced she got a wrong number. Again, the same ominous message.

"Something must have happened," she cried. "They wouldn't disconnect the phone unless they had moved. And Mama wouldn't leave without a good reason. Maybe Aunt Martha's sick, or—"

"Try calling your home in Willowbrook," said Robert. "There has to be someone there who can explain what's going on."

Annie dialed the Herrick house, her fingers trembling. She was stunned to hear the same familiar feminine voice explaining that the number had been disconnected. She looked up in askance at Robert. "Something terrible must have happened. My family—they're all gone. No one answers anywhere. It's as if they simply vanished from the face of the earth!"

TWENTY-FOUR

The Spring of 1946.

What has happened to my family? What has happened to Knowl?

Those were the uppermost questions in Annie's mind that April as she boarded a train at Union Station and began a whirlwind promotion tour set up by her publisher, Sanders and Browne. Those questions burned in her thoughts as she signed stacks of her popular novel.

Lines of people queued up outside bookstores waiting for her to autograph their copy of Pacific Dawn. Four weeks after the book was released, it reached number 14 on the New York Times Best-seller list. "You hit it right, Miss Reed," one bookstore owner told her. "We'll soon be celebrating the one-year anniversary of the war's end. People feel good about what we accomplished as a country and what our boys did for us over there. They want to honor their memory, and your book helps them do that."

Annie was grateful that readers found her book so helpful, but its success didn't ease her anxieties or alleviate her guilt. During lonely nights in unfamiliar hotel rooms, questions bombarded her mind: What happened to Knowl, to Mama, to Cath and little Jenny? Why did I ever run away from them? Why wasn't I strong enough to face the pain and work things out?

After a few days, the excitement of the tour muffled the questions. As her stage fright wore off and the anxieties abated, Annie began to enjoy her autograph parties. She thrived on meeting her fans and chatting with them about their lives and their war- or home-front experiences. Many clasped her hand and said, "My brother died in Pearl Harbor too," or "I had a father overseas," or "My son just came back from the war." Annie felt her deepest bond with those who had also lost someone.

For nearly two weeks, Annie obligingly took the train to San Francisco, Denver, and St. Louis, following the itinerary her publisher had arranged. But the stop she most anticipated was Chicago. It had been three weeks now since she telephoned Aunt Martha's home and the Herrick house, only to learn that both numbers had been disconnected. A cold dread had settled inside her, silencing the questions—a certainty that something terrible had happened, and she had no way of discovering what it was.

One possible source of information about her family was the Willowbrook News, where Knowl was perhaps still serving as managing editor. Annie considered telephoning the paper, but every time she imagined herself speaking to Knowl again, a knot of anguish twisted within her, overshadowing the questions. Whatever Knowl might be doing now, he undoubtedly wanted nothing to do with Annie.

When she arrived in Chicago several hours before her book signing at a large downtown emporium, Annie hailed a taxi and gave the driver Aunt Martha's address. In her mind's eye, she could already picture squat Aunt Martha on her porch, with a wreath of braided gray-brown hair framing her round face and a wry twinkle in her hazel eyes. She would be surrounded by her menagerie of cats, some mewing in her arms, some rubbing her legs, while others, with typical feline smugness, would be sitting guard inside the house on Martha's overstuffed sofas and chairs. Yes, Aunt Martha's home had always pulsated with surprise and whimsy.

After a half-hour drive, the taxicab pulled up to the curb beside a quaint old house Annie remembered dimly from her past. But this house was vastly different from the cozy clapboard residence she recalled. It stood gloomily silent, its windows boarded, a weathered "FOR SALE" sign stuck at an angle in the overgrown grass.

Impulsively, Annie ran up the porch steps and pounded on the door, knowing even as she called out for her mother and Aunt Martha, that there was no one inside to answer. Finally, she turned in disappointment and walked back down the steps. She was about to climb back into the cab when she spotted an elderly woman next door watering the plants on her porch. Annie walked over quickly and called out, "Excuse me, ma'am, do you know what happened to the people next door?"

The woman looked skeptically at Annie for a moment. "Who wants to know?" she asked as she continued her watering.

"I'm Annie Reed. My mother, Anna Reed, lived here with her sister, Martha. Now they're gone. Do you know what happened?"

The sprightly woman set down her watering can and shuffled down the steps toward Annie. "Martha took ill and died a few months back," she said, her expression softening with compassion. "Your mama took care of her right to the end. Then, after the funeral—and after she found all the cats good homes—she moved out. I don't have the foggiest notion where she went."

Numbly, Annie thanked her and returned to her taxi. Grief and recriminations assailed her. If only I had known! I could

have come and helped Mama with Aunt Martha. In trying to protect her mother from the painful events of her own life, she had missed out on helping Mama through what must have been a deeply trying time.

Dutifully, Annie kept her appointment for the autograph party at the book shop. She smiled brightly for her readers, exchanging polite greetings and chatty bits of conversation. Yet she sighed with relief after scrawling her name in the last hardcover volume, and, after bidding a hurried good-bye, she slipped out of the store, eager to become anonymous once more.

It was at that moment, as she gazed at Chicago's hazy skyline, that she decided she must take the train to Willowbrook tonight and face her past. Even if she stayed for only an hour, she had to glimpse again the house on Honeysuckle Lane, brimming with memories of love and hope, disappointment and despair. In her heart of hearts, she felt the Spirit's prompting, nudging her home, whispering soundless words that compelled her to return, however briefly, to her Indiana heritage.

The train ride from Chicago to Willowbrook was little more than a blur of swiftly moving images outside her window, so absorbed was Annie in her own private thoughts. Clanging signals echoed into the night, blending with the lonely train whistle, while quaint, storybook towns flashed by, bright as postcards for a moment until they were swallowed by darkness. The taxi ride, too, seemed fleeting and remote, except for the wizened little cigar-smoking cabby, who bombarded her with endless questions.

But, suddenly, even he was gone, and Annie found herself standing alone on Honeysuckle Lane, as if it were yesterday—except that it wasn't yesterday; it was now, the spring of 1946, and she was facing a house occupied by strangers—her fine old Victorian home with its peaks and gables and gingerbread trim, her beloved refuge, which, even on this rain-soaked night, still exuded an aura of sweet nostalgia and deep hurt.

And then, without warning, she heard the noise behind her—footsteps, a man approaching. She ran. He ran after her. And when she turned, terrified, and saw him, years of memories cascaded through her brain, like faded snapshots in a dusty album. In an instant she relived a lifetime, as she stood facing her husband for the first time in nearly two years.

"Knowl!" He stood there in the shadowed mists in trench coat and hat, towering and broad-shouldered, bigger than life, the brim of his hat shading his features, except where the street light caught the angles of his nose and jaw in a dramatic silhouette.

"Annie!"

Yes, his voice! He was real! "What are you doing here?" she cried. "How did you know I'd come back to Honeysuckle Lane?"

He stepped forward and answered with a sudden gesture, gathering her into his arms and pressing her slim body against his lean, solid frame. She felt the nubby roughness of his coat against her cheek and the sudden warmth of his torso sheltering her. For a moment her body warred within her, yearning to yield, yet wanting to pull away. Knowl's closeness, the familiar scent of his cologne, the minty warmth of his breath against her face swept away her objections. She felt an instinctive response moving through her frame, her limbs, a reaction as physical and elemental as breathing, a sensation of wholeness, of rightness, as if she'd endured a lifetime for this very moment.

"Annie, I prayed you'd come home!" He removed his hat and nuzzled his chin against her hair, then moved his mouth urgently over her cheek to her lips. She surrendered, meshing the curves of her body with his. Knowl kissed her longingly, and her face grew wet with tears—his tears, or were they hers? They were both weeping now, shamelessly. She couldn't speak, but it didn't matter, for she had no words anyway, no way of expressing this moment with language.

"Annie, dear Annie," he whispered against her ear, his words erupting out of a deep wellspring of anguish. "I thought I'd never see you again. Is it really you?"

"Yes, Knowl," she breathed. "But how—?"

His eyes were brooding through his wire-rim glasses, his raven hair wind-tossed, the rain-washed moonlight cutting across his angular features. He fingered the sodden minks on her stole. "No questions, Annie. You're home at last."

She reached up and touched his face—the straight line of his nose, the solid curve of his jaw—as if to assure herself he was real. An ache born of profound love and deep pain swelled behind her breastbone, making it difficult to speak. "Home?"

He turned her toward her cherished haven, his hand gently but firmly at her waist. He was handsome still, and yet something in his expression seemed eons older, as if his features had been sculpted afresh by a harsher chisel. "Come, Annie."

She held back, reason returning, prompting her to raise her guard, but he urged her up the steps and onto the sprawling porch, where lamplight spilled out in golden swaths. "We can't, Knowl," she protested as he reached for the familiar brass doorknob. "This is someone else's house now."

Ignoring her objections, he swung open the wide, paneled door and stepped back so that she could enter. She stared transfixed into the rosy glow of the home she would always carry with her in a pocket of her soul. Had Knowl made friends of the new owners? Didn't he realize how it would rent her heart to see these dear rooms that were no longer hers?

Compelled by a power beyond her own reasoning, she crossed the threshold into the marbled entryway. As if walking in a dream, she gazed around, her mind deliriously light-headed. She was home! Surrounded by familiar walls with their fine moldings and ornate beadwork. Incredibly, she was standing in the midst of Mama's favorite furniture—gleaming brass lamps, Papa's small writing desk with its silver blotter and inkwell, the cherry wood bookcase with Papa Reed's vintage, leather-bound books.

How can this be? Have I taken leave of my senses? Am I sleeping? Or suddenly deranged?

She could see into the living room and parlor—to the Queen Anne chairs and flowered love seat, the mahogany plant stand with its clawed feet, the Monet prints hanging beside the rustic brick fireplace. It was as it had been nearly twenty years ago.

Dazzled, Annie turned to her husband. "How, Knowl?"

"I did it for you, Annie," he whispered.

"But it's not possible. We sold the house and the furniture. Everything was gone."

"Not everything. Remember? We took many pieces to my house and stored several in the attic. I spent months seeking out other pieces that had gone to auction, and I purchased back many of them from their original buyers."

Annie walked awestricken to the dining room, her hands moving from item to item, as if she couldn't believe they were real. Her grandmother's hutch was filled with her Blue Willow ware and other heirlooms. Yes, even Alma Reed's antique crystal containers encased in ornate silver frames were here, filled with condiments and candy—one a blue mother-of-pearl satin glass, another tall and frosted, still another a cranberry glass with a hobnail pattern.

Annie could almost hear Papa Reed declaring, My Alma, my soul, she's here in every nook and cranny, in every quilt she stitched and curtain she sewed, in all her trinkets and treasures. I built this house for her and brought her here as my bride...

Annie's eyes welled with tears. You are here, Papa Reed, you and your dear Alma. I feel you here! And Papa and Chip! Your memories fill these rooms! Your voices sing in my head!

Come, Elizabeth Anne, let's read of Alice's adventures!

Look at you, daughter! You look pretty as a picture!

Hey, little sister, let's play keepaway or capture the flag!

She looked at Knowl. "Tell me I'm not crazy. I remember clearly. Mama sold the house. Someone else lived here—"

"Yes, Annie, but shortly after you left, the house came on the market. I sold my interest in the paper and bought it."

"You sold your ownership in the paper? Why, Knowl? Why would you do that?"

He approached her and touched her cheeks, wiping away her tears. "You meant everything to me, Annie. I loved you and knew how much you loved this house. I wanted it to be here for you when you came home. And I vowed I'd be here waiting, too."

"But how did you know I'd come home?"

"I knew. I knew whatever drove you away wasn't as powerful as what drew us together."

She stared at him in astonishment. "Whatever drove me away? You don't know? You really don't know why I left?"

His wide brow furrowed. "I suspect it had something to do with Jenny. You were heartbroken when Cath took her away. Your grief must have clouded your senses. You impulsively ran away without thinking what it would do to us."

He removed his glasses and cleaned the lenses with his handkerchief. "I admit, at first, I was bitterly angry that you would so recklessly throw aside our love, but with the passing of time, I realized your wounds must have been very deep to keep you away from Willowbrook. I want you to know, I've long since forgiven you, Annie."

"You've forgiven me?" She lifted her hand in a gesture of disbelief. "How can you say that? It's I who must forgive you!"

He replaced his glasses, adjusting them on the bridge of his nose. "Forgive me? For what? What did I do?"

She turned away from him, clasping her hands over her mouth. A wave of nausea swept over her. Is it possible he views the same reality from such a vastly different perspective? Is he trying to deceive me, convince me it was all some ploy of my imagination? Oh, God, don't let him play games with me, now that I've tasted his love again!

Knowl strode after her, whirled her around, and held her shoulders firm in his large hands. "What happened, Annie? What drove you away? What did I do wrong? Tell me!"

She began to weep. "In heaven's name, Knowl, how can you not know what happened? It was you! You and Alice Marie!"

He stared blankly at her. "Alice Marie? What—?"

The shock and shame of that dreadful scene flooded back. She wrenched out the words. "I saw you and Alice Marie— kissing—in the garden!"

He mopped back his tousled hair. "Great Scott! I never—!"

"But you did, Knowl!" The words spilled out with the pent-up force of two years of heartache and pain. "I'd just surrendered Jenny to Cath, and I desperately needed your comfort. But you were with her! Holding her in your arms. Kissing her. How could you do it, Knowl?"

He paced across the room to the window and stared out at the rain, dazedly shaking his head. "I'd nearly forgotten the incident. It meant nothing, Annie."

"Nothing?" She felt as if he had slapped her. "It meant everything! You killed me with that kiss, Knowl. You destroyed us!"

He came back to her and faced her squarely. She could see the tendons in his neck tighten and the pulse in his temples throb. The Knowl of her memories, so charming and young, lay hidden beneath this older, more intense man who spoke with the force of conviction. "If you saw the kiss, you must also have seen what happened afterward."

She stared questioningly at him. "Afterward? No. I turned away, distraught. I couldn't bear to look any longer."

His voice was ragged, filled with indignation. "Then you didn't see me push her away and reprimand her for her coy advances. She kissed me, Annie. I didn't kiss her."

Annie shook her head, tossing her tangled pageboy curls. She couldn't let him twist the truth, throw the blame back at her. "You speak in semantics, Knowl. I know what I saw."

"I've never been unfaithful to you, Annie. Never!"

"Perhaps not in deed, but I felt your betrayal, Knowl." She clasped the tiny mink heads on her fur coat. She felt warm. The house was warm, such a contrast to the weather outside—the brisk, nocturnal rain of early spring. In spite of the warmth, she felt a cold stone of doubt chilling her being.

Knowl removed his overcoat and tossed it over the back of a wing chair. "Let me take your coat, Annie. We've got to sit down and talk this out."

She handed him her fur and sat down in the flowered love seat. Knowl laid her stole over his coat and sat down beside her, turning sideways to face her. "Do you see, Annie, how you misunderstood that kiss?" He adjusted his glasses, his expression animated and eager. "What's so ironic is that Alice Marie packed and moved out a few weeks after you left. When I made it clear to her that there could be nothing between us, she took the train to New Orleans to join a jazz band. I haven't laid eyes on her for over a year, Annie."

"You told her there could be nothing between you?" Annie urgently searched his eyes. "When I called from Chicago, Alice Marie implied I should stay away so the two of you could be together."

"You called from Chicago?"

"Didn't she tell you?"

"No. Not a word. I didn't think you wanted to be found. Not that I didn't try. I searched everywhere on God's green earth for you."

"When you didn't return my call, I thought I was doing you a kindness to stay away."

"A kindness? Oh, Annie—!"

She swallowed a sob. "I knew you'd always loved Alice Marie. I knew I was second best—"

He seized her hand and held it against his chest. "Is that what you think? That you were second in my heart?"

"Wasn't I? From the time I was a child, you loved her. You would have married her. When she came to live with us, I saw how you favored her. You deferred to her, laughed with her, looked to her for approval. Oh, Knowl, are you so blind that you didn't know how much you loved her? I saw it every day."

He swiveled around and rested his elbows on his knees. "Oh, Annie, Annie." He put his head in his hands, his fingertips pressing his forehead. "I'm sorry."

"All the time we were married, you still loved Alice Marie, didn't you?" she said quietly. "Be honest with me, Knowl. Be honest with yourself."

He spoke over a surging wave of emotion. "It's true, Annie. I've never consciously admitted it even to myself until now, but you deserve the truth. A part of me still wanted her love."

Annie closed her eyes. *Dear God, why did I force his hand? I don't want to hear this. I can't bear it!*

Knowl was silent for several moments, his head still bowed. "Sometimes I felt the old stirrings of infatuation for her," he continued. "Not that I ever acted on it. But I suppose her attentiveness fed my—my masculine ego."

Tears slipped from Annie's closed lashes. *Did I come back to have my worst fears confirmed? Stop, Knowl, please!*

He looked at her, his own eyes red with unshed tears. "I never guessed how much I was hurting you, Annie."

She lowered her gaze as scalding disappointment washed over her. *There, I've done it—forced him to admit the truth.* "I suppose we have our answer then," she said dispassionately. "If you still love Alice Marie, we have no future together. I was right to go away."

"No, Annie." He squeezed her hand until she nearly winced. "You don't understand, my darling. There's more. So much more. After you left Willowbrook, I felt devastated. It was as if the core of my being had been ripped out. For the first time I realized how much I loved you. My fondness for Alice Marie was merely the remnants of a school boy crush. But my feelings for you run as deep as the blood in my veins. Don't you see? I need you, Annie. Next to God Himself, you're my life."

Annie felt herself mesmerized by his intensity. Had she heard right? "You love me?" she said wonderingly.

"Yes, my precious girl. I love you. Only you. Will you forgive me for all those years of trying to have it both ways? For loving you and yet setting a place in my affections aside for Alice Marie?"

Annie's heart pounded. "I want to forgive you, Knowl. But how can I be sure you won't be drawn to her again?"

"I can't predict tomorrow, Annie. I can only tell you I never realized what we had until you walked away from me. I never want to lose you again."

A sob rose in her throat. "Two years ago you stripped me of my trust in you, my security, my innocence. I don't know how to get that confidence back, Knowl. I want to, desperately, but—"

"Will you give me a chance, Annie? That's all I ask."

She searched his eyes. "Help me find my way back to you."

He wrapped her in his arms and sought her mouth, moving his lips over hers with an urgency that left her trembling. She sank against him, allowing his warmth to envelop her. Yes, at last she could begin to believe she was home where she belonged.

"I love you, Knowl," she whispered against his cheek. "I've always loved you."

"And I'll cherish you forever, Annie."

He stood up and was about to gather her again into his arms, when Annie heard a voice from her past that struck to her very marrow.

"Annie, my child? Is it really you?"

Annie looked toward the stairway, where an extraordinary vision from yesteryear stood by the old oak banister—her dear mother in a flowing red velvet robe, her silver tresses forming a halo around her head, a smile of surprise and delight on her rose-pink lips.

TWENTY-FIVE

Annie stared in astonishment at her mother, standing in quiet dignity by the staircase. Anna Reed no longer looked like an older version of her daughter, Alice Marie. Her beauty was still evident, but colored now by the years. Lines marred the porcelain face and silver strands replaced the gold locks.

Annie could hardly find her voice. "Mama—is it you? What are you doing here?" Then, without waiting for an answer, she ran to the stairs and the two women shared a long, tearful embrace. Like a lost child finally reclaimed, Annie savored her mother's comforting touch and the familiar fragrance of her lavender perfume.

"I tried to find you, Mama," she cried. "I didn't know where you'd gone after Aunt Martha died."

"Then you know—about Martha?"

"Yes. I was just there. I saw the house boarded up." She clasped her mother's hands as if she might never let them go. "How did you happen to come back home to Honeysuckle Lane?"

Mama cast a smiling glance at Knowl. "Your husband invited me after Martha died. He bought this house, intending to restore it to its original condition just for you. He told me someday you'd come back to Willowbrook to see your old home, and he wanted to be ready. He said he felt closer to you in this house."

"But how did you know I'd come home to Willowbrook tonight?"

"The newspaper—your photo," said Mama. "As soon as Knowl received your publicity release at the paper, he began making plans. He was sure if you got as close as Chicago, you'd be drawn irresistibly back to Willowbrook."

"You were right, Knowl. I couldn't resist. But if you knew where I was, why didn't you contact me?"

"I didn't know your whereabouts until I saw your photograph on the dust jacket of your book. Then I received the promotional write-up for the paper. I decided to wait and see if you would come home on your own. I didn't want to force you back."

"He's been fidgeting around this house for days," said Mama, "fretting over whether you'd come home or not. Tonight he was even out pacing the streets in the rain, looking for any sign of you. I finally got weary and went up to bed. I woke up when I heard your voices down here."

Annie gazed around in wonderment. "I can't believe I'm here in my own home once more. It's what I've dreamed of for years."

Knowl slipped his arm around her waist. "Would you like some hot tea and biscuits? Your mama has some fresh ones in the kitchen."

Annie followed her mother and Knowl to the kitchen like a child stepping gingerly through the wispy, insubstantial fields of a dream. This wasn't quite real; she couldn't be quite certain whether she was here or somewhere else, awake or asleep. Perhaps, in reality, she was slumbering in her hotel room in Chicago, and only imagining herself back within the cozy walls of her Willowbrook home. But if this was a dream, she sent up a silent prayer that no one awaken her.

She sat down at the sturdy oak table and looked around at the enameled cast iron stove with its warming ovens and the white porcelain sink with its shiny brass fixtures. Yes, this was real. She was indeed home again on Honeysuckle Lane. Gracing the table was a brass decanter of golden sunflowers, centered on one of Grandma Reed's crocheted doilies. China tea tins, a coffee mill, meat grinder, and several items of bisque crockery sat on the linoleum counter beside a large earthenware bowl of red-ripe apples. A family of Mama's handmade cornhusk dolls stood on the windowsill behind the antique lace curtains.

Mama served a pot of hot tea and flaky biscuits with her homemade strawberry jam. Annie ate hungrily while Knowl and Mama took turns catching her up on the news in Willowbrook. But more than anything, Annie wanted to know about Cath and Jenny.

"Cath's relationship with that Granger fellow didn't work out," said Knowl. "They broke up shortly after Cath took Jenny to New York."

"Was it because of Jenny—because he didn't want to raise her as his own?" asked Annie.

"I suspect so," said Mama, "although Catherine would never admit such a thing. Or perhaps her career keeps her too busy for a husband. No one knows exactly what happened. At any rate, she moved back here with Jenny the winter after you left."

Annie let out a little gasp. "Are they living here too?"

"No," said Knowl. "Cath wanted her independence, so she and Jenny moved into a little apartment in town. We see them often, especially Jenny. We keep her whenever Cath takes a trip to New York or London or somewhere else for an assignment or an exhibition. She's always off somewhere—a regular little globe-trotter—and doing very well with her painting. Did you see her Post cover of you and Jenny?"

Annie nodded. "I hung it on my wall at the mission where I stayed." When she saw Knowl's brows arch with curiosity, she added quickly, "After I've had some rest, I'll tell you all about my life in California."

Knowl reached across the table for her hand. "All I want to know is whether you've come home to be my wife again."

She smiled at him. "Yes, Knowl. I'm home for good." Turning to her mother, she said, "I'm both eager and fearful of seeing Jenny again. Should I telephone Cath? Will she want to see me?"

"Yes, of course, she will, dear. She's your best friend, isn't she?"

"I'm not sure if she considers me her friend or not."

"She knows about your book and my hopes for your return," said Knowl. "She didn't think you'd come, but I know she misses you immensely. We've all been lonely around here without you."

Annie sipped her tea, then murmured, "Tell me about Jenny. What's she like? How does she look? Is she happy?"

"She seems like a happy child," said Mama. "She loves coming over here and seeing her Uncle Knowl."

"And her Grandmother Reed," said Knowl with a wink. "She's nearly four—you know that, of course—and as bright as can be. She's a little carrot-top, the spitting image of Cath; but you can see Chip in her too. She's beautiful, Annie. So full of life and love and laughter."

Annie felt tears well in her eyes. "I never stopped loving her, Knowl, just as I never stopped loving you."

That evening, Knowl took his wife back into his bedroom and into his bed for a night that rivaled the bliss of their honeymoon. Scented candles burned on the bureau and Glenn Miller and Tommy Dorsey played on her father's old Victrola. They danced in the mellow glow of a flickering hurricane lamp and made love on silk sheets in their sturdy four-poster bed. They cuddled together under a calico quilt and fell asleep in each other's arms, while Frank Sinatra crooned, "I'll Be Seeing You."

The next morning, Knowl telephoned his sister and told her Annie was home. Cath agreed to come over for lunch and bring Jenny. Annie nervously paced the floor and fussed with her hair and gazed out the window until Cath pulled up in her new black DeSoto. Annie watched her stride up the walk to the porch, looking sleek and stylish in stacked heels, a slim, calf-length gray dress, and matching tam. She was leading Jenny—a miniature, auburn-haired version of herself—by the hand.

Annie greeted them at the door, her throat dry and palms perspiring. Strangely, she felt as if she were standing on the edge of a precipice, ready to topple over. Cath offered a tentative hug, then stooped down beside Jenny and said, "This is your Aunt Elizabeth. Can you say hello?"

The child stepped behind Cath and shyly lowered her gaze. She reminded Annie of a Kewpie doll, with large, thick-lashed brown eyes, fat, freckled cheeks, and a mop of curly red curls. She was dressed in a peach-colored pinafore with white ruffles.

Annie knelt beside her and smiled. "I'm very happy to meet you, Jenny. You're a very pretty girl. Would you mind if I had a hug?"

Jenny shook her head and ducked behind Cath once more.

"That's okay," said Annie, fighting back unexpected tears. "We have lots of time to get acquainted, don't we, Jenny?"

Mama came over and scooped Jenny up in her arms. "Come on, Sweet Pea. Come to Grandma. Let's go to the kitchen and get you some cookies and milk and take them out to the gazebo."

Cath looked around the parlor. "I thought Knowl was here."

"He had to get to the paper. He sends his love."

Cath sat down in the rocker. "So it's just the two of us."

Annie took the wing chair. "Yes. I guess that's best."

"It's been a long time." Cath looked more sophisticated than Annie remembered— her long hair cascading around her padded shoulders, her makeup flawless. But there was a hard edge to her features that wasn't there the last time they were together.

"We have a lot of catching up to do," said Annie.

Cath examined one long fingernail. "Then why does it seem so hard to think of anything to say?"

"I don't know."

"Maybe too much has happened for us to simply pick up the pieces and go on," said Cath.

"Maybe so," Annie agreed. "But do you remember all the fun we had in this house as children?"

Cath's expression remained noncommittal. "How could I forget? It was the only childhood I ever knew."

Annie gazed out the window. White, billowy clouds scudded along the skyline. Their loveliness belied the heaviness she felt. It was as if she and Cath were calling to each other across a great chasm, but neither could quite hear the other's voice. "I suppose we can't go back, can we?"

"No, we can't," said Cath. She looked frankly at Annie. "You should keep that fact in mind. In fact, I need to know why you've come back. Are you planning to fight for Jenny?"

Annie stiffened. "No, of course not. Why would you think such a thing?"

Cath's expression softened. "I just had to be sure."

"I'll always love Jenny, but she's yours now. I just want you both to be happy."

For the first time, Cath seemed to let down her guard. "We are happy, Annie. Jenny means the world to me. She's the only one who's never disappointed me. She loves and accepts me just as I am, and when I have to take a trip, she's there waiting for me when I come home."

Annie nodded. There didn't seem to be anything else to say, so she changed the subject. "How is your mother doing? The last time I called, the number at your house had been disconnected."

"Didn't you know?" said Cath in surprise. "My mother's in a sanitarium. She's getting the help she needs for her drinking."

"No, I didn't know," said Annie. "I hope she'll do well."

After a while, Mama entered the doorway with little Jenny in tow. "Come, children, it's time to eat. I fixed chicken sandwiches, vegetable soup, and peach cobbler."

Immediately after lunch, Cath prepared to leave. "Can't you stay awhile?" Annie asked. There was so much between them that hadn't been spoken yet. Annie yearned to feel the closeness

they had experienced in their youth, to somehow bridge the gap between them.

But Cath was firm. "I've got to get home, Annie. I've got a trip to New York coming up soon, and I need to start packing. Besides, the rain is starting up again, and I hate to drive on slick streets."

"You're right, of course," said Annie. "Take care." She hated this feeling of formality with Cath. They had once shared their deepest longings; now they struggled just to offer each other polite cliches. She gave Cath a searching glance. "I hope we can spend some time together soon, renewing old times."

"Yes, why not?" said Cath, a bit stiffly. After a moment, she relaxed a little and met Annie's gaze. "I wanted to tell you—I read Pacific Dawn, and it—it was wonderful—and painful—and it brought Chip back to me. No one could have written that book but you."

Annie flushed, suddenly close to tears. "Thank you for saying that, Cath. You don't know how much it means to me to know you liked the book. I wrote it for you as much as for myself."

"I know. I sensed that."

Annie felt an impulse to reach out and embrace Cath and tell her how much she still loved her and needed her friendship, but she resisted, sensing she might only embarrass or offend her.

Cath looked around and called Jenny to her side. "Time to go, sweetheart. Say goodbye to your Aunt Elizabeth."

The child looked up, wide-eyed, her rosebud lips pursed in curiosity. "Bye-bye," she said shyly.

Annie leaned down and gathered Jenny into her arms and bounced her up on her hip. As she savored the child's warmth and closeness, she felt a physical sensation of pleasure ripple through her arms. Her child. No matter what, Jenny would always be her child. "Good-bye, beautiful girl," she murmured, breathing in the fragrance of Jenny's hair. "Will you come see me again soon? And if you'd like, you can call me

'Annie' instead of 'Aunt Elizabeth.' Can you say 'Annie'?"

Jenny worked her mouth around the words. "Aaa-neee."

"That's right. And Annie loves Jenny very much."

"Time to go, Jenny." Cath reached out and took the child into her arms. She cast one last glance at Annie and said shortly, "I'll be in touch."

Annie stepped out on the porch and watched Cath and Jenny drive away down the cobbled, rain-washed street. A capricious wind whipped the rain into Annie's face, blending the downpour with her own swiftly falling tears. "Oh, God," she whispered aloud, her voice lost to the rain-swollen sky, "if only Jenny could be mine again! If only she were mine!"

TWENTY-SIX

The call came hardly more than an hour after Cath and Jenny had left. It was the emergency room at Willowbrook Hospital. We regret to inform you that there's been an accident....

Annie telephoned Knowl, who came immediately and drove Annie and her mother to the hospital. They paced about in the waiting room, stunned and silent, until a physician came with news. He introduced himself as Dr. Whiting and invited them to his office. When they were seated, he sat forward and folded his hands on his desk as if he were going to confide a secret.

Annie searched his face, trying to read his expression, desperate for clues. There were none. She felt as if her heart were being squeezed by invisible hands—hands that with just a word might crush her, shattering her fragile hold on reality.

"Tell us, Dr. Whiting," she pleaded. "Will Cath and Jenny be all right?"

He cleared his throat and said, "It appears that the child suffered only cuts and bruises. When the car crashed, her door flew open and she was thrown clear into some bushes. She's in X-ray now. If everything checks out, she'll be able to go home tomorrow."

"Thank God!" cried Annie. The child she cherished was okay! "And Cath? What about Cath?"

"Miss Herrick? We're prepping her for surgery."

"Surgery?" echoed Knowl. "What kind of surgery?"

Dr. Whiting spoke guardedly, obviously weighing every word. "Your sister lost control of her car on a slippery street, Mr. Herrick. The vehicle careened into a ravine, and she was thrown through the windshield head first into a concrete abutment. Presently, she's experiencing a great deal of brain swelling. We've summoned a specialist from Chicago who will operate to relieve the pressure. He's on the train to Willowbrook even as we speak."

"She will be all right, won't she?" insisted Annie.

"We don't know, Mrs. Herrick. Only time will tell."

"Are you saying—she could die?" asked Knowl.

Dr. Whiting's brow furrowed. "May I be frank with you, Mr. Herrick? With injuries like this, it's difficult to predict the outcome. We anticipate a good chance that your sister will survive the surgery. After that, she may remain in a coma for some time.

Naturally, the sooner she regains consciousness, the better—the less chance of permanent brain damage."

"And if she remains in a coma?" prompted Knowl.

"We'll cross that bridge when we come to it, Mr. Herrick."

"No. I want to know what we're up against," declared Knowl. "I want to know the worst we're facing."

"Very well—if you insist." Dr. Whiting's tone was grave. "In the worst case, if your sister lives, she could spend the rest of her life virtually as a vegetable."

Annie covered her mouth in horror. *Dear God, I didn't want to win Jenny this way!* "Not Cath!" she cried. "Not our Cath!"

Catherine was taken to surgery at seven that evening. The doctor warned it might be hours before there was news. Knowl drove Mama home for some rest and returned to keep vigil with Annie. They sat in the modest waiting room, drinking coffee, thumbing through worn magazines—Life, Look, Collier's, the Post—and staring at Winslow Homer prints on the pale walls. Annie kept thinking that Cath would like these paintings. She would comment on Homer's splendid sense of color or the drama in his seascapes. She might even say they were some of the best watercolors she had seen, although Annie couldn't be sure, since Cath was the art expert.

But, then the reality struck home. Cath might never paint again. Cath might be as lost to them as Chip and Papa and Papa Reed.

As the night wore on, Annie's spirits plummeted. She wondered, *Why does life always have to be a matter of counting one's losses? Why had she and Cath striven so hard to accomplish so much if it could all be snuffed out in an instant?*

Another thought occurred to Annie, a verse from somewhere in Scripture: *What shall it profit a man if he should gain the whole world and lose his own soul?* The idea stunned Annie. Through all the years they had been best friends, Cath had repeatedly rejected Annie's God. Annie had long since stopped pressing the issue, figuring each person had to live life as he saw fit. But now that truth took on ominous proportions. *What if Cath never had a chance to repent and know her Savior? Would she enter a hellish eternity, lost and alone, forever separated from God and those she loved?* The possibility was appalling.

"She can't die," Annie said aloud, under her breath.

Knowl looked at her through weary, shadowed eyes. "What? Are you talking about Cath?"

"Yes. I won't let her die, Knowl. God help me, if it's the last thing I do, I'm going to see that we have our Cath back again."

He hung his head in his hands. "I pray to God you're right."

It was nearly midnight before Cath was brought out of surgery. Dr. Whiting approached Knowl and Annie, still in his surgical gown. "She's holding her own," he told them as he peeled off his mask. "She'll be in recovery for about two hours. Then we'll move her to a private room with around the clock nursing care."

"When can we see her?" asked Annie.

"When they bring her down to her room. No more than five minutes, though."

It seemed forever before Annie was allowed to slip into the anonymous cubicle that contained Cath's high, railed hospital bed and a plethora of forbidding machines and equipment. Quelling her own searing panic, Annie stole over to the bedside and gazed down at the frail, ghostly figure lying amid a frightening network of wires and tubes. Certainly this couldn't be her beautiful, exuberant Cath. Her bright curls were gone; instead, her head was wrapped in bandages; her eyes were two dark shadowed spots on an expanse of white. Tubes ran into her nostrils and wrists, and another was taped to her mouth so that her lips were twisted downward in a loathsome grimace.

Annie felt a sudden revulsion deep in her belly. The pungent antiseptic smells permeated the walls of this sterile, airless room. An aura of death hovered everywhere. A gagging reflex seized Annie. She thought she might vomit, but gradually the sensation passed, leaving her weak and perspiring.

She reached out and placed a trembling hand over Cath's motionless one. Bending close, she uttered a promise, her voice raw with emotion. "I won't let you leave me, Cath. I will stand by you until you're well. I'll will my life into yours if I must, but I will not let you die. Do you hear me? We signed a blood pact, Cath. You've got to honor it. You've got to live and come home and be my friend again."

The next afternoon, Knowl and Annie picked up Jenny at the hospital and drove her home to Honeysuckle Lane. She had bruises and bandages on her face, arms, and knees, but, otherwise, she seemed as happy and full of life as ever. All the way home she jabbered, pointing out the window at houses or passing cars. "There Mommy," she chirped. "Mommy come home. Mommy have ow-ee. Mommy love Jenny."

Annie's heart ached at the child's guileless words. Fighting back tears, she assured Jenny, "Mommy will be home soon, sweetheart. I promise. Mommy will come home."

Once Jenny was settled comfortably at the house with Mama, Knowl and Annie returned to the hospital to take turns sitting with Cath. She looked the same as she had the night before—fragile, motionless, locked in a secret world of slumber from which she might never awaken.

Nevertheless, Annie sat by her bed, talking about the past, reading favorite Psalms, even singing familiar hymns. "Remember the games we played as children, Cath? You made the best paper dolls in the world, and you designed such beautiful clothes for them. Everyone in the neighborhood wanted your paper dolls."

"Keep on talking like that, Mrs. Herrick," said the stout, gray-haired nurse, sitting by the door. "Make her start thinking again. Make that broken mind work."

"I'm trying," said Annie tremulously. "But I don't even know if she hears a word I say."

"She hears. I got a feeling. You just keep on talking."

Annie bent close to Cath's ear. "Someday you're going to paint again, Cath. You're going to paint a splendid portrait of Jenny, and we'll hang it over the fireplace in the parlor. And when you're well, we'll sit in the rosebud room and talk like we did when we were twelve. Remember, Cath?"

The hours at Cath's bedside turned into days. Knowl returned to work, leaving Annie to keep her vigil alone. Sometimes she was so weary, she fell asleep in her chair. Occasionally, she sat in her chair and rested her head on the pillow beside Cath's, and slept, until the nurse startled her awake and urged her to go home to bed.

At other times, Annie sat and read aloud from the Scriptures, or from books of poetry or the classics, or even from the newspaper. Still, Cath made no response. Annie worried that she might remain a silent, slumbering angel for the rest of her life.

Annie prayed constantly—silently and aloud, as she tended Jenny in the morning, as she drove to the hospital, as she kept her lonely watch over Cath, and as she collapsed into bed late each night. She woke with a prayer on her lips and moved and functioned in a constant state of prayer—wordless, urgent, instinctive.

She began to feel that she wasn't sure where her own consciousness left off and the whispers of God began. She was keenly aware of His Spirit, sensitive to His subtle moving within her in a way she had never been before. She had emptied herself of all that was superfluous or frivolous. Nothing mattered now except that she hold on to His power, that she let Him spill Himself into her, washing her, cleansing her, purifying her in deed and motive, so that somehow she might pass on that spirit of life to Cath.

At the end of her second week in Willowbrook, Annie wrote a letter to Robert Wayne in California, explaining why she wouldn't be coming back to the mission. "I hope you'll be glad to hear I'm back with my husband," she wrote, "just as I hope you'll pray fervently for my dear friend, Cath. I only wish I could communicate in words the spiritual odyssey I've experienced in the hours I've spent reading Scripture and praying at her bedside. It's as if I've finally laid aside every burden and distraction that would hinder my communion with Christ's Spirit. Sometimes He is more real to me than my surroundings, more tangible than the people who pass like shadows in and out of my life these days. I've never been more aware that my faith is centered on a Person whose very essence occupies a place within my soul. Christ sits with me at Cath's bedside; He sings through me; He cradles me in the darkness. When I am empty of strength, He fills me with Himself.

"Why is it, Robert, that my senses are suddenly so acutely attuned to Him? Did I ever truly know Him before these crucial days? Surely, I did, but I was content with a lesser God than He who sustains me through these desolate hours. All these years, He was ready to be so much more to me than I asked, and I never knew, until now.

"Thank you, Robert, for all those months when you accepted me with all my neediness and nurtured me back to spiritual health. Pray now for Catherine. Perhaps some day the two of you will meet and you'll know why I cherish her friendship."

One morning, two weeks from the day of the accident, while Annie sat at Cath's bedside reading aloud from Alice's Adventures in Wonderland, she noticed the slightest twitch of Cath's little pinky. Her heart racing with excitement, she summoned the nurse. For the next ten minutes they hovered over Cath, their eyes darting intently over her unmoving form.

"Call her name," the nurse told Annie. "Call it as loud as you can."

"Cath! Catherine!" Annie shouted. "Wake up, Cath!"

Nothing.

"Try again. Make her hear you."

"Cath, it's Annie. Listen to me! Please come back. Jenny needs you. She needs her Mommy! I can't be her mother, Cath. Only you can. Do it for me. Do it for Chip. Do it for your daughter!"

The finger moved again, almost imperceptibly, but both Annie and the nurse saw it. "She coming," said the nurse. "She's got a long journey back, but she's finally begun the trip!"

In the weeks that followed, Cath inched back to consciousness with small successes, moving her fingers, then her hands, and eventually her arms. She wiggled her toes and blinked her eyes and made guttural sounds low in her throat. It was as if this person in a woman's body had been reborn as a helpless infant, and now she must begin again to discover and respond. Everything had to be relearned and mastered, from the simplest gestures to the most basic bodily functions.

Annie lavishly praised every small victory, urging Cath to try again, to tackle still harder tasks. At times Cath lay exhausted and disconsolate, tears streaming from her eyes. She still couldn't speak, except to utter a thick, throaty, No, no, no, no! It was her answer to everything that Annie suggested. But Annie always came back with, "Yes, yes, yes, yes!"

A chill, wet spring eased into a long, humid summer. Cath began an intensive program of physical therapy and speech rehabilitation. Slowly she regained sensation in her arms and legs and won back increasing control of her muscles. Her speech was garbled and unintelligible at first, her words dismayingly slurred, but gradually Annie could distinguish certain phrases and expressions. Me eat, go away, stay here, help me, kiss baby. Annie knew the spark that was Cath still flickered somewhere inside that fractured mind and broken body, and she was determined to find a way to ignite it.

As the stifling, sun-drenched days of August slipped away, Annie began to see glimpses of the old Cath. A rare moment of laughter. A sly gleam in the eyes. Her face upturned for a kiss from Knowl. A love pat for little Jenny. "You're going to make it, Cath," Annie declared the first time Cath held her daughter again. "No one can hold you back now!"

One morning just before summer's end, as Annie tediously coached Cath in the exercise room, Dr. Whiting called her aside and said, "I just wanted you to know, we'll be releasing Cath from the hospital at the end of the week."

"Release her? You can't be serious. She's not ready yet to live a normal life."

"We realize that, but we can't do any more for her here."

"Where will she go?" demanded Annie. "What will she do?"

His tone was matter-of-fact. "We're making arrangements to send her to a facility in Chicago where they're equipped to give her the kind of rehabilitation she needs."

Annie stared at him in astonishment. "Chicago? You can't! She needs her family, not strangers. She needs us!"

"Then perhaps you'd better take her home and hire your own physical therapist. But if you do, you'd better be prepared for the challenge of your life, Mrs. Herrick. Working with Catherine will take every ounce of strength and stamina and fortitude you have, and even then, it may not be enough. You may find yourself drained and spent long before Catherine is a whole person again. Is that a risk you want to take?"

Annie met his gaze unflinchingly. "I have no choice, Dr. Whiting. Cath and I are connected on an emotional level I can't begin to explain. If she doesn't come back whole, I'll never be whole either."

The physician looked skeptical. "Very well, Mrs. Herrick. I wish you extraordinary luck. You'll need it."

Annie was relieved when Knowl and Mama agreed with her that Cath should come home to Honeysuckle Lane for further treatment. "We'll bring in whatever doctors she needs," said Knowl. "What better place for her to get well than a home filled with those who love her?"

Annie prepared the rosebud room for Cath, decorating it with items from her own childhood that had languished for years in the Herrick attic—delicate porcelain dolls in exotic dresses, colorful posters and antique prints, handmade baskets and pretty afghans. Annie filled the room with vases of wildflowers—red phlox, white prickly poppies, sweet petunias. She placed a wicker chair by the window and a quilt stand by the bed. It was as homey and comfortable as Annie had ever seen it.

On Sunday afternoon, Knowl brought Cath home from the hospital and carried her upstairs to her room. He laid her on the bed and lovingly tucked pillows around her. She seemed pleased with the room, perhaps even recognized it, although Annie couldn't be sure.

Knowl brought home a wheelchair as well, so that Annie could take Cath on walks through the garden. But as much as Annie had anticipated having Cath home again, she found herself feeling vaguely disappointed. Seeing her friend in her beloved rosebud room underscored the fact that this new Cath, so silent and remote, was vastly different from the witty, fanciful Cath who once sat in this room regaling Annie with her extravagant dreams and outrageous ambitions.

This new Cath was moody, angry, irritable, and unpredictable. She often sat for hours, morose and withdrawn, refusing even to undergo her prescribed regimen of therapy. Her raging frustration could erupt over the most trivial incident—when Annie tried to help her feed herself and the food spilled, or when she tried to hold a pencil in her sluggish fingers and it kept falling to the floor. At times Cath simply sat and stared out the window, uttering over and over an anguished, No, no, no!

Annie didn't know how to exorcise the taunting demons of the mind that plagued Cath in her helplessness. As much as she tried to make her strength stretch to bolster Cath, her efforts were never enough. At every turn Cath seemed to resent Annie and resist her attempts to help. At times Annie felt as if the two of them were swimming together through an endless ocean. Actually, Annie was swimming and trying to hold on to Cath to keep her from going under. They were both exhausted and on the verge of collapse, but there was nothing they could do but keep on treading water. To stop would be to drown. And yet, more and more, Annie felt the waves washing up over her, carrying her down to the murky depths that already gripped Cath.

Late one evening as Annie slipped into bed beside Knowl, he leaned up on one elbow and looked at her, his expression grim. "Annie, we've got to talk. You can't keep on this way."

She lay down exhausted and stared up at the ceiling. "What way?"

"You know what I mean. We all want Cath to be well again, but not like this. You're killing yourself."

She turned her head toward him. "What do you want us to do? Send her to that sanitarium in Chicago where they'll let her lie in bed day after day and wither away, until she becomes a vegetable again?"

"She'd probably do very well there. Dr. Whiting says they work with the patients and give them therapy every day."

"It wouldn't be the same, Knowl. They wouldn't demand of her what I demand. They wouldn't will their very lives into her. They don't love her like we do."

Knowl reached over and drew Annie into his arms. "I know we love her, but I can't let Cath destroy your health and our happy home. I lost you once, and I vowed I'd never lose you again—even to a worthy cause like saving my sister." He nuzzled his chin against her ear. "I just want you to know, Annie, if I don't see some major improvement in Cath soon, I'm taking her to that hospital in Chicago."

TWENTY-SEVEN

The Fall of 1946.

"Look, Cath! Look, Jenny! The leaves are falling. Look at all the beautiful colors!" Annie scooped up a handful of crisp, dry leaves from beneath the sheltering walnut tree, walked over to the wheelchair, and placed them in Cath's open hands. Cath was still bone thin, her complexion pale as eggshell, and she wore a scarf around her cropped, auburn hair.

"Feel them, Cath," Annie persisted. "Run your fingers over their crinkly, brittle surface. Lift them to your nose and breathe in the sweet hickory smell of autumn."

Jenny joined in the game, scampering through the gold and russet piles, tossing orange and brown leaves into the air, rolling in them until she was seized by fits of laughter. She ran to Annie and cried, "Mommy, Mommy, come play with me!"

These days she called both Cath and Annie Mommy. No wonder. Cath was more the child than Jenny. Annie had become the mother of both.

Annie picked Jenny up and set her on Cath's lap. "Show Jenny the leaves, Cath. Tell her the colors. Red, orange, yellow—"

Cath pushed Jenny off her lap. "You—tell her!"

Jenny began to cry. Annie picked her up and soothed her. "Rub noses, Jenny. Come on, Sweet Pea, rub noses with me." Jenny stopped whimpering and rubbed noses with Annie.

Annie put the child down and said, "The breeze is getting chilly, Jenny. Run inside and tell Grandma Reed you need your warm coat. Or maybe you'd better stay inside and ask her to read you a story. That's right. Run along, sweetheart!"

Annie turned back to the frail figure in the wheelchair. "Let's walk in the garden, Cath." She reached for her hands. "We don't have many more days before winter will be here."

"I—don't—want to walk," said Cath, a slight impediment still evident in her speech.

Annie clasped her hands and pulled her up anyway. "We're going to walk, Cath. Come. You're walking very well these days. You should be pleased. You've made wonderful progress these past few weeks."

"I walk like—an old woman."

"No one is looking, Cath."

"I'm looking."

Annie steadied Cath with her arm at her waist. They ambled along the walkway toward Mama's flower beds. "You should try capturing these glorious colors on canvas, Cath. I'll bring out your oils or your watercolors, if you'd like to try."

Cath jerked away from Annie. "I can't."

Annie caught her arm. "Yes, you can, Cath. I know you can. But you have to want to more than anything."

"I tried. My hands—won't work."

"The talent's not in your hands, Cath. It's in your heart, and in your head. You can paint again, if you'll just try."

Cath's mouth twisted in despair. "No. I can't—do it!"

Annie stopped walking and turned to face her friend. She gripped her thin arms. "You're a survivor, Cath. From the time we were children, you showed me that. Look how you survived your parents' breakup, and Chip's death, and giving up your baby—"

"My baby? You have Jenny now," said Cath thickly. "She calls you—Mommy."

"She calls you Mommy too. She wants you back the way you were. We all want you back, Cath."

"No!" Cath shook off Annie's grasp and tottered clumsily through the grass, her arms swinging loosely at her sides.

Annie caught up and fell into step beside her. "Cath, I know you want to get well, so you can take care of Jenny again and be her mother. I know how much she means to you."

Cath shook her head. "My feet—don't work right. My hands don't—my head—!"

"But they will, in time. I promise!"

Cath pivoted awkwardly and glared at Annie. Her words came haltingly. "What do you care—if I get well? If I am—an invalid—you can raise—Jenny yourself. It's what—you always wanted."

"What I wanted?" As Annie stared back at her lifelong friend, something odd snapped inside. There was a gushing, rushing sensation deep in the wellspring of her emotions. She could feel the dam splintering like toothpicks in the wind. A sound was rising up out of the core of her, and if she released it, it might never stop—a scream of protest, of exhaustion, of lament.

Moving instinctively, Annie seized Cath by the shoulders and shook her. "Don't tell me what I want!" she cried. "I'd give my life to make you whole again! I've done all I can for you, and all you do is fight me. What's wrong with you, Cath? You wallow in self-pity and shut out those who love you most!" She was trembling now, her voice as raw as her feelings. "You—you may be suffering a grievous impairment, Cath, but you're as stubborn and pigheaded as you ever were! I'm through trying to help you!"

She released Cath and turned away sharply. She was already striding away when Cath reached out for her and lost her footing. She fell with a little exclamation of surprise, crumpling in a heap on the dry, crackling grass. Annie turned in alarm and darted back, kneeling with concern beside her fallen friend. Wordlessly, she gathered Cath in her arms and held her. The two swayed together, sobbing.

"I love you, Cath."

"I—love you—Annie!"

Annie sat down beside Cath on the grass. "Are you all right? Did you hurt yourself?"

Tears rolled down Cath's pale cheeks. She reached out and clutched Annie's hand. "Yes, I hurt." She touched her elbows and knees. "Not here, but here!" She patted her heart. "Why do I—always hurt myself? Pray—for me, Annie. Through you—I see God's love—for me. I want—to get well."

Annie moved over and put her arm around Cath's shoulder, protectively, reassuringly. "You will, Cath. You are! Look how far you've already come."

Cath's eyes were luminous. "I want my baby—my Jenny. I want to be—her mother again."

"You will be a wonderful mother to Jenny," Annie murmured, tilting her head amiably against Cath's. They sat like that for what seemed a very long time. The ground was cold and hard and scratchy with autumn's gusty harvest of scudding leaves, but Annie didn't mind. The earth was comforting and solid and dependable.

When she was a child she liked to stretch out belly-down and hold on to the ground, pretending to ride this gargantuan globe as it spun like a top through the heavens. At such times, she felt as if she were one with the earth, moving in perfect harmony. It was the same way she felt now, sitting here with Cath.

Annie watched the shadows lengthen across the grass and the October sky turn the color of slate. She was reluctant to speak, afraid of disturbing this unexpected aura of serenity. She and Cath had raged against each other and wept bitterly together, and yet, at this moment, the connection between them was stronger than ever. Cath seemed more at peace than she had been in months. Annie felt strangely at peace too.

As a blustery wind gathered, sending crunchy leaves into a skittish dance, Annie sensed the quirky, marvelous transcendence of time, when a commonplace moment takes on eternal significance and becomes branded in one's memory forever.

"Do you feel it, Cath?" she whispered.

"What, Annie?"

"The magic. This moment is crystallized for all time. We'll always recall how we felt right this second, sitting here together in Mama's garden. No matter what else happens to us, no matter where we go or how far apart we are, we'll have this memory to share."

Cath worked up a grin. "I won't forget, Annie."

Annie was silent a moment. Then she looked at Cath and smiled mysteriously. "May I tell you a secret, dear friend?"

Cath's brows arched. "A secret?"

"A wonderful secret." Annie took Cath's hand and placed it gently on her own abdomen. "Knowl and I—we are going to have our own precious baby. In six months, you will be Aunt Catherine. And in those six months, you will get well, dear Cath. I am trusting God for that, just as I pray one day soon you will trust God for your life."

Cath looked up and smiled wistfully. "A baby?" Wonderingly, she patted Annie's tummy. "A baby!"

Annie put her finger to her lips. "Don't tell. Knowl doesn't know yet."

Cath's eyes widened at the idea of such marvelous intrigue.

"I'm telling him tonight, when it's just the two of us, with the glow of candlelight, and Glenn Miller on the Victrola."

Cath let out a whoop of delight. "My brother—just wait!"

Annie stifled a ripple of laughter. "Knowl may already be home. Remember, don't tell him."

Cath pretended to button her lips. "It's… our secret."

Annie stood up, brushing dead leaves and grass from her simple shirtdress. Then she reached down and pulled Cath to her feet and helped her shake off bits of debris from her corduroy skirt. They exchanged conspiratorial smiles; then leisurely, arm in arm, like friends who had all the time on earth, they ambled back down the garden path to that beloved old dusty rose house, where Annie knew Knowl would be waiting.

"THE END"

Fiction

OTHER ELM HILL FICTION TITLES
Now Available

ANGELWALK and STEDFAST

BEN HUR

DEAD AIR

ESCAPE

NOW I LAY ME DOWN TO SLEEP

SERENITY BAY

THE THOR CONSPIRACY

Fiction

COMING SOON

ALWAYS IN SEPTEMBER

BEYOND A REASONABLE DOUBT

BREAD UPON THE WATERS

WOLF'S LAIR & ??? SANCTION

LONG TRAIN PASSING

QUO VADIS

SECOND CHANCES

THE COVENANT